FRACTURE EVENT

* * * * * *

WITHDRAWN

KATHLEEN O'NEAL GEAR
W. MICHAEL GEAR

WOLFPACK
PUBLISHING
— EST 2013 —

Text copyright © 2021 Kathleen O'Neal Gear, W. Michael Gear, All rights reserved.
Printed in the United States of America.

Published by Wolfpack Publishing
5130 S. Fort Apache Road, 215-380
Las Vegas, NV 89148

Paperback IBSN 978-1-64734-645-4
eBook ISBN 978-1-64734-644-7
LCCN: 2021941195

FRACTURE EVENT

******

To
Gerald and JoAnn Gerber
With fond memories of
Harleys, Beemers,
and
Long rides.

CHAPTER ONE

***

WIND SENT LITTLE WRAITHS OF SNOW DOWN THE DARK WYOMING STREET. THE FROZEN crystals seemed to slip, twist, and fly across the frozen asphalt. Wind and snow: They seemed a constant in Laramie while it was spring in the rest of the world.

Wrapped in his heavy coat, Simon Gunter hunched low in the driver's seat of his Toyota rental and watched the cars pass by. He'd followed the professor to the redhead's apartment building hours ago and had been listening to the party: music, laughter and loud talking. Apparently, the festivities were going to drag on late into the night.

Gunter considered himself to be a simple man. He liked simple things and simple assignments. Those kinds of assignments rarely came his way but this job had been simplicity itself. He'd met with the professor and communicated the offer. The man—as expected—had been dazzled by the money and luxury. He'd acted like a child suddenly given the opportunity to fulfill an impossible dream.

Gunter yawned and watched his breath condense in the frigid air. He looked out at the crusted snow on the small lawn of the apartment buildings. *It's April. When does this mountain country get warm?*

Periodically, Gunter ran the engine, using the defroster to keep the windows clear but, as the night wore on, he grew more and more agitated. He'd expected to be here late, but the lengthy celebration of the redhead's new doctorate degree was cutting into his schedule. Where was his wayward professor? People trickled away singularly or in pairs. With the exception of the older professors, who departed early, the revelers were young, most of them only moderately drunk, though a few had left staggering and supported by friends.

But the professor's sleek BMW, covered with a white hoar of frost, remained even after the apartment's lights went out.

So, Herr Professor spends the night with his redheaded student?

An unpleasant complication.

He'd already ascertained that the professor's wife and two young boys weren't in town. Poor fool. He'd better enjoy himself tonight.

Not that he blamed his quarry. The redhead was striking—tall and athletic. She'd been wearing a coat when Gunter first saw her but, from what he'd been able to see of her muscular legs, he could fill in the rest.

Gunter sighed and imagined peeling the redhead's clothing from her body, running his hands over her smooth white skin, teasing the pink nipples...

Headlights flared down the street and Gunter sank lower in his seat, watching as a dark Chevrolet sedan crept toward him; it slowed to a crawl when it passed the apartment building. The man behind the wheel craned his neck to study the cars in the parking lot. He slowed as he fixed on the professor's frosted BMW. Then the sedan rolled on and pulled to the curb no more than a hundred meters down the street.

Moments later, the driver's door opened and the parking lot lights illuminated a man in a black coat and black cap. As the door closed, the newcomer vanished into the shadows.

Someone else is interested in the anthropologist.

Things were no longer simple. The Big Man was not going to be happy.

Gunter leaned over and reached for a plastic case on the passenger floorboard. Clicking it open, he removed a stainless steel dart pistol from its recess in the cradling foam. He'd planned to use it on the professor. Ah, well, first things first.

When the intruder's silhouette appeared again at the edge of the parking lot, Gunter inserted a needle-pointed syringe into the pistol's breech and clicked the bolt home.

The intruder walked over to the professor's BMW, checked the license plate, and then looked up at the apartment building.

Easing open the car door, Gunter stepped out into the night. On silent feet, he ghosted toward his prey.

He would be faced with the task of disposal, but fortunately, the Union Pacific railroad ran through Laramie. He had used trains before. They sent an unmistakable message to the opposition.

CHAPTER TWO

***

THE FURNACE CLICKED ON WITH A ROAR OF AIR, WAKING ANIKA FRENCH. SHE GROANED,
rolled over on her couch, and wondered if something foul had died
in her mouth. She'd had way too much wine but what a great party!
The entire anthropology department had come to help her celebrate
receiving her PhD. As much as she'd like to drift back to sleep,
her bladder argued otherwise. She opened one eye to inspect her
small apartment.

Yep. She was on the couch, fully clothed, which meant she'd
refused to sleep in her own bed. That did not bode well for the man
in her bedroom.

God, I'm going to hate today.

As Anika sat up, strands of red hair fell across her face. Planting
her feet, she was delighted that the room didn't spin. She'd been there
a time or two in the past and didn't ever want to go back.

Rising, she studied the forests of empty beer bottles that covered
every flat surface—the coffee table, the open spaces in her bookcase,
the kitchen counter. Others lurked around the base of her plants; more
perched atop her speakers, like abandoned missiles.

She took two steps across the floor and her right foot squished.

"Oh… hell." She looked down and winced. What moron would
leave a half-eaten plate of nachos on the carpet?

Anika hobbled across the floor, leaving cheesy footprints all the
way to the bathroom, where she jerked off her sock and tossed it in
the hamper. To her relief, except for the empty wine bottle in the
shower, the bathroom almost looked normal. The hand towel hung
like a rumpled knot, the sink was soap-scummy, and the toilet seat
was up, but no significant damage.

She moaned to herself as she lowered the seat, dropped her pants, and surrendered to her complaining bladder. For moments, she lingered, feeling the dull ache behind her eyes.

When she rose, she studied herself in the mirror: green eyes- bloodshot, freckles barely visible on her straight nose. She had a good face, the kind men looked at twice. At least until she opened her mouth. Men rarely stuck around once her intelligence became apparent. The exception, of course, was the man in her bed.

Crossing the hall, she made two steps into her bedroom and stopped.

Dr. Mark Schott, chairman of her committee, lay on his stomach, head smashed into her pillow, naked down to where a twist of her sheets covered his lower half. One bare knee protruded.

Anika took a quick inventory of the wadded clothing on the floor: shirt, undershirt, tie, pants.

Memory returned and, along with it, his pleading blue eyes, the coaxing smile and clinging hands. "Come on, Anika. We're celebrating! *You're* celebrating."

"Yes, I am," she'd replied. "Remind me. Where are Denise and the kids tonight?"

"Denver. But—"

"Not a chance."

He'd paused. "It's not like you're still my student. Not after yesterday, *Doctor French!*"

"What part of *no* don't you get?"

"What if I told you I had something important to tell you?"

"What? That you're getting a divorce? You've used that one already."

"No, something *really* important."

She knew that look. The last time she'd seen it was when he'd been named department head.

"Anika, something amazing happened earlier today."

"More amazing than me finally getting my PhD?"

"Your degree is just icing on the cake." A gleam entered his eyes. "Come on. I'll tell you after we make love."

"Looks like you'll carry it with you to your grave."

"It's your future. *Our* future." He tried to pull her down to the bed with him, but she shook off his hand.

"Get out of my apartment, Mark."

"Well, sure, but let me tell you about the project first. You're a critical part of it. I need you."

She pointed to the door. "Leave."

He lounged back across the bed as though he owned it. "Not until I know you're in."

She walked to the closet and started stuffing clean clothes in her overnight bag.

"What are you doing?"

"If you're not leaving, I am."

"Listen! I know you need money. I'll pay you fifty thousand dollars if you sign a contract saying you'll work with me on this project."

Her breath caught. She straightened. He'd never have offered money unless her expertise was absolutely essential to him.

"This must be a computer modeling project."

"It is," he said with a smile. "This is right up your alley. You're perfect for the job as my assistant. Especially now that you have your doctorate. You finally have credibility."

Anika stared at him. He'd been stealing her work for years, publishing bits and pieces under his own name. When she'd first complained that she should at least be listed as a co-author, he'd convinced her that, without his guidance as chair of the dissertation committee, she'd have never come up with those ideas. So, in essence, they were his. At the time, she was twenty-three and scared to complain to anyone. She was just a student, a tiny cog in his research machine. And he'd assured her that working with him would have huge benefits down the road. Benefits that had never materialized. In fact, if he hadn't chaired her committee, she was sure she would have had her PhD two years ago. Now at the age of twenty-seven, she'd finally wised up.

"No, thanks." In disgust, she headed for the door.

CHAPTER THREE

***

THE ANTHROPOLOGY BUILDING WAS QUIET THIS AFTERNOON. ANIKA SIPPED COFFEE WHILE she stared at the charts taped to her office walls. The data clusters—the bases of the computer model, *her model*—stood out on the white paper. Each was clarified by a statistical formula.

It didn't look like much to the uninitiated but it was revolutionary. With the right data, she could detail the step-by-step decline and collapse of any culture that had ever existed. Once she published it, archaeologists would be able to understand exactly why earth's greatest civilizations had toppled.

She smiled at that, remembering the phone call yesterday after her dissertation defense. She'd called her father to tell him she'd passed.

"So, you're Dr. Anika French now?"

"I am. My dissertation will be printed and bound. You'll get a copy."

"That's okay, angel. I couldn't understand it any more than I could read Chinese. So, when's graduation?"

They called him "Red" French, a name he'd carried since his days as a Marine recruit. For much of Anika's life, he'd been the missing father, a lifer in the Corps. Now, he was Sheriff Red French of Converse County, Wyoming.

"You get me the date, sweetheart. I'll be there to see you get your diploma."

"That's for high school, Dad. For this…" she'd hesitated, *"They call it being hooded. I'm being hooded."*

"Oh, okay. You know, your mother would be so proud of you."

"Thanks, Dad."

Mother's interest and passion had been the ranch, a rawhide operation consisting of three sections of land on the Platte River in central

Wyoming.

"How are things?" she'd asked.

"Got a big case. Someone stole twenty bales of barbed wire from the Highway Department road crew last week. Got to go, honey. Love you."

"Love you, too, Dad."

She clicked END and, on impulse, reached for the photo on the corner of her desk. In this one, Red French stood in uniform, big, burly, a pistol on his hip. He was staring into the camera, a crooked smile bending his lips. Lines etched his florid face, the tiny scar on his cheek oddly white in the photo. She'd taken it the day he was sworn in as sheriff.

Dad had never liked Mark Schott: *The man's a weasel. You watch him.*

Anika sipped coffee and listened to the sound of students passing in the hallway before she turned to the stack of papers on her desk. In two weeks, she would leave the University of Wyoming, a newly minted PhD in anthropology. And then what?

Her gaze shifted to the model. Yes, it was brilliant but, since the economy had turned, finding a job in anthro had never been more difficult. A lot of anthropologists—every bit as brilliant as she—were out there pounding the pavement, sending *curricula vitae* to any university with an opening and there just weren't many out there.

Someone cleared his throat in the doorway behind her and she turned to see Mark. He'd clearly gone home, showered, and dressed in his best, ironed chinos, a tie, and tweed jacket. He looked like a scion of Oxford rather than the Head of Anthropology at Wyoming's only university. She wondered if Denise had made it back from Denver this afternoon.

"Can I come in?"

"What for?"

He stepped into her office and closed the door. As he seated himself in a chair, he pointed to the papers on her desk. "Job hunting?"

Coldly, she responded, "That's the next step, isn't it?"

"That's why I wanted to talk to you."

"Before or after orgasm?"

He winced. "Sorry about that. I can be an ass, as you well know. I had planned to have this conversation yesterday, before your dissertation defense, but I couldn't find you. Now, time is short. I have a meeting soon, then I have to be in Munich tomorrow." He glanced at his watch.

"Bye."

He gave her a tight smile. "How would you feel about taking my old position here at the University of Wyoming? You'd start as an assistant professor of anthropology."

Surprised, she blinked. "First of all, you can't just give me your old position. I'd have to compete for it just like everyone else. Second, what's the catch?"

"I *can* give you the position. You see, it will come with special project funding. I already have the president's and trustees' approval. I spoke with them an hour ago. You have the job if you want it."

Her instincts—despite being numbed by alcohol—kicked in. "What's the catch?" she repeated.

He pointed at the computer model spread across her wall. "You'll be doing exactly what you've been doing, but we'll be taking the model in a different direction."

"How?"

"Are you really saying you don't want this job?"

She leaned back in her chair. "I'm not the naïve young woman I was the last time you stole my research. I've learned who you really are."

"Now, Anika, we've discussed—"

"You're always working your own angle, Mark. What's in this for you?"

For a time he sat, apparently weighing what he should and should not say. Then he glanced at his watch again. "No matter what you think of me, you want to do more with that model, right?"

"Of course. It's critical for understanding why and how prehistoric civilizations around the world collapsed."

"I know that." He stared at her. "Here's the deal: You'll get a position here, a *nice* signing bonus that we've already discussed, other perks, and unlimited opportunity to work on aspects of the model that you're comfortable with. And all those survey courses that first-year professors get stuck with? You don't even have to teach if you don't want to."

Her eyes narrowed. "And in return?"

"All you have to do is plug in the variables I send you and run data." He hesitated. "Oh, and there may be some restrictions on what you can publish and say."

"I can't publish or talk about my work? That's a big catch."

He squirmed in the chair. "There are a few security clearances involved."

She hesitated while she considered the ramifications. "Is this a Department of Defense project?"

He looked at the door, then leaned forward and opened his arms. "Look, after you sign the contract, I can tell you everything but, right now, I can't. All I can say is that you can refine the model, add new data, publish anything you want to on any other subject. But the work you do for me? That will be different."

"Good Lord, Mark, I don't have the energy to unravel your twisted motives. Just tell me—"

"I've got a meeting. Sorry." Mark stood up and strode for the door.

"What meeting? About the project?"

He opened her door a slit and looked up and down the hallway before he stepped outside.

"Are you expecting someone?"

For an instant, he turned back to look at her. "Do not, I repeat, *do not* tell anyone about this conversation."

CHAPTER FOUR

***

DR. MAUREEN COLE STRODE ACROSS THE MAYFLOWER HOTEL'S FAMOUS LOBBY IN Washington DC, glancing at the ornate walls, the woodwork, and artwork. Everything bespoke grace and sophistication, even the uniformed doormen.

And smack in the middle of all that refined elegance stood the well-known southwestern archaeologist, Dusty Stewart—as out of place as a coyote in a petting zoo. In contrast to Maureen's immaculately fitted wool suit, Dusty sported a sweat-stained Stetson and cowboy boots that were worn down at the heel. Mirrored sunglasses hid his blue eyes but, in concession to the place and time, at least his blond beard was combed. His garish yellow t-shirt proudly proclaimed ARCHAEOL-OGISTS DO IT IN THE DIRT in big black letters.

As she headed for him, a stream of European tourists hustled by, dragging suitcases. When two of the young women spotted Dusty, they stopped short, eyes widening, and smiled at him. The young men in the group laughed and pointed, calling, "*C'est Roy Rogers, non?*"

"Non," Dusty called back, loudly pronouncing, "Are-key-ol-o-gist."

The group walked on by but the women kept shooting glances over their shoulders. The man drew female attention like a magnet. What woman wouldn't look twice? Dusty was, obviously, an untamed male as exotic as a Neandertal in western garb.

When Maureen walked over, Dusty said, "Why are there so many foreigners in DC?"

"It's the nation's capital? Home of the Smithsonian?"

"Don't look like museum people to me." Dusty gave them a squinty look and stuffed his thumbs in his belt. The t-shirt pulled tight across his muscular shoulders, hardened by years of shoveling, screening, and backpacking through rough country.

Maureen sighed. "I swear, if I can get you out of Washington without having to post bail, I'll call it a miracle of biblical proportions. You can't even go to Gallup without causing trouble."

"That wasn't my fault. Joseph Klah kept buying me beer. Haven't seen a single Navajo in DC, so I should be okay."

Maureen gave him a menacing look. "Let's go over the plan again."

"I know the plan." Dusty counted off on his fingers. "I take a cab to the Smithsonian. I ask for Brian O'Neil's office at the information desk. We look at the Anasazi artifacts, then I come back here and meet you." He hesitated. "Are you sure you don't want me to go with you to the FBI? I don't trust them. What do they want with you?"

"It's just a consultation."

"You're a Canadian citizen. You've got rights."

"Dusty, it's not like I haven't acted as a consultant to the American government before."

"Yeah, and it almost got you killed."

"That was the Department of Defense, not the FBI."

"They're all alike," he said in a low authoritative voice.

"At least they put us up in a nice hotel." She indicated the lobby.

"Yeah? The first time something explodes, don't say I didn't warn you."

Maureen gave him a sour look. "You really are annoying."

"I—"

"Dr. Cole?" the doorman interrupted. "Your car is here."

When she turned to leave, Dusty called, "Wish me luck."

Maureen examined his worried expression. "Just ask the doorman for a cab and give him a couple of dollars when he opens the door for you."

"I know that."

Dusty wouldn't blink twice if his truck broke down in the middle of the desert forty miles from the nearest paved road, but a cab ride in the big city terrified him.

"You sure you're okay?" she said.

"Get going, Maureen. I got things to do, too."

She walked outside to where a black Lincoln waited at the curb and climbed into the back seat.

"Dr. Cole?" the driver asked, staring into the mirror to get a good look at her.

"Yes."

"Welcome to Washington, ma'am. It's about a fifteen-minute drive to your destination."

"Thanks."

Maureen settled back, watching through the tinted window as the Lincoln pulled smoothly into traffic. She couldn't help but glance over her shoulder to see Dusty, obvious in his yellow t-shirt, talking to the doorman.

She leaned back and pulled her long black hair over her shoulders. Absently, she noted a few more long white hairs mixed in. She'd had them since her early twenties, but her Seneca Indian ancestry had limited them to just a few.

Fifteen minutes later, the driver turned off Pennsylvania, and down into the depths below the ponderous FBI headquarters. The driver lowered his window at the security booth and the uniformed agent glanced in before the barricades were lifted.

As the car pulled to the underground entrance, another agent, wearing a suit, opened her door. The African American woman, perhaps thirty, was smiling. She offered her hand.

"Dr. Cole? I'm Tony Jacobs. How was your trip in?"

"Fine, thank you."

Jacobs ushered Maureen through security where she passed the metal detector and her passport was inspected. Several halls and an elevator ride later, Maureen was led to a small conference room sporting a central wooden table, chairs, and overhead fluorescents that illuminated starkly white walls.

Jacobs asked, "May I have the secretary get you something to drink?"

"Coffee would be great."

"I'll send for it. In the meantime, please have a seat." Jacobs indicated the chair-lined table. The room itself was up-grade institutional with a whiteboard at one end.

As Maureen sat down, Jacobs produced a sheaf of papers, saying, "I'm sure you're familiar with our nondisclosure forms. The information we're about to discuss is classified and not to leave this room."

Maureen scanned the forms and signed.

Jacobs took them and left.

A few minutes later, two agents entered. The woman carried a laptop. They were professionally dressed, the man in a sport coat and tie, the woman wearing a gray, form-fitting skirt, a white blouse and gray jacket. On their heels came a young woman with a Styrofoam cup of coffee.

"Good morning, Dr. Cole." The man stepped forward, offering his hand. He looked to be in his mid-forties, blond hair graying at the temples. He appraised her with watery blue eyes. His belly suggested a desk job. "I'm special agent Phil Hart."

"Amy Randall," the woman said, shaking Maureen's hand. "Assistant to the Secretary, Department of Defense." She had a blocky face and brown hair.

The first inkling of unease went through Maureen. "Defense?"

Amy Randall gave her a smile completely devoid of humor and placed the laptop on the table in front of her. "Secretary Rivera was impressed with your performance on your last assignment."

Maureen quietly said, "Sure, and those radical jihadist factions still have *fatwahs* outstanding that call for my execution."

Randall seated herself opposite Maureen. "This has nothing to do with Islam and, to set your mind at ease, we're not setting you up to be a target."

"Good. Having done that, I don't care to play again."

Randall gave her a bland smile. "All we want is your opinion of an article that is scheduled to be published online six months from now in the *Journal of Strategic Assessment.*"

"I'm not familiar with the *Journal of Strategic Assessment.*"

As Randall opened the laptop and pulled up the article, she replied, "It's pretty specialized, catering to think-tanks concentrating on globalization, international law... what you'd call policy wonks. Most of the participants are NGOs, consultants, political hired guns. That sort of thing. You're here because of your anthropological expertise."

"The world is full of anthropologists. Why pull me off an archaeological excavation in the New Mexico backcountry?"

Randall was staring at the screen when she said, "Because mass murder isn't just academic for you. You've excavated the bodies from graves in Ecuador, Venezuela, Serbia, and Armenia. You've touched the victims, given them names and faces. You understand the stakes."

Maureen shifted in her chair. "This is about mass murder?"

Amy Randall pointed. "Please take a look at the article and let us know your opinion of its validity."

Maureen shifted the computer to read the title of the article: THE COLLAPSE OF THE NATION-STATE: A PREDICTIVE STATISTICAL MODEL. The author was Mark Schott, PhD. Maureen scanned the abstract.

"Interesting." She frowned. "I'm familiar with Schott's computer models for the collapse of prehistoric civilizations, but this…"

Her voice faded when she clicked on one of the figures and four maps appeared side by side with a timetable at the bottom. Africa, Europe, Asia, and America appeared in time lapse. She watched centuries pass in seconds as blue splotches swelled and shrank, spreading across the continents to show the rise and fall of civilizations.

"Hmm. That's a brilliant reconstruction but it's not new."

"Keep going," Randall instructed. "It's the next figure we're concerned about."

Maureen clicked on the next figure. The same maps appeared but, this time, they simulated the future rise and collapse of global cultures. Fascinated, she noted that America only had seventeen years left…

She got out of the figure and returned to reading the article in earnest. The complicated statistical equations that predicted the future made up more than half the paper and were slow going. Through it all, the others sat silently until she looked up.

"So?" Randall asked. "What do you think?"

Maureen straightened in her chair. "It's stunning. Radical. And, frankly, a little unbelievable."

"What do you mean?"

"Well—" she shook her head "—using mathematics to understand the past isn't new. Archaeologists have been doing this for decades. What is new is suggesting that four human emotions can be quantitatively measured to predict human behavior and, thereby, predict the future. But, frankly, his statistics are way beyond my ability to understand."

Agent Phil Hart leaned forward and braced a hand on the table to look over her shoulder. "So, based upon your initial assessment, you think it could be spurious?"

"No, I didn't say that. I said the math is beyond me."

Randall frowned. "What did you think about the section that suggests American's economic collapse is near?"

"I'm not sure that just plugging four variables into a model can predict that—but based upon the known course of human history, I suspect it's possible."

"Then you believe it?" Randall was watching her so intently it made her very uncomfortable.

Maureen touched the screen to scroll through the article again, reading the equations before she glanced up to meet their eyes. "Am I here because of my publications about how a human sense of deprivation—even something as abstract as a deprivation of justice—fuels Islamic fundamentalist movements that inevitably lead to cultural collapse?"

Amy Randall pulled a pen and small notebook from her purse to take notes. "Dr. Cole, our primary concern is that someone can use this model as a guidebook. If you follow the model step by step, plugging in specific variables, can it be used to plot the downfall of a nation?"

"As I said before, I'm not the person you need. It would take a very competent statistician to give you that answer."

Hart and Randall looked meaningfully at each other and some silent communication passed between them.

Hart said, "Let's assume, for the moment, that Dr. Schott's model can be used for that purpose. What then?"

Maureen saw uncertainty in his watery blue eyes. "Then you'd better prepare for the apocalypse."

Randall inhaled and held the breath while her gaze drifted around the conference room. Finally, she exhaled the words: "I see."

Maureen's gaze went to Randall. "By the way, how did you get this article six months before publication?"

Randall made an airy gesture with one hand. "We have people who monitor such publications."

"You said the article *was scheduled* to be published. Did you—"

"It's a matter of national security; of course, we pulled it. That article will never be published. I guarantee you that. It would be like publishing a guidebook on how to create a nuclear weapon."

The tension in the room was increasing. Maureen said, "May I keep the article to study it more thoroughly?"

"You may. But you've signed a nondisclosure agreement so, if you share the article with anyone, I'll have you shot," Ms. Randall smiled as though she was joking, but Maureen had the feeling she wasn't.

Pointedly, Maureen asked, "You're not considering using this model to plot the downfall of China or Iran, are you?"

Randall didn't answer for a few long moments. "Thank you for your expertise today, Dr. Cole. We'll have two agents escort you to your hotel. Have a nice flight back to New Mexico. We'll be in touch."

CHAPTER FIVE

***

MAUREEN GLANCED AT THE THERMOMETER IN THE DASH OF THE RENTAL CAR AS SHE TURNED off Speedway and into the University of Arizona.

"Good Lord, it's 103 and it's not even noon."

"Yeah, pleasant day," Dusty the desert-dweller replied from the passenger seat.

"People live here on purpose?"

"You should be here when the asphalt starts to melt. Now that's hot."

She found the parking lot Fred Zoah had suggested, took a ticket, and prowled for a space.

"So," Dusty wondered from the passenger seat, "you gonna tell Fred more than you told me?"

She glanced at him as she waited for a young woman to back out of a space. "What's to tell? We're going to get Fred's take on a few statistical data clusters."

"Then we're going to be here for days." Dusty pulled his sweat-stained straw hat down tight as she wheeled into the space. "Fred runs five statistical programs to decide if he has to pee in the morning."

Maureen pulled the pages of statistical equations she'd extracted from the Schott article from the console and opened her door. She would just be sharing equations, not the article. The heat hit her like a sledgehammer.

As they walked out into the sun, Dusty donned his mirrored sunglasses and led the way to the anthropology department. Maureen almost gasped in delight when they entered the air-conditioned building.

"I've read plenty of statistical articles modeling the collapse of pre-historic societies. Why would the Feds care about these data clusters?"

She gave him a sharp glance. "That's classified, Stewart."

"So you said." Dusty pointed to the building directory and found Zoah's room number. A flight of stairs and a hallway later, they stopped at Dr. Fred Zoah's door. It was plastered with statistical equations.

Maureen knocked.

They waited.

Maureen knocked again. "He said he'd be here, right?"

"Sure. But knowing Fred that was probably with five degrees of statistical freedom."

Maureen was raising her hand to knock again when a voice called, "Read the door! Office hours are Wednesday and Friday!"

"Fred!" Dusty bellowed. "It's us."

Maureen heard a chair squeak. A moment later, a gray-haired man peered at her as the door cracked open. Thick glasses in industrial frames enlarged his eyes to fish-like proportions. "Oh. Dusty, Dr. Cole, I didn't expect you until this afternoon."

"I said noon," Dusty reminded as he opened the door wider.

Zoah, dressed in a rumpled white shirt and chinos frosted with clumps of cat hair, checked his watch. "Oh. Well, I thought it was still morning."

As Maureen stepped into Zoah's cluttered office, she noticed that his shirt had been misbuttoned and the collar was askew. The man's fly was held together with a safety pin and he wore two different colors of socks visible above worn brown loafers.

The office, like the man, was a disaster. Towers of poorly stacked archaeological reports rose from the carpet and leaned precariously. A work table supported a small mound of statistics books that partially buried at least four coffee cups. The trash can overflowed with crumpled pieces of paper, most of which were covered with statistical formulae. Long sheets of computer printout had been taped to the walls, some coming loose where the tape had aged and lost grip. Obsolete computers formed a sort of edifice in one corner—an archaeological stratigraphy makes and models. Maureen craned her neck, sure that an Apple II and a Xerox 820 lay at bottom.

"I keep them," Zoah said soberly, seeing her interest. "Never know when I might need to recover an old program I developed years ago."

Dusty had an amused look, his blond mustache curled as it did when he was trying to hide a smile.

The two spare chairs were mounded with clutter. The desk, dominated by a glowing computer monitor, was piled equally high.

"How do you find things in here?" Dusty asked in amazement.

Zoah's eyes swam behind his glasses. "Like everything in life, it's a stochastically modeled statistical probability."

Maureen handed him the pages of statistics that she'd printed out. She wasn't exactly violating Randall's order. She wasn't sharing the article, just a bunch of equations. "This is what we're interested in. I was hoping you could take a look at these. I just need to know if the math is valid."

Zoah inspected the first page. "Hmm. Very specialized." He flipped pages, lips moving as he studied them. "Clever use of tau, don't you think? And that's an innovative application of correlation coefficients."

Dusty grimaced. "If you say so."

Zoah lowered himself to his chair, plucked up an old-fashioned calculator, and began dexterously tapping as he glanced back and forth between the pages and the digital display.

While she waited, Maureen browsed the titles of the books on Zoah's shelves. After thirty minutes, she finally asked, "Dr. Zoah?"

Zoah remained oblivious.

"Dr. Zoah?" she asked, louder.

"Hmm." He started, giving her a surprised glance through his bottle-bottom glasses. "Oh, yes. Sorry."

"What are your initial impressions?"

"Where's the rest of the data?"

Maureen frowned. "What do you mean?"

"I mean I'd *love* to see the rest of the model. So many deterministic variables are missing."

"Huh?" Dusty asked.

Zoah thumped the pages. "I'm saying the author is very clever. He's taken the best work in the field… I see some of my own here… and cherry-picked the statistics. But I don't know where these forced statistics come from. Nonetheless, they are incredibly elegant. He tailored each and built a synthesis, fitting them into a seamless whole. But he doesn't provide a linkage between some of the deterministic and stochastic assumptions. Nor does he elaborate on which initial conditions would precipitate an application of—"

"Hey, Fred," Dusty interrupted, waving his hand in front of Fred's face. "I'm a field archaeologist, okay? Give me an elementary explanation."

"Oh, well... of course. What I mean is the author assumes his audience is too stupid to understand he's left out critical details, statistically speaking. Without the other statistics, no one can reliably plan the destruction of a nation."

Maureen's sudden intake of breath was loud in the quiet room. Her eyes went wide. "You can tell from those equations that the author is—"

"Of course, I can tell. In fact, I assume this is the work of Mark Schott."

Dusty squinted when Fred looked up from the pages. "Mark Schott from the University of Wyoming? The guy is a swine. What's he doing plotting the destruction of a nation?"

Maureen felt her breathing go shallow. "How do you know that's what those equations imply?"

Fred adjusted his glasses. "Think of my work on the Hohokam. I compare data we've collected about the people who lived in the Phoenix basin here in Arizona. That includes archaeological material, environmental data, climate, soils, water supplies, total land area under cultivation, canal maintenance, transportation, storage, population estimates based on house size, village size, resource availability, and a host of other variables. From that, I attempt to model exactly how Hohokam society functioned—specifically so I can tell you why it collapsed. And in the end, based upon the variables I choose, I can compute the chances that my model is correct. For years, Schott has been doing the same thing, albeit with less sophistication than my models—" he tapped the pages with a finger "—until now."

Dusty asked, "Are you saying that Schott is taking archaeological models, like yours, and applying them to modern societies?"

"Certainly. Archaeology gives us the ability to study human cultural systems across time. Once you know that—"

"You can kill your enemy?" Dusty put it bluntly.

Fred nodded. "We call it diachronic evaluation. Think about it. For five hundred years, the Hohokam flourished in one of the most inhospitable deserts on earth. Then, in 1380 AD, they collapsed. Migration from the north, coupled with a natural disaster, exceeded their ability to produce food. Within a generation, the mighty canals ran dry, their once-green fields became nothing but wind-scoured dust, and the great towns were abandoned."

Dusty propped his hands on his hips. "Same as the Chaco Anasazi, Cahokia, the Lowland Maya, Harapan civilization, the Minoans, the Hittites, you name it."

Maureen whispered, "That's why Schott based his work on archaeological models. Because they've been derived from the study of failed cultures."

"That's right." Zoah plucked off his glasses and cleaned them on his shirt. "What Schott does so brilliantly is to take everything we've learned and apply the model to the modern world to predict the future."

Maureen blinked. "What is the probability that it actually can predict—?"

"That," Zoah stated, "is what I'm trying to tell you. Everything hinges on how the data are sampled. The variables, the types and quality of data employed, all are critical to assessing the predictive model's utility."

"I don't get it." Dusty pushed his hat back on his head.

Zoah gave him a fish-eyed look. "Measure the wrong things and Dr. Schott's model is nothing more than an intellectual curiosity. Measure the right things, and the model becomes a weapon of war."

Maureen was watching Dusty when he went pale.

It took a couple of seconds before he turned to her. "Department of Defense. Now, I get it. Who are we planning to kill?"

She just stared at him.

CHAPTER SIX

***

ANIKA WALKED, HEAD BENT AGAINST THE ICY WIND, AND GLANCED UP AT THE SCUDDING clouds. The University of Wyoming, in Laramie, sat in a high mountain basin. At 7,000 feet, it was perpetually subjected to west winds. She was a Wyoming native. She should have been adequately dressed in her coat but, even for late April, the day felt bitter.

She tramped up to the administration building door, opened it and stepped inside, curious about the summons she'd received upon arriving at her office that morning. The department secretary had stuck her head in the door and stated: "Your presence has been requested at the highest levels. Dr. Chambers wants to see you at his office at one."

"The president? Why?"

Mary Ann had shrugged. "It's his university."

Anika found the president's office, announced herself to the secretary, and was led to a small meeting room. To her surprise, Mark Schott sat at the table looking uncommonly lordly. The Dean of the College of Social Sciences, Bill Laslo, hunched like a vulture across from Mark. And at the head of the table, President Chambers rose, offering his hand and greeting, "Dr. French? Thank you for coming on such short notice."

She shook the university president's hand, trying to read his eyes. Chambers wore a jacket, tie, and white shirt. His placid face reflected nothing.

God, this isn't about Mark and me, is it?

But another glance at Mark set her mind at ease. He didn't look like a man about to be chastised for diddling a graduate student.

She seated herself. "Why am I here, sir?"

"Dr. Schott, why don't you fill Dr. French in on what we've

been discussing?"

Triumph glittered in Mark's eyes. "I have taken a position as an international consultant for the ECSITE corporation. It was a last-minute development."

"Yes?" Anika said.

Mark glanced at Chambers. "I was able to negotiate a rather lucrative deal with ECSITE. The university will be the recipient of a grant, under my direction, to help with various aspects of the research I will be pursuing in international development. That includes two hundred fifty thousand a year for the department. Half of that is designated to fund my research assistant."

"Me, I assume?"

Dean Laslo interjected, "Yes, Dr. Schott has suggested that you fill his position. Not as department head, of course, but as an assistant professor."

"I'm not sure I'm interested in the position."

Mark preempted the others. "Come on, Anika, you need this job and you have the expertise required for the research ECSITE is conducting."

"Designing statistical predictive models," she concluded.

"Yes. You'll be honing your research and actually having a chance to apply it. And it's a huge benefit to the university."

Chambers steepled his fingers, leaning forward. "Ms. French, the university has no problem with this. After discussing the situation with Dr. Schott, and to fulfill the terms of the ECSITE grant, we'd have to replace Mark with a person skilled in predictive modeling. Given your obvious expertise, we'd be hard-pressed to find anyone better on such short notice."

She asked, "How many hours would I have to teach?"

Laslo said, "Three courses—"

"Two," Mark interrupted. "Both graduate level in statistical modeling. The rest of the time you'd be working directly with me."

Anika glanced at Laslo who looked enraged.

"Dr. French?" President Chambers said, "Are you interested?"

Her chances of landing a position anywhere else were less than ten percent. Even then, the salary offered at another institution would be poverty level. Surely, she could figure out a way to make this work.

"Yes. I'll take the position."

Mark looked so relieved she thought he might faint as he flopped back in his chair.

Chambers replied, "Good. I'll have the paperwork sent over." He looked around. "Anything else? No? Then, Mark, I'll leave you to work out the details with Dr. French."

CHAPTER SEVEN

* * *

ANIKA CLOSED THE DOOR BEHIND HER AS SHE FOLLOWED MARK SCHOTT INTO HIS office. She wasn't surprised to note that most of it was already packed into boxes.

"Have a seat, Anika," he said and gestured to the chair in front of his desk.

She sat stiffly with her arms folded. "How are you planning to use *my* model?"

He shuffled through some papers on his desk. Without looking at her, he replied, "ECSITE is interested in putting their resources where they will have the most beneficial impact in building the developing world. You and I will be helping them choose the most advantageous places to invest. I'm looking at social structure, tribal mores, distribution systems. Can educational facilities be easily integrated into tribal society? Estimating religious flexibility… that sort of thing. And yes, it's based on *parts* of your model."

"You sound like a publicist. I want to know exactly what ECSITE does."

"ECSITE specializes in international finance—investors looking for opportunities in the developing world. They have discovered that economics is one thing, politics another. Where they seek an advantage is in understanding the native cultures. Most investment firms have no sense for indigenous rights or how a sudden influx of capital or technology will impact a tribal or kin-based society. You and I do. We'll be helping to protect native peoples while ECSITE builds their economies and makes their lives better."

She watched him for a moment, mentally applying the model in the ways Mark suggested. She couldn't dismiss the potential benefits.

"If this is all true, why do you have that guilty look?"

To avoid her eyes, he straightened his cuffs again. "I know I've made mistakes. I've tried to make it up to you. Hopefully, getting you this position helps." He raised a hand, forestalling her protest. "And I'm removing myself from the problem."

"What problem?"

"You bring out the worst in me, Anika." He smiled shyly. "Denise and I are moving to Europe so I won't see you much, if at all, after today. Now, take the job, tackle the research, and even if you stay in the university system, you'll be able to write your own ticket after two years."

"I have the gut feeling that something's wrong about this, Mark."

He gave her a soft look. "It's worth a try, isn't it? What if the model, *your* model, gives applied anthropology a tool that can sidestep the usual deleterious effects of development on fragile societies? Isn't that worth a shot?"

CHAPTER EIGHT

***

MAUREEN WATCHED DUSTY PACE THEIR ROOM ON THE SECOND FLOOR OF TUCSON'S HILTON Garden Inn. He was swinging his sunglasses, a familiar frown betraying his thoughts as he considered everything Zoah had told them.

Dusty muttered, "My tax dollars at work. The government is flying you all over because somebody wrote a statistical model to murder people."

"That remains to be proven," she answered and turned her attention to the window; relentless Arizona sunlight gleamed on rows of rush hour traffic inching down I-10. Beyond the buildings, across the San Pedro valley, saguaro-covered hills wavered in the distance as heat waves rose.

Dusty said, "And, of course, it's Mark Schott. He's slimy on the best of days. Wonder where the rest of the equations are that make the model work?"

"I wonder that, too."

Dusty watched her through suspicious eyes. "I was a lot happier when all we had to do was worry about Navajo witches and prehistoric serial killers."

She glanced at the clock. "I have to call Washington. Why don't you go down and get a beer?"

"I don't get to listen in?"

She pointed at the door.

He hesitated.

"My God, Stewart. The world just stopped turning and pink rabbits can fly."

"Huh?"

"You just turned down the opportunity to go for a beer."

He grinned, grabbed up his hat, mashed it on his head, and said, "Maybe I'll call the guys from the Institute of Desert Archaeology.

See if anyone's up for a little party."

"Sure. Just don't mention anything about the data clusters."

"I'm not that dense. I'm pretty sure there's a DOD hit squad watching our hotel." Then, donning his sunglasses, Dusty was gone.

Maureen stepped over to the hotel phone, read the directions for an out-of-state call, and dialed the Washington number she'd been given.

Amy Randall picked up on the second ring. *"Randall."*

"It's Maureen Cole."

"What have you found?"

"Apparently, Dr. Schott has taken the finest archaeological models and molded them into something applicable to the modern world. A predictable model that may be able to predict the future.

"May? Why only may?"

"The model presented in the article doesn't work. Key variables and the justification for many of the statistical functions are missing."

"Missing?"

"I mean a predictive statistical model is only as good as the data it's based upon. If you are measuring the wrong things, say the price of consumer goods, you can't make a statement about a family's living standard unless you compare it to household income. In this case, the article doesn't reveal which variables to plug into the statistics. It's like doing algebra without numbers. Just the equation."

"So it could be garbage?"

"Could be, but I doubt it."

Silence.

"Ms. Randall?"

"Call me Amy. Looks like we're in this for the long haul."

"Why don't you just get Dr. Schott on the line and ask him?"

"I'll have travel book you a flight to Laramie."

"Why me?"

"One, because you're our anthropologist. And two, you're the one who's up to speed on this."

Maureen frowned out at the desert visible through the window. Sunlight glittered across the hills. "I'm sure you have statisticians far superior to me. Shouldn't they be the ones—"

"And leave Stewart behind this time. That's an order. He's a loose cannon."

CHAPTER NINE

***

ANIKA CLIMBED THE STAIRS FROM THE CLASSROOM LEVEL TO HER OFFICE FLOOR, A HEAVY stack of term papers in her arms. Thirty students had handed in their papers, each twenty pages in length. That left her with 600 pages to read over the weekend.

She'd just begun to appreciate the learning curve for all of her responsibilities. It was daunting, to say the least, but she comforted herself with the knowledge that others had done it before her. What she really dreaded was Monday's coming faculty meeting. Just how was she going to handle that? In an instant, she'd become the new kid in class. Professors had already begun barraging her with questions she barely had answers to. Old friends were suddenly reserved, and the halls buzzed with speculation as to why Mark Schott had left, and why administration had elevated Anika French to a professor's position.

I'll deal with it, she promised herself. *Just do my work, be smart, and keep my nose clean.*

When she rounded the corner to her hallway, she stopped short.

Keep your cool. Be professional.

Anika strode toward the brunette woman, calling, "Hello, Denise. I thought you and the boys would be off to Munich with Mark?"

Denise Schott was an attractive woman, her facial features fine and dominated by large brown eyes. She dressed to emphasize her bust and long legs. Today, she'd chosen a fitted blouse and tan cotton pants belted at her slim waist. Her shoulder-length hair was curled as if fresh from the beautician.

Denise gave her a hostile look. "So, he left you, too?"

"Excuse me?"

Denise tilted her head toward Anika's office, indicating that she should continue inside.

Anika opened the door, placed the papers on the corner of her desk, and offered a chair as she lowered herself into her own. Heart pounding, she asked, "What can I help you with?"

"What's Mark into?"

"I don't—"

"Let's cut the crap, shall we? I just found Mark's note on the kitchen table. What's he doing in Germany? What's this all about?"

Anika stiffened. "All I know is that he took a position with this ECSITE corporation. I looked them up online. Apparently, they're a multi-billion-dollar investment firm. Consultants for the mega banks. The CEO is a Russian, a man named Mikael Zoakalski. Their head-quarters is in Zurich but most of their operations are run from a small town outside of Munich."

Denise gave her the same look she'd give a moldy sandwich. "Are you pregnant?"

"Pregnant?"

"Do you answer every question with a question? It's a simple yes or no."

"No! And wait a minute. I'm not sleeping with Mark! This thing caught me by complete surprise, too."

Denise seemed to lose steam, composure breaking. "Is it some other woman?"

"I don't think so."

"He didn't discuss it with you? You really didn't know what he was planning?"

"No."

"Is he in any kind of trouble?"

"Not to my knowledge." Anika took a breath to steady herself. "What I do know is that there's a lot of money involved. He told you that, didn't he?"

"Money, money, money. That's all he cares about." She sniffed. "Why fucking Germany? What was wrong with being a professor in Wyoming?"

"I have no idea. The first I heard of it was Monday morning. I swear."

She gave Anika a probing look. "Did he ask you to go?"

Anika felt her gut drop. "No."

"Don't lie to me." The woman looked ready to disintegrate.

"My involvement with your husband is research-related. Period. I have commitments here for at least the next year. And even if I didn't, and he wasn't a married man, I still would not be going to Munich with him. End of story."

"You didn't always feel that way."

Anika winced at the accusatory tone.

"I knew," Denise whispered. "Just like the other times. The thing is: He really fell for you. It was never the same afterward."

Anika, heart bleeding, said nothing.

"I've been living a lie since I married him."

"Are you going to Munich?" Anything to change the subject.

"He didn't ask me to go. Will and Jake… they're broken-hearted."

"I'm sorry, Denise. Really and truly sorry."

She nodded, eyes focused on infinity. "So, that wasn't your car?"

"Excuse me?"

"Stop doing that!" she snapped, eyes suddenly fiery.

"What car?" Anika asked in irritation.

"The one watching our house."

Anika shook her head. A car watching Denise's house? That made no sense. Maybe someone from ECSITE? But why? They'd know Mark was already on his way to Germany. She saw the worry reflected in Denise's eyes. "Listen to me: I've been overwhelmed since this all broke. I'm lucky to get six hours sleep a night. The last thing I have time to do is sit in a car outside your house."

Denise looked up. "Then who was it?"

"If there's someone watching your house, for God's sake, call the police."

"Maybe it's nothing. I could just be paranoid. Didn't sleep last night. I paced around trying to figure it all out."

"Did you tell anyone that Mark was leaving? That you'd be alone?"

"No one."

Anika stood. "Denise, call the police. Immediately. Meanwhile, go home. Keep the doors locked. Get some rest." She took a breath. "I'm not sure what I could do but if you need something…"

"I think you've already done enough." Denise stood. "Sorry to bother you."

Anika watched Denise Schott straighten her shoulders and walk out the door. Elbows on her desk, she dropped her head into her hands.

When she heard steps coming back up the hallway, she just closed her eyes. The person stopped in her doorway. Trying to keep the sound of defeat out of her voice she asked, "Yes, Denise? What is it?"

"Anika French?" the voice was controlled and definitely not Denise's.

Anika lifted her head. The woman was tall, long-legged, wearing a tailored jacket, matching skirt, and pale blue blouse. The woman's long black hair and face hinted at Native American, or perhaps Hispanic, ancestry.

The woman cocked her head knowingly. "Is this a bad time?"

"No. Sorry. What can I do for you?"

"I'm Dr. Maureen Cole."

Anika started at the name, did a double take. "Dr. Cole?" She stood, suddenly rejuvenated, and shook the woman's offered hand. "Wow! It's not every day that a celebrity walks into my office."

"A celebrity?"

"Well, not everyone gets shot at and nearly bombed in the name of anthropology."

"Yeah, well…" Cole glanced around, eyes fixing on the model that covered the walls. Anika noticed the leather binder under her arm.

"That's a—"

"A predictive model," Cole answered. "And a very sophisticated one."

"How do you know about my dissertation? It hasn't even been bound yet."

Cole turned. "*Your* dissertation?"

Anika felt her throat going dry and swallowed hard. "Yes, ma'am."

"Tell me about Dr. Schott. He guided you through this?"

Anika felt the pieces coming together in her mind. *The model. Everything revolved around it. Even the appearance of Maureen Cole in her office door. Why? What was the missing variable?* "Dr. Schott chaired my committee, but he had to go outside the department to mathematics to grade the statistics."

"Dr. Schott isn't a statistician?"

"Oh, he's got the basics. Better than ninety percent of the other cultural anthropologists working in the discipline. But, no, he couldn't understand most of my model."

Cole gave her that evaluative look again. "When I asked at the desk, they said he wasn't here and referred me to you."

"Mark... Dr. Schott's gone to Germany."

Cole walked forward to place the leather case on Anika's desk and open it. "Dr. French, I have permission to show this to you but you can't keep it."

"What is it?" Anika sat forward, trying to see it.

"Could you tell me what Schott was getting at here?" She touched a section of the paper. "There are apparently some missing variables."

"Missing...?" Anika skimmed the title page. *Journal of Strategic Assessment.* Scanning down the page she found the first of her statistics, then more. Frantically, she flipped the pages, seeing her work. Finally, she turned back to the title page where **Mark Schott, PhD** was prominently printed as the author's name, just below the title of the article.

"I feel sick."

Cole frowned at her. "What do you mean?"

She fought to control her anger. "This is my work, Dr. Cole, not Mark's. But I never intended for it to be used in this way!"

Maureen Cole cocked her head slightly. "Then may I ask you some questions about the missing variables?"

Adrenaline was flooding Anika's veins. "I'm sure Mark didn't understand the model well enough to realize he'd left out critical variables."

"Then, I'd appreciate it if you could explain this section..."

CHAPTER TEN

***

MARK SCHOTT STARED DOWN AT IRREGULAR GREEN FIELDS, STANDS OF TREES PLANTED IN rows like a garden, winding roads, and neat, red-roofed Bavarian villages as the Airbus banked on approach to Franz Joseph Strauss International Airport.

A sense of giddy excitement filled him. *It's really happening. And I'm doing it in first class!*

He couldn't believe it. He'd always hoped that he would end up in some emeritus position at one of the major universities. He'd told people Harvard but any of the Ivy League schools would have been acceptable. None of his fantasies had prepared him for this.

He glanced at Simon Gunter, sitting erect in the over-padded aisle seat. The man was locked in thought, his brown eyes fixed on the bulkhead before him.

The long plane flights with Gunter hadn't exactly been a joy. The man could be described as "conversationally impaired." To Mark's surprise, Gunter had no sense of humor. At least, none he could determine. He didn't like jokes and had no interest in discussing the attractive flight attendants who waited on their every whim. They'd supplied Mark with copious amounts of quality champagne.

Mark had never flown first class. Professors didn't fall into that socioeconomic bracket. If this was any indication of where his life was headed, well, he was all for it.

The big Airbus changed altitude, swooping down from the sky like a god.

The landing was perfect, but the taxi seemed to take forever before the plane finally pulled into the terminal. Mark gathered his bag and slipped into his jacket when the smiling flight attendant provided it to him. He gave her a wink that she shrugged off with another professional smile.

"A car will be waiting," Gunter told him. "I will meet you on the other side of passport control. You have the documents I gave you?"

Mark tapped his pocket. "All here."

"*Ja, ja.* Do not joke with the agents. Be professional. These people have no sense of humor."

"Right. Okay."

The process was efficient. Mark followed instructions, didn't even smile, answered their questions, and got his official stamps. Gunter was waiting upon his exit. His "green tagged" luggage wasn't even inspected when Mark handed his customs statement card to the officer. He followed Gunter through the final *Ausfart*-marked door.

A man and woman waited at the side of the crowd and stepped forward. Both were dressed in suits, of medium height, and, if Mark could judge, in their mid-thirties. He gave the woman a second glance. Trim, she had a great body and athletic spring in her step. The way she'd pinned her blonde hair, he couldn't tell if it was long or not. Then his limbic system flooded his brain as he really got a good look at her delicate face, full lips, and sparkling blue eyes.

Damn! Stunning. Don't tell me she's one of my new assistants?

As Mark struggled to keep from gaping like an idiot, the woman gave Gunter a smile and said something in German. Gunter replied, then turned. "Dr. Schott, this is Stephanie Huntz. She will be helping you to get acquainted with ECSITE. If you have any questions, or needs, she will be of assistance."

"Glad to meet you," Huntz said in slightly accented English. She offered her hand for a firm shake. "We are looking forward to working with you."

"My pleasure, Ms. Huntz."

"Please, call me Stephanie."

Unlike Gunter, she had a genuine smile. Perfect white teeth flashed behind full red lips.

Huntz nodded toward Gunter. "Anyone who survives a long trip with Simon and is still in a good mood must have unusual resilience."

Mark laughed, hoping he wasn't blushing and turned to the brown-haired man with broad shoulders.

Stephanie introduced him. "May I present Pierre LaFevre, from our Zurich office. He will be implementing your research."

"Good to meet you." LaFevre extended a hand. "I've been studying your work. As fascinating as the published material is, I cannot wait to get into the variables you were unable to include in such a small article."

"It's all coming," Mark told him, wondering what the man meant.

Stephanie Huntz interjected, "I checked just before your flight. FedEx tracking informs us that your materials should be delivered sometime tomorrow."

Gunter, without another word, gestured that they proceed.

LaFevre locked step with Gunter, speaking in German. Mark understood nothing, except a couple of *neins*.

"Our background research suggested that you don't speak German. Is that correct?" Stephanie asked, dimples of amusement forming at the corners of her mouth. Was there anything about her that wasn't charming?

"Somehow, I never got around to learning that one. Maybe it's something I can pick up."

"If you have the time. You'll find that most Germans have enough English to get along. Everyone you'll work with is fluent."

"Where did you learn your English?"

"My father was American. He met my mother while he was stationed in Heidelberg. When he was transferred to Virginia, mother and I went along." She shrugged. "He met another woman. Mother and I came home. A couple of years after the divorce, he was killed in an airplane crash." She gestured with a slim hand. "Apparently, his commitment to good aviation practice was as limited as his devotion to matrimony. I've never made that mistake."

"With matrimony?" Of course, she'd be married. German masculinity would be in question if they let a gorgeous creature like this run free.

"Flying," she said evenly. "I inherited my father's passion for fast airplanes. And, fortunately, my mother's level-headed devotion to self-preservation."

"So, you're from Heidelberg?"

"Have you been there?" She shot him a cool smile. "I thought you'd only delivered papers in Frankfurt and Berlin?"

"Uh... that's right."

"Heidelberg is one of the most beautiful cities in the world. Perhaps when things are under control, you'd like to tour the town, see the castle?"

"I would like that."

To Mark's further delight, a long black Mercedes was idling at the curb. The driver took both his bags and Gunter's and placed them in the trunk before opening the door. Mark slipped into the back seat with Stephanie and Pierre LaFevre. Gunter took the passenger seat.

As they followed the exit route, Mark craned his neck, staring at the terminal's great arching roof with its cable trusses. Then, he glanced around the plush interior.

Yes, I could get very used to this.

"Outside of delivering a couple of papers, have you spent much time in Germany?" Stephanie inquired.

"Just in and out to deliver papers on predictive modeling."

Then he got his first glimpse of the Alps, still mantled in snow. "Wow," he whispered.

"They are even more magnificent from the air. You are used to mountains?" Stephanie asked.

"Wyoming has its share. And we're just north of Colorado. I was born in Iowa. Mountains are still a novelty."

"You will like our offices. We're located outside of Oberau, at the foot of the Alps."

"I have so many questions," LaFevre interrupted. "How did you come by the stress statistic? Measuring stress in a social system is so subjective. I, myself—"

"Pierre," Stephanie interrupted, "Dr. Schott just finished a long flight. With Gunter, no less. Let him relax."

"Sorry," Pierre made an apologetic gesture. "I just have so many questions."

Stephanie laughed as if in relief. "Oh, yes. So many questions. All statistics and no life."

"I have a life," LaFevre protested.

"Yes, an intimate relationship with a computer." She glanced at Mark. "But he hasn't had a date with a woman since university. And even then, I've heard, it was with his mathematics professor."

Pierre made a face, smiled, and shrugged. "If God would make an attractive mathematician, perhaps I would be inclined to take her out for a delightful evening."

Stephanie whispered conspiratorially to Mark. "What a delight. Scribbling equations on the tablecloth all night."

He studied Stephanie Huntz from the corner of his eye, evaluating the swell of her breasts, the way her coat narrowed at the waist. Seated, the skirt had ridden up, revealing her perfect legs. She had no ring on her finger but, in this day and age, that didn't mean anything.

"So, what does a person do in Oberau? I mean, after hours?"

"I'm afraid you'll be occupied in the ECSITE compound for a while, but do you ski?"

"Never had the time to learn. I'd be a clumsy novice."

"Garmisch-Partenkirchen is just up the road. In winter, it's a skier's holiday-haven filled with restaurants and shops. The nightlife is all anyone could ask. But if you are enchanted by the city, Munchen, excuse me, Munich is a fast half-hour's drive. Theatre, opera, fine shopping, wonderful restaurants, museums and cathedrals: they're all right there."

She'd had him so enchanted, he finally realized they were flying down the left lane and moving at an incredible clip. *This,* he thought, *is the real autobahn.*

Even in Wyoming, with its wide-open spaces, he'd never come close to topping out his BMW. Too many chances of hitting a deer or antelope. And yes, there was always the Wyoming Highway Patrol waiting to write a hefty ticket to maintain the state coffers.

He declared, "I think I'm going to like being here."

CHAPTER ELEVEN

***

MAUREEN COLE WATCHED ANIKA FRENCH'S REACTION, SAW THE CONFUSION. "MIND if I sit down?"

"No, please."

Maureen slid into the chair. "You didn't know Schott had submitted this article for publication?"

Anika looked at her with pained green eyes. "I can't believe he did this."

"The article has created quite a stir. All the way to the FBI."

"The FBI?" Anika looked terrified.

"It's brilliant work. You should be proud."

"But..." Anika anxiously licked her lips. "I designed it to analyze prehistoric societies, not modern ones."

Maureen evaluated her with steady eyes. "The article's title implies that the model has utility for today's world. Have you tested it on modern societies?"

"Once or twice, but nothing like applying it to a nation-state."

"Why would Dr. Schott have suggested that it could be used that way?"

Anika rubbed her forehead. "We discussed it over beer one night. He thought I should test it on modern America." A pause. "I didn't want to."

"Why not?"

"I was afraid of what I'd find. No one wants to discover her country is hurtling headlong toward the abyss."

The situation was almost absurd. A bright young graduate student's committee chair had published his student's work. The article had caught the eye of the FBI and State Department, causing them to call Maureen in. After a cross-country chase, here sat the source of all the brouhaha: a startled, attractive, and worried-looking redhead in her late twenties.

Maureen checked her watch. "Tell you what, it's almost five. All I've had to eat was a so-called breakfast wrap in the Tucson airport this morning. Why don't we go find a meal somewhere and talk this over? My treat."

Anika glanced uncertainly at the stack of term papers piled on the corner of her desk. "I don't know. I've got a lot to do." And just as quickly, she looked up, horrified. "What am I saying? Of course, I'll go. The most famous anthropologist in the world just asked me out to dinner!"

Maureen shoved herself out of her chair and smiled. "Uh, the fame isn't all it's cracked up to be. If I had my way, I'd be back in the lab analyzing the skeletal pathology of a murder victim."

Anika stood and almost tenderly placed her dissertation on the chair. Then, she reached for her purse.

Maureen hesitated. "If you don't mind, could you bring your dissertation? I'd like to take a look."

"Of course." Anika grabbed it up, extending it like an offering.

Maureen took it and stepped out into the hall. As Anika locked her office door, Maureen noticed a man down the hall, inspecting one of the archaeological displays of Clovis points. Normally, Maureen wouldn't have given him a second glance but something about the way he stood, the close-cropped hair, his over-muscled shoulders, struck a chord. Definitely, not a student.

"Know him?" Maureen asked, inclining her head.

Anika looked. "No."

"Come on." Maureen turned in the opposite direction and hurried Anika down the stairs. At the bottom, she glanced back, reassured that the man wasn't following. *Probably just getting paranoid in my old age. Right. That doesn't mean I'm stupid, either.*

She turned her attention back to Anika. "What motivated you to combine psychology, chemistry, economics, and biology, with archaeology in the first place?"

They walked past the Anthropology museum and out the side door. As Anika led the way to the parking lot, she replied, "All hard sciences rely on mathematics. I just used them to model the evolution of biological processes."

"Specifically, psychological processes, correct?"

Anika nodded. "Sure. I mean, there are only four basic human emotions: happiness, sadness, anger, and fear—and nuanced variations, of course. These emotions are simple biology. They cut across sociocultural influences, meaning they're universal to all human beings around the globe."

She glanced at Maureen to see if Maureen was following her. "Your four variables. I see. Continue."

"Well, I'd looked at the models created from the Maya and Cahokia data and analyzed the psychological factors that likely motivated the people. Then, I tried to apply them to the collapse of the Mississippian polities in the American Southeast in the 1400s. Climate played a huge role but emotion was the key."

"Why?"

Anika lifted her shoulders. "Climate puts humans in a situation where they have to make decisions but it doesn't make the decisions for them. They do that based upon one of the four emotions."

"And you're saying we can mathematically chart how emotional responses cascade and descend into chaos?"

"Exactly."

"That's my car." Maureen pointed. "You just tell me where to go. Your choice. As a starving graduate student, there's got to be a place that's generally out of your budget."

Anika directed her downtown—well, as downtown as Laramie, Wyoming, gets—to a restaurant that specialized in steak and seafood.

"Don't eat the seafood," Anika suggested as they were led to a table. "But as a ranch girl, I can tell you that the steaks are the best."

Maureen smiled. "If you'll excuse me, I've got to make a quick phone call. Order me a cup of coffee but have your favorite drink."

She retreated to the small lobby, retrieved her cell phone, and pressed Amy Randall's number.

"Randall."

"Are you always in the office? It's after seven in DC."

"Of course I'm in the office. I work for the Secretary of Defense. What have you got?"

Maureen outlined everything she'd learned from Anika French.

"She's a newly minted PhD?"

"Yes. Her committee chair, Mark Schott, published her research without her knowledge. And under his own byline, which is distasteful, but not all that rare. He's in Germany, by the way."

"We know. What does French say? Is this model really a guidebook for toppling a nation?"

Maureen sighed. "She's never tested the model on a modern society."

"Why not?"

"Basically? She doesn't want to prove the world is ending."

Silence.

"I want her on the first plane to DC and bring everything she has. Charts, data, graphs, notes, everything."

"I'll ask."

"You'll succeed or I'll have the nearest FBI field office arrest her, clean out her apartment, and drag her here."

Maureen heaved a sigh. "Understood."

Maureen thumbed the "end" button and walked back to the table to find Anika poring over the menu, a tall glass of some amber beer on the table in front of her.

"So, you said you were a ranch girl?"

Anika looked up. "If you don't mind, I'm going for the porterhouse, medium rare." Another worried look. "Uh, you're not a vegetarian, are you?"

"In spite of what I know about the industrial red meat industry, no. I love a good steak, preferably bison."

Anika pointed at the menu. "Right there on the menu. Grass-fed, locally raised. No hormones or antibiotics. And, yes, I was raised on a real Wyoming ranch. That was Mom's first love."

"What does your father do?"

"He was a Marine for most of his life. When Mom was killed, he came home. I was just finishing high school. He took over but, well, the place is leased now. Dad's the county sheriff." Her eyebrow lifted. "He's chasing down barbed wire thieves as we speak."

"So, you're close?"

"Very." She sounded sad.

"Too long away from home?"

Anika nodded. "Dad served at the point of the sword. He's the bravest man I know. I really miss him."

"What led you to anthropology?"

"We had a ranch covered with archaeological sites. Mom taught high school history as a way of making enough to keep the ranch running. She invited a University of Wyoming field school out to excavate a Paleoindian site. I was hooked. Before that, I thought I'd be a mathematician."

"Rare combination, math and anthro."

"Well, given what I know about agriculture, it beats pulling calves, vaccinating heifers, and trying to get a dime's worth of value out of each nickel."

"That bad, huh?"

Anika gave her a weary smile. "Dr. Cole, the only reason the small farm exists anywhere is through huge government subsidies, be it here, Europe, or China. The only money to be made in agriculture is on large corporate farms where volume production and growth hormones make it feasible."

"I've heard that American agriculture is growing less and less sustainable."

"Not just America." Anika leaned forward. "Did you know that, in China, human food production accounts for 57% of the total biomass? There's virtually no wildlife or wild country left. Everything alive is there to feed the massive human population of one-point-five-billion. Believe me, there's a comeuppance in the future."

"Scary."

They ordered their steaks.

While they waited, Maureen looked around the restaurant and sipped her coffee. "Where is Dr. Schott in Germany? Do you know?"

"Munich. He took a position with ECSITE Corporation. You know anything about them? They're international investors. Until you showed up, it didn't make sense. Why hire Mark for an investment firm? And it was all so sudden." Her face fell. "And then you brought the article and the variables fell into place."

Maureen stared across the table at Anika. "Speaking of the Chinese," she said, "did they offer Dr. Schott a position?"

Anika gave her a penetrating look. "The Chinese? I didn't know anything about the Germans until Monday. This all came out of the clear blue sky." A pause. "If the Chinese are interested…" Maureen could see her mind running predictive models behind her eyes. "The global implications…"

Maureen's phone rang.

"Dr. Cole?"

"Hello, Amy."

"Can you check out Dr. Schott's office? Maybe take a look at his records?"

"What am I looking for?"

"Anything you can find out about Dr. Schott's contacts." She sounded tense. *"We'll have a team there in four hours but if you could get there sooner, we'd appreciate it."*

Maureen gazed at Anika and found the woman frowning back at her with unnerving intensity. "I'll see what I can do."

Maureen shoved her phone back in her jacket pocket.

"Would you mind filling me in?"

Maureen sighed. "Anika, when Dr. Schott published that article, it started a storm. Unfortunately, you're right in the middle of it."

Maureen watched Anika's face change as her clever statistical mind put the pieces together. Then a glimmer of fear reflected in her eyes. "Are you saying that the government—"

"Don't panic. You're not in trouble. I was called to Washington by the FBI. That was them. They want me to take a look at Mark Schott's office."

"It's been cleaned out. I turned off the lights after the moving company took the last box." Anika had a deer-in-the-headlights look.

"All right, for my next bombshell, an assistant to the Secretary of Defense wants you in Washington. Immediately."

"Me?" Anika gaped. "Why? What did I do?"

"The DC statisticians want to ask you some questions about your model. That's all."

Anika stammered, "B-but… I *can't* go! Look, I've just been hired as an assistant professor. I can't screw this up."

Maureen gave her an amused smile. "If I could take care of the university, would you agree?"

Maureen got a hesitant nod before she pulled her phone out and entered Amy Randall's number.

"Randall."

"I need someone in authority to contact the University of Wyoming and clear Anika French for immediate travel to Washington. Oh, and they need to make clear that this will not in any way affect Ms. French's employment status."

"You're kidding."

"I think if you handle this little snag, Dr. French will be eternally grateful."

"Do you want the call to come from the Secretary or the President?"

"Now you're kidding."

"Consider the university handled."

"Thanks. By the way, Dr. French informs me that Mark Schott's office is completely empty. He cleaned everything out."

"Try his home. I'll have someone join you with a warrant. Keep your phone on."

"We're in the middle of dinner. Give us an hour." Maureen ended the call as sizzling steaks were placed on the table. Maureen took a moment to inhale the aroma. "The university is taken care of. Before we fly to Washington, we've got a couple of stops to make. First, we need to go back to your office and retrieve all of your notes and data, then we need to—"

"All my notes?" Anika, still pale, swallowed a gulp of beer.

"Yes, but for now just enjoy your steak. You're going to need your strength for what comes next."

CHAPTER TWELVE

***

MARK'S TRIP TO OBERAU MIGHT HAVE BEEN A FANTASY. STEPHANIE HUNTZ ACTED THE gracious hostess, pointing out the BMW corporate building, asking about his car. The proper pronunciation, he learned, was *Bay Em Vey*. He fought the urge to stare out the window or to ask too-personal questions about Stephanie's involvement with men. But he did notice that when she talked about going places, it was always "I" never "we." That gave him hope.

What was even more suggestive was that he hardly thought of Denise or the boys. He'd gotten over the bitter arguments they'd had after he'd announced he was taking the ECSITE job. Somehow, his arrival in Germany felt like stepping out of an old life and straight into a dream.

As Stephanie made a witty remark, he shared her laughter, only mildly surprised to discover the dream to be so intoxicating. Denise and the boys, in comparison, were little more than a fading nightmare.

He blinked at the jet lag nibbling at his brain and body. The long flight was finally leaching his reserves.

So, how do I play this? Stephanie's father walked out on her mother. What do I tell her upfront to keep her from casting me in the same light?

That would take some planning. He stifled a yawn. "Sorry. Long flight. Should have grabbed an energy drink back at the airport."

"Oh." Stephanie gave him another of her radiant smiles, unbuckled from her seatbelt, and leaned forward to a leather console behind the driver's seat. She opened the lid, fished around among the bottles and cans, producing, of all things, Red Bull. "There's beer, wine, bourbon, and sodas, if you'd prefer."

"Red Bull will be fine."

He took the can as she belted herself back in.

Pierre LaFevre had been mostly silent since Stephanie had laid into him. "I'd like to have you and your team get to work as soon as possible. What I've seen so far is tantalizing. Even the Big Man is anxious."

"I think you're going to be surprised," Mark admitted. "And maybe a little shocked."

"Shocked how?"

Mark adopted his professorial demeanor with LaFevre. "You may not like what you find when you plug in all the variables."

"There are problems with the model?" LaFevre frowned, head slightly cocked as if computing the odds in his head. "I was concerned about the missing—"

"No. The model works perfectly." Mark gauged the man's reaction. "What I mean is that the world is rife with potential fracture events. It's not pretty out there."

"That's why you're here, Dr. Schott. ECSITE's goal is to predict when and where the fracture events will occur."

Mark gave him a confident smile. "I'm aware of that."

To the south, the Alps had been rising, white, pristine, and stark against the late afternoon sky. The effect was stunning. No wonder they were considered some of the most beautiful mountains in the world. The jagged and snow-covered peaks seemed to rake the sky, contrasting with the spring-green world below.

Mark watched the long Mercedes merge onto a two-lane as the freeway ended. Less than a kilometer later, the driver took a left onto a side road.

"Almost there," Stephanie said brightly.

LaFevre said, "Dr. Schott, how soon will the model be ready for implementation?"

"I have to refine some variables, then we'll test it. I don't know how long that will take."

LaFevre gave him a cold smile. "Sooner rather than later, Dr. Schott."

"Of course."

Mark turned away from LaFevre's vaguely inhuman eyes to watch the small, fenced pastures and neat houses pass beyond the window. Horses and a couple of cows grazed. Stands of conifers partially blocked the view of the Alps now.

The road ended at a large wrought-iron gate complete with a guard. A tall wall stretched to either side. As the Mercedes slowed, the uniformed guard leaned out. The driver rolled down his window, allowing the guard to inspect the occupants. Then he nodded, stepped back, and the gates swung open.

"This is the office?" Mark asked incredulously.

Stephanie replied, "Originally, it was an estate. The Big Man chose this location for several reasons. We're completely self-contained, away from distractions, and given the work we do, ensured an amount of security impossible in an office building."

Mark frowned. "Looks more like a prison. Why do you need—"

"Mark." Stephanie turned sober blue eyes on him. "You must understand, ECSITE handles billions of dollars for some of the world's largest multinational corporations. Much of the information we're privy to is highly sensitive. Were some of our client's financial details to fall into the wrong hands, it would signal the end of ECSITE. We'd be ruined overnight. As it is, the multinationals, governments, and the big banks can come to us with complete confidence. We've never had a security breach."

LaFevre added, "And God help the fool responsible if we ever do."

Mark glanced over his shoulder, watching the gates close as the Mercedes rolled forward. The drive wound uphill through trees and meadows that opened to a curving, circular drive. Across the grass, he could see what looked like a four-story palace. The architecture was definitely Bavarian with dark timbers crisscrossing the white walls. An ornate façade surrounded the windows and doors.

"It was a palace originally," Stephanie explained. "Various cardinals and princes lived here prior to the unification of Germany under Bismarck. Like everything else of value, it became home to a high-ranking Nazi industrialist. After the war, it housed some of the occupying Allied troops until the West German government was on its feet. The Big Man acquired it five years ago. He spends most of his time at the headquarters in Zurich, close to the banks, but the real work is done here."

Instead of driving up to the palace, the Mercedes followed a paved road around its side and through a screen of trees. On the slope behind the house, a neat and modern-looking three-story apartment complex was nestled in the trees. On either side, wood-roofed complexes had been dug into the slope. One, Mark was curious to note, looked exactly like a tavern, complete with neon beer signs in the window, a bicycle rack, a couple of cars, and three motorcycles out front.

"Yes," Stephanie said, following his gaze, "that's our local restaurant and bar. It stocks one hundred and four brands of beer and sits on top of one of the finest wine cellars in Europe. The kitchen is a masterpiece and the chef is world-renowned."

"Nice."

The Mercedes pulled to a stop before the apartments.

Mark waited for the driver to open the door before he stepped out into the cool afternoon. The air smelled of conifers and grass.

"I'll take you to your apartment."

Mark bid the others goodbye and followed Stephanie down the walk fronting the long building. At number 3, she stopped, opening the door.

He wasn't sure what he'd expected but when he entered the spacious living room furnished with a couch, music system, comfy looking recliners, and expensive carpeting, his eyes widened. Teak woodwork was polished to a shine. Behind an ornate divider, he found a model kitchen, six-burner stainless steel stove, giant refrigerator, stocked cabinets filled with fine china and crystal. The fitted wood floor had been waxed to a fine sheen. Four leather stools lined a marble breakfast bar.

"Must be a bitch to keep clean."

"Housekeeping takes care of that."

"Better and better." He might have found this level of opulence in one of the high-dollar houses in Jackson but never in Laramie. A glance into the bathroom shocked him. The fixtures were gold, the toilet a porcelain work of art.

"The best part is upstairs." Stephanie climbed the carpeted steps, Mark following as he shook his head.

The first floor was divided into two rooms. He just stared at the office. The walls were covered with walnut bookshelves above matching cabinets engraved with floral scenes. He almost sank in the carpet as he walked over to the central cherry-wood desk. In the States, he couldn't have touched anything like it for less than ten grand. The computer monitor and keyboard were unlike anything he'd seen at Best Buy.

"Where's the mouse?" he asked.

"Don't need it. The system follows your eye movements. Blink twice to left-click. Blink three times to right-click. Once you get used to it, a mouse becomes as primitive as a stone ax."

Two more of the impressive recliners had been placed strategically to face the solid glass wall that looked out upon the valley and the Alps beyond.

"Unbelievable."

A door led out onto the teak-wood deck that overhung the ground floor. Lounge chairs, a heavy glass table, and small refrigerator rested on the decking.

Stephanie cocked her head. "So, do you think you can work here?"

"No problem." He ran his fingers along the small wet bar and opened the cabinet to discover more crystal on one side, a line of bottles on the other.

Walking with a seductive sway to her hips, Stephanie called, "Bedroom is here, along with the master bath."

She led him to a large room with a huge bed. A plunge pool filled one corner, the blue water swirling. The wall to his right was mirrored but opened into a walk-in closet. The master bathroom had been finished in white marble. Thick glass enclosed the combination tub—big enough for two—and multiple-head shower. Gold-plated fixtures sparkled in the sunlight that streamed through a skylight in the ceiling.

Another of the expensive toilets stood next to a bidet.

Mark pointed across the bed to the glassy gray wall. "What's with that?"

"Anything you want."

"Huh?"

"The wall is a holographic projector. Any vista you can imagine or program: a beach in the Bahamas, the surface of the moon, Times Square in New York, a trip down the Amazon, the French Grand Prix? You name it." She tapped a key on the bedside console, drawing up a menu screen. After scrolling, she said, "This is my favorite."

A second after pressing a button, the wall erupted in color. Mark stared in disbelief at a rainforest waterfall. The sound of falling water mixed with the songs of tropical birds.

"Amazing."

She gave him a teasing look. "You have no idea until you're in the plunge pool, a cool glass of wine in your hand. Depending upon what you're doing in the pool, your fantasies can soar."

She pressed another button and the screen turned back to glassy gray. The sounds of the waterfall vanished.

"They'll bring your bags shortly." Stephanie walked past him. "If you're up to it, how about a glass of champagne to celebrate, and then I'll leave you to get some rest?"

"Oh, I'm always up for champagne."

Mark watched Stephanie walk to the office wet bar. When she bent to open the refrigerator, it was to display a perfectly toned ass.

His limbic system began leaking hormones.

Stephanie straightened, gave him a grin, and loosened the twist on a bottle of Dom Perignon. He opened the cabinet and lifted down two flutes. With a pop, the cork shot across the room.

She poured, set the bottle down, and clinked his glass in a toast.

"Welcome to the ECSITE team, Dr. Schott."

"It's quite the welcome."

"Your model has the potential to make this company a great deal of money. You've become a most important person."

She reached back to unpin her hair. A wealth of light blonde spilled onto her shoulders, answering one of his lingering questions. Then she unbuttoned her suit jacket and slipped it off, removing any doubt about her physical assets. Laying her jacket on the bar, she walked to one of the recliners, settled back and kicked off her shoes.

He retreated to the other, watching as she sipped, smiled, and closed her eyes to savor the taste. "So, have the worries started yet?"

To his surprise, the chair seemed to conform to his body, almost massaging. "Worries?"

"The niggling ones that say, 'This is all too good to be true? What's the catch?'"

"Not really, but… What's the catch?"

"Two things. First, your model had damn well better work. We take failure very seriously here. Second, we take security even more seriously than failure. No emails, phone calls, letters, or other unauthorized communication. The compound is monitored, and our technology shuts down everything that is not authorized. Understand? The consequences *will* be severe if you attempt to circumvent our security."

"With billions at stake? Of course, I understand."

"On the other hand, if you produce, the rewards will compensate for the other inconveniences. Yes, the room's nice. But you've only seen the tip of the iceberg, so far."

Confused, he said, "What do you mean?"

"I mean, don't ask any questions and deliver on your promises and nothing is out of your reach."

"Nothing?" he gave his most charming smile.

She sipped her champagne, then leaned toward him until their lips almost touched. "Nothing."

CHAPTER THIRTEEN

***

BY THE TIME ANIKA PUSHED OPEN THE DOOR TO THE ANTHROPOLOGY BUILDING, SHE couldn't even remember the taste of the steak she'd mechanically devoured as the implications of her work overloaded her normally analytical brain.

Behind her, Maureen Cole seemed unflappable as they climbed the stairs on the building's west side. When Anika turned into the hall, it seemed alien—a fixture from another world.

The Department of Defense is not simply afraid my model can forecast the end of the world. They want to use it to plot the collapse of one or more of America's enemies. It's the only logical conclusion for all the hullabaloo.

Dazed, she walked down the hall, fumbled for her key, and unlocked her door. Flicking the lights on, she stopped short.

The first thing that hit her was the bare walls where her intricate chart had been, then the fact that her computer was missing. The photo of her father lay where the monitor had been. Even the term papers she was supposed to grade were gone. Her trash can had been emptied; the missing file cabinet beside it left nothing more than an impression on the carpet.

Maureen stopped behind her. "Your books are gone, too."

"I don't understand," Anika murmured, shaking her head. "Who— who would do this?"

"Dr. Cole?" a male voice asked from the doorway.

A middle-aged man in a sport coat, brown dockers, and laced shoes extended a small leather wallet with a badge and photo. He had a pleasant face, pug nose, and wide mouth. "I'm Brandon Salazar, FBI. I was asked to assist you."

Maureen checked his credentials and handed them back.

"My research!" Anika cried. "Someone's *taken all of my stuff!* We were only gone an hour."

Maureen gave Salazar a cold look. "Did the FBI confiscate the contents of Ms. French's office?"

Salazar glanced around. "Not us, no. We need to maintain the integrity of the crime scene, okay? Don't touch anything. Both of you. Please, step into the hall."

As Anika backed out of the room, Salazar asked her, "Do you have any idea who might have done this?"

"No." Anika stood, weak-kneed and nauseous.

Maureen said, "When we left earlier, a man was staring at one of the displays out in the hallway. He didn't look like a student. Older, muscular, buzz-cut head, which is common enough, but the way he stood, well, it reminded me of the kind of man someone would hire to get things done."

Salazar glanced at her then looked down the hallway. "Hmm." He said thoughtfully. "Are you aware that the Sheriff's Office discovered a dismembered body south of town on the railroad tracks?"

"A body? Whose?"

"They're keeping it pretty quiet for now but the DNA recovered from beneath the victim's fingernails says his assailant was likely an assassin we've tangled with before."

Anika couldn't help herself. "There's a murder in Laramie, ECSITE is interested in my model, and my office was just trashed. The possibility that those three things are not connected is two-point-six-five million to one. That's based upon a population of three hundred and twenty million and the probability that… God, listen to me. People are committing murder over my model."

Salazar said, "The suspect was obviously waiting for you to leave before he stripped the office."

Maureen shook her head. "Thank goodness your dissertation is still in the car. But maybe we'd better get back to it. Fast. Then we have one other place to search, Agent Salazar."

CHAPTER FOURTEEN

***

SALAZAR PULLED INTO THE DRIVE BEHIND DENISE'S TAHOE.

"Um, you might want to leave me here." Anika felt sick. "I've seen Denise once today. My presence might not be helpful."

Maureen turned in the seat. "Sorry. After what happened at your office, I'm not letting you out of my sight."

"All right."

Anika stepped out of the car into the cool evening breeze and followed Salazar and Maureen toward the door. The darkness seemed to echo threat, barely mollified by the yellow light in the family room.

Salazar rang the bell.

They waited.

He rang it again and opened the screen door. Before he could knock, he frowned. "Step away from the door," he ordered.

Maureen didn't hesitate. She grabbed Anika by the hand and ran back to the car where she shoved Anika down behind the hood. "Stay there," she said. "Something's wrong."

Around the nose of the hood, Anika watched Agent Salazar draw his pistol and shove open the door, calling, "FBI, Ms. Schott, are you here? Is anyone here? I'm Agent Salazar. Hello? Anyone home?"

Anika felt faint as she watched Salazar shove the door completely open and step into the living room. The wide-screen TV was on the History Channel, the voice-over talking about missing ghosts.

"Do you smell something burning?" Maureen looked at Anika.

"Yes."

"Ms. Schott?" Salazar bellowed. "Hello? Anybody home?"

A couple of minutes later, Salazar appeared in the doorway again, and called, "Dr. Cole? Dr. French? No one's home. Please, come inside."

Anika, heart pounding, ran forward. "What happened? Where are they? What's burning?"

"A pot was left on the stove. I turned it off."

Salazar stepped out of the way to allow Anika and Maureen to enter. Anika hurried down the hall, pushed open the door, and found Mark's office empty of all but a few books. But he would have taken his things to Munich, wouldn't he?

"Denise?" she called in rising desperation.

But for the television in the front room, the house was silent.

"How many people live here?" Salazar asked.

"Just Denise and the two boys."

"How old are the boys?"

"Nine and fourteen."

Salazar holstered his weapon, looked around, then walked to a family picture hanging on the wall and stared at it. "Is this relatively recent?"

Anika nodded and Salazar pulled his phone from his belt, stepped away and spoke urgently to someone on the other end.

Anika, unnerved, whispered, "Where could they be? Are they all right?"

"There are two cars in the driveway, a BMW and a Tahoe. Did they have another car?"

"No."

Salazar tucked his phone into his pocket. "Laramie police are on the way. They're checking the hospitals and doctors in case someone had a medical emergency." He looked at Anika. "You said you saw Ms. Schott earlier today? Did she look distraught?"

"Yes." Anika swallowed hard. "She thought I might have been going to Germany with Mark. We... There were troubles between us. In the past, I mean."

Salazar took the implications in stride. "Did she say anything else? Perhaps someone had been bothering her?"

"The car."

"What car?"

Anika struggled to clear her thoughts. "She told me she'd taken Mark to the airport but she was so upset she couldn't sleep. She saw a car on the street. For some reason, she thought it was watching the house."

"Did she say what kind?"

"No. She thought it might have been me."

"Had you ever done that before?" Salazar asked it so reasonably.

"What? God, no! Why would I want to watch his house?"

"The question is," Cole said coolly, "Why would someone else?"

"Denise didn't know anything!" Anika protested. "She's just a professor's wife. She couldn't have cared less about his research. And she certainly didn't know the first thing about the model!"

Salazar shot a glance at the smoking pot on the stove. "Maybe not everyone was aware of that."

CHAPTER FIFTEEN

***

THE MEADOWLARK SINGING ITS FAMILIAR LILTING NOTES SOUNDED UNCOMMONLY CLOSE. Mark rolled over, and the fine silken sheets slipped across his naked body. He blinked his eyes open, caught movement, and stared at a herd of bison grazing in a green meadow no more than a few feet from where he lay. The mirrored wall was showing him Yellowstone National Park, no doubt about it.

He threw the bedding back, stood, and rubbed his back. Damn. Yellowstone looked so real. He shook his head and wandered into the bathroom. The first time he'd used the toilet, it had taken him fifteen minutes to figure out how it flushed. The shower remained a mystery, though he managed to get two of the upper directional heads to shoot cold water. Tapping the programmable panel, he somehow turned on three of the heads but the water stayed cold. The shower was quick.

Drying and shivering, he wrapped the towel around his waist and walked to the cabinet.

"Drop anything you want to wear tomorrow down the laundry chute. It will be in this cabinet tomorrow, washed, pressed, and folded," Stephanie had said on her way out.

Opening the door, he found his Dockers, shirt, tie, and jacket cleaned and perfectly folded on the shelf.

"How do they do that?"

Dressed, he walked out into the office, staring at the Alps through the window wall. Puffy clouds were piled up around the peaks.

"All this technology and no coffee up here," he growled as he started down the stairs, and hesitated, hearing the sound of frying bacon, smelling it and coffee—the sirens of breakfast.

Stephanie stood at the stove, a spatula in hand.

"There were buffalo in my bedroom," Mark greeted.

"I hope you don't mind my intrusion. Consider it your wake-up call. It's almost midday, and you've got a team so filled with anticipation that they're literally chewing their pencils in two. If you don't get over there, Pierre may burst a blood vessel."

He studied her as she handed him a cup of coffee heavy with cream and sugar. Nope, he hadn't been dreaming. She was every bit as beautiful as he'd remembered.

"The shower is smarter than I am."

"I'm sorry. I should have shown you."

"Oh, I like cold showers. Especially when the only nozzles that shoot are waist-high. Reminds me how tough I am."

That brought the dimples to the corners of her mouth. "How do you like your eggs?"

"I thought you got a continental breakfast in Germany."

"If you'd prefer." She turned toward the big silver refrigerator.

"No, bacon and eggs over easy will be just fine. Got Tabasco Sauce?"

"What do you think? We're barbarians? Of course. That cabinet."

Mark thought the ornate plates were much too fine to be eating breakfast on and watched Stephanie load his with breakfast. Concentration lines etched her smooth brow.

"What exactly do you do for ECSITE?"

"I take care of problems. Make sure things work. Ensure that we have the information we need."

"That sounds more like a handyman."

Her lips bent into a knowing smile. "Yes, I suppose that's exactly what I am. I take care of unforeseen trouble. Plumbing, cutting, digging, cooking breakfast, that sort of thing."

"I see."

"I hope you do." She sipped a cup of coffee. "After a night's sleep, and time for your subconscious to process, are you having any reservations about coming to work for ECSITE?"

"Just the big, locked gate out front."

"I don't want to sound indelicate, but we've invested a great deal of money in you and the model."

Mark picked up his fork and dug into his eggs. Between bites, he said. "I know you have."

"And if Pierre and his team are suitably impressed—how about you and I go up to Garmisch-Patenkirchen next Saturday for a delightful meal and a little relaxation?"

Mark wiped up what was left of his egg with toast, and started to pick up the plates.

"Leave them. Housekeeping will see to it. Come. Your notes and research boxes have been delivered to the working group. The time has arrived for you to show us just what this model can do and how you derived it."

"Headlong into the fire, huh?"

"For your sake, I hope you don't get burned."

Something about the way she said it sent a tingle of unease down his spine. *Cut it out, she's just teasing. This is foreplay...*

He laughed to let her know he understood.

CHAPTER SIXTEEN

***

MAUREEN STARED AT THE GULFSTREAM'S POSH CEILING, FEELING THE PLANE JUDDER slightly from turbulence. Amy Randall had booked a charter jet to get them to Washington as soon as possible. A sense of urgency had filled Randall's voice. No matter what was happening in Laramie, the Department of Defense wanted Anika French at the Pentagon by eight the next morning.

Now, the Gulfstream was winging east through the night. Out the window, Maureen could see scattered towns glittering. The frequency and size told her they were over eastern Nebraska. The clusters of light were growing closer together, indicative of a rising population.

"What's the word?" Anika sat across from her, seat reclined, legs outstretched, arms crossed. Anyone would know she was a Wyoming cowgirl. Her red hair was tied back in a ponytail, and she'd worn her best everyday clothing: a white, Western-cut, snap shirt with ruffles, new form-fitting Wrangler jeans cinched at her narrow waist with a tooled leather belt, and pointed western boots with a high riding heel.

Like most starving graduate students, Anika's wardrobe proved meager. Maureen had watched the woman pack the only two skirts she owned, along with a couple of blouses and her single jacket for Washington. A pair of shoes, underwear, and a toilet kit had gone into her battered suitcase.

Anika looked exhausted and petrified. Her green eyes sparkled with an unnatural brilliance, and worry hardened her jaw.

Trying to relieve some of Anika's tension, Maureen said, "The FBI's Evidence Response Team has finished with your office. No sign of forced entry. Either they had a key or picked the lock. Whoever took your stuff didn't leave so much as a fingerprint. They're moving to Denise's house next. Every Wyoming law enforcement agency, and half of Colorado, has been issued a BOLO for Denise. You know what a BOLO is?"

"'Be On Lookout' for. Dad's a sheriff, remember?" Anika jerked upright in the seat. "Oh my God! Dad! He's going to get that first thing in the morning. He knows Denise's name. He's going to panic!"

"The FBI has already contacted him to let him know you're safe. You can call him the first thing when we land. As to what you tell him…?"

"Dr. Cole, this is my father. You can't snow him with bullshit."

"Call me Maureen. We're in this together. And prepare yourself. There will be restrictions on what you can tell anyone. For all I know, your model just fell into the black hole they call national security."

Anika clenched her fists in her lap. "This is like a bad dream. For two years, I've dedicated every waking moment to the project. I was so proud that I'd made a real contribution to anthropological theory." Anika closed her eyes in defeat. "Now, people are missing. Mark published my work under his name. The model's been stolen, and all my work is about to be classified."

"We've still got the dissertation. Agent Salazar is running down your committee members. He's recovered most of the dissertation copies. Even the one at the printers. So far, all but Mark's copy seem accounted for."

Anika gave her an evaluative glance. "How do you stay so calm?"

Maureen leaned back, hand on the dissertation where it lay on the seat looking entirely innocuous. "Calm?"

"It's like you've done this all your life."

"No. I grew up in Ontario and have spent most of my time analyzing the skeletal pathology of archaeological specimens."

"You know, anthropology students really look up to you. Everybody says you're the new Margaret Mead."

She smiled. "I'm a lot taller."

Anika didn't share her smile. Instead, her expression dropped. "I'm worried about Denise and really worried about the boys."

"Is it possible that Mark asked ECSITE to escort them to Munich?"

Anika blinked at the ceiling. "I don't know. If I had to guess, I'd say no."

"You still care for him?"

Anika gave Maureen a startled look. "God, no. He's been stealing my work for years and now... this."

Maureen lifted the dissertation, opened the cover, and thumbed through the text and equations.

Anika watched her. "I wish I'd never developed that model."

"If it hadn't been you, someone else would have figured it out. Knowledge is like fire. Your model gives power to those who know how to use it. Being able to predict social unrest, crop failure, or regime change is of incalculable value." Maureen studied the elegant statistics, so far beyond her own understanding.

Anika said, "Why would ECSITE rob my office? If they'd wanted any information, I would have given it to them. Mark and I are working for them, right? And kidnapping Denise and the boys isn't likely to inspire Mark to help them. He's going to freak out when he hears they're missing."

"Maybe it wasn't ECSITE but a competitor. The motive isn't to spur Mark to greater effort but the opposite. Leave ECSITE or you never see your family again."

Anika's expression changed as she ran the hypothesis through her agile mind. "You're scaring me, Maureen."

"Good."

CHAPTER SEVENTEEN

***

STEPHANIE HUNTZ LED MARK ACROSS THE MANICURED GRASS TO ONE OF THE LARGE buildings flanking the clearing. The place had a distinctly Bavarian look: two stories with a wide, shallowly gabled roof. The upper story was walled in with ornately crafted wood, and had a balcony to each side, covered by the overhanging roof. Leaded windows were surrounded by ornate plaster scrollwork.

"We call this style '*Luftlmalerie*'. It's quintessentially Bavarian."

"Pretty," Mark said.

Instead of dark hallways, the inside was as modern as any office in the world with tiled floors, a couple of potted plants and a wide central hallway. Mark had a vision of aluminum, stainless steel, and glass doors through which he could see spacious offices where people in cubicles bent over computers. In one, a group of men and women watched an entire wall of stock tickers, the numbers rolling along proclaiming the status of the Dow, NASDAQ, FTSE, Hong Kong, BOLSA, and others he could only guess at. He barely had a glimpse before Stephanie paused in front of an elevator; the doors were brass and polished to a mirror surface. She pushed the down button. "For the time being, you're downstairs."

In the elevator, she punched 3, and the lift dropped.

Mark stepped out into another hallway, bordered with glass-walled offices. Here, too, he found a beehive of activity.

"I didn't think this many people lived here."

"There's another apartment building, larger than yours, just behind the trees." Stephanie gave him a wink. "The units are not as nice. And some of the analysts live in Munchen or its suburbs. They don't have your clearance. Nor will they be associating with you and your team."

"I see."

"I hope you do. From here on out, the only people you are to speak with are the members of your own team."

"Which includes you?"

"Of course."

She led him to the last door on the right where, unlike the other offices, the door appeared to be solid metal.

Stephanie produced a key card, swiped it through the reader and pressed in a code. Then she opened the door. "We will provide you a card and security code later. For now, meet your team."

Mark entered a room that reminded him of a war room in the Pentagon. The walls were covered with large monitors, computer consoles below them. In the center of the room was an oval table surrounded by black office chairs. His boxes—FedEx stickers prominent—sat stacked in the middle.

Pierre LaFevre stepped forward, hand extended. "Dr. Schott. Finally." After shaking, he turned. "While I will be called away to other duties, may I present your team. This is Jacques Terblanch."

Mark shook Terblanch's hand. The man was silver-haired, tall, with soft brown eyes and a narrow mouth. "Good to meet you."

"Wu Liu," an Asian man introduced himself. "My pleasure." He spoke with a thick Chinese accent. In his twenties, he had a chunky body, round face, and shaggy black hair.

"Francine Inoui," LaFevre announced as an anorexic-looking forty-something woman in sweats and a baggy pullover stepped forward. She had a severe face and long chin.

"Max Kalashnikov," the next man introduced himself. "And yes, I'm a distant cousin."

"Of whom?" Mark shook the thickly-built man's hand. He had a square face and light blue eyes.

"You have heard of Mikael Kalashnikov, inventor of the AK-47?" He smiled to show a gold tooth. "I am a much milder man."

"Pleased to meet you, Dr. Schott," a diminutive Indian woman said offering a hesitant hand. "I am Nanda Hashahurti." She gave him a shy smile.

Her shake was limp, little more than a touching of fingers.

Pierre pointed at the boxes, obviously anxious. "Shall we unpack?"

"Wait a minute," Mark said, smiling at the anxious ring surrounding him. "Let's sit down and discuss some things first."

"Discuss what?" LaFevre appeared annoyed by the delay.

"The basics," Mark said, striding to the table and lifting a box out of the way. "Look, Pierre, I understand your motivation, appreciate it, in fact. But before I turn you loose with the statistics, I need to know something about you guys. And until you know where the model comes from, you're going to be spinning wheels, and coming back to me for explanations that I can get out of the way now."

He glanced at Stephanie, who'd stepped to the back. She was watching, evaluating. Good. He'd show her just how competent he could be.

"Got coffee?" Mark asked as the table was cleared. "Let's all have a cup while we sort through this."

Nanda Hashahurti and Max Kalashnikov retreated to a Capresso machine in the corner.

Mark settled himself in one of the chairs as the others filled seats around him. Kalashnikov placed a Styrofoam cup before him along with cream and sugar. Across the table, LaFevre looked stressed out. Stephanie had taken a chair at the end, physically separated from the rest of the team. Interesting. Not only that, but no one seemed particularly anxious to be close to her.

"First," Mark said, falling into professor mode, "I need to know something about you. How many are anthropologists?"

No hands.

"Let me guess, your backgrounds are all in econometrics, right? Economic theory, statistics, forecasting GDP, that sort of thing?"

Everyone nodded.

"You are used to manipulating precise data. Following long-established economic statistical theory that evaluates manufacturing potential against monetary policy, interest rates, consumer demand, that sort of thing."

They nodded.

"To use a metaphor, you employ scalpels to dissect portions of the economy. From your perspective, creating and employing the model is going to be like turning in your scalpel for a stone ax."

"What?" LaFevre asked.

Mark leaned back. "I come from the bastard child of social sciences: anthropology. Anthropologists have used most of the last century to discover, to their horror, that mathematics are a rather imprecise tool when it comes to interpreting social data." He raised a hand. "I know. Economists decry the imprecision of their statistics. Too many variables, you say. How can you quantify election results against a dip in consumer confidence?"

"You're saying your model is even more imprecise?" Liu asked. "Then why are we even discussing it?"

Mark stared into his coffee cup. "I'll get to that in a moment. First, let's do a little review of the model's origins. Archaeologists have modeled extinct cultures for years. You've heard of the Maya civilization in Central America?" He got nods all the way around. "How about the Hohokam in Arizona?" No nods.

Mark sipped the coffee, anxious for the sugar and caffeine jolt. "What's important is that, especially in America, archaeologists have been modeling these vanished civilizations as a means of determining why they collapsed. In the process, while the rest of the statistical world has engrossed itself in ever more elaborate and elegant mathematical models, we've been improving the stone ax."

Francine Inoui raised a hand, asking in a French accent, "I do not understand this stone ax metaphor."

"Think about the archaeological record. Big chunks of it are missing. We've had to develop a host of descriptive statistics to manipulate the quality of data we can recover and, then, we fill in the missing pieces with *inferential* stats."

Jacques Terblanch cried, "But you cannot expect high levels of accuracy or predictability with inferential statistics."

"That's why anthropologists are said to 'worship at the point-oh-five level of confidence.' We accept that by chance, one in twenty studies is going to be wrong." He got a couple of nervous chuckles. "Hence the stone ax."

LaFevre looked nervous. "With such a high standard of error, why use this stone ax of yours?"

Mark dramatically sipped his coffee. "The reason the original stone ax was developed was because, by using it, you could *cut the tree down*. In this case, nations."

He cataloged the faces and read a great deal of skepticism.

LaFevre said, "I don't believe it's possible to quantify human motivation. Too chaotic."

"First principles, LaFevre. What do humans need? Food. Water. Shelter from the elements. Security for themselves and their families. Access to sexual partners. Threaten any of these things and the likelihood of sociocultural dysfunction increases. Once it gets past what I call 'the tipping point,' the society turns on itself and collapse is inevitable. Essentially, I'm saying that we're all human. We all respond in very similar ways when we are starving, or threatened, or terrified. And since we know that, we can model how humans will react."

"So what are the infamous missing variables?" Inoui tapped the table insistently.

"I'll get to that. But number one." He held up a finger. "Food. Does a nation's agriculture produce enough to feed its population? If not, the nation imports food from elsewhere to fill the shortfalls. Does it produce enough fuel to transport the food to where it's needed? If not, the nation imports the fuel to fill the shortfall. How is it distributed once it gets there? From grocery stores or out of the backs of trucks? How fragile is the system? That's what the model is designed to predict—when and how systems fail."

LaFevre said. "We're interested in how to make them fail. That's what your article was about."

"Correct. One small variable—say a change in precipitation or a new virus—thrown into a fragile system, and human anger and fear cause the economic infrastructure to crumble and collapse like falling dominoes. I can predict exactly how to push human beings past the tipping point."

LaFevre said, "Tell us about your Southeast Asian hypothesis. You claimed you could predict the level of panic and demographic relocation if a rice blight was introduced. Could you input the variables into your model and show us what would happen if a pathogenic fungus was introduced into America's corn belt?"

Mark blinked. "Sure, I mean, I could. But I have other things to explain first. For example—"

"We don't care about those other things." Pierre LaFevre drummed his fingers on the table. "We want to see the model work."

Mark straightened in his chair. "Let me repeat. You need to first understand the key variables: Do people have enough food to put in their mouths? Are their children safe? Are the lights on? Will tomorrow be like today? If the answer to any of those is a long-term no, things are going to get messy, nasty, and mean."

"We understand," LaFevre said impatiently. "Get to the point."

Mark reached into his pocket and removed a flash drive that contained Anika's dissertation. He'd prudently removed her name and substituted his own. "I want you to download this, read it, study it. In fact, I'd like each member of this team to work on a different variable."

As though annoyed, LaFevre snapped, "What variables?"

"Pierre," he said calmly, "why don't you take a lethal fungus introduced into cornfields in Iowa. Wu, experiment with a bacterial rice blight in China. Mikael, find the best way to destroy the wheat crop in Canada. Francine, start a plague in Moscow. Nanda and Jacques, hypothesize a virus engineered to bring about the extinction of cattle worldwide within twenty years. And have it start in India. This is all about modeling human behavior. I want you to see how the data clusters predict happiness turning to sadness, then fear, and finally anger, which trips the global dominoes to fall as chaos runs rampant through the system."

"Simplistic nonsense," Pierre grumbled, almost too low to hear.

Every person stared at Mark. "We will reconvene tomorrow afternoon to see what you've come up with. Consider this a first draft. We're going to need to refine, adapt, and revise the model as we go along. The question we all have to answer is where do we begin? Do we start with one country? Ten countries? Or tackle the entire world? It's just a model, after all. It's not like we're actually declaring war on anyone." He chuckled.

But no one else did.

CHAPTER EIGHTEEN

***

WHEN ANIKA TOOK HER SEAT IN THE SECOND-FLOOR PENTAGON CONFERENCE ROOM, Maureen could see grinding fatigue in the woman's eyes. Anika clutched an energy drink in her hand as if the sugary liquid could replace what she lacked in sleep.

All told, they'd had two hours in the hotel prior to the arrival of the car sent to pick them up. Crossing the bridge, passing through security gates, Anika had gaped as they were driven to one of the Pentagon's side entrances. Maureen, to be honest, had been a little overwhelmed as well. She'd never understood just how big the Pentagon was. At the door, they'd been met, issued visitor's badges, and ushered here. Coffee, fortunately, had been provided.

Maureen felt the warm threads of fatigue pulling at the back of her brain. But for Anika, who'd already undergone a week of stress, had her office robbed, and found an acquaintance and her kids missing? She had to be close to hitting bottom.

Two men in suits opened the door, leading the way for Amy Randall, Agent Hart, and the Secretary of Defense herself, Martina Rivera.

Maureen watched everyone rise to their feet and stood up, too. She thought Anika's knees were shaking.

Introductions were made. The Secretary shook Maureen's hand. The woman wore a neat gray suit, immaculately tailored in contrast to her celebrity predecessor's colorful but tacky wardrobe. Rivera's graying-black hair was neatly cut to brush her collar. "Good to finally meet you, Dr. Cole. I've followed your work. And let me extend, once again, this country's gratitude for your role in previous cases."

"You're welcome, Madam Secretary." She turned. "This is Dr. Anika French."

Anika shook the Secretary's hand.

"You both look exhausted." The Secretary gave them careful scrutiny.

"It's been a long couple of days." Maureen waited until the Secretary sat before she lowered herself into the chair.

The Secretary glanced around the table. "I'll try not to keep you. I'm on a tight schedule myself. And I need to brief President Begay the moment this is over." The Secretary fixed her eyes on Anika's dissertation. "Is that the document?"

Anika reminded Maureen of a rabbit with an eagle overhead.

Maureen said, "Yes. Everything else was taken. The FBI is working on recovering Dr. French's notes and graphs."

The Secretary waved it aside. "I've been briefed."

"Any news on Denise and the boys?" Anika blurted.

"No." The Secretary waited as the two suited men opened notebooks and, when they nodded, said, "Tell me precisely and succinctly what this model is all about. Why is it so important to so many people?"

Anika wet her lips and clasped her hands nervously. Hesitantly, she laid out the history of the model, how she'd discovered the equations to predict the emotional variables that would predict how prehistoric societies collapsed.

"The statistics are derived from both archaeological and climatic models?" Secretary Rivera asked.

"Yes. A—a breaking point is reached. What I call a 'fracture event'. Neighbors either band together for protection or turn on each other. Depending upon the size of the population, the resource base, and the level of demographic dislocation..." She sucked in a breath as though starving for air. "The entire system disintegrates into anarchy."

The Secretary didn't blink, just stared into Anika's eyes. "Your model can predict when and how this will happen? When a society is verging on collapse?"

Anika managed to nod. "By the numbers."

"You know this for a fact?"

Anika nerved herself and said, "It's worked with every prehistoric political entity I've applied it to."

"But in the case of the past, the result is always a foregone conclusion. After all, we know what happened to them. Our statisticians have been working with the Schott article, and they're a bit confused about the variables, but none of them see a threat to modern societies."

Anika paused. "It's in my dissertation." A wince. "Well, mostly."

"What do you mean, mostly?"

Anika spread her hands. "The model I presented was only designed to meet the requirements of a PhD. The dissertation is descriptive of a prehistoric society. In this case, Cahokia."

At the Secretary's confused look, Maureen added, "The largest prehistoric empire in North America, circa 1200 AD."

"Let's get back to the problem." The Secretary pinned Anika with a penetrating stare. "The Schott article asserts that the model is just as viable in the modern world. You seem to share that opinion. Why?"

Maureen could see little beads of sweat on Anika's pale brow as she leaned forward and said, "Because the cultures we study in the archaeological record follow the same fundamental rules as modern societies. Given the right variables, mathematics can explain the future course of human events, regardless of cultural complexity."

"Explain."

"Well…" Anika shook her head as though to clear it of fatigue. "I have to start at the beginning. Take any measure: Biodiversity loss? Atmospheric carbon? Ocean acidification? Ozone depletion? Nitrogen and phosphorous cycles? And the biggest of all: Population growth. Each generates fear, a predictable human response. The level of that response can be mathematically modeled. As fear increases, social forcings determine when and how society crumbles."

"Go on."

"Well, it's easier for me to show you mathemat—"

"Tell me. I don't want to see equations."

Anika exhaled a slow breath. "Okay. At the hunting and gathering level, when the animals are hunted out, people just pick up their tents and move to the next valley. The evolution of agriculture tied people to a specific plot of land. In Cahokia, the climate changed, the soil wore out and the corn crop failed. Two hundred thousand people couldn't just pick up and move. Instead, the entire polity crashed. Compare that with our modern world. What happens when eight billion people surviving on a just-in-time food and energy inventory suffer a catastrophe?"

"Such as?" The Secretary cocked her head, skeptical.

"Three years of heavy rain in the American Midwest cutting harvests by over forty percent. The Indian Ocean monsoons shifting north over Pakistan instead of dropping precipitation on the southern slopes of the Himalayas. The Atlantic Ocean conveyor shutting off entirely and dropping the temperature in Europe by four degrees Celsius. In that scenario, winter in Berlin would be little different than winter in Fairbanks, Alaska."

The room was silent. The Secretary shifted her attention to Maureen. "Dr. Cole? Your thoughts?"

"She's right."

The Secretary glanced at Amy Randall, then at the two men who had been writing copiously. "But, Dr. French, I'm told you've never tested the model on a modern, functioning society. So how can you know if this has any application to a highly-complex, industrialized and multinational economy?"

"I, uh, I guess I've run a few modern scenarios," Anika stuttered. "Well. Two."

Maureen saw Anika on the verge of shaking and took over: "And if you think the chaos that results from introducing a simple virus like COVID is bad, imagine what would happen if the virus was not targeted to infect all humans but only humans with certain genetic traits? Say Asia is suddenly devastated by a disease that affects only people with Han Chinese genes? The feeling that we're all in this together drops away. The search for a culprit begins. Suspicions lead to accusations. Denials to threats. Threats to war. Dr. French can model precisely how fear and anger descend into—"

"I understand." The Secretary checked her watch and rose from her chair. "Randall? I want Dr. French and Dr. Cole in my conference room this afternoon at 14:00 hours."

CHAPTER NINETEEN

***

MARK'S TEAM YAWNED, SOME MASSAGED THE BACKS OF THEIR NECKS, AND OTHERS rubbed bleary eyes. But, Mark, his body still on Wyoming time, found its circadian rhythm. He'd finally started to perk up and was just hitting his stride.

Stephanie stepped in the door, arched a questioning eyebrow, and pointed suggestively at her wrist.

"People," Mark called, "you're looking tired. Let's call it a day."

Smiles greeted his announcement and, to his delight, everyone went about cleaning their workstations and locking their materials in drawers.

Goodbyes were said as they filed out, leaving him in the suddenly quiet office with Stephanie.

"How did it go?" she asked.

"I think they're catching on." Damn, she was even more beautiful than he remembered. What would it be like, coming home to a woman like this every night? He gave her his charming grin as he placed his copy of the dissertation in the space provided and locked the combination.

"And what is your plan?" she asked as they stepped out into the hall.

"We're going to work through each of their hypotheses until we've honed the relevant variables. I'll know they've got it as soon as they start suggesting nuanced refinements to the model."

They stepped into the elevator and she asked, "How long will that take?"

"That's when things get a little more complicated." He motioned her out before him. "With a prehistoric or historic society, we're dealing with a closed system. In the modern world, the levels of sophistication increase exponentially. We live in a world economy. Everything, and I mean everything, is tied together. Social unrest in India affects accounting firms here in Germany, the US, and most of Europe. A typhoon hitting Taiwan can impact the just-in-time delivery of aircraft guidance computers for Airbuses waiting on the assembly line in France."

At the door, Mark was surprised to walk out into darkness. When had that happened?

"I explained to Gunter that I'd need to rely on my people back in Wyoming. We've got to have the right data. When I developed the idea for the model, Anika French was instrumental in helping me define the variables. As we figure out which questions to ask, I'll ship some of the research to her." He smiled. "About time she earns some of that salary you're paying her."

Stephanie accompanied him across the grass; the Alps were glowing in the crescent moon. "Yes, well, there have been some complications there."

Mark shot her a questioning look. "Such as?"

"The American government has taken her to Washington." She gave him a sidelong glance through blue eyes.

Mark stopped short. "The government? Why?"

"Apparently, they're also interested in the model."

Stunned, he just stared at her.

"They never contacted you?"

"No. The only person was Gunter." They resumed walking. "So, what does this mean?"

"It means they've taken your research assistant, and the last thing we want is to have them following the direction of our research here. So, how does losing Ms. French impact your schedule to make the model operational?"

The first threads of panic prickled through him. Could he do it without Anika? He felt suddenly sweaty.

Stephanie said, "As I understand it, the essential drivers are food and energy production. Not exaggerated estimates but actual production."

"That's right."

"We can obtain any data you need." She sounded very sure of herself.

At Mark's apartment, she opened the door and stepped inside. The delightful odor of boiling lobster filled the air. Mark closed the door behind him, shocked to see a cook in his kitchen.

Stephanie asked, "How are we doing, Eduard?"

"Five minutes, Ms. Huntz. If you and the gentleman would freshen up, I'll have the plates on the table."

Mark lifted an eyebrow.

Stephanie smiled. "If you'd rather eat alone, that will be fine."

"No, no. Happy to have company."

Her twinkling eyes, the dimples at the corners of her smile, preceded her suggestion. "Why don't you go wash up? I need to make a call."

"Sure."

Showered, and in a change of clothes, Mark returned to lowered lights, a candlelit table, and exquisitely prepared lobsters, blanched asparagus, little potatoes boiled in spices, and another bottle of Dom Perignon. Stephanie seated herself across from him, the candlelight doing marvelous things for her wavy hair.

After seeing to their comfort, Eduard bowed and stepped out the door.

"So, am I to expect a meal like this every night?"

"If you like." Stephanie picked up a fork, speared one of the potatoes, and nibbled it. "Um. Cardamom. Delightful." She swallowed. "But it can get old after a while."

Mark cracked his lobster claw and tried to figure out how to prepare his new boss for a possible failure. "Stephanie?"

"Humm?"

"Your boss, the Big Man, I don't think he's going to like the results when we finally work the kinks out of the model."

She gave him a level stare. "Why not?"

Mark sighed with satisfaction as he washed the lobster down with champagne. "The final word? On a planet that can reliably sustain a maximum of two billion people, we've passed eight, and the population's still growing. The grim news is that the entire planet is running on borrowed time. We're past the tipping point."

Her blue eyes never wavered. "Yes. We know."

"If you know, why hire me to prove it?"

"That's not why we hired you, Mark."

He fiddled with his fork. "What do you mean?"

"Your job, once you make the model work, is to determine where the global system will break. The fracture points, I believe you called it."

"And after that? I mean, what's left? People are going to be hungry, frightened, rioting in the streets. Governments are going to disintegrate in turmoil. Trade routes will collapse. The entire industrial complex will come tumbling down."

"Of course." She delicately placed a piece of lobster on her tongue. The candles cast a golden glow on her face. "Everything will go to the devil, right?"

"That's a medieval way of putting it."

She gave him a saucy grin. "Then, the devil has the most to profit from what will come. That is your ultimate task, Mark. To help us figure out how to strategically place ECSITE so that when the fall comes, we're left standing."

"I don't think you got my point. There won't be much left standing. Billions of people are going to die, first from epidemics, then starvation, and finally warfare. It's not a pretty picture."

She shrugged. "You knew that when you took this job. Like us, you opted to make the best of a bad situation. There will be survivors when this is all over. We intend to be among them. Ultimate evolution, don't you think?"

Mark's eyes narrowed. He had no idea what she was talking about.

She read it. "Mark, like the Big Man, you are an ultimate pragmatist. Why else would you have left your wife and children behind? They don't fit in the coming world order and you know it. We do."

He glanced down at his plate, unsure what to say.

"Relax. Don't take this so seriously. You are among like-minded friends here. The best time for saints is when civilization is building, when there is optimism for the future. If you had been a saint, Mark, we would have found someone else."

"I suppose." He was thinking of Anika.

"A toast." She lifted her champagne glass. "To those who are unafraid to seize the future." The glasses clinked.

"Have I sold my soul to the devil?"

"Absolutely." She gestured toward the plates. "But there are nice perks associated. And, once the dominoes begin to fall, what would you rather be doing? Eating ECSITE's lobster by candlelight or scrambling around some village in Asia, desperate for a handful of infected rice?"

Attempting to quote from the movie *Casablanca,* he said, "It appears that you are the only person with less scruples than I."

"Kindred souls," she agreed, her eyes seeming to enlarge into violet pools. "All you have to do is build ECSITE the kind of predictive model that will help us to anticipate the best way to survive your coming collapse."

Mark chewed a bite of lobster, then said, "It will be a little more difficult without French. I've been working with her for years."

Her eyes literally danced. "Don't panic yet."

"It's not panic. I'm just accustomed to having her input while I run variables and—"

"Forget about Anika French for the moment. Let's set tonight aside for exploration."

"Exploration?"

"Curiosity always leads to exploration, doesn't it? Come on." She stood, offering her hand.

He took it, letting her lead him up the stairs to the bedroom. She crossed to the console that controlled the holographic wall, accessed the menu, and selected the tropical waterfall. As the sound of cascading water and birds filled the air, she turned, stepping up to him and placing her hands on his shoulders. "I did some research. This was recorded on a Caribbean island called Dominica. I haven't been able to get it out of my head."

He stared down into her eyes, aware that her lips had parted. "Me either."

He kissed her, her tongue sliding past his lips, darting and teasing. Moments later, he felt her peel his coat back and unbutton his shirt. As he shrugged out of the sleeves, her nimble fingers undid his belt and fly. Artfully, she pushed his pants and underwear down to pile around his feet.

By the time he kicked off his shoes and extricated himself, she was barefoot, her skirt fluttering down those shapely, athletic legs.

Heart pounding, he unbuttoned her blouse and reached around to unsnap her bra. As the clothing fell away, his breath caught. She stood proudly before him, head cocked, eyes sparkling. Framed by the waterfall, the plunge pool at her feet, she'd become mythic: A Venus that stopped the breath in his lungs.

"Damn," he barely whispered.

She stepped forward and slipped her arms around his neck. Her body pressed against his and she playfully bumped his straining penis. "We've both sold our souls to the devil. Now let's see what kind of demonic pleasure we can conjure."

CHAPTER TWENTY

***

MAUREEN WATCHED THE SECRETARY WALK OUT THE DOOR AND TURNED TO AMY RANDALL who had her gaze fastened on a half-panicked Anika French.

"How was Dr. Schott supposed to contact you?" Randall asked.

"I don't know, ma'am. He just said he would." Anika swallowed hard. "He's in trouble, too, isn't he?"

Randall barely nodded. "ECSITE has reputation for disposing of individuals who have served their purpose. Call it a way to keep the competition from reproducing or even understanding their methods." She leaned toward Anika. "You'll inform us the moment he tries to get in touch, understand? Meanwhile, can you test the model on a modern society?"

"The pertinent data and statistics…" Her face dropped. "…are in my stolen notes."

"But you know a lot of it from memory, correct?"

A subtle communication passed between Randall and Maureen.

Anika nodded. "Yeah, I guess so."

"I'll see that you have a place to work, computers, data. Tell me what you need, I'll see that you get it. Understand?"

"Yes, ma'am."

"How soon will you have an answer for me?"

"Working by myself, I don't—"

"We don't have time to fool around. Dr. Cole will be your go-to person. Anything you need, anyone you need, just ask her. Recruit anyone you want." Randall shifted uneasily and her brow furrowed. "If you have to move heaven and earth, get me an answer by Friday."

Anika looked like fish gasping for air.

Maureen reached out to touch Anika's arm. The young woman's

eyes were fixed on infinity.

"Anika? Do you want Fred Zoah?"

"Yes. He—he'll immediately understand the archaeological model."

Randall said, "I'll have him on a plane tonight."

"He's a little eccentric," Maureen said. "You might have to gag him and haul his entire office with him."

"Not a problem."

"How about data?" Maureen asked Anika. "What kind do you need?"

Anika frowned. "This is happening so fast. Landsat images. Economic reports, water quality, population densities, cumulative world energy production figures, infrastructure analyses, diverse stuff. In Laramie, I had a whole library at my disposal."

"We've got one down the street," Randall said dryly. "They call it the Library of Congress. And the Pentagon has runners who can fetch anything you need. As to farm production, hectares of cropland, infrastructure analyses, that's what the State Department does. If they don't have it, Langley can get it."

"What about security?" Maureen asked. "If I have any say in this, I want Skip Murphy. There's no one else I'd trust."

Randall looked at Hart. "Get Murphy."

"Understood." Hart turned and strode from the conference room.

Maureen watched Anika's eyes widen. The woman's dry swallow sounded loud in the quiet room.

CHAPTER TWENTY-ONE

***

THE MELODY OF NANCY GRIFFITH SWEETLY RELATING THE WOES OF A FORTY-ACRE FARM issued from the battered stereo atop the tool-cluttered workbench. The garage door was open, adding bright spring sunshine to the output of the overhead fluorescents as Sean "Skip" Murphy bent over the valves on his BMW RT motorcycle. Religiously, every six thousand miles, he unbolted the crash guards, pulled the spark plugs, and loosened the aluminum rocker box covers.

Real mechanics undid the complex bodywork, took off the timing cover, and rotated the engine to top dead center with an allen wrench. Skip, unwilling to undertake the effort, put the transmission in third gear, turned the back tire, and watched while a vernier rod was pushed out by the piston.

That done he used thickness gauges to test the clearance in the valve tappets, adjusting intake down to .15 mm and exhaust to .30.

He was in the process of fiddling with the adjusting screw and lock nut on the left exhaust when his cell phone chirped.

Growling, he found a shop rag, wiped his fingers as best he could and pulled out his phone. "Skip Murphy."

"Hey, Skip. It's Phil Hart. Are you available?"

"Got a Saudi family coming in at the end of the week but I can assign that job to one of my people. What are we talking about?"

"It's high profile. I'd prefer to tell you in person. When can we meet?"

Skip chewed his lip for a moment, then said, "I'm out in Manassas. Give me about an hour. Where do I meet you?"

"An escort will be waiting at the main entrance."

CHAPTER TWENTY-TWO

***

THROUGH THE PENTAGON'S GLASS DOORS, ANIKA WATCHED SKIP MURPHY WALK UP. HE wore brown dockers, athletic shoes, a tan sports coat that did little to hide his broad shoulders, and a blue shirt with matching tie. The sunlight played on his black hair and neatly trimmed beard. Even walking, the man communicated competence, his step springy, back straight, head shifting as his alert brown eyes absorbed the surroundings.

"That him?" she asked Agent Hart.

"That's him."

Skip met her eyes through the glass, giving her a crooked smile. After passing the second set of glass doors, he walked up, and Hart said, "Thanks for coming, Skip. This is Dr. Anika French."

Skip nodded to Anika. "Good to meet you, Dr. French."

Hart stopped in front of the security station, and Anika watched Murphy surrender his pistol and permit, knife, flashlight, and keys, then pass the metal detectors and body scan. He was issued a coded visitor's badge. They kept his pistol.

"If you'll both come this way, please." Hart turned and led the way toward the conference room where Anika had spent most of the day trying to absorb the sudden traumatic changes in her life.

"What do you do, Dr. French?" Skip asked as they followed Hart down the hall.

"I'm an anthropologist."

"Got it. I've acted as security for anthropologists before so I know a little about your field."

Anika gave him a sideways glance. "I guess I'm in trouble, Mr. Murphy."

He gave her a warm smile. "Anthropologist, huh? Figures. Just what kind of trouble are you in, anyway?"

Anika folded her arms protectively over her chest. "I developed a model that describes how and why ancient civilizations collapsed."

"That doesn't sound so bad."

"Not if you only apply it to prehistoric cultures. The problem is that it can be applied to the modern world."

Skip's brows lowered while he considered that information. "I gather this model of yours is considered a national security threat?"

"I guess."

Murphy walked quietly at her side for a few seconds, then said, "Starting to wish you were off digging up Neandertals or futzing around stealing the Ark of the Covenant?"

Anika smiled despite the anxiety running wild through her veins. "Unfortunately, I'd be out of my league there, too. I'm not a field person. I'm a kind of library anthropologist, more of a mathematician."

When they stepped into the elevator and Hart pressed the button to the second floor, Murphy turned to look at him. "Who's in charge?"

"Secretary of Defense. She's off briefing the president as we speak."

Murphy blinked. "That resets my switches when it comes to understanding the stakes."

"We're going to set you and Dr. French's team up in a safe house where she can work and just disappear for a while."

"A team? How many people?"

"Not sure yet. Maybe six or seven."

Anika watched Murphy's face go dark before he replied, "No safe house, Phil. I want the St. Regis, sixth floor. One block of contiguous rooms. The building is freestanding, used to the needs of security, and we can cover access with three people. Nice circle drive out front with a good field of view. From 16th and K streets, we've got unlimited routing options. If we use early and late travel times, we can avoid rush hour traffic."

"Defense isn't going to spring for the St. Regis, Skip."

"Let me speak with the Secretary. I'm sure I can explain the security situation to her."

Hart gave Murphy a skeptical look, then led the way to the conference room and held the door open for Anika and Murphy to enter.

Anika walked around the table and dropped into the same chair where she'd been sitting for hours. She noticed that Randall was watching Murphy with narrowed eyes. When she looked back at him, he was still standing in the doorway staring at Maureen Cole with a surprised expression.

Murphy said, "Hey, Doc! They didn't tell me I'd be working with you. How ya been? Where's that scruffy archaeologist you hang out with?"

Maureen replied, "Digging up a pueblo in New Mexico. Have a seat, Skip. This is going to be a complicated briefing."

Anika asked, "Are you two friends?"

Given the way Maureen and Skip embraced, there was a lot more to their relationship than "just friends".

Nevertheless, Maureen's simple, "Murphy's saved my life a time or two," was clearly an understatement.

"Ladies and gentleman," Amy Randall announced. "This is Sean Murphy. He'll be providing security. Sit down, Skip."

Randall waited until Skip and Hart retreated to the end of the table and seated themselves, then she said, "The Secretary wants this done fast and quiet. And people, that's how it's going to be handled."

But the butterflies in Anika's stomach just got worse.

It's just a model. Why is this happening to me?

CHAPTER TWENTY-THREE

***

THE BLACK LIMOUSINE PULLED UP AT THE ST. REGIS'S MAIN ENTRANCE, AND SKIP TOOK one last look around. This early in the game, the threat level should still be low. The only people who knew Anika French's location had been in that Pentagon conference room.

The doorman opened the Lincoln's rear door and Maureen stepped out, followed by a haggard Anika French.

Skip stepped forward, giving Anika a hand. "Everything's set."

He led them through the ornate lobby to the elevators. Inside, he pressed six. "Sixth floor isn't the most expensive real estate, but it's the most secure. Your luggage is already in the rooms."

Anika yawned and he had the feeling the young woman hadn't slept in days.

Skip led them down the hall, going to Anika's room first. Inside, he flicked on the lights and inspected the room, checking the closet and bathroom, before he said, "Dr. French, please sit down and let me explain how this works."

"Okay." Anika dropped into the chair.

Skip crouched to meet her eyes. "One. No phone calls. None. Period. If you absolutely have to call someone, you find me. I'll work something out. Two. Until we're totally secure, you don't answer the door for anyone. Not police, not maids, nor room service. If someone knocks, you call me before you even look out the peephole. If you need room service, you call me. If you need personal items, you call me. Even if you think it's silly, I'll get anything you need. No matter what you've asked for, you don't open the door unless you see my cheery face staring through the peephole. Understand?"

"Sure. Got it."

"Rule Three. You don't leave this room for any reason unless you're in my charming company. Even if the hotel's on fire. You stay put until I come to get you. Four. Stay away from the windows. Do not open the shades. Ever. Understand?"

Anika swallowed hard. "Yeah."

Skip stood up. "Lock your door after we leave."

"Yes, sir."

Skip led Maureen out and waited until he heard the lock click, then he turned to her but before he could speak, she said,

"Yeah, Skip. I know the drill."

"Good." Skip followed her into her room, made his check, and paused at the door to stare hard into her eyes. "Good to see you again, Doc. You're looking good. How have you been?"

"Good, Skip. Even the nightmares have faded and I've stayed as far as I can get from motorcycles, bombs, and snipers." She paused, "And until today, bodyguards who might lead me astray."

"I've got no regrets, Doc."

"I was sorry to hear about Jenn. Heard that she really came through at the end. I'm so sorry."

"Yeah." He squelched the pain, took a breath. "Be honest with me, Maureen. What aren't they telling me?"

Maureen's mouth tightened. "You mean what secrets are they keeping that might compromise your ability to protect Anika?"

She walked a few paces to the middle of the hotel room and looked at the small desk and chair in the corner. When she turned back, her expression had turned dire. "Let's just say the situation would be very bad if someone took Anika alive."

Skip paused to consider the ramifications. "The things in her head are like unexploded bombs?"

"Nukes, Skip. Nukes."

CHAPTER TWENTY-FOUR

* * *

"DAD, I'M SAFE BUT I CAN'T TELL YOU WHERE I AM," ANIKA SAID. **"IT'S CLASSIFIED."**

"Classified? How does an anthropology student—"

"I've got to hang up, Dad. They won't let me talk too long."

"They're afraid your calls are being traced?"

She glanced at where Skip Murphy stood on the other end of the conference room, arms crossed, checking his watch, while Anika's team filed into the room. "Don't forget that I love you very much and don't worry about me."

"Can't stop that, sweetheart. I love you, too. You watch your six, understand?"

"Loud and clear, sir."

She hung up the phone and stared thoughtfully at it. Skip had allowed her the call, figuring that if anyone was cagey enough to be listening in, they'd have already figured she was in DC.

"All right, people," Amy Randall called, clapping her hands. "Let's be seated."

Anika found her chair. *My team.* The notion still left her dumb-founded. Dr. Fred Zoah, a man whose work she'd admired for years, sat across from her in a rumpled sweater—never mind that it was seventy-five degrees in here. He nervously peered around through his thick glasses like a demented owl.

Beside him sat Maureen Cole. Next to her was Gale Wade, perhaps the finest modeler of climate change in the world. Gray-haired, dumpy, she looked more like she should be knitting and raising cats than predicting droughts halfway around the world.

Phil Sinclair was thirty, a rail of a man with thick-rimmed glasses, a receding chin, and a bobbing Adam's apple.

And somehow, I'm in charge of all these experts. They should be in charge of me.

Amy Randall stood at the head of the table, meeting each one's gaze. "People, you've all signed your security and confidentiality agreements. You've been briefed, seen the Schott article. Most of you have at least had a chance to skim Dr. French's dissertation. Your job is to actually put Dr. French's model to the test on a global level to identify any and all threats to America's national security. My job is to see that you get that done as quickly as possible. So anything you need, see me or Dr. French, and you'll get it."

Around the room, quizzical glances fixed on Anika. She figured she knew what they saw, a twenty-something redhead with terrified eyes.

Randall said, "On that note, I'll turn this over to Dr. French."

Anika tried to calm herself. She was about to try and lecture experts with far greater abilities than hers.

Time to be Daddy's girl. She stood. "From here on out, I guess this is deadly serious. Our job is to see if the model reliably predicts anything relevant about the modern world. There's a… a hypothesis I've been toying with for about a year but was afraid to test. I discussed it with my former professor, Mark Schott." She sucked in a breath and finished, "So I'm afraid the bad guys are already working on it."

CHAPTER TWENTY-FIVE

***

MARK SCHOTT SWORE HE'D FALLEN INTO PARADISE. STEPHANIE AWAKENED HIM EACH morning in a most erotic manner. After showers and a quick breakfast, he accompanied her to the office, or lab as he'd come to call it, where he immersed himself in the work.

His team had proved astonishing, pouring themselves into the task. Days later, they had the Cahokia model down and, true to his prediction, were making refinements beyond his ability to understand. He would have given anything to have Anika's take on what they were saying.

Leaving the lab each night, his head spinning with permutations of the model, he returned to his apartment where Stephanie redirected his thoughts to prime rib, escargot, steaming mussels, and other delicacies. Then, they would retire to the bedroom, sometimes to explore the kind of exotic sex that exceeded even his fantasies, other times to simply hold each other on the bed, while staring at some impossible landscape. On a dare, they even made love in the middle of a virtual Champs Elyse, mindless French passersby walking within inches of their heads.

And back to the lab.

He'd lost count of the days and was pondering a correlation coefficient with Terblanch when Stephanie stepped into the lab. He hardly noticed the man who accompanied her and absently checked his watch. Damn, time just seemed to fly.

"Mark?" Stephanie called.

He gave her a half-hearted wave, his attention centered on the statistic. "I'm just not sure these correlations are actually significant," he growled. "Remember Schott's rule?"

"Thou shalt not infer a causal relationship from statistical significance," Terblanch muttered. "It's just that these social systems aren't clean. Give me solid economic data any…" His voice trailed off as he glanced at Stephanie's companion. Then Terblanch was on his feet, almost standing at attention.

Mark made a face and turned. The man was tall, big, but not necessarily fat. He wore an immaculate Italian suit that seemed to shimmer, the shoes polished to a luster. But it was the face that grabbed Mark's attention. It was almost bulldoggish, heavy of jowl, and hard-lipped. Something about the man's skull kindled the image of a blunt artillery shell topped with a wealth of thick white hair. The eyes were blue, slightly squinted, over a flat nose.

The Big Man. He stepped forward offering a callused hand that enveloped Mark's. The grip was just short of crushing.

"Dr. Schott, I am pleased to meet you. The reports on your activities here have been refreshing, to say the least. You are ahead of schedule, yes?"

"Mikael Zoakalski?" Mark guessed. "Pleasure to meet you, sir."

"Excuse me." A cold twinkle animated his eyes. "I sometimes forget to introduce myself."

"There have been some setbacks but, yes, we're making progress. I think, sir, that by next week, we'll be able to run a test on a modern state. I'm thinking Indonesia."

"Why Indonesia?"

"It has one of the world's largest populations. Close to two-hundred-seventy-five-million people in a closed geographic area. The country's economic profile, income spread, percent of urbanization, and internal resources almost match the global median. The added benefit is that it's an island nation and, hence, isolated from easy immigration. But there are a few problems."

"What?"

"The accuracy of their economic reports for one. We think the agricultural production figures are inflated. We're also unsure about median family income."

"You will have the real figures by tomorrow morning."

"Uh, that may not be as easy as you think. Certain ministers keep those closely guarded. Call it job security."

Zoakalski's smile was hard-edged. "It won't be a problem."

Mark hesitated. "You're aware, right, that we're exploring new ground here? The first test might indicate that the variables we're using may require substantial reevaluation on our part. Our results will not be concrete by any means."

"Understood."

"Good." Mark rubbed his hands together, oddly unsettled. The guy was spookier than Gunter. Something was cold and efficient about his posture. If those blue eyes looked icy now, what would they be like when the guy was mad? "I don't want expectations to be too high. I've found that when they are exceeded everyone can crow and be happy. When they are met, people slap each other on the back, roll up their sleeves, and continue. But when the results are below expectation... Well, I don't want to find myself in that circumstance."

Zoakalski's smile thinned. "I understand you perfectly, Dr. Schott. Tell me. Have things here been to your liking?"

"Yes." He fought the urge to glance at Stephanie.

"Good." Zoakalski half turned. "We have great expectations for your work, Dr. Schott. You have already taught us a great deal, given us insights we've never explored before. Knowledge, especially in the world to come, will determine a great many advantages to those who provide it."

"Thank you."

Mark noticed a curious excitement sharpen in Stephanie's eyes.

Turning to her, Zoakalski said, "Reward the good doctor tonight, my dear."

And with that, he walked out.

Mark's team promptly relaxed, some venting sighs of relief. The effect was as if the room were suddenly warmer, safer.

Stephanie gave him a satisfied smile, then turned to the others. "Why don't you all wrap things up and leave early? It's Friday night. As hard as you've been working, no one would say anything if you didn't convene until noon tomorrow."

Terblanch, Liu, and Kalashnikov, instead of looking relieved, almost looked cowed as they began putting their things away.

Stephanie waited while Mark stowed his work, then took his arm as they left the lab.

"Special night," she murmured.

"Every night with you is special. What's Eduard cooking up

this time?"

"Nothing," she replied as they exited the elevator and strode down the hall. "Change of plans."

"Really?"

"Just wait," she promised.

To his surprise, she led him to a sleek silver Jaguar XKR parked at the curb. "Get in."

He slipped into the passenger seat, delighted by the mechanically perfect snick of the door as it latched. He wiggled in the form-fitting seat, clicking the seat belt.

Behind the wood-finished steering wheel, Stephanie pressed the start button. The Jaguar gave a throaty roar as she slipped it into gear and gave it gas. She added, "Supercharged. Five-hundred-horse engine. She's my toy."

"Nice toy. Where are we going?"

"I promised you a night on the town. You've earned it."

"The team did," he replied. "They're good people."

As they rounded the palace, half of its windows glowing with yellow light, she gave him a sidelong glance. "Are there any who aren't working out?"

He shrugged. "Francine Inoui is a little intense. The forcing statistics drive her a bit nuts. She insists on absolute certainty and only gets probable responses."

"Should I remove her?"

"What? No. I mean, she's all right. I don't mind a skeptic. Her critique keeps us focused."

"What else?"

"Oh, nothing. Really. I'm mean, I'm always a little irritated when Pierre goes off task, but—"

"He goes off task? How?"

"He veers into genetic vulnerabilities when I've assigned him a different—"

"For example?"

Mark made an airy gesture. "For example, yesterday I told Pierre to analyze the effects of a change in precipitation patterns in California's San Joaquin Valley, decreasing average rainfall by two inches. Instead, he used the model to analyze what would happen if a deadly virus was engineered that only killed people with the EPAS1 variant."

"What is that?"

"Tibetans, mostly. That's what I mean." Mark rolled his eyes to display his frustration. "It's a waste of my time to model wild hypotheses that will never be implemented."

"Would such a virus also affect the Chinese? They're related to Tibetans, aren't they?"

"Tibetans diverged from the Han Chinese about 4,725 years ago, so targeting EPAS1 wouldn't significantly—"

"Explain what that variant does." It was an order, not a request.

A little annoyed, he replied, "It's a genetic adaptation to hypoxia, specifically the low oxygen levels experienced by people who live at high altitudes, like Tibetans. Red blood cells carry oxygen through the body, right? People who live at high altitudes undergo evolutionary pressure to produce more oxygen-carrying red blood cells. That's what the EPAS1 variant does."

"Interesting. Then it would be a clean way for China to eliminate its Tibetan problem, wouldn't it?"

He turned to frown at her.

Stephanie gave him a disappointed look. "Oh, come on, you're not that naive. Do you still think COVID was an accident? The Chinese have been using genetic surveillance since 2019. That's how China identified and detained Uighur Muslims so they could be interred in concentration camps. Though, of course they called them "re-education" facilities. It was called 'total surveillance'. The instant scientific papers began being published that identified genes unique to different ethnic minorities, human beings began using it to weed out the undesirable elements of their society."

Mark's chest suddenly constricted. He knew about the Uighurs. But, somehow, it had never occurred to him that genetic surveillance would be systematically used around the world as an authoritarian tool. It was the twenty-first century. "Surely, the world community will stop this sort of—"

"Surely you jest."

Mark ran the probabilities, observing the cascade of events if nations banded together to try to halt such activities in other sovereign nations. War, of course. Economic devastation. For most countries, it would simply be less devastating to turn their heads.

"Please tell me that's not where ECSITE is headed."

"Of course not," Stephanie insisted. "We're not monsters. I'm just saying there are no safeguards on this kind of technology, and ECSITE must model what will happen if someone—say a nation-state—uses it as the Chinese have in the past."

A little relieved, he exhaled the breath he'd been holding. "I guess that makes sense."

"All I'm suggesting is that you allow Pierre to run his models. What harm is that?"

"None, I suppose."

As she slowed down at the gate, Stephanie's blue eyes glittered in a way that made him distinctly uneasy. She rolled down her window when the guard stepped out and shone a light inside to check the occupants.

As they pulled away, Mark added, "Is this security really necessary?"

"We can't be too careful, and having a secure retreat will turn out to be a comforting thing when the dominoes begin to fall, don't you agree?"

Mark just looked around at the massive high-tech security. He hadn't really noticed it when he'd arrived but, now, it occurred to him that ECSITE employees were virtually prisoners. Extremely well-paid prisoners... but prisoners, nonetheless.

She stopped at the highway, waited for a break in traffic, and made a left, flooring the Jag.

"Yaa hoo!" Mark cried as tires shrieked and he was pressed back in the seat. Stephanie, it seemed, liked driving hot cars.

"What did you think of the Big Man?"

"I wouldn't want to piss him off."

"Good, you will live longer that way." She steered smoothly around a truck and paddle-shifted into third. "More than anything, Mikael values loyalty and rewards it accordingly. That is one rule you must understand. He *demands* results."

Mark's stomach began to crawl. Damn, just how fast was she going? It wouldn't be macho to crane his neck to see the speedometer. But nervous as he was, Stephanie was as cool behind the wheel as if they were doing thirty. "So, what's his story?"

"He came up through the ranks in the old KGB."

"Why did he leave?"

"He got crossways with his best friend, a fellow named Vladimir Putin."

Mark frowned. "What happened?"

"I have no idea. Whatever it was, Mikael thought it was a prudent time to flee Russia. You can relax. His specialty was as an analyst, not a field agent. He understood trends. How nations were developing, where opportunities for sound investments could be found. He made a killing in both Afghanistan and Iraq working for the American government. They needed ways to move men and material into both countries and he facilitated.

"Smart guy."

"Brilliant, actually. Never underestimate him. He thinks five steps ahead." She shook her head. "It's almost uncanny."

"No wonder he's so interested in predictive models."

"Of course. Your model can apparently predict human actions, and the consequent economic fallout, hundreds of steps ahead in any direction. That's impressive. Of course, we need to test verify that."

As they entered Garmisch proper, she took a right, pointing. "Traditional Bavarian? Braustuberl is the best."

"It's your town."

She parked, stepping out. Mark took a deep breath, aware his heart was still pounding from the trip. The Jag beeped as Stephanie set the alarm. He took her arm as they walked, heels tapping on the sidewalk.

"Charming," Mark noted as they stepped through the crowd at the door. To the left, he saw a traditional beer hall, straight out of the movies. And just as loud. Stephanie led him right, to the restaurant. After chatting in German with the host, they were led to a table beside a great enameled stove. The waitresses wore cute Bavarian dress and all seemed young and athletic.

"Skiers mostly," she noted. "They work here to pay for their habit." A pause. "Do you trust me?"

"What kind of question is that?"

"Then let me order."

He grinned, leaning back in his chair. "I'm game."

In short order, two large glass mugs of beer appeared and Stephanie leaned forward, offering hers in a toast. "To the future."

"Which isn't all that bright."

She shrugged. "Those who keep their heads find opportunity where others find disaster."

"And that's what Oberau is all about?"

"Can you imagine a better place to spend a global apocalypse?"

He cocked his head. "So, how does this work between us? Down the road, I mean."

Her eyes narrowed the slightest bit. "Don't get maudlin on me."

"I'm not. It's just that, well, I have to admit, I like your company." He raised a cautionary hand. "I'm a big boy, Stephanie, and I'd just like to know the rules."

The frost melted from her eyes. "Fair enough. And, yes, if you're wondering, I'm completely mercenary. My job was only to ensure that you landed on your feet. The sex was entirely my decision."

He sipped the beer. "So, what happens when I'm fully settled in? You just go away?"

She studied him, fingers slipping down the sides of her mug. "Mark, just what kind of woman do you think I am?"

"Just so we're clear, why don't you tell me?"

"Never forget that I'm known as a heartless bitch. For which I make no apologies. I told you once, I'm a problem solver who's very good at what she does. My loyalty is to ECSITE, and they pay me accordingly. The work is challenging, demanding, and I enjoy the hell out of it. What you really want to know is will I be sticking around? The long and complicated answer is no." Her intent blue eyes held his. "Please tell me that won't be a problem."

"Like I said, I'm a big boy. But I'll miss your company."

She gave him an ironic smile. "Your bed won't be empty for long."

"Really? I hope whoever she is, she knows how to run that waterfall program again."

"I've developed your profile. I know what kind of women you like. Tell me if I'm wrong. Intelligent, worldly, and educated, poised, attractive, and sexually adventurous, interested, but not clingy. You've had your share of subordinate females as a college professor and the wife thing didn't really work for you. In fact, one of the reasons I chose to sleep with you is because you're not inherently monogamous.

What I don't know is do you prefer blondes, brunettes, or redheads?"

"For tonight, I'll take blonde." He sipped the beer. "Is it really that easy? I get lonely and ECSITE provides a woman? They've got a name for that where I come from."

"Actually, given where you come from, they don't. You're in an entirely different league now, cowboy."

Plates were set before them. Mark leaned forward. "Okay, looks good."

"You're about to enjoy *schweinebraten*. On the side is *weisswurt*. Dip it into the sweet mustard. Black rye, I assume you've had before."

"Delicious. I think I could survive here."

"For as long as it lasts."

"Amen."

After polishing off *zwetschgenstrudel* for dessert, Mark found his way to the *herren* room. He stepped up to the urinal, totally absorbed by Stephanie Huntz. Intuitively, he'd known that she wasn't sticking around long term. But hearing it had bruised his ego. How did a man let a woman like that just walk out of the room?

But there would be other women? Attractive and poised? Sexually adventurous? Intelligent and interested, but not clingy?

"Nirvana," he whispered as a man, singing to himself in German, entered behind him.

As Mark stepped away from the urinal, he glanced at the newcomer: Tall, blond, wearing a sports jersey and denim pants. The fellow was obviously drunk. He gave Mark a silly grin, almost toppled sideways, and started headlong for the urinal.

As they passed, the man careened against Mark, almost knocking him off balance. Mark grabbed him, steadied him. "Easy there."

The man pawed at him and, in the process, raked his ring across Mark's hand.

"Danke!" The man gave Mark's hand a hard shake, grinning foolishly, his watery eyes bright. Then, he released Mark's hand and staggered to the urinal.

At the sink, Mark washed, staring irritably at the red scratches the man's ring had left. His assailant was braced over the porcelain, still singing in German.

Back at the table, Stephanie gave him a curious look.

"Friday night in Garmisch," Mark muttered, staring at his raked hand.

They were sipping a dessert wine when he had the first hint that anything was wrong. Blinking, he felt hot, then experienced a slight dizziness.

"You all right?" Stephanie asked.

Mark rolled his head, took a breath. "Yeah. Weird. Just a little lightheaded is all."

"I've seen you drink. It's not the alcohol." Her gaze narrowed. "You're bright red and sweating."

"Yeah, and my heart's racing the way it does when we have sex." He grinned, blinked again. "Maybe something I ate?"

"We're going," she said. "Come on. Let's get you back to Oberau and have the clinic check you out."

He swallowed hard, let her take his hand. Another dizzy spell hit him. "Whoa."

By the time they were on the sidewalk, he was leaning against her. "This is like a bad case of the flu all at once."

"Let's hope that's all it is," Stephanie growled, something dark in her voice. "You didn't take anything? Drugs? LSD? Ecstasy?"

"I don't do drugs." The street lights were smearing in his vision, and the feeling of vertigo worsened.

Two men in leather coats were approaching. Their white sneakers gave Mark the impression of white rabbits hopping along the concrete.

Stephanie leaned Mark against the wall as they passed, her right hand partially inserted in her open purse.

One of the men said something, Stephanie answered, "*Nien, danke,*" in a clearly hostile voice.

At that moment, Mark's stomach lurched. He bent double, vomiting onto the sidewalk.

He wasn't sure how it happened but Stephanie jerked, spasmed, and collapsed. Mark fell to his knees and watched Stephanie kicking and jerking beside him.

Then, in the swirling vertigo, the two leather-coated men had him by the armpits, dragging him toward the street.

A black van lurched to a stop; the side doors swung open like wondrous flower petals. Two more men leaped like magical dancers, their feet sounding hammer taps on the pavement.

Mark felt himself lifted, tossed. The sensation of sailing, dropping, and thudding on the van floor made him retch again.

He caught a vision as the doors were being swung closed. Stephanie was wobbling to her feet, leveling a silver pistol. Mark saw the muzzle flash, heard the bang, and felt the man holding him jerk. Two men dressed in sports jerseys were sprinting past Stephanie, racing for the van, guns in hand. Then the doors slammed shut.

A voice shouted in German. The van lurched forward, tires squealing. *Tink! Tink! Tink!* The sounds like taps on metal, sent heavy bodies crashing down onto Mark. Curses filled the air.

He and the bodies were pitched sideways. Then they were thrown back as the tires shrieked around a corner. The engine roared. Mark Schott felt something warm and sticky soaking his clothes. Then, he began to float away into darkness.

CHAPTER TWENTY-SIX

***

AS ANIKA LEANED OVER SINCLAIR'S SHOULDER, THE NUMBER BURNED INTO HER BRAIN: 0.002.

"Terrifying, eh?" Sinclair said.

"Maureen?" Anika called. "You might want to see this."

Maureen walked down the table, stared, and wet her lips. Her black hair shone in the lights. "We're not wrong."

"No," Anika said.

From down at the end of the table, Amy Randall called, "What is it?"

Maureen took a breath. "The model was designed to prove the null hypothesis. You remember what that is?"

"Sure. Situation normal. No problem. Israel will not launch a full-scale nuclear strike. The world is safe."

The sensation was akin to a lump of lead in her belly. Anika said, "Sinclair's calculations demonstrate that we must reject the null hypothesis. The chances of us being wrong are only two in one thousand."

Amy Randall's face lost its color. She nodded, walked over to the phone, and pressed in a number.

The others crowded around to gaze somberly at Sinclair's screen.

"Maybe if we took another look at airborne transmission and global wind currents," Wade suggested.

Sinclair replied, "You mean we could wrong about the viral carrying capacity? Yes, we could. But I don't think so."

Anika heard Amy Randall say, "Yes, ma'am. Right away."

Fred Zoah adjusted his glasses. "After seeing this, I'm not sure I even want to look at the social forcing data. Somehow, it's no longer a valid pursuit."

"French? Cole?" Randall called. "You're with me. The rest of you, keep working. See if you can knock a hole in this model."

"Do we bring the printout?" Anika asked.

"A copy is already in the Defense database. A printout is waiting for us. Let's go, Murphy. Time to keep us safe."

Anika glanced down at the computer. Of course, Defense was monitoring every keystroke they entered into their laptops. Why wouldn't they be? It just… made her uncomfortable.

As she followed the rest out of the room, the question needled her: *How is America going to use this information?*

It would start as something small. Seemingly insignificant. The general public wouldn't even realize the first domino had toppled. The government would use a misinformation campaign to keep the media busy while the next dominoes were quietly knocked over around the world.

The goal wouldn't become apparent until it was too late.

CHAPTER TWENTY-SEVEN

***

SKIP MANAGED A CROOKED SMILE AS HE WATCHED ANIKA FRENCH'S REACTION WHEN they pulled up to the gate at 1600 Pennsylvania. The redhead was all large eyes and cowed expression as the guard took Amy Randall's credentials, checked them against his database, and took IDs from the rest of them.

As they waited in the idling Lincoln, the great gates before them, Anika whispered a reverent question: "I'm going to the White House?"

"What did you expect?" Randall asked. "You've just proved the end of the world is coming. You thought no one would notice?"

The car dropped them at the West Wing entrance where they went through additional security. Skip—used to the procedure—had left his HK pistol, knives, and Leatherman in the car, produced his *bona fides*, then passed through the metal detectors.

Maureen had a wry smile. Anika looked like she was about to hyperventilate.

Skip knew the room they were led to. He'd been there before. But last time, it had been with Jenn Royce. He bit off a curse and forced the spear of grief from his heart.

Amy Randall told them, "Wait here for the moment." Then she was off, walking at a brisk pace.

An aide asked if they needed anything. Skip promptly asked for coffee, gesturing the others to do the same. Anything to help Anika relax, to get his mind off Jenn and the ache in his gut.

After the aide left, Skip forced himself to grin as he paced around looking at the familiar paintings on the walls. "I always liked this one," he said, pointing at a Bodmer painting of the Upper Missouri.

Anika, almost quaking, noted, "You've been here before?"

"A few times. Not so long ago, I was here with Maureen after a terrorist tried to blow her up with a letter bomb."

"You're joking."

"I wish he was," Maureen said dryly. "My advice? Take a load off, enjoy the artwork. And if things get hairy, Skip will start earning his exorbitant fee."

Skip smiled.

An aide leaned in: "Follow me, please."

Skip gestured Maureen and Anika ahead of him, then brought up the rear. The aide led the way down elegant halls, past paintings and doors. The fates of nations had perched precariously on the shoulders of the men and women who had trodden this same hall. It never ceased to humble him.

The big shock came when the aide opened a door and Skip followed Anika and Maureen into the Oval office. To his amazement, it was smaller than it looked on television. In the center of the room, two couches faced each other on a carpet depicting the Presidential seal. A copy of the infamous printout sat perfectly square in the center of the polished coffee table between the couches.

Skip glanced at the two Secret Service agents standing watchfully on either side of the room, then at the three people huddled around the magnificent desk: President Jonathan Begay, Secretary of Defense Martina Rivera, and National Security Advisor Juan Zapatero. When Secretary Rivera looked up, she nodded at Cole and pinned Anika French with reserved eyes. Then she glanced at Skip, a flash of recognition in her eyes. "Mr. Murphy. I'd heard you were back. Why is it that when there's trouble with anthropologists, you're in the middle of it?"

"You keep hiring me, Madam Secretary."

Rivera arched an eyebrow but the man behind the desk chuckled and stepped around. President Begay was tall, fit, and gray-haired, and his Navajo ancestry was clear in the sculpted lines of his face.

"Mr. President," the Secretary said, "May I present Dr. Anika French and Dr. Maureen Cole. Accompanying them is the security contractor Sean Murphy, better known as Skip."

"My pleasure." President Begay shook hands in turn, his smile warm and reassuring. He pursed his lips for a moment, frowned, and said, "Why don't we sit on the sofas? They're more comfortable." He led the way to the three pale blue couches, arranged around a large square table, and said, "My aides have been briefing me on parts of your model for days, and I just reviewed the printout, but I don't understand it and none of my people seem to be able to explain it to me. That's why you're here."

With Maureen and Anika on one side, the President and Secretary on the other, the printout was spread on the table between them. Dr. Zapatero, National Security Advisor, sat alone on the third couch. Skip took a position behind Anika, his hands clasped in front of him.

The President leaned forward and propped his elbows on his knees. He pointed at the printout. "All right, what does this mean? I don't want to waste time on background, why or how it was developed; just give me the bottom line."

Anika opened her mouth but no sound came out.

It was Maureen who calmly said, "Mr. President, global civilization as we know it is headed for catastrophe."

"Uh-huh. I've heard all this before. Why does this particular model have everyone trembling in their boots?"

Maureen didn't even flinch. "Because this isn't religion, it's science. Not speculation but statistical certainty."

"Science says the world's about to end?"

"It... it's a mathematically derived probability based on a sampling of the data," Anika finally found her voice.

"So this is all just based on sampling, on statistics? Sort of like our infamous political polls? Like the ones that said I wouldn't win the presidency in the last election? What was it that Mark Twain said, 'There are three kinds of lies: lies, damned lies, and statistics?' "

Maureen smiled and answered, "Yes, sir, but Dr. French has demonstrated that we have two chances in a thousand of being wrong. Specific genetic information will be used in Israel to—"

"I don't buy it." President Begay touched the printout and looked at Anika. "If someone was about to launch nukes, my analysts would inform me first. And they haven't."

Maureen nodded. "Yes, sir, I know they would if they understood the probable chain of events. Please, let us explain."

"That's why you're here. Dr. French? It's your model."

The President turned to Anika but when she stared into the eyes of the most powerful man in the world, she froze. Her mouth opened but nothing came out.

Secretary Rivera glanced at her stunned face and said, "Sir, this is all nonsense. Economists, the Department of Defense, State, professors of political science, foundations like the Brookings Institute, have been creating models for years. They've had limited success and produced nothing but conflicting results."

Maureen answered, "Yes, the difference here, Madam Secretary, is that Dr. French's model was derived from a long line of archaeological models based on failed systems."

"Archaeological models? If they're so good, why haven't I ever heard of them?"

"Is the *Mid-Continental Journal of Archaeology* high on your reading list?"

"The what?" Rivera made a face.

"A small pool of American archaeologists has been refining models... testing them on closed systems... for thirty years now. They've slowly, but surely, determined which categories you keep, which you throw out, and the statistics you need to fill in the blanks. But, because they were archaeologists, no one paid them any attention. Who, in the Department of Defense, or State, would have thought we had anything to learn from the collapse of the Lowland Maya in the mid-ninth century?"

President Begay asked, "So, you're saying the perfect model was under our noses all along?"

Maureen shrugged. "Not even the archaeologists realized how pertinent their research was. At least, not until Dr. French put it all together. Her brilliance was applying climatic forcings to social and behavioral data. In short, human emotion. After that, the last piece of the puzzle was in place. We can finally look down on the forest and clearly identify the specific trees that will fail, know where the system is likely to break or has already broken. We call these 'fracture events'."

President Begay stood, walked over to the wall, and stared up at the portrait of Abraham Lincoln. Rivera and Zapatero exchanged worried glances. The room was silent but for the ticking of an antique clock.

Finally, the President asked, "You're here because of the model you ran over at the Pentagon. Amy Randall said it all came down to Israel.

That was where this fracture event might be. Based on your statistics, how much time do we have to turn this thing around?"

Anika stammered, "Maybe days."

"You said it would be a virus? Why a virus?"

"It makes the most sense. No one wants to get into a military conflict with Israel. The lessons taught by COVID-19 have been learned. A targeted virus, coupled with cyberattacks, has the highest probability of bringing Israel to its knees. But the attackers haven't calculated the behavioral variable."

The President's body tensed. "Then give me something I can use to stop it. Anything."

Anika began, barely audible, "I think—"

Maureen cut her off: "The key is not with stopping Israel, but convincing Iran and Syria not to launch missiles into—"

"No," Anika murmured. "That won't work."

Rivera interrupted, "It would actually be easier for us to work with Israel's government. They're rational if you give them the hard data."

Anika insisted, "Not given the current ties you're building with the PLO coupled with the senior housing crisis. Throw in an epidemic and that would be devastating. Conspiracy theories based on pandering to the Americans would run wild. They'll feel even more threatened and likely to—"

"Mr. President, this is ridiculous." Juan Zapatero said, "Wishing no disrespect to Dr. French, here, but *if* there's going to be a crisis in Israel, we should consider working with Russia to put pressure on Syria…"

The President held up a hand. His gaze had fixed on Anika, who was twisting her hands in her lap. For several moments, he just studied her. "Dr. French, sheerly out of curiosity, have you ever modeled the collapse of America?"

Skip unconsciously tensed, loosened his arms, and perched on the balls of his feet. The silence in the room was palpable.

Anika nervously glanced around the room. In a small voice, she answered, "I completed one model for America."

"Tell me about it. It might help us all to have an example that's closer to home."

Anika inhaled a breath and let it out slowly before she said, "In the case of America, an attack that obviously came from a foreign power would unite the American people against the threat. The one small act, the fracture event, is more likely to come from inside."

"How so?"

Anika looked petrified to continue but said, "If you tried to ban guns with a capacity of more than six rounds, it would be the fracture event."

A chuckle went through the room. The President squelched a smile. "My administration is hoping to ban *all* guns, Ms. French."

"Yes, sir, but that won't work."

He gave her an annoyed smile and folded his arms. "I'm sure you know that I have a majority of the American people behind me but I'm listening."

She quoted the Second Amendment, "'A well-regulated Militia, being necessary to the security of a free State, the right of the people to keep and bear Arms, shall not be infringed'."

"I'm well aware of the language, Dr. French. Show me the fracture event."

"Democratic originalists."

"What?"

"You only need another two percent of the nation to support you to achieve your goal in Congress. Here's how you get that two percent. You back the original technology in place during the adoption of the Bill of Rights: black powder, single-shot guns, double-barrel shotguns and rifles were the weapons of the day. The weapons used by the signers of the Bill of Rights in 1789. That's what they meant when they said you can have guns. You'd be supporting the democratic intent of the original founders of America," Anika took a breath and exhaled the words, "and that argument will sway another two-point-three percent to your side."

"Sir," Zapatero said with a frown, "limiting capacity to two rounds would also effectively ban ninety-eight percent of all weapons in America. Your constituents would see that as a huge victory."

Rivera said, "Turn the constitutional originalist's argument against them? You know, that might actually work. We just added a new member to the Supreme Court—"

"Once again, Dr. French. Where's the fracture event that will bring down America?" President Begay impatiently tightened his arms across his chest.

"Across America, guns and ammunition will sell-out as people hoard—"

"We know that. Every time we suggest a ban—"

"Fifty million Americans will probably abide by the law and, though they resent it, will let the government 'buy back' their guns. For seventy million Americans, however, it will be a fracture event. They will feel betrayed by the government. Local militias will grow and gain power. Western and Southern state governments will declare themselves Second Amendment sanctuaries. Municipal and rural law enforcement—like my father—will refuse to obey orders to confiscate weapons and will instead side with citizens. Red states, already feeling alienated from Washington and federal policies, will feel vindicated when they vote for secession. The Rocky Mountain States of America will emerge first, then the Southern states, followed by the Midwestern States of America. Others will follow. Civil war is inevitable. America will collapse."

The President stared at her.

Almost too low to hear, Anika whispered, "Sorry."

"You're telling me that taking guns away, in an effort to make our streets and schools safe, ends in just the opposite? Civil War?"

Anika nodded. "The emotional groundwork is already laid. You know how the national media portrays rural Americans. The 'Deplorables'? They feel scorned and disenfranchised. Deprivation leads to hate. And given other variables, I can predict that China will support the 'will of the people' in each new American nation and back them economically against any retaliation on your part. Russia will offer military support, though Europe, Japan, and Southeast Asia will back Washington. Canada will remain neutral, adopting a wait-and-see attitude."

Maureen Cole sat back in her chair, drawing everyone's attention but she didn't say a word, just looked at Anika with narrowed eyes.

Zapatero said, "Sounds like you're predicting World War III."

Anika nodded. "It's one of the possible outcomes, yes, sir."

Skip's scalp was tickling, nervous sweat beginning to bead his forehead.

Secretary Rivera leaned over and tapped the printout. "Okay, I admit that it's interesting that a single variable, banning guns, could fracture America, but the President needs to know how to keep Israel from launching nuclear weapons. Do you understand?"

"Yes, ma'am," Anika said. "If you'll give me a few more days, I think I may—"

President Begay said, "Have you modeled any other modern fracture events, Dr. French?"

"I—yes. I've also modeled what would happen if someone genetically engineered a virus that killed only women."

Rivera did not smile when she said, "Just for fun?"

Anika didn't seem to know if she was joking or not, so she said, "Uh. No. I just thought, you know, it would be interesting."

"Really?" Rivera glared at her, checked her watch, and stood up. "Mr. President, you have a luncheon with the Prime Minister in fifteen minutes. Would you like to freshen up?"

President Begay studied Anika, lips pursed, face emotionless. "Thank you, Dr. French. I'll be eager to hear what you come up with in the next few days."

"Yes, sir. Thank you, sir."

As the oval office emptied of important people, the aide appeared and led Anika and Maureen down the hall. Skip marched in the rear.

As they neared the first security station, Maureen put an arm around Anika's shoulders and said, "How about cheeseburgers for lunch?"

Skip called, "I know a great place, but…" His voice faded when he saw the Secret Service officer walking toward them.

The man stopped in front of Maureen. "If you would all follow me, please. Just one more stop for today."

"God," Anika said with a sigh, "Tell me it has beer."

The man did not respond, just led them down the halls to an elevator where they were joined by a Marine guard in dress uniform. In the elevator, the Secret Service officer inserted an electronic key, pressed a button, and the cage dropped.

CHAPTER TWENTY-EIGHT

***

THE BASEMENT CORRIDOR WAS NOTHING LIKE THE ORNATE UPSTAIRS. THIS WAS FUNCTION-al. All the doors had little plaques on the front.

They were ushered to one marked **Situation Planning.** Inside, the expected long table dominated the center. The walls, however, were covered with large monitors, many with maps, others with lines of numbers. Some displayed empty conference rooms, others were dark. Below them were individual workstations with keyboards and telephones. Young men and women sat at the stations, their attention fixed on the computers before them.

Then, Anika got a good look at the room's occupants and swallowed hard.

The Secretary of State, Frank Card, stepped forward, saying, "Come in, please."

Anika passed down the line, shaking hands, her head reeling.

"Bob Mason, Chief of Staff. Pleased to meet you."

"Dr. French, I'm Frank Card, Secretary of State."

"Admiral Jim Stark, Joint Chiefs, Dr. French. My pleasure."

"Bill Garcia, Dr. French. Director, Central Intelligence."

"And I'm Monica Scalia. Director, Federal Bureau of Investigation."

Behind them waited a congregation of aides and advisors who could apparently remain nameless.

"Have a seat."

Anika's heart pounded as she shot a look over her shoulder at Skip, who stood at parade rest with the others. He looked just like a combat vet would in the presence of his superiors.

Anika and Maureen were directed to two chairs in the center. The table itself was a huge thing, studded with phones, monitors, piles of paper, notebooks, and bottles of water. Several copies of her print out had been opened and the big pages marked up with notes.

Secretary Card started: "Dr. French, your report has caused quite a stir. We're here at the direction of the President to investigate your claims, determine how probable they are, and formulate a policy to handle the situation."

He looked at Maureen. "Dr. Cole, as a Canadian citizen, you are here because you have worked for the United States of America in the past and faithfully honored your word when it came to non-disclosure of sensitive information. You will find additional non-disclosure documents in front of you. The French Model, as we have come to call it, now falls under the category of National Security." He smiled. "Top Secret. As a Canadian national, with allegiance to that government, do you have any problem with the restrictions about to be imposed upon you? If you have any questions about what your oath entails, feel free to ask them now."

Maureen frowned slightly, took a breath, and said, "I'm sure that for the moment, at least, I have a better understanding of the security implications than you do. I accept and agree to the non-disclosure terms." She retrieved a pen and signed where little yellow sticky arrows had been affixed.

Around the table, people sipped coffee and whispered.

Frank Card spread his hands. "Dr. French, how much does Dr. Schott know about your model?"

"Mark chaired my dissertation committee. He understands the basic model. Given time, and the right people and resources, he'll know it as well as I do."

"Where is he now?" Garcia asked.

"ECSITE has him," Monica Scalia said. "He's in Oberau, Germany."

Garcia sighed as he wrote a note and passed it over his shoulder to an aide. "And you wait until now to tell me? Zoakalski is protected on high by members of the German political and corporate machines."

"We know that." Scalia gave him a cool look. "We've had him under surveillance for quite some time."

"What else do I need to know?" Garcia gave her a flat stare.

Scalia related the information on the break-in at Anika's office and the fact that Schott's family was missing.

Garcia kept writing notes and passing them over his shoulder. They were taken to the aide, now on one of the telephones.

Frank Card said, "So ECSITE understands the value of the model and is trying to reproduce it? If they do, it'll be all over the world. Sold to the highest bidder."

The Secretary of State grunted uncomfortably. "Chinese intelligence is interested. They might even be behind the break-in where Dr. French's notes were taken. The day after this broke, one of their contractors was found dead on some railroad tracks south of Laramie, Wyoming."

Anika started. *China?* One of their people dead outside Laramie? Her mind began calculating the variables...

Garcia shook his head. "This gets better and better. Why not just post it on the internet?"

"Schott as good as did." Scalia went on to discuss the article that Schott had submitted to the *Journal of Strategic Assessment.*

"But we quashed it, right?"

"Absolutely."

Garcia fingered his chin. "The good news, if you can call it that, is that when Schott's no longer of use to ECSITE, they'll simply eliminate him."

Anika stammered, "I—I need everything you have on Mikael Zoakalski. DNA profiles, ancestry, detailed history of where he has lived, his childhood illnesses—"

"We'll make sure you get them."

Anika used a shaky hand to shove red hair behind her ears. "They'll really kill Mark?"

Garcia turned sympathetic eyes her way. "I'm sorry, Dr. French. But that's the kind of people we're dealing with."

"Any chance to get him out?" the Secretary asked.

"From Oberau? Not without sending in the Marines and causing an international incident. Half the politicians in Europe are in his pocket."

"What about Denise and the boys?" Anika asked. "Any word?"

Scalia shifted uncomfortably. "Not yet. No communications, no evidence. Nothing."

"So they're being held as leverage?" Garcia asked.

"Most likely." Scalia gave him a lidded stare. "We just don't know who to blame yet."

Bob Mason leaned forward. "All right, so we're taking the model's validity on faith. At least three parties, maybe more, know of its existence. What about those notes and flow charts stolen from Dr. French's office? As I understand it, they're the real gem."

Anika nodded. "A lot of my best ideas were in those charts and the notes in my file cabinet."

Garcia took a deep breath. "Stealing secrets sounds like ECSITE."

No, not ECSITE. Possible but improbable. Anika was running the numbers in her head. *Another player. Not a group. A nation.*

Anika flushed as all eyes turned in her direction.

"All right, people," Frank Card said, "We're sitting on our very own little bomb. What are we going to do to keep it from going off?"

Anika felt a cold wave go through her. *The model itself could be the fracture event.*

CHAPTER TWENTY-NINE

* * *

THIRSTY.

Damn.

And my bladder. Please, just go away.

Mark tried to return to shredded dreams that guttered and died like exhausted flames.

He worked his tongue, rubbing it dryly across the roof of his mouth. Piss-poor engineering that his bladder was chock full when his mouth was like a desert. Evolution should have seen to it that water could pass by osmosis through the bladder wall. Packrats did that, concentrated their urine.

Opening his eyes turned into a heroic struggle. At first, he could see nothing but a blur. He managed to get a hand up, rubbed to restore vision, and blinked at an ornate room. Immediately above him, two white-robed angels hovered on still wings over a partially naked man, a simple sheet wound over his hips. The man was reaching up, hand open, as if asking for assistance to rise from the tan rock upon which he reclined.

Now, who'd have that *on his ceiling?*

The great painting was surrounded by intricately carved wooden molding that curved down to blue-plastered walls. A window opened to his right; white gauze curtains barely masked a glimpse of tall snow-capped mountains framed by two great trees. A slight breeze swayed the curtains, and the smell of roses was carried in on the air.

Mark shifted, pulled back soft white bedding, and stared around. He lay in a great bed, buck-ass naked. A wardrobe crafted of some dark wood stood against one wall. An antique chair perched next to it. The huge wing-backed thing looked impossibly comfortable. Closed wooden doors were framed in both of the two walls.

"Which one's the bathroom?" He slipped his legs over the side of the bed, wobbled slightly as he stood, and walked to the closest. Opening it, he found a toilet, sink, and an ornate bathtub.

"Right the first time," he muttered, rubbing the back of his neck as he gratefully emptied his bladder. Turning on the faucets, he splashed water on his face and paused to gulp all he could from his cupped hands. Feeling better, he noticed a nagging headache and dried his face on the hand towel. Then he stared into the mirror, wondering at his stubble-coated cheeks and bloodshot eyes.

"All right, Mark, where are you?"

"Italy," a female voice called from his bedroom. "I brought you clean clothes. They're on the foot of the bed."

Mark tilted his head out the door and squinted. A lanky Asian woman, dressed in form-fitting black, now reclined in the great chair. One long leg was pulled up and held by the ankle. Her other arm was over the chair back, her supple body curled into the chair's padded recess.

She was watching him with curious dark eyes. Glossy black hair spilled over her shoulders, its length hidden behind her. He'd call her a classic: heart-shaped face, with large dark eyes at an Asian slant, delicate chin, petite lips, with a perfectly proportioned nose.

"Sure, Italy," he muttered, supporting himself on the door frame. "And how did I get here?"

"By van." She tilted her head inquisitively. "The drug has mostly worn off, but your memory will come back. You had supper in Garmisch last night with Stephanie Huntz. Some sloppy drunk staggered into the men's room while you were taking a leak. He scratched you with his ring."

Images began forming in Mark's memory. "I got dizzy… felt sick."

"Sweet Stephie tried to get you out. It happened so swiftly, her two shadows were caught by surprise in the middle of their beer. Fortunately, the waiter grabbed them before they were out the door and made them pay up.

"By that time, you were on the street hurling that wonderful meal all over the sidewalk. My people helped you up and tossed you into the van."

"Stephanie," he mumbled, a hazy memory of her staggering to her feet, raising a pistol and firing.

"We think she twisted away when Teo hit her with the stun gun." Her brow furrowed as she glanced absently away. "The jolt should have flattened her. You just can't underestimate that woman."

"Where are my clothes?"

"Washing. Getting Chin's blood out of your jacket may be a lost cause."

"Who's Chin?"

"One of the men in the van. He took a bullet in the side. Dr. Santiori removed his kidney last night. He might make it. Too early to tell."

Mark swallowed hard, remembering the metallic tinking sounds, the sticky liquid.

"What the hell is going on?" He shook his head, impossible memories conflicting with the greater impossibility of waking up here, naked, in this room. *In Italy?*

"You've been rescued from certain death, Dr. Schott. I hope that you show us a little gratitude. But then, you really don't know much about ECSITE, the evil Mikael Zoakalski, or the charming Stephie, do you?"

His back was starting to complain from the angle of peering around the door.

The woman smiled. "I wasn't aware that you were so bashful. Your file suggested that you had few scruples about being naked in a bedroom with a woman."

"Who *are* you?"

"Michelle Lee." An amused smile curled her lips. "If you're that shy, wrap a bath towel around yourself. Unless, that is, you've got something other men don't. Having some familiarity with male anatomy, I'd be really surprised."

He considered, glanced at the neatly folded clothes on the bed, laughed at himself, and strode into the room. Her eyes were mocking as he seated himself on the side of the bed and plucked the socks from the top of the pile. "So, *you* saved *me*?"

"They would have killed you. Probably within a week of proving to themselves that the model was up and running."

"Why the hell would they *kill* me? I gave them the damned model?" He pulled on the pants.

"For which they will be eternally grateful," Michelle replied. "It's just that good ole Mikael burns dead wood almost immediately. That and there's no sense leaving someone alive who could slip away and reproduce the model for someone else. He's big on having the best insurance possible. For that very reason, he holds the majority share in some of the biggest insurance companies in the world."

Mark inspected the shirt, a classy Robert Graham, and pulled a sleeve over his arm. "I've fallen through the rabbit hole."

She laughed musically. "I'm almost sympathetic. Almost."

"Wait a minute. They gave me a stunning apartment, took super care of me. Why do all that if they were going to kill me?"

She gave him a knowing glance from under delicate brows. "Tell me, Dr. Schott, would you have worked your heart out for them if they'd put you in a cell? No? I thought not. Sometimes, people who have guns put to their heads figure out that there are no happy endings. So, if they're dead already, why assist their future killers? Besides, from all accounts, Stephie likes playing with her victims first."

"Huh?"

Michelle was studying him thoughtfully. "I wonder how she would have done it? Slow poison so she could savor your inevitable decline? But then, if she was just tired of you, it might have been a bullet. My bet is that she'd pick a moment guaranteed to have the greatest shock value. Maybe just after a heart-pounding bout of sex."

"You're twisted."

"Me?" She broke out in hysterical laughter. "Oh, that's rich. Compared to Stephie?" The amusement died as rapidly as it had come. "Pay attention here: Zoakalski calls her 'his problem solver'. Any time he needs something from a male, he turns sweet Steph loose from her leash. The woman lives for the chase. Get them in bed, suck whatever she needs out them, bank account numbers, top secret schematics, financial reports—or sometimes a predictive model—and leave. If the victims are expendable, she gets her rocks off killing them in inventive ways."

Mark felt himself slumping on the bed. "I don't get it."

Her dark eyes seemed to soften. "No, you probably don't. Mark, you're in the middle of a game where trillions are at stake. If Zoakalski can figure out the model, he'll have a tool that allows him to topple nations. A ruthless man could make a killing if he knew how to trip, then manage, fracture events."

"So, who are you? Who do you work for?"

"CIA," she said evenly. "We wanted to get you out before too much damage was done. Which leads me to my next question: How much does Zoakalski know about the model?"

"Everything," Mark muttered, angry with himself. "Well, mostly."

She nodded. "That's why Stephie took you to Garmisch. Your usefulness was over."

"How'd you know I'd be at the *Braustuberl* last night?"

"We'd been watching her usual haunts all week. We had one chance and, even then, it was a near thing."

He thought of the mysterious Chin who supposedly took a bullet and remembered bodies piled atop him.

"So," he asked, "if you're CIA, how come I'm not at some posh safe house?"

"And just where do you think you are?" She spread her hands wide, staring around the room as if to emphasize the point. "We'd like to extract you back to Washington. But right now, we have a problem."

She stood, unwinding her long body from the chair and walking toward him. Shining black hair swung in time with her sexy hips, her form-fitting black suit emphasizing high breasts, flat belly, and feline grace.

Squatting so her eyes were level with his, she propped long and delicate hands on his knees. "You're in Europe, ECSITE's back yard. Zoakalski has sources in every major metropolitan police force, personnel in all the airports, and most of the customs and immigration control offices.

"If you'd just walked away on your own, he'd be mad enough. But we snatched you out from under his nose. To Mikael, that *demands* a response. But for Ms. Huntz? Ah, it's even more intense. We took you right out of her arms. She's seething. As we speak, ECSITE is turning Europe upside down looking for you."

"Lucky me," he mumbled, rubbing a hand over his face.

"As soon as they get the faintest whiff of where you are, damn the consequences, they're coming." Michelle's eyes narrowed. "It is said that when Stephanie 'hunts', may God help her victim. She's pissed,

Mark. And killing you is now a matter of honor."

"So, what do I do now?"

"You lie low. If you're not moving, you can't be seen."

"Where am I exactly?"

"A private villa in the Dolomites."

"Okay, right. And just what am I supposed to do here?"

"First, we'll have breakfast. Then I'm going to help you work on the model."

"Are you… an anthropologist?" He looked her over.

She smiled. "No, my original training was in chemistry. Actually, chemical warfare."

CHAPTER THIRTY

***

I DON'T GET IT," MARK SAID AS HE CUT A PIECE OFF HIS BREAKFAST PASTRY. "YOU WANT me to work on the model? Here? Just off the top of my head?"

Michelle Lee sat across the table from him, athletic legs crossed in her chair, a small cup of coffee cradled in her hands. "We have documents coming. Copies of Anika French's notes. We'll be able to supply you with any data you need."

Mark looked around the dining room and up at the high ceiling overhead. The walls had been painted a pale orange, and open windows allowed the morning breeze in, fluffing out the curtains. He could see a delightful garden beyond the mowed grass, yellow and red roses, fruit trees in bloom, and neat flower beds.

"I'll need to be in touch with Anika. She's almost a necessity when it comes to adapting the model to modern societies." He gave Michelle a smile. "She's part of my team. That's why ECSITE put her on the payroll."

"Not anymore," Michelle told him. "Agents from the Department of Defense flew her to Washington a week ago. She's been locked away in the Pentagon."

"Can't I just get on the phone and call her?"

"No. Apologies. Zoakalski will be monitoring everything."

Michelle sipped her coffee, dark eyes on his, promising... what? She lowered the cup.

"Look, I'm a patient guy but I have to co-ordinate with Anika. If I'm right, we're talking inevitable dark ages: The fall of Rome. Barbarians terrorizing a world you'll hardly recognize. Considering the archaeological models, you'll be lucky if people are existing at a Neolithic level of culture when this is all over."

Her smooth brow furrowed, eyes penetrating. "That's being a bit extreme, don't you think?"

"It's the Flat Earth, Michelle. Everything's tied together by multinationals and economic interest. Eighty percent of the accounting firms in the US process IRS tax returns in India. Thirty countries around the globe make parts for Boeing aircraft. China manufactures eighty percent of American household goods, and at the same time its vehicles run on Iranian and Saudi oil. Multinational corporations run twenty-four-hour shifts as workforces on four continents electronically trade projects back and forth in real time. Indonesia manufactures Japanese motorcycles with machines built in Korea and run by American computer programs. European homes are heated with Russian natural gas coming from wells drilled by Canadian rigs. Italian clothing, designed in Milan, is manufactured with Japanese sewing machines in Vietnam from cloth woven in Pakistan. Get it?"

"Zoakalski understood this?"

"Hell yes." Mark replaced his cup and picked up his fork again. "Maybe he didn't quite get the gist of it. He's planning on making a few trillions during the collapse. What the poor son of a bitch doesn't understand is that he can make all the money he wants? But it's just paper. There's going to be nothing to spend it on."

He cut another piece of pastry and put it in his mouth.

"Evidently, you're right. He didn't understand. Otherwise, he'd have shot you himself."

Mark stopped chewing and forced himself to swallow.

Michelle smiled. "Do you really think the world is that vulnerable?"

"More so. Start with the simple things. That van that brought me here runs on a fuel injection system controlled by a computer. What happens when the ECU fails… and there is no spare part on the shop counter? Hmm?" He leaned forward, taking another bite of the pastry.

"The CIA just wants to know—"

"That's why I took the ECSITE job, left my family, and decided to live big for a while. It's because we've built such a bloody complicated, interconnected economy served by hyper-sophisticated technology, providing just-in-time commodities to an over-populated world. Knock one prop out from under it—just one—and all those levels of complexity come tumbling down."

"Who do you see surviving? Industrial giants like China?"

He shook his head, chewing. "Too many people and insufficient distribution of commodities. The Chinese, in their wisdom, are replacing the water buffalo with GPS directed tractors, shifting millions from rural poverty into manufacturing. They're feeding a billion people by transporting their imported food in diesel trucks powered by foreign oil. They're replacing the town farmer's market with grocery stores as fast as they can. Then, to complicate their problem, these days they store food in refrigerators made in Korea. Do you see a potential problem here?"

"So, what's the answer?"

"Simple is better. Subsistence farmers in marginal environments like sub-Saharan Africa who are used to feeding themselves, grinding their own grain, and eating their own chickens are the potential survivors."

Her expression slowly changed. "That's depressing."

"You people in the CIA are such morons. All this time you've spent spying on Iran, the Taliban, the North Koreans, and the Russians? All the jockeying for geopolitical advantage? You should have been running anthropological models."

She tilted her head in a condescending manner. "We have experts who do nothing but run models."

He shrugged, then sat back, everything striking home at once. "Without my model, you're just rearranging the deck chairs on the Titanic."

She was about to say something when a gunshot sounded, then two more.

"Get up! This way!" Michelle leaped up.

She wheeled and sprinted for the door. Mark lurched to his feet, knocking his chair over, and threw a quick glance out the window. Two black-garbed figures were ducking around the flower beds, carrying machine guns. One of them was Simon Gunter...

CHAPTER THIRTY-ONE

***

AS THE LIMO DROPPED THEM AT THE FRONT DOOR OF THE ST. REGIS, SKIP WAS SURPRISED to see two suited men standing on either side of the wood-and-glass main entrance.

"Bill," he said to the driver, "when I get out, lock the doors behind me. Anika, you and Maureen stay inside. Bill, if I give you the sign, get the hell out of here, and run straight for the FBI building. Surrender yourself to the guard and have them call Scalia. Got it?"

"Got it, Skip."

Skip stepped out, slammed the door behind him, and walked up to the first suited man, who nodded.

"You Skip Murphy?"

"If you're a bill collector, try my house."

The man grinned, extending credentials. Skip didn't take the folder, even when the man said, "Agent Mike Gallagher. FBI. Monica Scalia sent us over to take responsibility for Dr. French's security."

"Your supervisor is Matt Parkinson?"

"Matt retired last week—which I'm sure you know."

Skip exhaled, walked back to the car, and gestured for Anika and Maureen to exit.

As they walked into the lobby, Skip picked out two more agents in casual dress, trying to act as if they belonged there.

"Come along, Agent Gallagher. We're going to have a little meeting in the control center."

Gallagher introduced himself to the women after they stepped into the elevator, offering his credentials.

Anika shot Skip a questioning look.

"Later," he told her.

On the sixth floor, he used his key to open the control center where Maxine Martin sat at the room desk, a cup of coffee half-drunk in her hand. Normally she worked as a plainclothes DC cop but didn't mind pulling in a little overtime doing security details when female principals were involved.

"Max? Anything cooking?"

"All quiet. The drivers called. The group from State is *en route*, ETA fifteen minutes."

"Keep Agent Gallagher here happy while I see the principals to their rooms."

"Yes, boss."

Gallagher stepped in, and Skip followed Maureen and Anika down the hall. Another suited FBI guy waited at the stairway door. The man nodded, the wire for his earpiece visible.

"Let's talk." Skip motioned Maureen in after him as they entered Anika's room.

"The Bureau?" Maureen asked.

"Yeah, so it seems." Skip did his usual room check, then seated himself on the corner of Anika's bed. "Apparently they've got reservations about the private sector keeping you safe."

"What does that mean?" Maureen asked.

"I've got a hunch Agent Gallagher is going to tell me I'm out of a job."

Maureen narrowed an eye. "All right, let's go see what's up."

Skip stood, leading the way back to his control center. Gallagher was sitting on the bed sipping at the insipid coffee made by the room's coffee machine. He looked surprised when Maureen and Anika followed Skip in.

"Agent Gallagher, it seems my principals wanted a cup of coffee. That and they're as interested as I am to hear what you've got to say."

"My orders are to assume responsibility for Drs. French and Cole. Your employment by the Department of Defense has just been terminated." He gave Skip a hard look. "End of discussion."

Skip turned. "You heard the man, Dr. Cole."

Maureen nodded. "Twenty bucks?"

"That would do it. I'll have Nancy draw up a contract."

"Wait a minute," Gallagher cried, standing up. "What the hell is going on here?"

"Dr. Cole just hired me for twenty dollars to provide her security."
Skip shrugged. "She's my client."

"I'm in," Anika added. "Same price."

"Accepted," Skip agreed.

"Not funny." Gallagher walked up to Skip. "You don't want to try
and jerk me around."

"Agent Gallagher," Maureen added, stepping up. "I'm a Canadian
citizen working for the benefit of, and with the blessing of, your government. Am I to understand that I am now being placed under the
restrictions of the United States without my consent?"

"Think what you want, ma'am."

Maureen replied, "I need the number for the Canadian embassy,
please."

Gallagher placed a hand on the desk phone. "No one is calling
anyone."

Maureen added, "You are refusing me the right to call my government? In front of witnesses?"

"Whoa!" Skip said calmly. "Agent Gallagher, could we step outside
for a moment?"

Gallagher was glaring daggers at Maureen, who calmly stared back.

"Come on, Mike. Let's step out into the hall and have a chat."

Gallagher chewed his lip, stewing, then nodded.

In the hall, he shoved a finger into Skip's chest. "What the fuck are
you doing? Getting yourself thrown in jail for obstruction of a Federal
agent in the execution of his duty?"

Skip calmly stepped back. "Wouldn't think of it." He leaned against
the wall and cocked his head. "You wouldn't want to charge me with
that." He jerked his head toward the room. "I've got two witnesses who
will testify that I never so much as hinted to them that I needed a job."

"Then what was that twenty-bucks shit? Cole didn't just think
that up."

"She thought of that all by herself. But I do have a history of keeping
Cole alive when the whole fucking world—including Amy Randall's
predecessor—was trying to kill her. Let's work out a compromise that
lets you do your job and me do mine."

"You always this smooth, Murphy?"

"Just practical. Assuming we can work out the dick-swinging macho shit between us, two of us thinking is better than one. We'll be less likely to miss anything. You're a Federal agent. You've got rules that you'll adhere to because that's the system. And they're the rules. And you play by the rules. As a private security professional, I've got more… shall we call it… latitude? You with me here?"

"Yeah, but you haven't sold me."

"Did Scalia brief you on *why* this matter is so sensitive?"

"Not my job, Murphy."

Skip turned and opened the door with his card. As he stepped in, he said, "Anika, Maureen, no need to stir up international incidents tonight. Come on. Let's get you to your rooms."

Maureen gave Gallagher a hard look. "It's settled?"

"It will be by tomorrow morning." Skip jerked a thumb in Gallagher's direction. "No one bothered to brief Mike or his detail before they were sent over. For the time being, he's not cleared, so no one discusses anything in front of him or his team. Got it?"

Both Anika and Maureen nodded.

A knock came at the door. Skip stepped over to the peephole. Amy Randall stood in the hall.

Skip opened the door. Randall seemed surprised to see Cole and French. "No wonder you weren't in your rooms."

"Yeah," Skip said. "We had some details to work out with Agent Gallagher here. What do you need, ma'am?"

She circled her finger, saying, "Murphy, French, Cole, you're with me. We need a place to talk."

"I'd say the terrace." Skip glanced at Gallagher. "Can your people do a quick advance? Ensure privacy?"

Gallagher's demeanor had changed with Randall's arrival. "You've got it." He lifted his sleeve mic and spoke to someone.

Anika and Cole were giving each other uneasy glances as Skip led the way to the elevator. Moments later, they stepped out into the pleasant Washington night. Three of Gallagher's agents stood on a sort of perimeter.

"What's wrong?" Anika asked.

"It's Schott," she said. "Someone took him right out from under ECSITE's nose on a public sidewalk in Garmisch. The police there are saying it was a drug deal turned sour. Shots were fired. When it was all over, Mark Schott was gone."

Skip frowned.

Anika's gaze had gone vacant as she considered the implications. "So, the Chinese have everything now?"

Skip asked, "Amy, where did you hear this?"

"CIA. Garcia was a little irritated by what Scalia dropped on him during the session. I just checked with our consulate in Munich. They were aware but didn't understand the significance."

"Aware how?" Maureen asked.

Randall turned to look out at the city. "It seems that Mark Schott's face and description are in every police station, checkpoint, and passport control office in Europe. Interpol has him listed as a known drug kingpin with orders to detain and hold."

"A drug dealer?" Anika's expression changed. "Oh, that's smart. Every agency in Europe will be on the lookout. The Chinese will have to hide him unless he's already in an embassy somewhere."

Skip looked at Randall. "Who'd have the balls to grab Schott off a sidewalk?"

"Someone who figures having Schott is worth pissing Mikael Zoakalski off. He's not the kind who will take this lightly. Nor will the agent who grabbed him."

"Anyone I know?" Skip asked.

Randall barely smiled as she said, "I'll get photos to you in the morning. If she's spotted in Washington, I'm flying all of you to Cheyenne Mountain in Colorado, locking you safely underground, and throwing away the key. Just to be safe."

"So," Skip mused, "does Zoakalski have any competitors to speak of?"

Randall laughed. "Hundreds. A lot of powerful and influential people hate his guts. Could be any of them."

Skip followed Randall's gaze to the gleaming lights. "I've got a friend in Munich, Helmut Rath. If anyone was hiring professionals, he might know. Want me to call him? Ask around?"

"Do that."

"You've got it."

Maureen had been listening, now she spoke. "Amy, we've got

another problem."

"What, Dr. Cole?"

"The FBI just tried to fire Skip. Murphy remains in charge of my personal security or I'm gone. I don't mind him cooperating with the FBI, but when it comes to Anika and myself, we want Murphy."

"May I ask why?"

Anika quietly responded, "I've calculated the statistical probabilities that I'll end up as a case study in terminal ballistics on some coroner's slab. That reason enough?"

Randall nodded. "Point made. I'll call Scalia in the morning. But for tonight, Gallagher is in charge." She turned to Skip. "Acceptable? Otherwise, this is going to turn into a nasty little turf war that I'd rather avoid."

Skip took a deep breath. "Understood."

CHAPTER THIRTY-TWO

***

MARK HAD NEVER HEARD FULL-AUTOMATIC LIVE FIRE. DESPITE THAT DEFICIT IN HIS EDU-cation, he immediately recognized the sound when a submachine gun chattered, and bullets slapped into the building like angry bees.

"Mark, *come on!*" Michelle paused at the door only long enough to tap in a security code before swinging it open.

Bullets made a snapping sound as they pounded into the wall, dust puffing. Bits of plaster pattered around. Mark stared at the blasted plaster, then glanced back at the open window; the curtain looked shredded.

Michelle grabbed him by the arm and dragged him through.

She pressed the door closed and shot a heavy steel bolt home. Mark only had time to contemplate the stone stairs before she was dragging him down into darkness.

Mark tripped, recovered, heels hammering down the steep steps, his hands brushing rough brick walls.

At the bottom, Michelle flipped a light switch, keyed another lock pad, then led him into a wine cellar, its racks filled with bottles. Without hesitation, she shot another heavy deadbolt home, then led him across the room. Panicked, his heart pounding, he watched her long fingers dart along the side of one of the racks.

A bang shook the room, rattling the bottles.

"That can't be good."

"Nope," she agreed. "There." She pulled a lever. "Help me."

Mark grabbed the wood, following her example and pulling. The wine rack slid out, revealing an illuminated room filled with computers, desks, and chairs.

"Help me!" Michelle ordered, struggling to pull the heavy portal closed. Mark got a hand next to hers, heaved. The portal clicked solidly.

Turning, he saw that the walls were covered with maps, and two Asian men were emptying entire file drawers into a giant shredder against one wall while they shouted to each other in Chinese. At least, he thought it was Chinese. Could have been Korean. Sophisticated electrical equipment and large metal cabinets were stacked to the ceiling. Through an open cabinet door, Mark recognized night-vision goggles but couldn't place the other pieces of equipment.

Another boom shivered the very floor.

"This way," Michelle called, grabbing his hand. Even as she led him around the desks, the computers were smoking, the plastic melting. An acrid stench rose on the air.

She paused at a table, searching through documents until she found a passport. She opened it, nodded, and tossed it to him.

"Put that in your pocket."

At the opposite end of the room, Michelle paused to input her code, then turned a knob on a thick metal security door. This opened onto another flight of stairs that led down to a large, illuminated garage. As he hurried down the steps after her, he recognized the black van; fresh bondo had been smeared over the bullet holes, the surrounding paint sanded down to bare metal.

Other vehicles included a Mercedes, a couple of nondescript Fiats, and an Alpha. Two small delivery trucks were parked in the rear.

As Michelle led him along the wall beside the van, he was shocked to see an open weapons locker. Two ugly black submachine guns remained on a rack that should have held ten. Michelle paused only long enough to grab a black pistol from a lower rack and a couple of magazines. She jammed the magazines into her belt, racked the slide back, and let it snap home.

"This way," she called, sprinting around the cars. On the far wall, she snagged a backpack down from a hook, quickly shoving the pistol inside. Tossing it to Mark she led him to a locker beside a racy-looking red motorcycle and threw open the doors. After a moment's hesitation, she thrust a heavy black jacket at him.

"Put it on," she ordered. "Now."

He did, only to have her toss him a full-face helmet. "What the hell are we doing?"

"Saving your life," she snapped. "Put it on!"

As she spoke, she jerked out a red jacket and shrugged it over her shoulders, then lifted down another black helmet and tossed him the backpack. "Put it on."

Mark donned the coat, then slipped his arms into the backpack. He winced as he pulled the helmet over his head. The room darkened as he peered through the smoked visor and fiddled with the chin strap, trying to figure it out.

Michelle straddled the bike and flipped up the side stand. A staccato rumble sounded as she hit the ignition. Then she threw a look over her shoulder as if waiting.

This time the loud *bang* was accompanied by dust trickling down from the ceiling. Any hesitation on Mark's part vanished. He gingerly climbed on the tiny pillion seat, feet pawing awkwardly at the high passenger pegs.

"Hold on!" Michelle called. Mark wrapped his arms around her middle.

Accompanied by a bellow of exhaust, the force of the acceleration tried to pull him backward. Leaving the lighted garage, the world went black as Michelle shot down a dark tunnel. The headlight seemed dim as Mark held on for dear life and peered over her shoulder.

A sliver of light appeared as doors swung open and they were out, Michelle barely hesitating as she leaned the bike around a blind turn.

Craning his neck, he looked back to see a cloud of smoke rising above the trees in the direction of the villa.

"Where are we going?"

"Hang on."

The winding blacktop snaked into a series of curves. Mark swallowed hard, fear paralyzing him as Michelle leaned into the first corner, then the second, each one deeper, the lean more severe. He felt the g-force squashing his butt onto the tiny saddle.

The motorcycle seemed to slingshot around the corners, a drop-off to the left, an implacable rock hillside to the right. When Michelle braked for corners, he was pitched forward, and then back as she found the right gear and rolled on the throttle. He saw the machine's nose rise as brutal acceleration lifted the front wheel.

Cresting a hill, he got a look at the tall peaks around them, the jagged summits white with snow. At any other time, he would have marveled at the scenery. Now the dizzying drop-offs left him petrified.

Michelle managed to stop a couple of feet shy of the Carabinieri who stood beside a police car with flashing blue lights.

One of the officers walked up and asked Michelle a question. She fired back in Italian, not too kindly.

The officer said something else.

Michelle rattled on, then jabbed a thumb over her shoulder at Mark.

The officer laughed and waved them past.

Michelle flipped her visor down, clicked the bike into gear, and with a blast of the exhaust, almost wheelied again as she rocketed away from the two cops.

"What was that all about?" Mark bellowed as she caught second gear.

"Looking for an American drug dealer. You, I suspect. Thank God you kept your mouth shut."

"What did you tell them?"

"I told them you were my boyfriend up from Milan and that we had a room waiting in Cortina where I hoped you'd fuck my brains out."

Ordinarily, he would have laughed. Instead, with the wind ripping at his helmet, he shot a look over his shoulder. ECSITE had just declared war on the CIA.

Over him?

CHAPTER THIRTY-THREE

***

ANIKA TOSSED ON HER BED, BLINKED HER EYES OPEN, AND STARED AT THE BEDSIDE CLOCK. The numbers 3:13 glowed as if mocking her.

She rubbed her face and whispered the key variables: "Filipchenko. Lundborg. Eugenics. Imperial Russia. 1900…"

For hours before she'd climbed into bed, she'd been working on her DOD laptop, modeling everything they'd given her about Zoakalski. She needed to refine it before she presented it to her team but she felt certain, even in its rough state, Maureen and Fred would understand.

She could hear her father's voice inside her head: *"This ain't your first rodeo, honey. Just hang on."*

Anika massaged her burning eyes. She'd grown up with rodeos. Mom had taken her to the local ranch rodeos, the one at the State Fair in Douglas, even the big one at Cheyenne where she'd watched the Professional Rodeo Cowboy Association cowboys and bull riders.

An ache began to twist her gut. God, what she'd give to be home in that small worn-out ranch house where life consisted of waging war on the field mice that climbed in through the cracks in the foundation and struggling to make the bills.

Off and on throughout the night, she'd been jotting notes on her bedside notepad, calculations, trying to run models in her head to determine Zoakalski's ultimate goal and decipher how to bring him down. *He's Russian. The key is there, just haven't figured out…*

A soft knock came at her door.

Anika groaned, climbed out of bed, and peered through the peep-hole. A man in a suit stood there, holding a tray covered with a round silver cover in his hand.

"Who is it?"

"FBI, Ms. French." He raised his credentials to the peephole. "Wake-up call. I've got breakfast here, and you'll have to be ready to go in fifteen minutes."

"It's *three fifteen*," she cried.

"White House wants you, ma'am."

"Okay. I'll… just give a minute." She wobbled back to her clothes, pulled on her pants, and tucked in her long sleep shirt. Yawning, she walked back to the door, flipped on the lights, and squinted as the agent entered and placed the tray on her desk.

"Sorry, ma'am," he said as she stepped over and lifted the lid. A sandwich lay on a plate.

"Breakfast?" she asked, turning to give the agent a scowl.

Even as she focused on the small aerosol can he held, the thing shot spray into her face.

Anika took a step back, reeling, clapping hands to her face. Then the room spun and the man caught her as her legs turned to rubber. As he eased her to the floor, he was lifting a tiny radio to his lips, saying, "Got her."

Then everything grew misty, soft, and faded into gentle clouds…

CHAPTER THIRTY-FOUR

***

MARK STOOD IN THE SHOWER, RUBBING HIS BUTTOCKS, DELIGHTED TO HAVE FEELING BACK in his knees. Michelle had checked them into a small hilltop hotel overlooking the harbor and city of Venice.

What the hell has happened to me? Who the fuck have I become? He wondered what Denise would say. Probably that he'd gotten exactly what he deserved.

Mark sighed, thankful that she, Will, and Jake were safe back in Wyoming. But for the boys, he'd have ended the marriage years ago. He missed them.

He stepped out of the shower and toweled off. Rubbing the steam from the mirror, he stared at himself. Shit like this didn't happen to anthropology professors.

Picking up his clothes from the counter, he dressed and stepped out into the bedroom.

Michelle sat on a corner of the great four-poster bed, sorting through the contents of the backpack. "Feel better?"

"Yeah, and it turns out I didn't have a childish accident on that mad ride."

She gave him a crooked smile. "First time on a motorcycle, huh?"

"I always thought they were dangerous."

"So you took up sleeping with sociopathic women like Stephanie Huntz as a safe alternative?"

He walked over to the bed. "I saw her back there. Following Gunter through the garden."

"Yes. She always follows along behind to cap off the wounded."

Michelle handed him a thick fold of bills. "That's two thousand Euros for emergencies. We'll go down to San Marco in the morning and buy you a billfold and a couple of sets of clothes."

Mark walked to the window and peered out at the city. Even from this height, he could see Venice's Grand Canal in the distance. The gondolas could have come from a movie set. Across the boat-dotted lagoon, white-domed churches and classic Venetian architecture rose against the skyline.

From the backpack, Michelle had retrieved a cell phone and called a cab. Twenty minutes later, they were deposited dockside at the pier. It was a beautiful sunny day. The water glinted for as far as he could see. A water taxi sped them across the opaque brown waves to the canal-side entrance of a grand historic hotel that sat at the water's edge.

"This place is stunning."

"The Hotel Danieli is very famous." Michelle was sorting through a series of credit cards as she walked toward the front doors. "Not the kind of place Zoakalski will expect us to hide out."

Mark pulled his new passport from his pocket. "Brian Joseph Meyer. Date of birth: 1980. Place of birth, Cleveland, Ohio." In the picture, he looked drugged. Probably because when the photo was taken, he had been. He had no memory of anything between Garmisch and the villa.

He was supposed to call Michelle 'Shelly', which was close, and easy to remember. They were supposed to be married. The very notion made him wonder just how far the charade was supposed to go.

"What do I do for a living?" He asked as they entered the magnificent lobby and headed for the registration desk.

Michelle said something in Italian, gave the desk their passports and a credit card, and waited for the key to be presented.

As they headed for the elevator, she answered, "That's up to you. Pick something you know that isn't anthropology or even university related. Something you can discuss offhand and answer questions about intelligently."

He paused, thinking. "Travel writer?"

"Who's your publisher? What's your editor's name?"

They stepped off the elevator and headed for their second-floor room. When Michelle opened the door, the scene was amazing. Antique furniture spread across the floor, but Mark went straight to the big window overlooking the water and fabulous ancient cathedrals.

"Breathtaking."

Michelle dropped into a chair and sorted through her credit cards. He'd watched her go through them three times now—what was she doing?

Her cell phone rang. *"Si."* She walked to the far end of the room, head tilted as she listened. Mark watched her give slight nods, then her gaze darted to him. Finally, she lowered the phone and stabbed the *End* button with a pointed finger. For long moments, she just stood, head down, staring at the gorgeous red carpet.

When she walked back, Mark asked, "A lot of people are dead back there, aren't they?"

"Of course."

"The man just attacked the CIA," Mark reminded. "No one does that and gets away with it." He gazed out at the *Riva degli Sciavoni* and the glittering water beyond. "I wish I'd never said yes to Simon Gunter."

"They'd simply have taken you off the street."

"They'd have kidnapped me?"

"Grabbing you isn't all that hard. We pulled you right out of Stephanie's arms."

He stopped short. "What about Anika? Are they after her too?"

She gave a faint shake of the head, eyes focused on an infinity beyond the window. "Will you still help us with the model?"

"Can you keep me alive?"

As if in answer, she walked over and removed the black pistol from the backpack, pulled back the slide to check the chamber, and released it. She said, "Hope so," as the slide slammed back with a final click.

CHAPTER THIRTY-FIVE

***

SKIP'S CELL PHONE CHIMED. HE SAT UP IN BED, DISCONNECTED IT FROM THE CHARGER, AND glanced at the clock: 4:18. Tapping the call icon, he said, "Murphy?" and tried to collect his thoughts.

"Skip? It's Maureen. You'd better get down here. Anika's missing."

"What?" Turning on his light, he began fumbling for his pants.

"No one's talking. They just did a bed check on the rest of the team. I was told to stay in my room and keep the door locked. But looking through the peephole, listening at the door, I can tell you Anika's gone. Agents are scurrying in and out like roaches."

"I'm on the way." He ended the call and jammed the phone in his pocket. Next, he clipped his holstered HK pistol in its accustomed place inside the back of his belt.

Rushing to the garage, he almost scraped the top of his vintage Charger on the garage door as it was opening.

Fifteen minutes later, in defiance of speed limits and red lights, he rolled to a stop behind a line of three black government Tahoes parked in front of the St. Regis. He tossed his keys to the bellman as he burst through the door, only to be stopped by a serious young agent.

"Sorry, sir. No one is allowed—"

"You tell Mike Gallagher that Skip Murphy is here and Anika French had better be present and accounted for."

The agent talked softly into his sleeve, nodded, and said, "Go on up."

Skip, fuming, nodded curtly at the agent who stood before the elevators, and fumed some more waiting for the doors to open on the sixth floor.

The door to the command center was open. Mike Gallagher stood

before the desk. An older man was seated—suit coat hanging open—as
he talked on the phone. The man laid the handset in its receiver and
leaned back. "Okay, everyone's alerted. Washington PD is receiving
French's description as we speak. Every Field Office in the country is
alerted, Border Patrol, Customs and Immigration, Langley, everyone."

"So, you haven't found her?" Skip's heart sank.

"You're Murphy?" The man gave him a slight nod.

"I am." Skip pulled out his ID and handed it over.

As he handed it back, the agent said, "Glad to meet you. Ms. Randall said I was to fully cooperate with you. I'm Stew Ortega. Special
Agent in Charge, Washington Metro Field Office." He leaned forward,
rubbing his face. From his sloppy dress, Skip figured he'd just been
yanked out of bed, too.

"What happened?" Skip asked.

"Delivery truck pulled up at the kitchen loading dock at two
fifty-eight. A woman with an invoice rang the kitchen entrance
bell. One of the night cooks let her in. At three-oh-seven, all the
cameras went down."

Skip's heart began to pound. "How'd she incapacitate your agents?"

Ortega continued. "Still working on that. Probably a somnolent
gas."

"They only took Anika French?"

"She's the only one unaccounted for. I've got ERT going over her
room as we speak. The place, so far, is clean. The bed is rumpled,
so we know she slept there. Other than that, her suitcase, toiletries,
toothbrush, everything is gone. The only thing remaining is a sandwich
on a delivery tray. ERT is sending it straight to the lab."

Skip straightened, feeling sick. "Professional job."

"Yeah," Ortega said and glared at Mike Gallagher. "Top fucking
notch."

Gallagher looked as if he longed to crawl under the couch. But for
the burning rage, Skip could almost have pitied the man. "Maureen's
just across the hall. Did she hear anything?"

Ortega glanced at Gallagher. "Go get Dr. Cole."

Gallagher left.

Ortega said, "I haven't had a chance to talk to her yet. I've been
busy at damage control."

Gallagher leaned in the door. "Dr. Cole said she won't leave the room until Murphy tells her it's all right."

Skip strode out of the room and walked to Maureen's door where he knocked. "It's all right. We just need to talk to you."

Maureen unlocked the door and followed Skip down the hall.

Once in the control room, introductions were made. Skip asked, "Did you hear anything, Maureen?"

She shook her head. "No. I was sleeping soundly. When the FBI finally woke me, they nearly had to hammer the door down."

Ortega said, "They must have had a passkey."

"No passkey," Skip said, seething. "Anika used the security lock. Which of your agents is missing his credentials?"

"Shit." Ortega looked at Gallagher.

Skip could picture it clear as day. Anika had been there when he'd turned control over to Gallagher. She didn't personally know all the agents. She'd have looked out, seen the badge and ID, and turned that last critical lock.

"You're going to want to alert Bill Garcia at Langley right now. Before you even brief him, tell him to center his search on the Top One Hundred database. He'll know what you mean."

Ortega hesitated. "Calling the DCI, that's above my pay grade."

"Do it on my authority. Tell the operator to put you through on an NSA Alpha One."

Ortega's eyebrows raised but he picked up the phone and started dialing.

Maureen had a wounded look. "Anika must be terrified."

"They want her alive," Skip said. *Or they're eliminating the competition.*

"Murphy?" Ortega called. "The DCI would like to speak with you."

Skip took the phone. "Murphy, sir. This is not a secure line."

"What's your assessment?"

"Top of the line professionals, probably trained by us, Russian intelligence, Israel, or maybe the Chinese or Germans."

"What's the chance of recovering the young woman?"

"Barring a miracle or random event, she's already out of the country. You had best notify the President."

"That's my next call. What was the FBI doing there?"

"I was informed yesterday that they were in charge, sir."

"Monica?"

"Washington Metro Field Office."

"Christ."

"Sir, I have some ideas but this is not a secure line."

"I'm sending a car. Here's my personal number. Got a pen?"

Murphy wrote it down, folding the paper and slipping it in a pocket. He hung up.

"The *President?*" Ortega asked. Sweat was beading on his forehead.

Skip took a breath. "SAC, you want my advice?"

The man gave him a hollow look.

"From here on out, Dr. Cole's team should be relocated to Andrews Air Base, maybe Quantico. Someplace it would take a division to get to them."

At the door, Gallagher, looking humble, stopped Skip. "You tried to warn me. Thanks for that."

Skip gave him a nod. He figured it was a lot more politically expedient than decking the guy.

CHAPTER THIRTY-SIX

***

FOR SUPPER, MICHELLE SUGGESTED THE DANIELI TERRACE, THE RESTAURANT ATOP THE hotel where they could watch evening settle on the Marco basin. As they were seated at a table, the setting sun slanted across the Lido with its white domes, casting it in a golden light that seemed ethereal.

Mark fingered his hair, oddly unsettled with the black color. His stubbly beard itched but he'd been encouraged to let it grow. Earlier, Michelle had left him with the pistol, taken the backpack, and vanished for nearly a half hour. When she returned with clothing and hair dye, she'd led him to the bathroom sink for a makeover.

"The tide is changing," she said as she lounged back in her chair. "Each time the tide goes out, it drains Venezia."

He watched the lights come on across the lagoon. Looking to the west he could see Santa Maria della Salute at the mouth of the Grand Canal.

Michelle stayed quiet for most of the evening. They ate, shared a bottle of wine. Only after the plates had been cleared did she finally say, "It really hasn't been a cheery day."

"Want another bottle of wine? I find that if I drink enough the fear goes away."

She shot him a speculative glance. "You did better than I thought you would in a crisis. I thought you'd seize up, panic."

"I did. First thing when we got to the hotel, I checked to see if I'd crapped my pants."

Her look went distant again. "Let's talk about something irrelevant. What are you going to do when you get home?"

He swirled the wine in his glass. "Give Denise the house, the cars, and the divorce she deserves. Try and make peace with Will and Jake.

After that, I don't know. Watch the world die, I guess."

She waved an arm at the lights now reflected on the water, the boats in the lagoon, and the surrounding buildings. "So, all of this is doomed?"

"The buildings, the history, and the passions of the people who created them, yep. Everything goes back to the earth after it wipes us clean."

"Then what's the purpose of art and beauty?"

"Our own amusement, I suppose. We're a selfish species."

"That's not much of an epitaph for humanity."

He sipped the wine. "Human survival has always hinged upon a balance between the selfish and altruistic parts of our psyches. When we weren't beating our neighbors over the head with a club, we were offering a hand to pull them up from the mud. If we hadn't been the exploitive and violent bastards we are, our ancestors would have died out two million years ago. And if we hadn't been able to create mutually beneficial alliances, share our resources, and see ourselves in another's shoes, we'd have gone just as extinct. Funny creatures, we humans."

Her gaze roved over the water, enjoying the beauty of Venice. "Maybe we should just focus on the present, then."

He looked at her, her face softened by the restaurant lights. Michelle had transformed from the single-purposed, Ducati-driving Kamikaze into a startlingly beautiful woman.

She pushed her chair back, stood, and pulled her long hair over her shoulders.

He rose, acknowledged the waiter's "*Gratzi e buona sera.*" Then followed her.

They didn't speak as she led him down the stairs, passing classic artwork and sculpture. The wooden hand railings under his hand reminded him of age and the thousands of people, famous and not, who had trod these passages.

At their room, she checked the little wedge of paper stuffed in at the bottom of the jam, assuring herself that no one had entered.

Once inside, Michelle propped a chair under the doorknob, turned on a desk lamp, and faced him. Placing her hands on his chest, she stared into his eyes, as if trying to read his soul.

Who is she seeing?

Whatever her conclusions, she lightly kissed him, lips moving on his. As his arms went around her, the memory returned of how solid she'd felt on the motorcycle.

"Are you sure you want to do this?" he asked softly.

"Tonight, I need the 'now' more than any illusion of 'tomorrow'."

She led him to the bed.

Later, he wondered where time had gone. The pealing of distant church bells shifted his attention from her to the world at large.

She lay curled against him. His arms were wrapped around her, right hand cupping her breast, the nipple, once so hard, now smooth and soft. His head was pillowed on the silky swirl of her hair. It smelled of woman and shampoo.

She'd said nothing the entire time. Her only utterances had been the explosive gasps each time he'd brought her to climax.

Finally, she asked, "What advice would you give the government? What plan? What could the US do to ensure that something was saved?"

"First thing?" He thought about it. "Decentralize authority. Begin manufacturing simple machines that can run on vegetable oil, string telegraph lines again, or old-fashioned wind-up phones." He sighed. "Force people out of the cities and back onto the farms. Anything to reduce the reliance on technology. But that will result in revolt and blood running in the streets."

"Could someone more autocratic, like the Chinese, manage?"

"I'm not an expert on China, by any means, but they've promised too much to the people. You can't tell a billion people, 'We're going modern' then tell them, 'Forget the dreams of a car and your own businesses. Forget going to college and start breeding water buffalo because you're going back to the fields.'"

"I see. Where do you see the geopolitical advantage ending up?"

"There won't be any geopolitical advantage. Any semblances of governments that remain are going to be concerned with local problems, get it? Not national, or international, just local. My best guess: It'll be a feudal system. Lords, their warriors, and the farmers who feed them. So, CIA agent, welcome to the new dark ages."

"The material you need to work on the model will be here tomorrow by FedEx." Her tone sharpened. "You'd better be able to show me why you think this way."

Mark grimaced at her. "So, Langley can FedEx us stuff but they can't get us the hell out of here and back to the good old USA?"

"Not yet. Not with Zoakalski's tentacles everywhere."

CHAPTER THIRTY-SEVEN

***

THE CAR GARCIA HAD SENT TOOK SKIP ONLY AS FAR AS THE WHITE HOUSE. ONCE MORE HE declared his weapon and surrendered his keys, flashlight, Leatherman, and knife before passing through the detectors. He didn't get to inspect his paintings or order a cheeseburger. The Marine guard ushered him straight to the basement situation room where he'd observed the meeting the afternoon before.

Coffee and doughnuts were provided and he munched them as he waited while the guard stood "at ease" in the back of the room.

The first to enter was Bob Mason, followed by Frank Card. After introductions, Skip answered the questions he could. Then, a prickly Monica Scalia charged in, fire in her eyes.

"How the hell did you let it happen?" she demanded.

"Ma'am," Skip replied, summoning battle-field discipline, "I was officially relieved by Ms. Randall. She left Agent Gallagher in charge."

"Back off, Monica," the Secretary of State called as he walked into the room. "I've just had a talk with Amy Randall. This is *your* mess, now."

Skip raised his hands, aware that Mason and Stark were watching. "With all due respect, it's too late for blame. The people who took Dr. French were outstanding professionals. They'd advanced the St. Regis, done their homework, and used the arrival of the FBI brilliantly."

"*Used* us?" Scalia barked.

"Used you." Skip perched on the table. "Gallagher's team had no idea what they were getting into. Guard a bunch of professors? From what? To them it must have seemed like plush duty. Hang out in a Five-Star hotel and keep unauthorized people off the sixth floor. They had no familiarity with hotel staff or procedures and no established operational instructions on threat detection or identification."

Monica Scalia walked over to the coffee pot, still seething.

"The question is," Bob Mason said, "who took Dr. French?"

Skip slipped his butt off the table and took his seat. "Had to be ECSITE. Zoakalski had Mark Schott working on the model, probably making progress, until he was snatched in Garmisch. It doesn't do for a man with Zoakalski's reputation to let someone snatch a resource like Schott from under his nose. He has to prove to the world that he's not taking it lying down, and he has to have a new scientist to replace Dr. Schott."

"So he grabs French right out from under the FBI," Card agreed. "Brassy."

Bill Garcia strode in with a file under his arm. Two men in suits followed him. One walked over to one of the empty wall corrals. He seated himself and began to tap on a keyboard.

Scalia asked, "What about the organization that took Schott? This mysterious third party? The Chinese or whoever they are."

The DCI was staring at the computer screen when he said, "Things continue to get more interesting. John? Got it?"

"Coming up now, sir."

The image that formed on the screen appeared to be a white-stuccoed mountain villa. From the vegetation and angle of sunlight, Skip judged it to be a southern exposure somewhere in Italy. Smoke rolled out of the windows and doors; a fire company kept pumping water into the rambling main structure. Their hoses and boots were ruining expensive landscaping.

"What's this?" Card asked.

Garcia said, "According to the regional Carabinieri, a local drug lord just got taken down by his competition. Fifteen dead, mostly by nine-millimeter small arms fire. At least four bloodstains indicate other casualties were evacuated by the perpetrators. Preliminary pin tests indicate MP5 HK subguns were the main weapons. The explosives used to breach the doors were all NATO spec C-4. A fine powdering of heroin was recovered from the dining room table. Next image."

The screen flashed to show the damaged remains of the interior. Bodies sprawled here and there, smoke stains visible.

"Next."

The image showed a blasted door leading down a stairway.

"Next."

This shot was of what looked like a control room, the walls covered with maps, the surrounding desks exhibiting the melted and charred remains of computers. A smoking bin stood next to an industrial-grade shredder. Two men lay sprawled on the floor.

"This was a real surprise for the Carabinieri. They're calling it the operations center. Their story is that a major European drug ring was operated from this room. Next."

The shot was of a large garage filled with vehicles. Prominent among them, a black van splotched with bondo.

"Watch the van, people." Garcia said. "Mark Schott's fingerprints were lifted from both the van and one of the villa bedrooms."

"Oh, I get it," Card murmured. "Zoakalski caught up with the snatchers. Paid them back. But who is 'them'?"

Garcia said, "John, go back to the control room."

Skip stared at the wrecked room. "Looks more like a military facility, doesn't it?"

"Yeah." Garcia walked over to the monitor, pointing. "Drug lords don't usually install this grade of incendiary to destroy computer equipment." He pointed to another smoking piece of equipment. "They don't utilize passive radar receivers. The dish, incidentally, is on an adjacent high spot disguised as a water tank. The surrounding trees are studded with incredibly sensitive receiving equipment. The charred steel cabinet you see to the left was obviously incinerated but enough remained to identify the equipment inside as very sophisticated surveillance devices. In short, spy stuff." He paused. "We think Chinese intelligence."

"Spying on whom?" Scalia asked.

"Best assumption?" Garcia looked around the room. "This was a monitoring station to keep track of NATO activities around Aviano air base."

"So the heroin on the table was a plant?" Skip suggested.

"That's our operative assumption," Garcia replied. "Because of potential NATO security concerns and because an American citizen is involved, State has asked if the Italians will allow FBI's ERT to inspect the villa. They're already *en route*."

Skip was chewing his thumb, studying the image. "So, does this mean Zoakalski's got both Schott and French?"

"Not necessarily."

"Mr. Murphy," Mason said, "anything you're planning cannot be associated with this country or administration."

Skip straightened. "Of course not."

The room was silent.

Finally, Garcia said, "If you're caught, we've never heard of you."

Skip nodded. "This isn't the first time I've stuck my neck out for this country. God willing, it won't be the last."

CHAPTER THIRTY-EIGHT

***

AT THE BREAKFAST TABLE, "RED" FRENCH, DULY ELECTED SHERIFF OF CONVERSE COUNTY, had just finished a hearty breakfast of eggs over black beans seasoned with strips of green chili.

Raising a cup of coffee to his lips, he sipped and felt an eerie sense of loss. The battered kitchen around him had last been refinished in the early sixties. The only renovations had been done by his wife—and that consisted of a coat of off-white paint. He'd thought about redoing it, replacing the old white gas stove with a modern unit, ripping up the worn linoleum and replacing it with shiny vinyl flooring or that modern stuff that looked like wood.

Every time, just as he'd talked himself into it, he'd resisted the urge. Doing so would have been just another betrayal of the two women he'd loved—and let down so many times.

Looking out the old double-hung windows, he could see the ranch yard, the barn, and the low-hanging electrical line.

Would it have made a difference if he'd been home? Would he have been the one to take the ladder?

His attention focused on the light fixture atop the barn door. It had been raining the day his wife walked out, a light bulb in her pocket, her hands struggling with the aluminum ladder.

Maybe it was a gust of wind. Or she might have slipped on the muddy ground. Whatever the reason, she'd touched the top of the ladder to that damned power line.

Anika had found her, pitched on her side, her staring eyes filled with rain and splattered mud.

Red expanded his lungs, exhaling. Then he tossed off the last of his coffee and carried the plates over to the sink. They'd never had an automatic dishwasher. Any extra money had gone to the ranch, the bank, or the feed bills.

Washing his plate, Red placed it in the drainer and checked to make sure he hadn't splashed soap or water on his crisp uniform.

At the door, he reached for his broad-brimmed hat, placed it on his head, and turned when the phone rang.

"Yeah, Red here," he said as he picked up the handset. *What was it this time? Loose horses? Some kid rolling an ATV?*

"Is this Major Red French?" an unfamiliar voice asked.

"Yeah."

His door burst inward, sending splinters flying across the living room.

CHAPTER THIRTY-NINE

***

ANIKA STOOD WITH HER ARMS WRAPPED PROTECTIVELY AROUND HERSELF AND WATCHED low surf rolling onto the white beach. A warm sea breeze ruffled her red hair as she gazed at the distant horizon where the impossibly turquoise water met the sky.

Behind her—just back from the beach—stood a plush, glass-fronted house nestled in a grove of mangroves and palm trees. The place dominated the island. Two boats, both moored to a dock in the sheltered canal behind the house, and a helipad appeared to be the only means of egress. The boats were guarded and Anika didn't think she'd be able to sprout rotors.

No way off without swimming. But even so, they still didn't trust her. The two muscular guards stood, one on each side, ten feet away, close enough to grab her if she ran for the water. Close enough to shoot her with their damned taser pistols.

The last thing she remembered of DC was the FBI agent, her hotel room, and looking down at a crummy sandwich. The next had been waking up here, on this island.

Did anyone find the notes I left on the bedside table?

At the sound of a helicopter, she turned, watching the thing materialize over the palms. White and sleek in the sunlight, it circled, then settled on the heliport behind the great house's red-tiled roof.

"That's probably your ride," one of the guards said. "Come on. Let's go meet them."

Resigned, she turned and trudged through the sand to the wooden steps that led up to the house. As the guard opened the door, she heard the helicopter spool down.

The house interior was a marvel of teak flooring, ocean-view windows, and walls decorated with what was probably expensive artwork. The ceilings were high, slanting affairs, from which hung ornate fans that whirled lazily. A fancy glass table with chrome-framed chairs and several comfortable couches were the only furniture.

Voices came from the rear and, within moments, an athletic blonde woman strode in. She was dressed in a loose white blouse that barely disguised a full bust. Spray-tight Levis accented muscular legs. She fixed Anika with gorgeous blue eyes, her smile warm and welcoming.

"Dr. French? I am so glad to meet you." She offered a hand Anika refused to take. "I'm Stephanie Huntz. Please excuse my appearance. Things have been busy for the last couple of days. I was only able to get some sleep on the flight over."

"Where am I?"

Stephanie gave the guards a questioning look, then chuckled. "Rude of them, isn't it? Not to have told you, I mean. You're in the Bahamas. We thought you might like a bit of time to relax and recover after that grueling schedule the Americans have had you on. You've been treated well, I hope?"

"If you can call kidnapping being treated well. No one's beaten or raped me yet. So I guess I've still got that to look forward to."

"Nonsense," Stephanie's slight Germanic accent slipped through. "We'd hardly be gracious hosts if we resorted to such sordid tactics. Come, sit." She gestured to a great glass table overlooking the beach. "There are some things we need to discuss. Gunter?" She turned, attention on a black-haired, muscular man who entered from the rear. "Bring us some of that delicious mango juice. I've been dreaming of it all through the flight."

The man padded off to the kitchen.

Anika reluctantly seated herself, leaving plenty of space between her and Stephanie. The woman slouched, looking relaxed as she fondly gazed out at the water. "I don't come here enough. I miss the peace. The snorkeling is awesome. An old fishing boat sank just over there. The most marvelous fish inhabit it."

"When are you going to get to the point?"

Stephanie gave her an amused look. "Please, relax. I told you, my name is Stephanie."

"I've been running possible variables," Anika said as the man called

Gunter placed two glasses of mango juice on the table, turned, and left the room. "I suspect you no longer have Mark. You're stumped on the model, so you grabbed me."

Stephanie's eyes turned chilly for a moment as if revisiting something unpleasant. Then she nodded, saying, "You're a smart woman. That saves me time." She picked up the mango juice and took a long drink. "This is so marvelous. It's made fresh here." Her expression hinted at irritation as she noticed Anika's untouched glass. "At least try it. Just to be polite if nothing else."

Anika looked down at the glass and shook her head. "No, thanks."

"Very well," Stephanie said. "If you insist on delving straight into business, here's the truth: Our interest in the model is purely mercenary. No sense in denying that. What my employer seeks is to position himself for the best possible outcome when the inevitable collapse occurs."

"Lucky him." Anika waited for the rest.

"You're familiar with dark ages? The rise of feudal societies? That's the future, isn't it? Foreknowledge will allow those pragmatic enough to save something." Stephanie shrugged. "My employer is no saint but the alternative is chaos and complete social collapse."

"So Zoakalski only wants to save a small piece of the world for himself?" Anika asked sarcastically.

"It's limited, I know," Stephanie confided. "But the end of global society somewhat precludes world domination, don't you think?" She gave Anika a teasing look. "Oh, come on, that's a joke."

"Not laughing."

"Needless to say," Stephanie continued, "we were a little annoyed when we discovered that Mark wasn't the creative genius behind the model. Still, with his guidance, we believed that we could finally figure out its intricacies."

"You discovered you could not?"

She hesitated, eyes icy. "Here's the thing: You *can* come out of this as a very rich woman. You'll live a pleasant and enjoyable lifestyle— Mark particularly relished the lobster and champagne. You won't believe the apartment you'll be housed in. And there are numerous amenities. Salary consists of five hundred thousand a year and, once you've proven your reliability, vacations to locations such as this." She spread her arms to indicate the house. "We reward our people well."

"But it sounds like you kill them once they've served their purpose."

Stephanie lifted a skeptical eyebrow. "Why would you say that?"

"Highest probability is that Mark's dead. Tying up loose ends, ensuring no one can duplicate your work, saving five hundred grand a year."

"Wouldn't pencil out."

"Excuse me?"

She studied Anika. "If you could devise something as sophisticated as the model, what other miracles might that bright mind of yours conjure given the proper inducements? Contrary to what you may have heard, we don't *waste* valuable assets. It would be a nonproductive business practice."

Anika kept her mouth shut. She was running statistical permutations, trying to arrive at conclusions without sufficient information.

"Number two is not as pleasant. If you insist on an adversarial relationship, we will motivate you by any means necessary. Because we have sophisticated means of ensuring cooperation, you will be a very unhappy woman. So much so that you will find yourself complying with our requests just to bring an end to the misery."

Stephanie gave her a pleasant smile. "Now, please. Drink the juice. It's really quite good."

CHAPTER FORTY

***

IN THE WORKROOM, MAUREEN PACED THE FLOOR. BEHIND HER, THE TEAM SAT AT THE conference table, misgiving on all of their faces. The trip to the Pentagon that morning had been in a convoy, complete with Washington DC traffic police blocking intersections.

Amy Randall stood in front of the giant world map that covered one wall. She looked angry. But then, she wasn't alone.

"So tonight, you're not going back to the hotel." Randall propped hands on hips. "We're relocating you to Andrews Air Base. Your bags will be there when you arrive."

The team members greeted the announcement with silence, then angry murmurs started to eddy through the gathering.

Randall raised her hands. "Look! I don't like it. You don't like it. But there's more at stake here than Anika's kidnapping."

Maureen stopped pacing. "What do you mean?"

Randall clenched her teeth and glared around the room at the scientists. "There's a crisis in Israel. Just like Anika said there'd be."

"What crisis?" Gale asked.

"The President got an urgent call from the Israeli Prime Minister an hour ago. A strange new virus seems to be sweeping the country. From initial reports, it attacks only certain men."

Maureen said, "Which men? What genes are being attacked?"

"No information yet. The initial symptoms include high fever, trembling, and rapid breathing."

Maureen watched Fred Zoah's eyes narrow behind his thick glasses. "Well…" he said softly. "Only certain men? That's an interesting choice by our opponent."

Randall walked over to the table and stared down at him. "Explain, please."

Gale was staring straight at Zoah when she suddenly stiffened in her chair. "You think they've targeted the Y chromosome variant R1a?"

Zoah seemed to think about it. "If so, it will be devastating. Not just for Israel but vast sections of the world. The R1a-M558 mutation affects one third of men in parts of Russia, and the R1a-Z93 haplogroup is common in South Siberia, so—"

"So," Gale said, "ECSITE must be targeting a specific R1a mutation that affects only certain men. We just have to figure out which mut—"

Randall slapped the table hard to get their attention. "If one of you doesn't explain this to me in the next five seconds, so help me God, I'll have you all locked away."

With rising anxiety, Maureen stepped forward. "Women have two X chromosomes, right? And men have a Y and an X chromosome. ECSITE, or whoever, may have targeted men with the R1a variant, which is a common variant for Ashkenazi men. But a good deal of European men in general have this lineage, so it's a poor choice. Israel has some of the best geneticists in the world. They're already cataloging the genome of the virus, trying to verify that it's engineered and not just a natural mutation of a known virus."

"What happens if they do verify it?" Randall asked.

Zoah calmly leaned forward and propped his elbows on the table. "If Israel discovers the virus is engineered," Zoah calmly added, "they'll consider it not merely an act of war but an act of genocide. God help us if the ayatollah claims responsibility. As panicked as Israel is, they could launch their bombers and it's all over."

Randall paled.

"For obvious reasons," Fred said, "they will act quickly."

Around the room, people looked back and forth.

It was Sinclair who said, "Call the Secretary of Defense right now. Tell her that we need every resource you can give us so that we can model the dominoes about the tumble. Before it's too late."

Fred Zoah removed his glasses and cleaned them on his shirt. "It's probably already too late. We've run the genetic warfare variable before. We know what happens next."

CHAPTER FORTY-ONE

***

MARK RUBBED HIS ACHING BACK AND GLANCED UP FROM THE PHOTOCOPIED NOTES WHERE they lay strategically placed on the hotel room's rich red carpet. To one side lay the opened FedEx box, the return address on the label from somewhere in New Jersey. Reading the photocopies was difficult. He often had trouble deciphering Anika's handwriting because the copies weren't very clear. He wondered where her original notes were? In some CIA vault?

He looked at Michelle. "Why didn't the CIA just scan and download these notes onto a flash card or—"

"Analysts are already working on them back at Langley. But what gives with Anika French and all these notes scribbled on paper? She's supposed to be a fricking Millennial, for God's sake. You can't make half the notations out in a digital scan. Her shorthand looks like code. She even uses different colors of ink. Is that for a reason? We couldn't take the chance of missing anything. You're her professor, you tell me."

Despite the cushioned rug, his knees hurt and squinting at Anika's script almost had him seeing double. "Sorry, I wasn't looking over her shoulder when she was putting these worksheets together. Anika works in a kind of creative chaos. But I'm beginning to get an inkling of where she was headed with her calculations."

Michelle sat up straighter at the table, where she'd been scanning one of Anika's papers on prehistoric witchcraft. "I'm listening."

"Her reasoning is almost hypnotic."

"How so?"

"She was formulating calculations for the tiniest differences in wind patterns and air temperature," Mark said and straightened up.

"Why is that important?"

"I don't know yet."

"I thought you said you had an inkling?"

"Yes, but I'm starving and my brain has stopped working. It's been a long day. Let's find food."

"Sure, Brian. First things first."

Brian. He had to remember he was Brian Meyer. He and Michelle... Sorry, he and *Shelly* had gone from boutique to boutique, buying clothes, inspecting jewelry, Morano glass and the wonderful crystal chandeliers—spending other people's money.

Okay, so he died tomorrow. Today might have made it worthwhile. He had a stunning Prada suit, extra pair of pants, Ferragamo shoes, Zegna shirts, a fine felt fedora, and new Nikes.

He'd hated shopping with Denise but watching Michelle, er Shelly, try on Dolce and Gabbana dresses, Escada suits, and Rodriguez outfits had been a revelation. The effect had been startling; the clothing accented her long body, her wealth of her shining black hair gleaming in the lights. Not only that, the lady instinctively knew what looked good on her, and better, how to wear it to maximum impact. It was the little things, the cant of her hips, the slight angling of her shoulders, and how minute changes in posture accented the entire outfit.

She's done this before. She appeared completely comfortable in designer high fashion. It was curious knowledge when compared to the way she'd ridden the Ducati and the competent way she handled her pistol.

Michelle placed the report on the table and helped him carefully pick up the papers in just the right order before replacing them in the box. Then she taped it shut, adding a tiny sliver of adhesive.

"Anyone opening the box will miss that." She pointed. "If that strip of tape is broken, you tell me. Understand?"

"Oh, yeah." He stood, making a face as he straightened. "God, I'm not as young as I used to be."

"None of us are, Brian."

She grabbed her purse, heading for the door, pausing only long enough to insert the tiny bit of paper at the bottom. Straightening, she gave him a smile. "Italian tonight?"

"Is there anything else in Venice?"

"Thank God I know you're joking." She bumped him playfully

with her hip.

Taking her hand, they descended the stairs to the lobby and walked out onto the Riva degli Sciavoni. At the top of the Ponte della Paglia, she stopped to point at the covered bridge visible on the narrow canal. "They call it the Bridge of Sighs. It was originally covered so that criminals being taken from the old prison to the Doge's Palace couldn't escape by jumping into the water. Another explanation is that political prisoners could be passed in secret, hidden from the crowds, on their way to their executions."

"How refreshing."

Skirting the Campanile, they entered the Piazza San Marco and mingled with the crowd. Hundreds of pigeons strutted across the ground.

As they wandered, part of the fun was inspecting the menus. Michelle finally picked a *ristorante* in the *Fenice* district and they were shown to a table in the rear.

Michelle selected a local wine and helped Mark order. Then, in the light of the table's candle, she leaned forward and the soft yellow flicker augmented the gleam in her large eyes. "We have to start making progress on the model."

He sighed. "Sure, but working on it in the hotel room is like trying to paint the Mona Lisa with a twig and flower petals. At Oberau, I had computers, a team who understood statistics, and access to data. But at least I'm getting an idea of the variables Anika thinks are important." He shook his head. "Damn! She had all this stuff and it was right under my nose."

"Would it have made a big difference?"

He gave a disarming shrug. "Zoakalski would be a couple of years ahead of where he is now."

Her cell phone picked that moment to chime. "Excuse me. I'll be right back."

He watched her stand and walk gracefully around the tables to the door. It pleased him that every male eye followed her willowy body as she passed. Through the window, he could see her standing in the lighted street, the phone to her ear.

She nodded, almost hunched against the phone. Periodically she'd shoot glances at the restaurant. *Talking about me?*

Mark thanked the waiter when he placed the plates and waited until Michelle returned. She had a dancer's grace, an almost sinuous movement to her stride.

"Trouble?" he asked.

She seated herself, replaced her napkin, and arched an eyebrow. "Complications. Turnabout, it seems, is fair play. Someone managed to snatch Anika French right out from under the FBI in Washington."

Mark stiffened. "Is Anika all right?"

She gave him an amused look as she speared a mussel with her fork and wound pasta around it. "Apparently."

"Who snatched her? ECSITE?" Fear curled around his heart.

"Unknown, but that's a good guess."

"Is the United States trying to get her back?"

Michelle chewed another mussel and smiled. "Again, unknown."

Mark frowned and his gaze slowly went over the room, then returned to Michelle. "How can you not know? You're CIA and you're on the phone constantly."

"Use your brain, *Brian*. Do you think the CIA discusses its next moves with anyone over the phone? I'm getting general information, things no one listening in will care about, and most of it is explained in code words." She pointed with her fork. "Stop looking horrified and try this *vongole*, it's marvelous."

Mark speared a clam and thought about Zoakalski. The man was ruthless and Anika would be completely vulnerable. "They're going to kill her, aren't they? When she's told Zoakalski what he wants to know?"

Seeing his dismay, she said, "Not for a while. Every extra day is a day the government can use to plan her rescue."

He suddenly wasn't hungry. He placed his fork on his plate and leaned back in his chair. *I did this to her.*

"Developing a conscience?" Michelle asked.

Mark reached for his wine and took a drink.

When he didn't respond, Michelle said, "Look. French is alive. You don't need to engage in self-recriminations. Yet, at least." Her expressive eyes turned thoughtful. "But it means ECSITE is going to push your girlfriend for every detail of the model. We have to figure out what they're doing first."

"I... I think I know."

She lifted suggestive eyebrows. "Then tell me."

Mark made a lame gesture. "Mass death by targeting ethnically unique genetic populations."

Michelle leaned across the table and smiled. "After dinner, we're going back to the room and you're going to show me how."

***

They worked long into the night, then collapsed into bed without a second look at the other's naked body.

Sleep, however, eluded him. Instead, he lay in the darkness, staring at the ceiling, remembering Anika. He pictured her in his classes, that thoughtful look on her face. Memories of her in her office prodded him. How, once, she'd looked up with excitement and joy each time he entered her door. He'd been so in love with her.

He relived the first night he'd kissed her and ran his fingers through her thick red hair. Surprisingly, he could remember every detail of the few times they'd made love.

Why the hell did I ever write that damned article?

Nothing but misery had come of it.

His fault. All his fucking fault.

He barely realized when Michelle eased from the bed, whispering, "Mark?"

He feigned sleep, compelled by a desperate desire for solitude.

From the corner of his eye, he watched her dress in the darkness, slip to the door, and ease the lock back. Opening it to a crack, she slipped through and was gone.

Mark was on his feet, pulled on his pants, and dragged a t-shirt over his head. A sliver of light at the door showed him the washrag she'd left to hold it ajar, and he eased out.

On bare feet, he padded along the hall, peered around the corner, and made his way to the stairs.

Where would she have gone? It was the middle of the damned night.

He descended the stairs and glanced out at the historic lobby. Michelle was off to the side, standing in the darkened lounge entrance. She was talking, making small gestures with her hands.

He could make out a dark silhouette inside the lounge, a shadow in the darkness. The man was obviously issuing orders as he emphasized each point with a finger. Michelle nodded.

Then he handed her a small plastic case. Michelle snapped it open and removed a syringe that shone in the dim light. She squinted as she checked the contents, nodded, and reinserted it into the case.

A bitter chill surged through Mark's blood as the thing's purpose hit home.

The unknown man rose from his chair. Heavyset, he wore a long coat and had a beret on his head. He might have been fifty, looked Asian, with a hard face and square jaw. But the most outstanding trait was a slight limp in his left leg.

Mark turned and bolted, trying to keep his feet from slapping the ancient marble.

Flying down the hall, he had a sudden feeling of horror. He had to grab Michelle's motorcycle keys and escape! They were still in her motorcycle jacket pocket, right? As was Michelle's phone and wallet? Well, hell, he took them too.

After that, what would he do? He had no idea where to go...

CHAPTER FORTY-TWO

***

SKIP EXITED CUSTOMS AT ZURICH'S UNIQUE AIRPORT WITH A SENSATION OF RELIEF. THE
steel, glass, and tile floors inside the gray monster had had a depressing
effect. The officer at passport control had routinely scanned Skip's
passport and COVID status and added another stamp.

Skip glanced around the shiny baggage claim, seeing the man with
white-blond hair leaned against the wall next to the women's restroom.
As he met Skip's eyes, the man lowered his phone and walked over.

Helmut Rath had a blocky face and alert blue eyes. Even as he
walked up, his roving gaze cataloged the surroundings.

Helmut gave Skip a slap on the back. "Good to see you, old friend.
And thanks for the opportunity to take a drive. I've been spending too
much time in the office."

"Tough job, administration." Skip clasped Helmut's hand in a
vigorous shake. "You must get such an adrenaline rush while you're
sorting through bills."

"Oh, it is stimulating, *ja*. Especially when I wonder how I will
pay them all." Though Helmut surreptitiously watched the crowd, he
managed a sidelong glance at Skip. "You bring work, *ja*?"

"Maybe." Skip tightened his grip on his single suitcase. "Your
car clean?"

"Freshly washed yesterday but I hit snow on the pass."

"I mean, *clean* clean." He gave Helmut a suggestive look.

"Oh, that. It is a rental, picked up yesterday. Random chance
dictates a high level of privacy without unknown listening devices."

"Then let's go. I've got a problem you might be able to help
me with."

Helmut grinned. "I just thought you flew in to borrow my Moto

Guzzi again."

Skip slowly shook his head as they walked out into the cloudy day. "Not this time."

At the end of the covered walkway, they stepped out into the misty rain, and Helmut led him to a long, sleek BMW sedan. The locks clicked open. The thing was a gun-metal-blue four-door. Skip tossed his bag on the plush-looking white leather seats in the back.

"It is a 750Li," Helmut explained as Skip climbed into the passenger seat and clicked the seatbelt. "Four hundred horsepower, all-wheel drive. Very advanced suspension."

Skip heard the engine roar to life and Helmut grasped the shifter—a thing that would look more at home on the bridge of the Starship Enterprise.

"And you rented this? No wonder you can't pay your bills."

Helmut grinned. "*Ja*, but you bring work. I can count on you, Skip. You don't just come for a social call. Not when I have to pick you up in Zurich and drive you back to Munchen."

Helmut shot him a look as he paid the airport tolls. "Goes on your account. I have to scrimp on every Euro for car rentals."

Skip waited until they were on the A-1, heading for Bregenz. Helmut was in the left lane, enjoying all the benefits of the car's four hundred horsepower, flashing slower traffic with his brights.

"Tell me about Mikael Zoakalski."

The evaluative study Helmut gave him was long enough to be more eloquent than words. And Helmut never liked to take his eyes off traffic. He turned his attention back to the road and took a deep breath. "Not a man to mess with."

"I know he was Russian intelligence, but I don't know specifically what he—"

"Along with banking and extortion, he was in charge of the biological warfare program, my friend. The experiments he authorized frightened enough of his scientists that, at the first opportunity, several defected to different countries around the world. They are all dead now, of course."

"He hunted them down?"

"Every single one."

"Has he ever hired you?"

Helmut puckered his lips, frowned, then said, "Yes. Always very anonymous: Someone important is coming to Munich. I am to keep him safe while he visits the city, sees the sights, gets laid. I've been in the compound outside Oberau. You don't want to try it. Top-of-the-line security. The perimeter fence is wired. Motion sensors, lasers, IR and thermal imagery, and human patrols. You wouldn't stand a chance trying to infiltrate."

Skip's brows lowered as he stared across the car at Helmut. "I have to try. He snatched one of my clients from right under my nose. This isn't one I can let pass," Skip said softly. "If you have another obligation, I'll understand, and we'll just discuss the weather." He glanced up at the low ceiling of clouds obscuring the Alps. "What you can see of it."

Helmut finally asked, "Who is this client?"

"A very important young woman who made a discovery that a great many people are interested in. Think national security. Here's the thing: She's a good kid, an innocent who's in way over her head. The Americans want her back and they'll do all the usual stumbling government things that may or may not work."

Helmut gave him an annoyed smile. "You are a fucking romantic, did you know that, Skip?"

"It's part of my legendary charm."

"Are you bringing in a team to attempt the extraction?"

"Just me. Or just the two of us. Unless, that is... you want to talk about the weather?"

Helmut skillfully navigated the curves, while Skip gazed out the window, feeling the g-force as the big BMW hugged the road.

Helmut finally said, "I do not tell this story to just anyone. My grandfather was a *soldat* in the Sixth Army. He went into the war as a good Nazi. In those days, everyone did. No matter what the morality of the war, Hitler abandoned the entire Sixth Army when the Russians surrounded Stalingrad. For months, my grandfather fought, starved, and despaired as the men around him died."

"Obviously, he survived."

"Fifty thousand finally surrendered. He was with them as they were marched all the way to Moscow and paraded through the center of the city, shuffling along through horse dung in rag-wrapped feet. It was there that he rescued a little abandoned dog.

"German prisoners were split up, marched all over Russia, and put into work camps. Grandfather somehow managed to stay alive—even at the expense of sharing his food with the little dog, who he called Schatzee."

"I hate stories where the dog dies."

Helmut spared him a glance. "He was put to work building a factory in the Urals where the Russians were going to make airplane parts. He and the others lived in tents in the mud, working seven days a week hauling cement, sand, and steel. Those who became too sick to work were simply shot. And one day, Grandfather became too sick to work.

"Before he was going to shoot Grandfather, one of the Russian guards who had been tormenting him, decided to kick little Schatzee to death in front of grandfather's eyes. He told me the little dog squealed and squealed, unable to understand. But the guard just kept kicking.

"When Schatzee was finally dead, Grandfather crawled over and wrapped the little dog in his arms. As the Russian was lifting his rifle for the final shot, Grandfather staggered to his feet, clutching Schatzee's body, and forced himself to return to work.

"He buried Schatzee in the foundations of the factory and finally recovered enough to stay alive. He was one of only five thousand who made it back to Germany in 1955."

Helmut's knuckles were white on the steering wheel. "I was there the night he died. The last words he uttered were 'Schatzee? I am so sorry. Schatzee, where are you?'"

Skip stared at the road.

"The point of my story," Helmut said, "is that I've known many Russians. Most are just people like the rest of us. The only time I met Mikael Zoakalski, the first thought that ran through my mind was, 'A man like this one kicked Schatzee to death.' And now he has a compound—like a gulag—almost in my backyard."

Skip admired the buildings as they passed St. Gallen. The twin domes of the historic cathedral rose above the rococo architecture of the monastery with its world-famous library.

Helmut's hard blue eyes narrowed. "After thinking about Schatzee and my grandfather, I do not want to discuss the weather."

"Thanks. I'll owe you one."

CHAPTER FORTY-THREE

***

THROUGH THE OVAL WINDOW, ANIKA WATCHED RAINY GERMANY EMERGE AS THE GULFST-
ream dropped through the low ceiling of clouds. Green pastures and
fields surrendered to houses as the jet's nose lifted and the wheels
touched down on the runway.

"There is something you need to know," Stephanie said from
across the aisle.

"What is it?" Anika asked dryly.

"It's about passport control and customs."

"You haven't bought them off yet? I noticed the officer in Nassau
just let us walk from the helicopter to the jet and, the entire time, he
looked at everything but us."

"He considered ignorance to be in his best financial interest,"
Stephanie told her. "Munich is a little different."

Stephanie handed her a package of papers. "Your passport, work
visas, and other documentation. The name is an alias, of course, it
claims that you are Louisa Velasquez, a citizen of Mexico. The officer
will take them, stamp them, and allow you to pass. We have arranged
that he will not ask you questions. You, for your part, will say nothing."

Anika tried to keep her face neutral, having already considered
making a scene in customs. In fact, she'd been counting on it if they
gave her the least opportunity.

Stephanie continued, "A silly woman might be tempted to scream
'I'm Anika French, abducted from Washington DC' Hoping to draw
attention to herself. But you won't do that."

Anika ground her teeth. "Why not?"

"Because," Stephanie said pleasantly, "if I don't give you the
antidote, the slow poison you drank along with the mango juice

will turn you into a raving psychotic in another forty-eight hours."

Anika turned to stare at her. In her entire life, she'd never felt true hatred until this moment.

Stephanie seemed unconcerned as she continued, "Upon arrival at Oberau, you'll be given the antidote. It binds with the toxic molecules, rendering them inert and harmless."

Anika tried to feel any effects. Nothing. Or maybe she couldn't feel anything because fear had numbed her wits.

The jet stopped and the whine of the engines diminished.

Simon Gunter unbuckled his seat belt and pulled his phone from his pocket. He was speaking softly in German when the flight attendant looked out the door, then undogged the locks.

Stephanie stood up, stepped into the aisle, and loomed over Anika. "The poison was not my idea, by the way. I thought we should bring you here locked in a casket. Unconscious."

God, she's good at this.

"Just be a good girl, Dr. French, and you'll be fine. Now stand up and follow me."

As she slid across the seat and stepped into the aisle, Anika felt sick. She lowered a hand to her stomach.

Stephanie glanced at her hand and checked her watch. "You still have six hours before the molecules begin to attach to your nerve cells. Plenty of time. You're just nervous."

Anika walked to the plane door and followed Stephanie out into the rainy afternoon. Simon Gunter strode closely behind her as they crossed the tarmac.

CHAPTER FORTY-FOUR

***

THE FIRST OF THE BOXES WERE DELIVERED EARLY IN THE MORNING. THE BLACK, HIGH-IMPACT plastic was marked with stenciled letters that proudly proclaimed MOTORCYCLE EXHAUST SYSTEMS.

The building Skip had chosen, high on the slope above Oberau, had formerly been a small factory involved in the manufacture of ski gloves. The concrete floor in the shop still showed signs of the machines that had previously been bolted there.

An office was accessed by a door that led off the shop area. The previous occupants had left a serviceable desk and chair. Two toilets—men's and women's—were located there. Along with a roomy closet for supplies, the floor had a trap door.

The thing was accessed by lifting a handle, which revealed a stairway that dropped down to a small concrete-walled room. Not a bad addition for someone on a covert operation. In a pinch, it might make the difference between life and death.

Skip pushed the heavy crate to one side just as a second lorry arrived bearing a collection of ratty and junked motorcycles. One by one they were lowered on the hydraulic tailgate and rolled into the building on flat tires and bent rims. By noon, Skip had taken the delivery of sixteen wrecks in various states of repair.

Just after one, two mechanics—Jurgen and Lars—arrived in yet another lorry bearing benches, motorcycle lifts, and toolboxes. As soon as these were muscled into place, the mechanics began disassembling motorcycles and laying parts onto the benches.

Neither Jurgen nor Lars had any idea of the true purpose of "Alpen Motorrad" as Skip had decided to call the business. They'd been hired as window dressing to fix bikes.

Helmut arrived next. Skip felt a tinge of sorrow as the silver Moto Guzzi Norge rumbled into the parking lot. The last time he'd seen the machine, it had been in Amsterdam, and Jenn had been on the back.

Helmut stepped off and removed a full-face helmet. His hair was now dyed brown and he sported a handlebar mustache. Helmut no longer looked like Helmut. The box strapped on the passenger saddle turned out to be a cheap radio and CD player. Helmut plugged it in and rock music began filtering through the cavernous shop. Lars and Jurgen both cheered, giving a thumbs-up. You can't have a motorcycle repair shop without a radio.

Helmut shot Skip a look and, together, they walked over to the open shop door. From their vantage on the western slope above Oberau, they could glimpse the ECSITE compound where it lay, partially visible, nestled among the trees across the valley. Jagged and rocky, the slope above was spotted with trees and pastures.

"What do you think?" Skip asked, tucking thumbs into his belt while he scanned the scenery. Sunlight cast shadows down the mountainside.

Helmut stood, one booted foot forward as he studied the distant compound, then he walked very close to Skip to whisper, "By now, they know the building has been rented. Someone will be here to check us out. Perhaps even tonight. Zoakalski's security will want to know who we are and what we're about."

Skip took the hint and his gaze subtly surveyed the building, searching for cameras. Even if he didn't see any, they could still be there, well-hidden, and the parabolic microphones would be invisible. "I'll be ready."

Barely audible Helmut added, "Zoakalski does not take chances. Oberau is *his* town. Take for granted that he owns this property. It is right where a spy would come to watch him, *ja*?"

"*Ja.*"

As if on cue a battered Ford delivery van rattled up the winding drive. A young man in coveralls stepped out and wrapped a tool belt around his waist. From the rear, he removed a toolbox and walked up to Skip and Helmut.

"You in charge?"

Skip looked the skinny kid over. Yep, just the sort of techie Langley would send. Right down to the jet-lagged blue eyes and mussed hair.

Skip leaned close. "The place may already be dirty. Expect sophistication."

As they walked into the building, Helmut took over in German, saying, "We will want to hang tools on the walls, so you must be careful where you route the telephone and computer wires. We don't want to drill into the electrical wiring."

"There will be no problem." To Skip's ear, the kid's German was flawless.

He watched as the tech opened his toolbox and removed what looked like a detector wand. He started around the doors, moving carefully, eyes on the readout.

Skip turned up the music to cover any suspicious sounds. Then, to play his part, he walked over to a wrecked green Kawasaki ZX6R, found a power screwdriver, and began taking off cracked bodywork. He was removing the tank when the tech appeared at the office door and gave him a beckoning finger.

Skip grabbed a rag, shot a glance at Helmut who was wrenching on a KTM, and they met the tech at the door.

"What's wrong?" Helmut asked in German.

"I can put your telephones in but the computers should be wired for reliable backup if the electricity goes off. Come to the truck, I'll show you the equipment you need."

They walked back through the shop with Lars and Jurgen glancing curiously at them, then the techie opened the back doors and stepped in. "Come, there's room. You can look at the catalogs."

Skip climbed in, followed by Helmut. It was a tight squeeze.

The techie gave them a serious look. "Your office is wired for sound. So far, I haven't found anything in the shop, but I can't get to the ceiling or the heater. As far as optics, I got a slight spike when I brushed past the office heater duct. Want me to neutralize anything?"

"No," Skip said wearily. "That would tip them off."

"Maybe we will hire a secretary," Helmut shrugged. "It will ease their suspicions."

"What about our own surveillance?" Skip asked.

The tech tapped the box he was sitting on. "Tomorrow's generation. How you got authorization to use this stuff for an op like this, I don't know. But you've got clout. I can have it installed in a couple of hours.

They'd have to be smarter than me and have trickier equipment than mine to find it."

"What about data transmission?" Helmut asked.

The tech pointed a finger upward. "Satellite relay, tight-beam, line-of-sight. The sender's new. Works on virtually paired particles. Any monitoring degrades the data stream cuing the receiver that someone is listening in."

"Okay, do what you need to do. The sign is coming tomorrow morning. We're putting it on the roof, so you'll have an excuse to climb up there and wire in lighting."

The techie nodded. "I'm going to put most of the equipment in the dead space between the ceiling and the roof. There's about a meter of clearance. Someone can lie up there, observing the compound for days with no one the wiser. To transmit, you just open a hatch I'll cut in the roof and send on line-of-sight to the satellite. That stuff is *en route*. You'll be James Bond in two days."

"Thanks, Q," Helmut added dryly.

The techie arched an eyebrow, pleased. "I like that. And since you've got to call me something, let's go for it."

Skip shot a glance at Helmut. "How's the safe house in Munich coming?"

"Ready. When you finish here, why don't you follow me back to Munchen? I'll show you where it is. Consider yourself at home. Q can set up his entire station in one of the bedrooms."

Q grinned. "By the end of the week, we'll have eyes all over that compound. I'm looking forward to it."

Skip rubbed his chin. "I need eight days."

Q said, "I'll make sure you've got it."

CHAPTER FORTY-FIVE

***

SKIP WAITED UNTIL JUST AFTER DARK TO PLACE HIS BEDROLL IN THE SHADOW OF low-spreading fir branches. The location lay less than fifty meters up-slope from the shop and allowed him a perfect view of the parking lot and shop building.

Then he laid out his equipment: The latest starlight binoculars, motion detectors, an infrared camera attached to a twenty-power lens, microphones, and a digital recording device. All of this he covered with a cold sheet—a tarp designed to hide his infra-red heat signature. The sheet might have been overkill, but Skip Murphy would never be guilty of underestimating Zoakalski again.

When everything was in place, Skip crawled into his bedroll and fell asleep.

The faint beep of the motion detector brought him awake. Skip blinked to clear his vision and glanced at his watch to discover it was 03:42. The starlight binoculars gave a faint whine as he energized them and pushed them out from under the cold sheet.

A Mercedes, lights off, rolled up the drive, the tires rasping on the pavement. The black car whispered its way to the parking lot, stopped, and the engine was shut off. For long moments, the driver sat, then opened the door.

Thoughtful prep, Skip noted. The interior lights had been deactivated. A man stepped out and carefully inspected the premises. Skip studied the intruder: muscular, dressed in black, and light on his feet. Switching to the camera, Skip adjusted the focus and started snapping.

The intruder walked to the office door, inserted a key, and the high-tech microphone recorded the click as he unlocked and opened the door.

In the Munich safe house, Helmut and Q would be monitoring his every move as the intruder wandered around examining the motorcycles, bike lifts, tools, beverage cans, parts, and greasy rags.

Five minutes later, the door opened and the man walked straight to the Mercedes. The car backed around and Skip snapped another photo. Then the Mercedes, accented by a flash of brake lights, whispered its way down the drive.

Anika, hang in there. I'm coming.

CHAPTER FORTY-SIX

***

MARK SLIPPED ALONG, EASING FROM SHADOW TO SHADOW. IT TOOK ALL OF HIS EFFORT TO keep his hands from shaking.

Cutting behind a plumbing supply shop, he eased up to the back of the building where Michelle had left her motorcycle and began peering through windows. Yes, the motorcycle was still in there. He searched his pants pocket and pulled out the keys he'd stolen from the pocket of her motorcycle jacket, along with her wallet and cell phone, then he waited until a Fiat rolled past. Heart in his throat, he tried different keys in the door. On the third try, the lock turned and he hurried inside.

It took him a while to find the motorcycle key in the darkness, then he fumbled it into its slot and turned it. Little lights flashed on the instrument cluster.

Mark pulled in the clutch, stabbed the starter button, and brought the beast to life. Rolling the bike forward, he leaned off and pushed the button that lifted the door. As it rose, his heart thundered.

By now, Michelle knows I'm gone, and she's madly searching for me. She could be right outside waiting for me...

He tried to ease off the clutch but the bike pitched forward and, with his feet slapping the pavement, he lurched out of the shop and weaved his way down the street.

Sheer, blind luck allowed him to navigate the couple of blocks back to the A-27. The traffic light was in his favor, and he even managed to get the turn signal on. As he entered the freeway, turn signal still blinking, he pulled in the clutch, pressed down, and pitched forward, still in first.

No matter what he did, pressing down didn't give him second gear. Traffic was rushing around him as he stabbed at the shifter.

All right, first it was.

He ran the tach up to ten thousand, the Ducati wailing.

The turn signal equally baffled him. He could make it blink left or right, but not cancel. Then, jabbing at the button, he finally figured it out. Press the button in, idiot, and it will cancel.

This just left him with the gear problem.

Think.

Down was first. Up would be neutral again, right?

What the hell, nothing to do but try. He damned well remembered Michelle hammering away at the thing.

He pulled in the clutch, keeping his revs up, and lifted, hearing a reassuring click.

Then, snapping the clutch out, the Ducati reared up on its rear wheel, and the front end pawed for the sky as he hung on for dear life.

CHAPTER FORTY-SEVEN

***

MAUREEN GLANCED AROUND THE SECURE CONFERENCE ROOM AT FORT ANDREWS AIR BASE where the rest of the team labored over laptops and sorted through piles of documents. The room was nondescript with three lines of overhead fluorescents. One entire wall consisted of a whiteboard, now filled with notes, diagrams, and underlined questions. The other walls were blank, the monotony only broken by the single, heavy, metal door.

Coffee, drinks, and food could be had by simply opening the door and asking one of the Air Force security personnel who stood outside. Beyond that, their world consisted of the fifteen-minute walk to their barracks.

She glanced up from the intelligence report she was reading. The top line of block-red letters on the whiteboard read: "Zoakalski."

Maureen rocked her jaw back and forth. She'd been gritting her teeth for so long, her face hurt. The satellite image of the Oberau compound spread across the table. Skip was out there right now, trying to find a way to get Anika out. The young woman must be terrified.

She took a deep breath and pointed to the satellite image. "The fences and walls make it look like a prison."

Gale Wade, a sagging cigarette in her mouth, slapped the table where she was thumbing through economic reports. "I'm a climatologist. If you want me to project the viral spread based upon environmental criteria, I'm your scientist. So, what am I doing looking at banking statements? This is like a foreign language to me."

Fred Zoah didn't even look up. He just kept tapping his calculator keys. "Fascinating. Did you know that Zoakalski has a ninety-three percent chance for success on any of the business ventures he enters?"

Sinclair removed his reading glasses and rubbed his temples.

"Who cares, Fred?"

"You should care because inherent probability would indicate that the number of failures—"

"Focus, Fred, will you?" Sinclair's forehead lined as he returned to his study, penning notes in a yellow legal pad.

Zoah smiled benignly. "I am. Focused. His only failures have come from catastrophic and unpredictable events: A luxury resort wiped out by the Christmas tsunami in Ache; an earthquake in Columbia that destroyed an emerald mine; a hurricane that sank a drilling rig. See what I mean?"

Sinclair peered over his glasses. "No."

Zoah blinked. "An investment banker who never loses?"

"Do you really think he's an investment banker?" Gale asked.

"That's what this document says." Fred pointed to a folder marked, "Security One, Eyes Only" in large red letters. "And according to this report from the CIA, one of his bigger investors is the North Korean government."

Maureen said, "Where's this going, Fred?"

"His Korean investments revolve around missile guidance systems."

"He's an expert at mass death. We already know that, Fred. Do you have anything new to add?" Sinclair asked.

Fred looked chastened. "Well… that's what I was trying to tell you." His shoulders hunched as he returned to tapping his calculator.

Maureen focused on the Oberau compound. The place was built to be impregnable with an emphasis on keeping some people in and keeping other people out. But it still ran on the basics: food, water, energy…

She sat back and fished for her cell phone, pressing the call button.

"Randall," the familiar voice declared.

"We need an update on what's happening in Israel."

"The virus makes men with the Y chromosome R1a variant very ill but it's only lethal in five percent of the cases. However, preliminary testing suggests it may result in male sterility. Israelis think Iran is behind it. Making matters worse, Tehran doesn't deny it. Says it's Allah's judgment. Threats and denials are the order of the day. But it's escalating as we speak—"

"They seem fixed on Iran, correct?" Zoah, who could only hear

Maureen's side of the conversation, called from across the table.

"Yes," Maureen answered, then said into the phone: "Hold on, Amy. I'm going to put my phone on speaker."

Zoah continued, "Tell Ms. Randall that within the next seven or eight days, Israel will accuse Iran of genocide, then seven variables come into play."

Maureen held her phone out to the room. "Did you hear that, Amy?"

"*Yes. Keep in mind, Syria has already sided with Iran and both nations have threatened war if Israel takes any aggressive actions.*"

Fred propped his elbows on the table: "It's not Iran or Syria that you have to worry about. At least, not until the very end."

There was a long pause before Amy replied, "*Explain.*"

"It's what numerous anti-Israel groups call The Final Showdown," Fred said.

Gale said, "You mean governments? Terrorist groups?"

Behind his lenses, Fred's eyes were bug-like. "No, governments will hesitate to launch World War III for fear of repercussions from the US and its allies. These are civilian groups that advocate non-violent means of overthrowing Israel. Primarily, they push for the use of sanctions, boycotts, and divestment in Israel, but, behind the scenes, their hackers—"

Amy broke in, "*We monitor these groups constantly. How are they a threat?*"

"The best model I've configured thus far has seven probabilities," he politely repeated.

"*What are they?*"

Maureen frowned, wondering when Fred had worked all this out since he had not presented this hypothesis to the team yet. For days, he'd been entirely absorbed in his own world and almost silent, compared to everyone else, rarely throwing out possibilities. All she'd seen him doing was ferociously tapping away on his calculator.

Zoah responded, "First, as more and more men become sick, Israel will rush into vaccine production, trying to stop the epidemic. Second, global anti-Israel groups will see Israel's weakened state as the opportunity they've been waiting for and will join forces to launch a massive global campaign using phishing emails that contain malicious codes to glean people's log-in credentials. Third, the attackers will precision target vulnerable elements of the vaccine chain. Number four: Iran and Syria will sabotage the chain to keep Israel busy while they prepare. Five—"

"You mean prepare for war?" Sinclair asked.

"Of course," Fred replied as though annoyed by the question when the answer seemed obvious.

Sinclair shook his head. "I disagree. My model starts with Iranian Quds forces attacking Israel from Syria, so I don't understand how you came up with—"

"Allow me to finish?" Fred said. "Five, Iranian Quds forces will launch rockets into Israel from Syrian sites. Six, fearing the worst, the Israel Defense Forces will make preemptive strikes against all known nuclear sites in Iran." Fred paused to take a breath. "Seven, Israel will simultaneously be attacked by Iran, Syria, and Gaza."

Around the room, expressions tightened.

Gale said, "Eight, Israel launches nukes."

Fred's brows drew together. "Probably, but I haven't—"

Amy Randall's voice sounded loud coming out of the speaker: "*How do we circumvent the chain of events?*"

Fred looked down at his calculator and began tapping keys again. "Death by a thousand cuts."

Maureen lowered her phone to examine him. "What do you mean?"

"He's an investment banker with hundreds of supply chains."

Frustrated, Sinclair called, "Would anyone like to hear the rest of my model because I don't buy this stuff about interrupting the vaccine chain..."

CHAPTER FORTY-EIGHT

***

IN MARK SCHOTT'S LEXICON, THE PLACE WOULD HAVE BEEN CALLED A TRUCK STOP.
Ablaze with lights, signs, a restaurant, and a canopied set of gas
pumps, the facilities beckoned him like an oasis in the night. He
flipped on the turn signal, tapped the brakes, and slowed the Ducati
as he took the exit ramp.

He wheeled up to a pump, grabbed the front brake, and almost
dumped the bike when he locked the front wheel.

Muscling it straight, he killed the ignition with the key and gasped
for breath.

"*Benzina?*" a uniformed young man, perhaps in his late teens, asked
cheerfully as he trotted over.

Mark lifted his face shield, legs trembling, his body nothing but
nerves. "Huh?"

"*Benzina?*" the young man repeated, pointing at the fuel tank.

"Uh, *Si. Si.*"

He stared stupidly at the tank, realizing he needed the key to unlock
the cap as the young man reached for the fuel hose.

For the moment, Mark was delighted just to sit on the machine
and let his heart slow. He glanced around, seeing cars and another
motorcycle in front of the restaurant.

God, a cup of coffee wouldn't hurt. And his stomach—mostly
ignored in the downright terror of trying to ride the snarling murder-
cycle—definitely needed a meal.

After the attendant topped off the tank, he asked something unintelligible in Italian.

"Oh, how much?"

The young man smiled, "Ah, American. On Ducati." He made a

clench-fist gesture of approval as Mark fished out his wad of Euros and handed the man one of the hundreds.

Receiving change, Mark snapped the fuel cap closed, inserted the key, and started the bike. Tapping the shifter down, he managed to ease the clutch out without killing the engine. Feet dragging for balance, he paddle-walked the Ducati over to park it beside the other motorcycle: a yellow BMW with windshield and curious box-like bags attached to the rear.

Sighing relief, he took the keys and marched dejectedly into the restaurant.

The place was clean. Plastic bench seats were arranged around tables. He barely noticed the handful of patrons eating and sipping coffee.

"*Buona sera,*" a man seated at the window said softly and nodded his direction. A helmet and riding jacket were piled on the bench seat beside the man. Obviously, the BMW rider.

"*Buono sera,*" Mark replied awkwardly.

"With an accent like that, you're another American," the rider replied, indicating the seat opposite him. "Sit down. Let's talk."

Panic built in his breast.

The rider offered his hand. "Harry Rau. Columbus, Ohio. You here on vacation?"

"Uh, yeah." Mark overrode his caution, desperate for someone, anyone, to talk to. He slid into the seat opposite Harry. "Wow. What a day."

Rau had to be in his mid-fifties, white-haired, with a mustache. He wore riding pants, boots, and a sweatshirt emblazoned with the words, **Alpen Motorcycle Tours**. His face was lined, the jaw firm, and a thick nose was dominated by twinkling blue eyes. He cradled a cup of coffee in capable-looking hands.

"Great ride?" Rau asked. "Where'd you ride from today?"

"Up from Venice."

"Saw the sights, huh? Me, I live for the Dolomites." Rau studied him thoughtfully, taking in the fine pants and button-down Zegna shirt. "Isn't it a little cold out there dressed like that?"

Mark smiled sheepishly. "The bike... Not the smartest thing I ever did."

"What do you normally ride?"

"I don't. This is my first time."

Rau arched a silvered brow. "So, you decided to start with an eleven-nine-eight? You got a death wish?"

Later, Mark would chalk it up to the stress he'd been under but he burst out in hysterical laughter. The fit left him exhausted, tears leaking from his eyes. Catching his breath, he managed to say, "I've been hearing that a lot lately."

Rau had watched with amused curiosity from behind his propped coffee cup. "Let me guess, you just got out of a bad relationship?"

Mark fought a battle with more hysterical laughter, barely keeping from crying. "You have no idea."

"So... you decided to come to Italy, find one of the fastest, meanest, scooters on earth, and really tempt the gods, huh?"

Mark rubbed his eyes, nodding. "When you get right down to it, yeah, that's pretty much the story in a nutshell."

"Okay," Rau confided, "I think I've got the picture."

"Close enough," Mark muttered, a sense of futility rolling through him. He grabbed up the menu, staring. "So here I am. Without a single damn clue as to what I'm doing or where I'm going."

"What's your name?"

"Brian," Mark said instinctively. "Brian Meyer. I used to teach high school social studies. In Iowa. Then later in Colorado out west. You?"

"Mufflers. For cars. I ran a string of eight shops in Columbus and Dayton. Mostly to support my habit."

"What's that?"

"Motorcycles." Rau grinned. "I've got a garage full. That, and I'm an MSF instructor."

"Huh?"

"Motorcycle Safety Foundation. We teach new riders how to enjoy the sport safely... and not end up in hospital emergency rooms like you're about to. You've got way too much motorcycle for a novice."

"Tell me about it. The thing acts like it's possessed by Satan. But... well, you might say it's my only choice."

"Where you headed tonight?"

"Me? I don't have the foggiest idea."

CHAPTER FORTY-NINE

***

ANIKA PACED THE LURID CONFINES OF SUITE NO. 3 IN THE OBERAU COMPLEX. THE WINDOW looked out over the great palace below and the Alps beyond.

As a Wyoming ranch girl who tramped around the backcountry to shoot her own food for dinner, she found the opulence distasteful, but Mark must have been swept away by the furnishings, the holographic wall, and the plunge pool. Oh, they'd exploited every one of his weaknesses the same way Isaac Perlman played a violin.

She'd been awake most of the night, her brain racing as it collated data, analyzed, and studied.

Stephanie had explained the compound's defenses in great detail, emphasizing the extent to which any attempt at escape would be futile. Nonetheless, Anika was calculating the odds of given actions.

"You'll eventually be allowed to go home," Stephanie had assured her as she'd given Anika a clear liquid to drink—allegedly the antidote to the neurotoxin she'd been fed in the Bahamas. "You're much too high profile. The US won't give up on you. On the other hand, there are diplomatic considerations they must abide by, which means obtaining your release will be a long and drawn-out process of threats, negotiations, and diplomatic pressure. Might take years."

Unless, of course, Anika pitched in and complied with ECSITE's wishes. Once she'd modeled several variables for them, Stephanie assured her that ECSITE would have no further use for Anika French.

Her preliminary model suggested the highest probability was another infusion of the neurotoxin that would kill her only after she stepped off the plane in DC but the second-highest probability was plutonium in her food that would ensure a death from malignant cancer after months of suffering. Her death would be a slap in the face to the United States and a reminder that Zoakalski had the power to kill anyone he wanted to.

The downstairs door opened, and Stephanie's cheery voice called, "Hello? Ready to go meet your team?"

When Anika did not instantly come down, Stephanie's feet sounded on the stairs. She was smiling when she stepped into the magnificent room. She'd dressed in gray wool and a light blue blouse.

Stephanie read her perfectly, her voice dropping as she asked, "Got your escape plan all worked out?"

Anika crossed her arms. "Before I make up my mind about anything, I want to see Zoakalski."

Stephanie's dimples formed. "Turns out, you're in luck. He wants to see you, too."

CHAPTER FIFTY

***

SKIP USED A RAG TO WIPE THE GREASE FROM HIS HANDS AS HE STOOD IN THE SHOP DOOR.
Business hours were over, and the late spring sun was beating down on the green valley. The workday finished, Jurgen pulled on his helmet, fastened the chin strap, and donned his gloves. Lars climbed onto his Triumph and thumbed the starter, bringing the big Thunderbird to life. He waited while Jurgen straddled his big blue Yamaha Tenere and started the bike. Together they rode off down the steep winding drive.

Skip took a step out, staring up at the big sign now dominating the roof. **Alpen Motoraad** stood out in ten-foot orange letters. A framed and enclosed wooden structure supported the tall letters, effectively screening the observation post that would be assembled there after dark.

Right on cue, a green delivery van appeared from the buildings below and climbed the drive, its engine and gears complaining.

Skip stuffed the rag back in his coverall pocket and walked into the shop where Helmut was putting away tools. Passing his own work-bench, Skip inserted a disk into the radio and turned up the volume. The loud sound of an air wrench blatted before the noises of a busy shop could be heard.

Turning, he watched the delivery truck back up to the door and stop. A man in a blue workman's uniform stepped out, a clipboard in hand. At the rear of the truck, he unlatched the back and rolled the door up. Grabbing a box, he walked into the shop, depositing it on the table.

"You're late." Skip propped hands on his hips.

"Had a flat," the driver replied.

"Left rear?"

"Right front."

The code was correct. Skip smiled, offering a hand. "Skip Murphy."

The man's firm grip and crooked grin added character to an otherwise forgettable-looking human being. "Gordon Gerber. GG for short."

"What have you got?" Skip looked at the box.

GG cut the tape, opened the box, and lifted out a thick folder. "Langley identified your mouse as Simon Gunter, 39. Gunter got his start in life in the Bundeswehr after a rocky start as a teenager. He'd survived a broken marriage and the suicide of his father. After service, Gunter worked in South Africa for a while, then tried to make it as a professional hunter in Namibia, but he beat a Belgian client half to death over a trophy fee.

"Gunter dropped out of sight for a couple of years until he was identified as a person of interest smuggling diamonds out of West Africa. A year later, he was on Zoakalski's payroll, quickly working up through the ranks. While no hard evidence exists, Gunter has a habit of showing up and, within a week, someone Zoakalski is involved with—or has crossed swords with—is found dead. Generally, from suspicious causes."

"Assassin, then?"

GG shrugged. "Among other things. Call him an expediter. For instance, we know he was sent to Afghanistan in 2003 when kinks began to develop in the opium trade. From there, he moved on to Uzbekistan, then to Ukraine. Within a month, opium supplies on the streets were plentiful and the price dropped. Curious one-to-one connection there."

"So he's a handyman?"

"That's as good a description as any." GG flipped open to a photo of Simon Gunter. "Even more interesting, he was in the US a couple of weeks ago. And you're going to love this: His destination was Laramie, Wyoming. He left on the same flight as Mark Schott."

"Anybody show up dead?"

GG's smile went crooked again. "Funny you should ask. A Paul Fetzer was found run over on the railroad tracks. Forensics determined he'd been anesthetized first. A cocktail of something called Diprivan and Propofol. It's used by surgeons."

"Yeah, I remember from the briefings. Who was the victim?"

"That's where it gets even more interesting." GG rubbed the side of his nose. "Hired muscle. Trained in China and probably in the employ of Chinese Intelligence."

"I remember. Most likely the people who jacked Anika French's notes." Skip nodded, putting the pieces together. "Gunter somehow realized that he had competition and took it out before they could sour the deal with Schott."

"Yeah. That's our best-guess scenario. Leaving his victim on the tracks is one of his favorite disposal methods. Like a signature. Generally, the authorities don't think twice about it and the body's a mess." GG winced as the soundtrack on the CD player broadcast the blatting air wrench again.

Skip waved a finger around indicating the building. "They told you we're wired for sound?"

"Yep. You're sure the background's loud enough?"

"Oh yeah. Your guy—we call him Q because that's the way he likes it—monitors them monitoring us. They listen from the office so we're secure in the shop." Skip made a happy face as the recording played the musical sound of a wrench dropped on concrete. "But I could turn it up if you'd like."

"Thanks, just the same." GG flipped a couple of pages in his file. "Our buddy Gunter hasn't just been to the US recently. The Brits had him in the Bahamas a couple of days ago. Zoakalski's got a private island there. Allegedly, that was Gunter's destination. Vacation, he said."

A spear of anger stirred in Skip's breast. "The Bahamas. That's how they got Anika French out. How'd he get back to Germany?"

"Zoakalski's private jet."

"Okay, so Gunter's not just a bad guy but a very clever and talented one. The Cliff Notes version is Be careful and don't underestimate him."

"There's more."

"Of course there is."

GG pulled a second file from the box. "Gunter doesn't always work alone. He has a female counterpart."

Skip took the folder, opening the page to the photo. He whistled, raising an eyebrow as he took in the attractive blonde.

"Stephanie Huntz," GG said softly. "In another universe, she'd have been a supermodel. In ours, she's Zoakalski's favorite psychopath. She cleared Bahaman customs at the same time as Gunter. Sweet Stephie, as she's known, likes life fast and rich, including her cars, planes, and men. She's a licensed pilot and pharmacist. Her *modus operandi* is to seduce her victim, obtain whatever she's been sent for and, depending upon her orders, kill him or leave him panting for more."

"A cuddly playmate."

GG shrugged. "She's multilingual, trained in intelligence gathering, martial arts, weapons and explosives, and the use of various toxins and amnesiacs. Guns or poison, each is equally thrilling to her. She's the one who lost Mark Schott to the Chinese. Word is that she and Gunter were both involved in the attack in Italy."

"No sense of humor, huh?"

"Not that you'd notice."

"Any word on Schott?"

"Everybody in Europe is looking for him, including us. Nothing. *Nada* and zero. It's like he's stepped off the earth. No word on his wife and boys, either."

Skip nodded as Helmut walked over. Using degreaser on his hands, he caught a glimpse of the photo Skip was studying. "Ah, Stephie," he said.

"You know her?" Skip asked, turning.

"She used to date a client of mine. He was involved in developing weapons… computer-guided targeting systems for the latest NATO tanks. Very sensitive. I provided security for them a couple of times."

"How'd it work out?"

Helmut's eyes went dull. "He died in a skiing accident. Probably an accident. Not sure. His body was found the following spring. Avalanche, they said."

"If I bump into her, maybe I'll introduce myself."

"Bad idea, Skip." Helmut narrowed an eye.

"Why?"

"After they find your corpse, I'll be left to rescue Anika French alone."

CHAPTER FIFTY-ONE

✱✱✱

AS STEPHANIE LED HER DOWN A LONG HALLWAY, ANIKA SILENTLY STUDIED THE LABORA-tories they passed. Behind the glass walls, people in hazmat suits moved around tables.

One lab made Anika stop walking. There were no people behind the glass, just row after row of small vials that looked like something you'd see in a biological weapons storage facility. She expected to see the vials labeled anthrax, ricin, and other deadly compounds. Unfortunately, they were too far away for her eyes to read anything.

"What is this place?" she asked Stephanie.

"Vaccine storage. One of our goals here is to develop vaccines against genetically engineered viruses. It was one of Zoakalski's specialties when he was in Russia. Now, keep walking. Trust me, you do not want to be late."

At the end of the hall, Stephanie swiped a key card, punched in a code, and an elevator door opened. "You first," she said gesturing to the door. When Anika stepped inside, Stephanie punched the button for the second floor.

Anika stepped out into another hallway. There was no more see-through glass, just blank white walls and metal doors.

Stephanie led her to the third door on the right, swiped her card again and entered another code. As she did, she said, "Everything is monitored. Security knows who has been in which room. All access is checked against the central computer. Anyone acting outside of clearance is immediately flagged."

"What happens to the people acting outside their clearance?"

"You don't want to find out." Stephanie opened the door and ushered Anika into a wonderland of desks, computer workstations, and frenzied activity. People in white shirts, the men wearing ties, bent over keyboards, eyes on the screens before them. Most wore headsets. Every wall was covered with monitors. Numerical sequences scrolled across the bottoms of the screens. Anika's first impression was of a NASA control center.

Stephanie noted her expression. "Welcome to the ECSITE nerve center. From here, the staff keeps track of global financial markets—banks, commodities, and the various stock markets." She indicated the large wall monitors. "These data reflect what our analysts are processing." She pointed to a large computer room. "Not even the New York Stock Exchange has a larger system."

Anika's eyes narrowed. "You're analyzing the data using portions of my model, I see."

"All preliminary," Stephanie replied. "Your former professor was not particularly helpful when it came to the finer details of your model but our people got the gist."

Anika continued to follow her down an aisle, glancing at the screens as she passed. Most made no sense. They were just strings of numbers, graphs, and text flashing across the screen. But occasionally she caught a piece of her model in action.

At the far end of the room, a single wooden door had been set in a blank wall. Stephanie knocked.

A muscular man, head shaven, with hard black eyes opened it. He wore a black suit, white shirt and tie, and a clear wire ran from his earpiece to disappear behind a thick neck.

"Anika French has an appointment with the Big Man." Stephanie said it deferentially.

Bullet Head nodded. His blunt face betrayed no expression. He just stepped back to allow them to enter.

The room might have measured ten by ten paces; the walls, like those in her room, were holographic. The images, however, were not of scenery but other offices, most occupied by men behind desks who watched her enter with interest. She seemed to have stepped into the midst of a virtual conference where she was the topic.

"Stand back here for the moment," Stephanie instructed.

Most of the men, Anika noted, were Asian. Two wore North Korean military uniforms. Pictures of the North Korean dictator hung on the walls behind them. The others, dressed immaculately, reminded her of corporate executives.

Then she turned her attention to the man who sat behind the room's single, incredible desk. The polished and carved wood almost dazzled. Even the size of it conveyed wealth and power. Sixtyish, he had white hair. She'd never seen a picture of Mikael Zoakalski but his imposing presence left no doubt about his identity. She took in his wrinkled face and sagging jowls. The man's nose might have belonged to a barroom brawler. The glinting blue eyes, however, cut through her like a Siberian wind.

"I see you've noticed my desk. It once belonged to Ludwig the second," the Big Man said. "After his death, it was disassembled and shipped to the Vatican. Four popes sat where I now do. By curious circumstances, it ended up here."

Zoakalski waved a hand and the walls went blank, the faces vanishing to be replaced by a soft green luminescence.

Then Zoakalski stood. He was a little over six feet and his blue silk suit was too shiny for her taste.

Stepping around the desk, he offered his hand. "Dr. French, I ask you to forgive the rudeness of your abduction and transport to Oberau."

"Your supply chains are being devastated. Anything I can help with?"

He smiled at that. "Just walking past the computer monitors, you gathered that?"

"You're using my model to analyze how it happened. Of course, I noticed."

"Well, that's excellent! Actually, you can help. The meeting you just witnessed concerned a delivery problem. One of our clients claims that the components we delivered are not correct. The factory that produces them claims they delivered what was ordered. What was received was definitely a different part than that which was placed in the boxes at the factory. We are tracking the delivery route to determine if someone made a mistake. Unless it was the shipper, an unknown party has made a substitution."

Anika nodded and absently said, "Supply chains are particularly vulnerable. From what little I gathered, your problem is centered in India."

His thick white eyebrows lifted. "Yes, I think so too. Can you hypothesize who's behind it?"

"Not America, if that's what you're worried about. Someone who knows you better. They've programmed my model based upon your known reactions. Your emotional psychology."

Zoakalski sank down on the edge of his desk. "You really are a master at understanding how to manipulate emotional variables."

Careful, Anika. "As you have just observed, no matter how precisely you plan, the frequency of random errors will increase exponentially as complexity increases. As the inevitable becomes apparent, predictability decays at the same rate that social dysfunction escalates."

His eyes narrowed. For a time, he just studied her. "You are very different than your predecessor, Dr. Schott."

"How so?"

"He was a pedigreed buffoon."

She nerved herself enough to shrug. "He didn't really understand the model or how it uses four human emotions to predict outcomes."

"Did your American team use my emotional psychology when it tested the model in Washington?"

She shifted uneasily. "Why would you think we tested the model?"

The corner of his lip quivered. "Subterfuge is not necessary, Dr. French. Why else would the Defense Department have rushed you straight to the White House? A great deal of time passed before you left. You must have been doing important work while there."

She didn't answer.

He flicked a hand as if shooing away an irritating fly. "Don't worry. The things you worked on in DC are irrelevant to me."

Anika stared at him. His psychology was everything. Why would he say that? "Then what is relevant?"

Zoakalski reached up with thick fingers to stroke his chin, and the frown lines deepened across his brow. "Dr. French, unlike your American colleagues, I know how fragile civilization is. It doesn't take much to bring it down. My Russian heritage goes back to the 1400s in Bessarabia. My beloved grandfather was in the small town of Kishinev, the capital, when the anti-Jewish rioting broke out in 1903. It was based on the false belief that Jews used Christian blood in rituals. The massacre was a festival of murder, bludgeoning, and rape. Grandfather barely escaped with his life."

"What's your point?" *Filipchenko. Lundborg. The search to create a true genetic elite...*

Zoakalski's white brows lowered. "I learned valuable lessons from my grandfather. First, everything boils down to how misinformation warps into mythology. Second, every act we take is a byproduct of what we believe and feel, not what we know. Without an understanding of these critical elements, men are nothing more than pawns in the hands of governments."

"Hence, my model."

He leaned closer to her. "Hence, your model. Let me be straightforward. Myths lead to unthinkable acts. You're going to help me create what people believe. You may do it—"

"For what purpose?"

He glared at the interruption. "You may do it from the pleasurable surroundings of your current apartment, enjoying fine food and decent clothing. Or, shall we say, under less desirable circumstances."

An adrenal rush flooded Anika's brain.

"Now," Zoakalski straightened, "I have to find out what happened in India that caused the error in the guidance systems we sold the North Koreans. Once you're settled, I'll expect your expertise in this matter. Stephie, please escort Dr. French to our conference facility and introduce her to her new team."

"Of course, sir."

Just before they reached the door, Zoakalski said, "Oh, forgive me, Dr. French. I almost forgot. Your father asked me to tell you hello and let you know that he's fine."

"My... my father?"

The Big Man off-handedly sorted through pages on his desk. "Don't worry about him. He's being well-cared for."

CHAPTER FIFTY-TWO

***

MAUREEN WATCHED FRED ZOAH REMOVE HIS BOTTLE-BOTTOM GLASSES AND LOOK AROUND.
Data files had been streaming in all morning, some to their laptops, others delivered in box after box, all marked 'Top Secret'.

The conference room seemed filled with despair. All but Zoah, who had an oddly euphoric expression on his face. Maureen shared everyone else's sense of being overwhelmed. Where, in this mountain of data, was the key to stopping ECSITE? Surely another genetically targeted virus was on the list to be released in the near future.

"Most interesting," Zoah said at last.

"Finally, a word from the maestro," Sinclair said.

Maureen asked, "Do you have something, Fred?"

Gale Wade had a sour look on her face as she ignored them to pore over a folder full of tables.

"Did you know that most of Zoakalski's accounting is handled by a firm in India?" Fred asked.

Maureen pulled her hair back, arching her back where it had cramped. "Many large companies transfer their accounting work electronically to firms in India. The savings in labor is huge. What does that have to do with Israel?"

Wade thumped a pack of cigarettes, pulling one out. "So his accounting is in India? That means… what?"

Zoah tilted his head back, lost in thought.

"Fred?" Maureen prodded.

"Oil."

Baffled glances met Maureen's. "Go on."

"He has a significant presence in the Indonesian petroleum extraction business. One of his clients, an energy minister, defaulted on a loan. The oil was collateral."

Sinclair's Adam's apple bobbed as he swallowed and shook his head. "And the Pleistocene led to the Holocene. For God's sake, Fred, we're trying to stop a nuclear war. What's your point?"

"Paychecks," Zoah said as if it explained everything.

Maureen took a deep breath. "Fred, you're way ahead of us. Tell us what you're thinking."

Zoah gave her a report he'd been reading. "Systems. The flow of information. Information leads to production and distribution."

"And?" Her skin had begun to crawl from sheer frustration.

"Zoakalski's in Europe. His administrators on the ground are in Jakarta, a whole world away. The computers that monitor production, labor, and accounting are in India."

"So?" Maureen said sharply.

"Computers run on programs," Fred said with satisfaction. "What happens if the computers are told production is dropping? Then, a day later, an administrator sends an email to the personnel office to reduce the labor force to bring it in line with the latest production figures?"

"You want us to hack into his email accounts to disrupt his distribution system?" Sinclair said.

Fred blinked at people around the table. "No. I want the CIA to."

CHAPTER FIFTY-THREE

***

ANIKA MADE IT OUT THE DOOR BUT HAD TO PROP HERSELF AGAINST THE WALL. SHE was breathing hard, her legs trembling to the point that she had to lock her knees.

Stephanie said, "He's good, isn't he? He's perfected the subtle art of intimidation. Actually, you didn't do too badly. I expected him to turn you into a sobbing mess when he told you he has your father."

Anika's thoughts were drowning in a haze of neurochemicals. She couldn't find words.

Stephanie smiled. "I do hope you don't force him to 'encourage' your creativity and genius. I'm not sure what would be left of your father."

CHAPTER FIFTY-FOUR

***

SKIP HUNCHED OVER Q AND WATCHED THE MONITOR. THIS WAS AS CLOSE AS HE COULD GET, given the cramped desk on which the monitor stood. The white-walled room, with its curtained window and small kitchen, looked about as nondescript as an apartment could.

From the street outside, it was just another suburban row house with a small walled yard, gated at the street. Two upstairs bedrooms could be reached by a narrow staircase.

Q carefully tilted the joystick, and the image on the screen veered slightly. "That's the access road."

Skip bent closer to the monitor with its greenish image. Technology still amazed him. The tiny drone was no bigger than a sparrow, but it could fly for six hours before its electric motor exhausted the battery. Under the plane's belly hung an infrared camera that broadcast, via an antenna, to a receiver that decoded the digital data and displayed it on the monitor.

"There," Skip said, craning forward. "That's the compound."

As the drone sailed over the gated entrance, Skip felt his heart begin to pound. "You're recording this?"

"Oh, yeah." Q jockeyed the stick as the image wiggled. "Bit of wind there. Afterwards, we can pore over the images, study every detail. Right now, we need an up-close view of how things are laid out. Think she's in the palace?"

"Got me. From what we've seen through the scopes, most of the activity is behind. Up in those apartments. Hardly anyone comes or goes from the palace."

"My call is to inspect the perimeter first. See if they've left any weakness. Then, we'll do the buildings."

"Yeah," Skip tugged his beard. "Let's pick this place apart. Before I go in, I want to know everything."

"You'd better because what I'm seeing so far... well, it's state of the art." The image showed a top-view of two armed men walking along the fence line. "Old school, too. We'll clean up the image later, but I can already see they've got earpieces."

For the next hour, Skip forgot the pain in his back as the little airplane crisscrossed the night above Zoakalski's compound. Mostly, he didn't like what the camera showed him.

CHAPTER FIFTY-FIVE

***

FOR TWO DAYS, MARK SCHOTT RODE THE DUCATI, FOLLOWING BEHIND HARRY RAU'S BMW.
The long hours, alone inside the helmet, left him with a growing sense
of clarity. He'd been over and over everything his team at Oberau had
worked on, trying to find the variables to decipher what Zoakalski was
up to, and he was just beginning to get an inkling.

He'd heard on the hotel TV last night that there was a strange new
virus that only seemed to attack men with the Y Chromosome R1a
variant and resulted in sterility. Speculation was running rampant
around the globe. One conspiracy theorist said the virus had been
created by Iran and was designed to wipe out all Jews worldwide.
Another theory claimed it was an Arab plot to get Israel to attack Syria
and Iran, thereby leading the United States into a direct conflict with
their ally Russia, and ridding the Islamic world of two opponents at
once. Both were ridiculous. The variables didn't add up. But human
actions were rarely based upon facts. Stir up enough fervor, and
passion would win out every time. Anika's model proved it over
and over again.

The only thing that made sense was that ECSITE was responsible
for the virus, but he didn't have enough information to work the variables to discover Zoakalski's desired outcome.

Mark pulled into a petrol station and paid in cash from his dimin-
ishing stack of Euros. He was running out of Michelle's money fast.

He got back on the motorcycle and rode away.

As Mark learned the proper use of throttle control, clutch, and
brakes, he added Austria, Liechtenstein, and Switzerland to his list
of countries. He stared longingly at the spectacular scenery and experienced moments of sheer joy. But after each bout of delight, he

felt guilty. He was running, scared out of his wits, but free. Anika, on the other hand...

Rau was returning that evening to drop off the bike and catch a ride to the airport to fly home.

By six o'clock, Mark would be on his own.

To do what?

An image of Anika formed in his mind. This was all his fault. What were her chances?

When he pulled off the road and stopped, Harry rolled to a stop just ahead of him, lifted his face shield and called, "Problems?"

Mark took a deep breath and removed his script-filled tablet to scrawl a note, then he walked forward to Harry's BMW and handed it to him. "Will you do me a favor?"

"Of course, Brian." He took the note and glanced at it.

"My name's not Brian Meyer. I'm Mark Schott, an anthropology professor from the University of Wyoming, and I'm in real trouble."

Rau's eyebrows shot up, disbelief in his expression.

"Yeah," Mark said, "sounds crazy, huh? But the favor I'm asking is if you'd get to Munich a little early. There's an American consulate in the city center. If you would go there, tell them who I am, and deliver that note, I'd be eternally grateful."

"What kind of trouble are you in?"

"Tell the people at the consulate that I know Anika French was abducted because of me. That ought to really get their attention. Anika French. Got it?"

"Anika French," Rau repeated. "Abducted. Because of you?"

"On the back of the note is my wife's number in Wyoming. When you get to a phone, could you give her a call? Tell her... tell her I'm sorry. Tell her I'm going do everything I can to make things right."

"What did you do?"

"Too much."

"Look, why don't you just ride into Munich with me and give this to the consulate yourself?"

"Because, Harry, my chances of dying of old age are getting slimmer by the day." He grinned, a cold shiver of fear running through him. "Anika's in the ECSITE compound in Oberau. I'm going to go try and get her out."

"I've never heard of ECSITE. What's that?"

Mark pulled his helmet on, stepping over to the Ducati. Raising the visor, he smiled. "Take care, Harry. And thanks for being a true friend."

Mark straddled the bike, zipped up his jacket, and turned the key. As the big Ducati thundered onto the road, Mark smoothly caught second gear. He had a glimpse of Harry Rau in the mirror, standing with sunlight gleaming in his white hair.

CHAPTER FIFTY-SIX

***

MAUREEN RUBBED HER TIRED EYES. SHE HADN'T HAD A SHOWER IN TWO DAYS, BUT NEITHER had any of the rest of the team sitting around the cluttered table. They were all bleary-eyed and irritable.

A knock came at the door before Amy Randall stepped into the room. She'd pulled her hair back and pinned it. The light brown pantsuit she wore looked freshly ironed, and she carried a brown leather case in her right hand.

"Morning, Amy," Maureen greeted, rising and arching her back. "What's the word?"

"A small victory." Randall slung the case onto the table. She unsnapped it, extracting a sheaf of papers. "These are communications we've intercepted. Substituting the missile guidance chips looks like a base hit. Zoakalski's turning his network upside down, trying to find the culprit. Whatever the North Koreans said really got his attention."

"Does he suspect us?"

"Undoubtedly."

Gale Wade yawned before she said, "As a next step, we should have an operative approach the Iranians and offer them the guidance chips for a couple of million more. You know, chips with the same specifications as the ones the North Koreans were supposed to receive?"

Sinclair caught on, adding, "So that Zoakalski learns of it?"

"Exactly."

"Another good distraction. But we still don't know what he is ultimately trying to do, folks." Randall cocked her head, retrieved a notebook from her case, and scrawled notes.

Maureen had been thinking about Anika constantly. This made it hard to keep her mind on models and statistics. "Any word about

Anika's status?"

"No updates."

"Schott, his wife and kids? Nothing?"

Randall shook her head. "Focus on your job, Maureen. What's the status of the model you were working on?"

"Fred and I think ECSITE's ultimate aim is to tie the R1a virus to Russian bioweapons research. Do you recall the big anthrax outbreak forty-five years ago that exposed the Soviet Union's biowarfare activities?"

"Of course, there's long been speculation that the recent smallpox outbreaks around the world can be tied to the Russian facility, one of only two in the world that houses the variola virus. But—"

"We're working out the mechanics of the model to disable that threat. While we do, we have another distraction that we think will delay ECSITE. We're calling it 'Operation YE'."

Randall gave her a curious look. "What is Operation YE?"

Maureen said, "It stands for the bacteria *Yersinia enterocolitica*. It's an enterotoxin."

CHAPTER FIFTY-SEVEN

***

A MISTY RAIN FELL FROM THE NIGHT SKY AS MARK SQUISHED ALONG THROUGH THE DARKness in his Ferragamo shoes and fought the urge to shiver. Damn it, if only he could see! So far, he'd blundered into fences, been slapped half silly by tree branches, and nearly broken his neck. Against the rain, he wore his motorcycle jacket and the heavy helmet. Sure, he must look ludicrous but his head was dry, even if the pattering rain on the hard shell drowned any other sound. He kept the visor up to see better—as if he could in the pitch blackness.

But then, if he could see, so could the compound guards. No, it was better this way. If he could get close to the gate, watch it through the night, perhaps he could find a flaw in the system.

And do what? Play James fucking Bond?

He wanted to turn right around and run straight back to Oberau where he'd parked the Ducati. After that, he wanted to ride like a madman until he reached... where? And therein lay the problem. Half of Europe was searching for Mark Schott—known drug dealer and killer.

Anika's in there.

He wondered if Harry Rau had delivered his note to the American consulate. And wondered some more if it made any difference.

Of course, they would have grabbed poor Harry by now. They'd be interrogating him mercilessly for every detail he could remember about the infamous Mark Schott. They would know he was riding a Ducati, that he'd dyed his hair, that he now had a scruffy beard.

So, if I survive the next couple of days, what next? Dye my hair red? After that, he'd be out of colors unless he opted for green, pierced his ears and eyebrows, and traded the fabric riding jacket for black leather with studs.

"Somehow I've got to get into that damned compound and get Anika out."

He stumbled over humped grass, vaguely aware of a white-painted fence to his right. Did he remember that fence lining the road into the compound?

Why didn't I pay better attention?

Because on the first trip in, he'd been jet-lagged. On the trip out, he'd been drooling over Stephanie and wondering if she was going to kill him when she wrecked at a hundred and fifty.

His next step came down on empty air. Mark dropped, water splashing as he fell forward, hit wet grass, and toppled sideways into a ditch.

Floundering and spitting, he clawed his way up the side of the ditch, slipped on the grass, and rolled length-long into the water.

"Mother fucker!" He battled his way back up the embankment and stood, dripping, slinging his arms around to drain the water. Unlatching his helmet, he poured water out, using his fingers to press out the lining. As if that did any good with rain pattering on his mostly dry hair.

Dripping, cold, and shivering, Mark Schott stood in the night, head raised to the rain-black skies, and whispered to himself, "What the hell more could go wrong tonight?"

He had the faintest sense of motion before an arm clamped around his throat like a steel band. A leg snaked around his and jerked his foot from under him. Weight smashed the breath from his lungs as he hit the ground.

Mark struggled to cry out as something sharp pricked the skin of his neck. In the corner of his eye, the shine of a polished blade glinted. Paralyzed by fear, he opened his mouth, emitting no sound.

"What more could go wrong?" a voice whispered in his ear. "You could run into *me.*"

CHAPTER FIFTY-EIGHT

***

ANIKA EXAMINED THE CONFERENCE ROOM, NOTING THE MONITORS, DISPLAYS, MAPS, AND people. She could barely remember their names: Pierre LaFevre, Jacques Terblanch, Wu Liu, Nanda... Hash-something. The other name was a blank.

Everyone stared at her, expecting her to speak, but all she could do was try to control her shaking.

"Please, sit down," a soft voice intruded into her reeling thoughts. Terblanch.

Anika clung to his kind eyes, then caught the slight nod from the older woman. Inoui, she thought. She gave Anika a solicitous gaze. "Excuse me. Who are you again?"

"Francine Inoui," the woman said through a thick accent. "You just met with the Big Man. We sympathize. He holds something over all of us."

"It is how he works," the man with the blocky face said, voice dripping Russian. He smiled, flashing a golden tooth. "As long as I work here, my wife and children live well. If I do not produce," he shrugged, "information is presented to the state police and people I love go to prison... or worse."

"And you?" she asked Pierre. Pierre... she couldn't recall his last name.

The man glowered at her. "It's none of your business, but I have a daughter with a very rare medical condition. It can be controlled with the right pharmaceuticals. As long as I produce results, her medications arrive with regularity. She is sixteen. Instead of lying paralyzed in a bed as her body eats itself, she plays football with her friends."

The Russian—*Max?*—drummed his fingers on the table. "When

Mark was here, he told us how instrumental you were to developing his research. You are not him. We understand. But we have so little time to understand the intricacies of his model."

Anika stood there stunned. "*His* model?"

"You are familiar with it, *oui*?" Inoui asked, her pointed chin jutting out.

"I created it." She watched her fingers clasp and unclasp, her body draining of energy as the fear began to subside.

"*You*?" Pierre asked sarcastically and looked her up and down.

"Yes."

Murmurs went around the room.

Finally, Pierre said, "Then you understand fracture events? Social forcings? The basic mechanics of the model?"

"Better than Mark ever will."

A man whose name she couldn't remember responded, "Good. We are currently attempting to model how a virus spreads so that we can propose a way to manage the spread. Can you help us understand the nuances of your model? We have used data from previous global pandemics, but it's like modeling the motion of a school of fish. We can't—"

"What's your name again?"

"Max. Max Kalashnikov."

Anika fought to focus, to summon even a trace of brainpower. "Yes, that's right. Good analogy, Max. It's all about modeling collective motion in biological systems. Collective behavior. Microscopic mechanisms can lead to the same behavior in different schools of fish... or people."

"I don't understand," Terblanch said.

"Traffic."

"Traffic?" Mikael squinted.

Anika nodded. "The school of fish is engaged in synchronized swimming. People moving through an airport are engaged in synchronized walking. The behavioral mechanism that allows them to efficiently move through the airport is signs. Baggage claim, this way. Taxis, that way. So, the first step is to identify the signs that govern human movements in small systems. Once you understand how each small system operates, you can tie them together into a large system to manipulate behavior. Do you understand?"

Mikael stared at her with glowing eyes. "You can alter collective behavior simply by changing signs? Sounds simplistic."

"I hope so. That's what makes a large system manageable. Simplicity of motion. Always start local. First, manage the signs in the local school, then traffic patterns in town, then key airports around the world, then global vaccine distribution channels. Do you see?"

"Ah…" Max said with a sigh. "I do."

Stephanie had moved to the rear and sat with a phone to her ear.

Terblanch lifted a hand to get Anika's attention. "If we put the right signs in place, we can manufacture what people believe, yes?"

"Yes. Absolutely."

"And how long will it take before the virus causes a fracture event?"

The Israeli virus? Was that what this was all about?

Anika glanced around the table. Fear paralyzed her ability to speak but her brain was running data. Collating… collating. Where were the largest repositories of Level-4 toxins in the world?

She softly said, "With the right signs in place? Days."

CHAPTER FIFTY-NINE

***

BLINDFOLDED AND GAGGED, HIS HANDS TIED BEHIND HIM, MARK ALLOWED HIS CAPTOR TO drag him along the trail until the man said, "Stop."

A metal door thunked open, then Mark was unceremoniously pitched onto a cold metal floor. God, it was freezing in here.

The man said, "If you don't want to be killed, you'll do as I say. Roll to your side and lift your feet so I can tie your ankles to your hands."

Mark did it.

After his ankles were bound to his hands. The man rose and walked away. The door slammed shut, an engine started, and Mark realized he was in the back of a truck. The vehicle bounced and jolted for... well, he had no idea how long.

Then the truck stopped, a door in front slammed, and he heard the rattling of metal as the rear door was opened.

"You have arrived," the man said, came across the bed of the truck, severed Mark's bindings, and ripped the tape from his mouth. Then, strong hands pulled him to his feet. "Walk."

"I can't walk!" His jaws ached. "My legs are numb. Give me a minute."

A hand steadied him while blood returned to his legs. While the painful tingling ran its course, he tried to figure out where he was. He smelled pines and the smoke from chimneys.

"Now, walk," the man ordered. He held tight to Mark's arm as he guided him forward. "There are stairs here. Step up."

Mark used his foot to feel for the steps and climbed the stairs.

A house door opened. Mark was guided into blessed heat. Then, step by step, he was forced to climb another staircase. At the top, he was turned to his right. Marched forward and a door slammed behind him.

Moments later he was shoved down into a chair. "If you scream or call out, I'll be back. You don't want that."

The man's boots thudded across the wood floor and he was gone.

Shivering and terrified, Mark waited. On top of the terror, his bladder was full.

Dear God, what are they going to do to me?

He imagined a pistol being placed to his head, Stephanie or Gunter aiming down the sights. Would he have any warning?

Hot tears beaded against his blindfold.

Denise, Anika, Will, Jake… I'm so sorry.

He was sound asleep when his blindfold was ripped away and he gasped and scrambled to sit upright. "Where… who—who are you?" It was still pitch black.

"Don't ask questions. Just answer them," his captor said.

"You going to kill me?" Mark managed hoarsely.

"Depends. Who do you work for?"

Mark licked his lips. "The University of Wyoming."

"In what capacity?"

"Professor. Uh, department of anthropology."

"Sorry, Mr. Meyer. Nobody there by that name."

"I'm Schott. Mark Schott."

"That's not what your passport says."

"It… it's a fake. That was given to me."

"By whom?"

He struggled to place the hard voice… and came up with a complete blank. All he could see in the dark room was a swaying black figure, like a silhouette. "She called herself Michelle Lee. It was in Venice. After she got me away from ECSITE. We were hiding there. Actually, I—I was her captive." He tried to keep from crying. "Look, I'll give you anything you want!"

"Where's your wife?"

"You mean Michelle?"

"You have more than one wife?"

"I don't know where Michelle is," he answered cautiously.

"Who's Denise?"

Who are these people? "She's in Laramie. Look, she doesn't know anything about this. It's all *my* fault!"

"What were you doing sneaking around the compound in the middle of the night?"

He narrowed his eyes, glaring. "Trying to figure out how to get in, all right?"

"Why?"

Mark pursed his lips, slowly shaking his head. "Doesn't matter."

"Thought you'd plead for Zoakalski's mercy? Try and get your old job back? Maybe hope Stephanie didn't put a bullet in your brain?"

"If that was the case, I'd pretty much ride up to the front gate and ask to be let in, wouldn't I?" Mark managed to swallow hard. "Look, who are you?"

"That's going to depend on how you answer the question. Why were you sneaking around the compound?"

Mark dropped his chin onto his chest. "Fuck you. Go ahead. Shoot me. I'm tired of all this. And I'm sure as hell not getting out of it alive anyway."

A male hand switched on a flashlight and held a photo in front of Mark's face. "Who is this?"

Mark squinted at the image. "That's Michelle Lee. The woman who had me prisoner in Venice."

"How did you meet her?"

"In a villa in the Dolomites the day after I was grabbed away from Stephanie in Garmisch. She got me out when Zoakalski's people attacked. Said she was CIA at first, but I figured out later that she wasn't."

"You know who she works for?"

"No. There was a man. She went to meet him in a bar. Looked Asian, I think." Mark didn't think he ought to explain about observing the meeting and the transfer of the needle.

"Why didn't you go to the American consulate in Milan and beg for US mercy?"

"They think I'm a drug dealer running product out of the Italian villa. Which they would probably believe instead of any wild story that I'm a professor running from Zoakalski." *Do I dare tell the rest? Maybe it will keep me alive.*

"But I did send a complete set of notes to the consulate. It's too late to stop it. It would have been delivered this afternoon."

"Where?"

"Vienna," Mark lied to buy time. "The American state department has it by now. And it explains everything."

"Do you have any idea where Denise and the boys are?"

"Laramie. I told you." He glanced up, puzzled. "She's irrelevant to you. Just my wife. She doesn't have the foggiest idea about the model."

"She and both of your boys vanished the night after you left for Germany. Did any of Zoakalski's people mention that?"

"What?" A terrible foreboding grew in his chest. "Vanished? Denise? Jake and Will? Are you sure?"

"Has anyone try to use them against you?"

"What do you mean, *vanished*?"

"It's as if they dropped off the face of the earth. If they'd been kidnapped and were going to be used against you, someone would have said something by now."

Mark sagged in the chair. "God, I'm a total fuck up."

"Oh, I don't know. You got away from a Chinese intelligence operative and managed to avoid being spotted or arrested while half of Europe, Zoakalski, and the US government have been looking for you. Not bad for a civilian." A pause. "That bit about sneaking into the compound, however, was lacking in any kind of good sense. Which brings us back to the question: Why were you trying to sneak in?"

Mark sagged. "A friend of mine is being held hostage in there. I was going to try and get her out."

"Who?"

He winced. "Anika French."

"How'd you know she was in the compound?"

"Michelle told me."

"How did you think you'd get her out?"

Mark shook his head, squinting in the lights. "I don't have the foggiest idea. But I had to do something." He worked his lips, sweating in the blinding glare. "You're sure my family... I mean Denise and the boys...?"

The room lights went on and he could see the colorful glare of a TV screen in the rear of the building. It actually hurt his eyes. Mark squinted as the burly man with a trimmed beard clicked off the flashlight.

The man walked over, his brown eyes curious, short dark hair gleaming in the light. He wore a black sweater over muscular shoulders.

Tactical pants—the pockets stuffed full—clad his legs. Mud and bits of grass covered the black boots on his feet.

Mark suffered another moment of terror as a knife appeared in the man's hands. But his captor only bent and severed the bindings on Mark's hands and feet.

"Who the hell are you?" The TV news anchor was speaking in English, but Mark couldn't make out the words.

"Skip Murphy. SSM security." He pulled a photo from a desk. "Is this Michelle? I got a picture of her today in Oberau. She seemed to be paying a great deal of attention to Zoakalski's compound. The rest of the time she drove around town, spent a lot of time in her car watching the main road. She was obvious enough that a couple of Zoakalski's people drove out and found an opportunity to talk to her. Through the scope, I saw that she had a real estate brochure. She's good. Talked to them for a half hour, periodically pointing at the brochure."

"Yes, that's Michelle. She's after me."

Skip seated himself on the bed. "Why would that be?"

Mark rubbed his sore wrists, seeing where the restraints had eaten into the flesh. "She must have figured out I stole her Ducati."

Murphy shook his head. "Stealing a woman's Ducati definitely rates as a killing offense, but I suspect she's really after the model."

"She is." Mark dropped his head into his hands and closed his eyes. "Everybody is."

On the TV screen in the back, Mark saw words scrolling across the bottom: *The State Research Center of Virology and Biotechnology in Koltsovo, Novosibirsk, Oblast, Russia, better known as VECTOR was attacked today…*"

"I'm pretty sure," Murphy said, "that she—"

"Wait! Turn the news up!"

Murphy frowned at him, then reached for a remote on the desk and turned up the volume.

The anchor said, "This is the same disease research lab that was attacked in September of 2019 by unknown agents. VECTOR was once the world's leading facility for weaponizing viruses."

"Hmm," Murphy said and sat on the edge of the desk. "That's interesting."

"Why?" Mark said.

"VECTOR was a maximum containment lab or biosafety-level-4 lab."

"Is that the really bad stuff?"

"You could say so. It's the stuff that can wipe out every human on the face of the planet. It's estimated that they have two tons of weaponized smallpox." He used the back of his hand to rub his beard. "Though, supposedly, in recent years they've been focusing on developing vaccines against genetically engineered viruses."

"Weaponized viruses? Like COVID?" In his mind, Mark was plugging variables into Anika's model and watching the dominoes position themselves. "Like the one that's ravaging Israel?"

Murphy's eyes narrowed. "Yeah. Maybe. In the beginning, some in the US government hypothesized that the COVID-19 virus had escaped from VECTOR during the 2019 explosion. Why not something novel today that targets the Y chromosome of your enemies?"

His tired brain was tracking variables, stumbling, trying to configure the model. "I—I need to eat and rest, please. There's something... something I'm missing."

CHAPTER SIXTY

***

HELMUT RATH DROVE INTO THE WAREHOUSE PARKING LOT AND KILLED THE IGNITION on the BMW sedan. For a moment he sat, letting his eyes roam the paved lot; sodium lights illuminated the white metal sides of the warehouse and the line of delivery trucks—the latter neatly backed into spaces along the rear fence. Yellow light gleamed on their windshields and chrome.

No one approached and nothing moved.

After five minutes, Helmut slipped a rubber Halloween mask over his head, aligning the eye holes so he could see. Then he tugged a brimmed hat over the whole.

Grabbing the package from the seat beside him, he opened the driver's door and walked to the building's side entrance. Leaning down so he could see, he inserted picks into the lock. Once he'd been an expert at the task. Now he muttered, "Out of practice."

Five minutes later, Helmut felt the final tumbler give and the door swung open. Retrieving his package, he stepped inside.

Only three banks of fluorescents—the night lighting—illuminated the warehouse interior and cast dim shadows over the large plastic-wrapped pallets.

So, which ones do I need? Keeping to the shadows he ghosted his way to the office, seeing a clipboard hanging from a hook. This he took down, studying it in the dim light.

Then, taking the clipboard with him, the package under his arm, he started down the aisles in search of the right shipping tags.

CHAPTER SIXTY-ONE

***

FROM THE OBSERVATION POST BUILT BEHIND THE SIGN, SKIP WATCHED THE WHITE DELIVERY truck wind its way up to the compound. Through the scope, he saw the guard at the gate step up to the truck, inspect the papers, then get out with the driver, open the back, and look inside.

Moments later, the gate rolled back and the truck entered.

Skip followed it as it wound its way to the back of the compound, delivering the weekly food order. Then he slid a piece of roofing back and crawled over to the satellite antenna. Plugging his phone in, he pressed the send button.

"This is Warren."

"Jackrabbit." Skip said. "The delivery is made."

"Roger that, Jackrabbit."

"I need a line to Amy Randall."

"Roger that. Hang tight while I connect you."

A moment later, a voice said, *"Randall."*

"Jackrabbit here."

"Glad you called. Was the delivery made?"

"Roger that."

"I've got a curious development to relay. Mark Schott checked in. He sent a series of notes scribbled on a pad to the American consulate by means of an American traveling abroad. The man apparently rode around on motorcycles with someone calling himself Brian Meyer. The notes delivered supposedly detail Mark Schott's recent adventures." A pause. *"As a heads up, the notes say that he's going to try and free Anika French."*

"Roger that." Skip grinned. "I've got him in the Munich safe house under guard as we speak. Should we try and get him out of the country?"

A pause. *"What's your call?"*

Skip rubbed his nose. "Personally, I'd rather wait. With the delivery made, I have enough on my hands."

"What's your opinion of Schott?"

Skip related what the man had told him. "I think he's telling the truth. Oh, and I sent a photo of a woman through the link yesterday. She's apparently the one who grabbed Schott away from Stephanie. Schott says she calls herself Michelle Lee." He spelled it. "Can you see if anyone can make an ID?"

"Already done. She's Mi Chan Li." Randall spelled it. *"Trained by the Chinese. But there's a catch. According to rumor, she cut ties with Beijing a couple of years back. Been freelancing ever since."*

What the hell did that mean? "So, we may have a fourth party interested in the French model? Or she's back on the Chinese payroll?"

"Your guess is as good as mine."

"I see." Skip frowned.

When he ended the communication, Skip crawled over and lifted a heavy pair of Swarovski fifteen-power binoculars to glass the town, then he focused his attention on Li's car.

Moments later the drone of a small plane could be heard. Skip watched Li step out of her car and stare off to the north, shielding her eyes with one hand. As the airplane approached, Li lifted a cell phone to her ear. Skip could just make out that she was talking, watching as the airplane flew up the valley.

Skip shifted, trying desperately to swivel his scope, blocked by the confines of the roof and sign. Using the binoculars, he was able to get a good look at the plane but couldn't place the make or model. The registration had been taped over. The thing flew over the compound, then it was droning off toward Garmisch.

Li stood beside her car, long black hair gleaming in the morning sunlight. Her attention was on the south. No more than ten minutes later, the plane made a return run, again passing over the compound. Skip watched Li talking, nodding. As the sound diminished, Li tossed her long hair back, slipped her phone in her pocket, and climbed back into her car.

So, was she hunting Mark Schott? Or someone else?

CHAPTER SIXTY-TWO

***

ANIKA WAS JUST BEGINNING TO GRASP ECSITE'S GOALS WHEN WHISPERS CAUSED HER TO raise her eyes and glance at her team members around the table.

Terblanch was muttering uneasily to Kalashnikov.

"What's wrong?" Anika asked, noticing that Hashahurti and Liu had their heads together, speaking in hushed tones.

"Don't know," Terblanch said in a low voice. "All the department heads are being called to the Big Man's office. The tension has been building all day."

"I've never seen it like this." Inoui shot a nervous glance toward the door. "We just received an email to the effect that some staff may not be going home tonight."

"People are worried," Terblanch agreed. "You could feel it in the cafeteria this morning. I ate breakfast there and, I swear, you didn't hear laughter anywhere."

"Did you notice the cars parked down at the palace?" Liu asked. "All expensive. Half have Swiss plates. Most of the Zurich office is here."

Kalashnikov rubbed his face, staring at the sheet of paper he'd been studying. "The fact that they are here, and not on a virtual conference, tells you how important it is. Whatever is wrong, the Big Man can't trust communications. They are meeting face to face."

"Any of you hear anything about missile guidance systems?" Inoui asked.

Glances went around the table.

Anika shuffled her notes. "Zoakalski depends on systems. Perhaps, he's just identified his own personal fracture event."

"And," Inoui asked, "what might that fracture event be?"

"Not enough data to hypothesize." But she was hypothesizing anyway.

Instantly, a cold shiver ran down her spine. If she didn't help them, they'd murder her father. She couldn't...

Stephanie straight-armed the door, stomping into the room. "Dr. French? You're with me. Now!"

Anika shoved herself out of her chair and half-stumbled toward her.

CHAPTER SIXTY-THREE

***

THE SAFE HOUSE CEILING LAMP CAST A CONE OF YELLOW LIGHT. SKIP LEANED OVER A table, his arms braced on its edge, and considered the high-resolution photos spread over its laminate surface. Every feature of the compound could be discerned with remarkable detail when a magnifying glass was employed.

Across from him, Helmut was staring thoughtfully at the compound, expression grim. Mark Schott had just finished pointing out where he'd been held and the path he'd taken to his lab. With a finger, he had pointed to where the guards had been and what he'd observed while inside.

The electrical technician they called "Q" came walking down the stairs, a Mylar tube in his hands. "Latest analysis from Langley is in. I've marked the overlay."

Skip yawned, straightened, and rubbed the back of his neck.

"Need more coffee?" Mark Schott turned his attention from the photos to study Skip's tired face.

"No. I've got to get some sleep when we're finished here." He glanced at Q. "How about the overlay?"

The technician slid a rubber band from the Mylar tube and unrolled it. He carefully placed the clear plastic over the aerial photos and aligned reference marks. Bright yellow lines had been drawn on the clear surface, delineating the compound perimeter. Other features, such as buildings, were outlined in various colors.

Q tapped the yellow lines. "These are the defenses I've been able to detect. The parallel lines along the compound fence denote the electrical signature from sensors. Probably both IR and motion detectors. The blue dots are camera locations. Careful analysis indicates the cameras are remotely controlled, allowing the guys in the security center here"—he pointed to a red square overlaying a building—"to track anything they see."

Skip chuckled softly. "Looks like they've done a thorough job."

Q added, "And the electronics we've been able to identify are top of the line. Expense wasn't an issue. They've got security for their security. The dotted lines are patrol paths. They run them randomly. No pattern that we can discern. The dogs seem to be well trained, and the guards are not hesitant about checking something if a dog goes on point."

Mark Schott made a face. "So, they'd have had me."

"Probably before you even made it to the perimeter fence. The good news is that given what we know about Stephanie, capturing you would have made her whole day." Skip tapped a little silver square parked just back from the palace. "Look. There's her souped-up Jaguar parked right next to the trees. But I don't think she'll take you for another ride. At least, not the kind you'd enjoy."

Mark's expression fell. "Yeah, well, she's had practice playing me like a puppet."

"Something to keep in mind," Skip said thoughtfully, "since getting in is easy." He glanced at Q. "My special equipment coming?"

"Arrived this evening by special delivery."

Schott was giving him a wary look. "What do you mean, getting in is easy?"

"Well, it is. Getting out, however, that's a whole different can of fish."Skip studied Mark thoughtfully. "You willing to play bait? Give sweet Stephie a reason to go for a joy ride?"

"Stephanie?" Mark asked incredulously. "You want me to ride with her? The woman wants to kill me! You out of your mind?"

"Yeah," Skip answered reasonably. "Haven't you heard? Being crazy keeps you from going insane. But the question stands: Are you willing to act as bait for Stephanie? Willing to call her? Sound bitch-assed scared? Ask her for help?"

"To do what?" Mark demanded incredulously, arms spread wide.

In return, Skip crossed his, propping his butt against the table as he inspected Mark Schott. "Traffic is way up in that compound. Bankers, investors, manufacturers, we've been running the plates on every vehicle going in and out of the place. Zoakalski's under a lot of pressure right now. Kind of a siege mentality. Stephanie might be stressed out, playing to all the big wigs. Maybe a nice spring drive would make her feel better. You know, relieve some of her tension."

"Her tension? I wouldn't give a rat's ass if she was desperate to the point of screwing a doorknob."

"Yeah, poor Stephie. I think it's time she worked for us for a change. You know, kind of like a puppet."

"Why not?" Helmut was staring at her silver Jaguar. "Psychologically, she views herself as a predator, an ultimate hunter, not a potential target." He turned his attention to Skip. "You thinking about how Rasheed got out of Kandahar?"

Skip shrugged. "You got a better idea?"

Schott took a deep breath. "Look, I've seen the lady use a machine gun. Even Michelle is afraid of her. You're out of your mind if you think she'll go down easily."

Skip fingered his chin as he looked back at the Mylar overlay. "Yeah, well, we've been watching her comings and goings. She really needs a reason to leave that compound."

Helmut was giving him a serious look. "Do you want me to count all the ways this could go wrong? I could use up all my fingers and toes."

"Hell, no! If you go over twenty, you could be busted for indecent exposure."

"Kandahar?" Schott asked. "What the hell happened in Kandahar? Who's Rasheed?"

Skip was back to staring at the daunting compound security. "He was a guy we needed to slip past Taliban security. Getting to Anika isn't going to be all that tough. But getting out...?"

"How are you going in?" Helmut asked.

"On the wings of an angel. But with Anika? Getting out's not so easy."

Q said, "We could pick you up with a helicopter."

Skip shook his head. "As careful as they are, I wouldn't be surprised if they had a very effective countermeasure. So, I'm thinking about how Stephanie likes manipulating people. Maybe it's time we turned the tables on her."

"She'll kill you," Mark insisted bluntly. "And I've just told you, every door in that compound has a key card and code lock. If there's an alarm, the whole place will be locked down."

"Yeah, well, we've implemented a distraction." Skip glanced at his watch. "And right about now, it's in its initial phases."

"My guess," Mark replied, "is that these folks don't get distracted easily. They put a bullet in one of the guys who grabbed me. Then they got even. Hard and fast. Michelle and I barely got out with our lives."

"Good," Skip said thoughtfully. "The more stressed she is, the better this will work."

Helmut arched an eyebrow. "Will she fall for it?"

"The trusted officers are always the weak link." Skip turned to Q. "There are some things I'm going to need."

"By when?" Q had been listening quietly.

"Anika comes out tomorrow night," Skip said softly. Then he glanced at his watch. "I've got a meeting in a half hour."

"At this time of night?" Mark asked.

"Insurance agent," Skip muttered. "I'm taking out a life insurance policy."

"Better make it a big one,"—Helmut's dubious blue eyes met Skip's—"and please list me as the benefactor because I'm not sure you've got long to live."

CHAPTER SIXTY-FOUR

***

STEPHANIE MARCHED ANIKA STRAIGHT TOWARD ZOAKALSKI'S OFFICE. SHE TRIED TO prepare herself for what would come next by clenching her fists to still their trembling. But this time, instead of meeting with the Big Man, Stephanie opened a door that led down a flight of stairs. At the bottom stood two guards, each with an HK-MP5 submachine gun hanging from a shoulder sling.

Anika stopped short, only to have Stephanie grasp her by the elbow and squeeze. The nerve centers screamed and Anika gasped.

"Come on," Stephanie growled. "We're going to the security center. I want you to look at some photos."

"Photos of what?"

"Faces," Stephanie insisted.

Anika allowed Stephanie to lead her down the rest of the stairs. The guards had been watching her, obviously entertained by her hesitation. Both men nodded professionally to Stephanie before she swiped her key card and punched in a code.

48732, Anika noted. Different from yesterday's 53719.

They change the codes every day. Maybe every hour... That was sobering. So, even if she managed to get Stephanie's card, she'd have to have the latest code.

The metal door opened automatically, swinging on silent hinges. Anika felt a tickle of fear-sweat as she was led into a cubicle with a similar door on the other side. Immediately, she understood. The Converse County jail was constructed the same way. Only one door at a time could be opened. A mirror (obviously one-way glass) and curious slits lined the walls. The second door opened to another cubicle similar to the first.

"This is the security center?" Anika indicated the steel room around her.

"Yes, but if you think this is secure—" Stephanie informed as she nodded at the mirror "—you should see the sensitive records room. Oh, and if you're wondering, the slits are designed for shooting through. One word from me and, well, we use a particularly nasty hollow point. You've seen fresh hamburger?"

Anika gave the mirrored glass a curious look. "Only this one way in, huh?"

Stephanie didn't bother to answer.

A rather mundane hallway lay behind the final door. Anika immediately picked out the line of security cameras mounted in domes. The doors she passed were solid, the walls paneled in white, the floor polished to a shine.

Second from the last door, Stephanie stopped and swiped her card. Blocking Anika with her body, Stephanie punched in a code and opened the door.

The room was small with a single occupant. Simon Gunter sat at a small table lined with six chairs. He held an accordion file, perhaps two inches thick on the wood-veneer table. Overhead, two of the cameras were the only features beyond two rows of fluorescent lights.

"Have a seat," Stephanie indicated the chair next to Gunter. Stephanie dropped into a chair beside Anika.

"We want you to look at photos," Gunter said in his accented voice. "Tell us if you know any of these people?"

Anika nodded and watched Gunter unwrap a bit of twine from a button that held the file closed.

Gunter pointed to the cameras overhead. "Do not lie. We are recording your respiration, heartbeat, and pupil dilation."

Anika glanced nervously up at the camera. "Good luck. I'm already half-panicked."

Gunter gazed at Stephanie through hard black eyes. The muscles in his shoulders seemed to bunch under the immaculate black suit he wore.

"It's not my fault if she's frightened," Stephanie almost hissed.

Gunter grunted and pulled out the first photo. "Who is this?"

The woman in the photo was pretty, Asian, with long black hair and a triangular face. "I've never seen her in my life."

"And this one?"

The next photo was of a gray-haired man, blocky faced, perhaps in his late forties.

"I don't know."

"He walks with a limp," Gunter added. "Left leg."

Anika shrugged. "I've never seen him."

"How about this man?" Gunter showed her a young man, mid-twenties, wearing a mechanic's uniform. He stood next to a motorcycle of some kind.

"Never seen him before."

"And this one?"

The photo was of a black-haired man with a curled mustache, late thirties, tall and muscular. She could see lines around his eyes as if he'd lived outdoors. "I don't know him."

"And this one?"

Anika willed herself to relax as she stared down at Skip Murphy. Then she glanced up, forcing herself to tense. "I have no idea."

Stephanie slapped a hand to the veneer hard enough to make Anika jump. "Forget the photos, Gunter."

"One more." Gunter reached out another. "Who is this woman?"

Anika frowned. "Assistant Secretary of State Amy Randall. Not that you'd need me to identify her. Her face is on every TV screen."

"Tell me about her."

"I was developing the model for her."

"Did she mention ECSITE during that time?" Gunter's dark eyes barely hid annoyance.

"Yes. She knew that Mark Schott was working for ECSITE. I was supposed to inform her immediately if he tried to get in touch with me."

Some subtle communication passed between Stephanie and Gunter. Then Stephanie made a gesture toward the file. "Give her the rest."

Gunter pulled out a sheaf of papers. "These are engineering reports, studies of Conn Edison utilities, and traffic planning reports." He reached down and produced a shipping tube she hadn't seen from under the table. Popping off the top, Gunter coaxed a thick roll of maps from inside. He laid them out and Anika immediately recognized a Landsat image of New York, north of Manhattan.

"What are these for?" Anika asked, shooting Gunter a wary look.

Gunter said mildly, "You will study the reports and maps and tell us how to manipulate signage to best manage the traffic patterns in Rockland County, New York."

Anika murmured softly, "Why?

Stephanie leaned in close, her blue eyes almost crystalline with purpose. "I understand your father likes his steaks rare."

Anika clenched her fists tighter.

Gunter pulled one last photo from the file.

The image was unmistakable. Beneath a half-dressed man, his pants wadded around his knees, lay a naked woman, chained spread-eagle atop a large metal table. Three other men stood watching, one bending down for a better look. The woman's face was turned toward the camera, expression one of anguish, eyes closed, her mouth twisted.

Denise... Dear God, where are the boys? What's happening to them?

Anika pushed the photo back with a shaking hand. "How long do I have?"

"Twenty-four hours."

CHAPTER SIXTY-FIVE

***

FROM THE ALPEN MOTORRAD SHOP DOOR, SKIP WATCHED AS MARK SCHOTT'S RED ELEVEN-nine-eight, along with two full-face helmets, was carefully loaded into the delivery truck. Helmut carefully used tie-downs to strap it in place.

Jurgen and Lars, having attended to their last duty of the day, rode off on their bikes, headed back to Munich. Jurgen had been euphoric, stating he had a date with a drop-dead gorgeous BMW rider that night.

Helmut, satisfied, leaped down from the rear of the truck and pulled the tailgate closed. "All is well?" he asked.

"Totally," Skip agreed, grinning up at Helmut. "Q called in. There's been a steady stream of people on the way to the infirmary. More than the usual number are taking off early."

"Phase one," Helmet noted, thrusting thumbs into his belt loops and staring across the valley toward the compound. "What was it called again?"

"*Yersinia enterocolitica.*"

"Charming name," Helmet mused. "You'd think it was a Verdi opera."

"Yeah, well it has its own unique movements." Skip made a face. "Us vulgar types call it the screaming shits."

"And if Anika has enjoyed the benefits of the lunch room?"

"I'll know when I get there."

"Be careful, Skip."

"You, too. See you at the rendezvous."

They shook hands and Helmut, his black hair shining in the sun, his odd mustache turned up, walked to the cab, got in, and fired up the diesel engine.

Skip watched the truck start down the curving drive and pressed the button that closed the shop door. The heavy metal rattled down and closed off the outside world.

Whistling, Skip walked to the CD player and ran the recording of shop sounds for background noise.

From a belt pouch, he placed an earpiece in his right ear and lifted a throat microphone. "Q? How we doing?"

"All's well. No sign of Anika, though. She's still in the security building." A pause. *"Is that a problem?"*

"I won't know until I get there."

"Roger that."

"Is Schott doing all right?"

"Yeah. He's worried stiff about his family. But I think he'll manage. It's just a phone call, after all."

"Yeah," Skip said with a sigh. "All right, Q, keep your eyes and ears open. Anything looks weird, you give me the heads up."

"Good luck, Skip. Watch your six."

"Always. Women tell me the view from back there is splendid."

He bent down and pulled a toolbox from under the workbench. Spinning the combination on the lock, he opened the box, lifted out a shallow tray of wrenches, and began removing the pieces of equipment.

These he lugged over to a rebuilt KTM 450 dirt bike and began lashing packs to the luggage rack. From a box marked "Riding Gear," he took what looked like a two-man tent in a nylon stuff bag with accompanying telescoping poles. Skip used bungee cords to fasten the nylon bag to the rear of the seat.

"Gonna be a long and interesting night," he confided to himself. "So, Mr. Zoakalski, am I as good as I think I am? Or are you going to turn out to be better?"

As he changed into black tactical gear, the butterflies—old companions before any operation—returned and begun to flutter around in Skip's gut. He glanced at his watch: three hours until dark.

The wait, as it had through the years, seemed interminable. Nevertheless, Skip finally pressed the button and watched the shop door clatter up to reveal fading twilight illuminating the mountains.

Skip rolled the KTM out, propped it on the side stand, and waited while the heavy door rolled down. Then he locked the building, set the security, and straddled the bike.

The four-stroke single lit on the fifth kick. Skip pulled on a helmet, let the engine warm, and snicked it into first. Letting out the clutch, he motored off into the growing darkness.

The lights of the distant compound seemed to mock him as he descended the long drive, took a right on the highway, and accelerated to the south.

A kilometer and a half later, he made a left onto a side road that turned to dirt, followed the deteriorating track up the mountain, and stopped long enough to pick the lock on a chained gate.

Then, killing the headlight, Skip reached into one of the packs and fastened night-vision goggles onto his helmet. He put the bike in gear and motored off, the single cylinder's muffled engine puttering in the darkness.

CHAPTER SIXTY-SIX

***

ROCKLAND COUNTY PROVED EASY. FEW PLACES ON EARTH WERE AS VULNERABLE AS THE area around Manhattan. Hong Kong perhaps, or Tokyo, might prove to be just as precarious but Rockland County wasn't even a challenge.

Anika looked up as a white-faced Stephanie stepped through the door. The woman didn't look well, and the hand she pressed to her abdomen added to the effect.

"I'm finished with the Rockland model." Anika stood wearily.

Stephanie, her hair uncharacteristically disheveled, eyes red, walked unsteadily to the table and stared down at the map Anika had left on top. Yellow stick-it arrows pointed here and there.

"I'll inform the Big Man," Stephanie said and Anika saw the sheen of sweat on her face. Where the woman had looked blanched when she entered, her face had now reddened.

"Do you have a fever?"

"Half the compound is down. Food poisoning." Stephanie glanced at Anika with bright watery eyes. "You eaten anything?"

"Microwave sandwich out of the machine." Anika backed away when Stephanie gasped from pain and made a face. "Shouldn't you be in bed?"

The woman tensed. "I've got to hit the ladies' room." She made a face, wiping her lips. "If I can make it that far. Stay here. I'll be back."

Stephanie left at a run and Anika gazed hollowly at the maps covering the table. While she'd been studying the street maps, it occurred to her that Rockland County seemed to have a high proportion of synagogues.

What have I done?

CHAPTER SIXTY-SEVEN

***

SKIP LEFT THE KTM IN THE TREES AND SHONE A RED-LENSED FLASHLIGHT AT HIS GPS. HE shouldered the nylon-sack with its poles, unhooked the pack from the luggage rack, and began to traverse the side of the mountain.

The way was steep and his circuitous path rounded trees and outcrops of rock. Periodically, he caught a glimpse of the valley lights below. The chilly air was rich with the scents of grass, spring flowers, and fir trees. Overhead, the sky remained dark, cloud-covered.

He checked his watch again, then picked his way across a cracked-and-tumbled boulder field.

An hour later, he found the spot he'd picked out from below. Here, a rounded outcrop of weathered rock jutted from the slope. On the top, he found a sparse cover of grass, some flowers, and a couple of small conifers that had taken root. He checked the GPS and, doing a little math, calculated that he was just over three hundred meters above the compound.

Skip unslung his backpack and laid it to the side. Then he withdrew the telescoping poles and carefully fitted them together in the greenish glow of his Gen III goggles.

From the nylon bag, he withdrew a thin graphite composite sheeting and, despite the breeze, managed to stretch it over the pole frame. The thing created a large wing with a tail, a type of a hybrid paraglider. Next, he withdrew a series of straps, clipped them together and created a harness that slipped over his shoulders and buckled at the chest and over both thighs.

When he had assembled it, he clicked the harness to the wing, strapped his pack onto his chest, and fought the night wind blowing down the valley as he maneuvered onto the crest of the rock.

I'm out of my fucking mind. The thought went through his head as he stared down at the ghostly green lights of Oberau. Then he turned his attention to the well-lit compound below him.

A gust almost toppled him and, at the last instant, Skip launched himself into black space.

For a moment, panic froze his muscles. Then, remembering his training, he used his legs, and arched his back, feeling the wing catch air.

In the eerie glow of his night vision, a tree top slashed past and Skip arched, catching air as he went soaring out over the dark valley.

Fifty-fifty I screw this up and break my damn neck.

Hopefully—if he ended up falling like a damned rock—he'd land on Zoakalski.

Spears of conifers passed below and Skip glided quietly down toward the compound. Despite the silence, the air rushing past his ears almost obscured the sound of an approaching airplane.

Slowing his glide, Skip turned his head. Through the glow of his goggles, he made out the dark form of the approaching plane, its engines bright points in the IR spectrum.

As Skip silently dropped toward the compound, the plane passed overhead. Something bailed out the side door. As the airplane droned up the valley toward Garmisch, a parachute unfolded, a body dangling below.

So, I'm not going to be alone down there.

But who was this new intruder? And how was his presence going to complicate Skip's mission?

CHAPTER SIXTY-EIGHT

***

DESPAIR SPREAD THROUGH ANIKA AS STEPHANIE WALKED HER BACK TOWARD HER APART-
ment. The sky above appeared as dark as her soul. The compound
lights cast cones of yellow in the misty air. She smelled freshly mown
grass which triggered odd memories of haying as a girl on the ranch.

Desperate to think of anything except what she had done with the
New York data, she let her soul drift back to the past. If only she could
be sitting in the hot cab of the swather, bouncing slowly along as the
blades tucked tall grass over the cutters. She'd hated the swather back
then. They'd never been able to afford to fix the cab air conditioner.
Even with the windows open, the late June sun had turned the tin box
into an oven. And the thing had constantly been breaking down, its
parts worn past tolerance as a hedge against expensive new ones.

*Please, God. Just let me go back to cutting hay and I'll never set foot
off the ranch again.*

Stephanie's stomach made a loud gurgle and the woman winced.

"How bad is it?" Anika asked. "The attack rate, I mean."

"Attack rate? What are you talking about?"

Anika gestured as she walked along. "It's an epidemiological term.
How many people has the enterotoxin affected?"

"We're running on half-staff. The rest are in the clinic or have
been sent home and told to stay put until we figure out what it is. The
lab's trying to run down the source. But they…" Stephanie stopped,
listening to something in her earpiece. "Come on. We've got to hurry."

"What's wrong?"

"One of the dog teams found a parachute. Security is going wild."

Anika glanced around, a sudden desperate hope building in her
chest.

"Don't even think it," Stephanie muttered, reaching into her purse and withdrawing a stainless steel semiautomatic.

"What do you shoot?" Anika asked, uncomfortably gazing at the pistol.

"Nine-millimeter Sig. Why would you care?"

"As sick as you are, you'd better keep the safety on. If you get the shakes, I don't want to get shot."

"Oh. Right. Wyoming girl. Of course you're familiar with guns." Stephanie gave her a cold look through fevered eyes.

When they reached Anika's apartment, Stephanie fumbled the lock twice, then shoved the door open and gestured for Anika to enter first. Closing the door behind them, Stephanie carefully looked around the room.

"With an intruder alert, guards should have been posted. But with most of them crapping and puking, we don't have the personnel." Stephanie clutched the pistol high and close to her chest and started forward. "Keep back until I clear the place."

Anika watched Stephanie step forward and glance quickly up the stairs before she walked wide around the kitchen divider. Then she checked the bathroom.

"Clear."

"Why would they come here?"

"To try and take you back."

Anika felt her heart race. She followed behind Stephanie as the woman started slowly up the stairs, pistol in a competent two-handed hold. No doubt about it, the woman knew what she was doing.

Anika swallowed hard. *Don't hesitate. Grab Stephanie by the belt and jerk her backward down the stairs.*

Anika opened her hands, heart hammering, mouth gone dry. A distant part of her brain thought: *This must be how Dad feels each time he puts his life on the line in Converse County.*

Just as she made her grab, Stephanie leaped upwards out of reach, taking the steps two at a time.

In a crouch, Stephanie rounded the corner at the head of the stairs. Moving quickly, the woman advanced on cat feet, the closely tucked pistol swinging with her body as she covered the office.

"Stay," she ordered, then advanced to check behind the desk.

Satisfied the room was clear, she crept to the bedroom door and darted inside.

Stephanie stepped out, pistol lowered, a look of disappointment on her excitement-flushed face. "No one here."

Anika watched Stephanie cross to the wet bar, kneel, and retrieve a bottle of water from the little refrigerator. The woman rummaged in her purse, removed a pill bottle, and tossed two tablets into her mouth before she cracked the cap and chugged water.

"Antibiotics," Stephanie told her. "My own concoction."

Anika took a deep breath, walking to one of the chairs and flopping into it. "You're not seriously going to attack Rockland County, New York, are you? Use your head. Run the permutations. The US *will* retaliate."

"That's the idea."

"What?"

Stephanie dropped, exhausted, into the opposite recliner, but managed to chuckle. "The dominoes of your beloved model are rolling down the hill like big rocks." She pointed to her gut. "If the Big Man weren't occupied with other things, he'd be euphoric."

"Other things?"

"Deals that are suddenly on hold. Investors dumping assets. Someone clever has figured out exactly how to hurt us. It's like nothing I've ever seen. Little things that would seem insignificant. A supplier of a critical part suddenly unable to deliver. Money transfers held up. Investors offered more lucrative deals at the last minute. Always at the weakest link. Zoakalski's experts are baffled."

Maureen and the team. Has to be. Modeling how to derail the chain of events...

"What about the parachute?"

Stephanie gave her a flat glare. "Anyone who thinks they're going to get you out is in for a surprise. Assuming they could get to you, they'd never make it past the first perimeter. Even on half-staff, security is alerted. Whoever the intruder is, the second he moves, the cameras and motion detectors will spot him. By now the dogs are tracking his scent." She smiled victoriously. "Poor fool."

"Why do you think they're after me?"

Stephanie's eyelids were drooping from exhaustion. "In your

words, you're the highest probability." She listened to her earpiece. "We've got guards on your door. A perimeter is being formed around this building as I speak. Since they aren't here already, they're not going to be coming."

Anika's heart sank.

Stephanie continued. "Too bad, actually. I'd have liked to take him down myself." A pause. "We'll be fascinated to find out just how he expected to get you out."

"Helicopter?"

"Not possible." Stephanie listened to her earpiece, nodding. "I'm placing security with you. You're to be under constant surveillance until this thing is concluded."

Stephanie climbed wearily to her feet, pistol dangling from her right hand. "The guard will be up momentarily."

Anika watched the woman walk to the stairs and listened as she descended to the ground floor.

In an instant, Anika was on her feet, running to the head of the stairs to peer down. Then she hurried to the refrigerator, removing a heavy bottle of champagne.

As soon as the guard walked up the steps, she had one chance to brain the man. A tremble ran through her muscles. *I have to kill him. I can do it.*

She whirled as the sliding door to the deck opened. Turning, she gripped the bottle by its neck, ready to swing.

Skip Murphy, dressed in black, gave her a stern look. "Put down the Dom Perignon, okay?" He slid the door closed behind him and quickly crossed the floor on silent feet.

"*Skip!*" Anika lowered the bottle. "A guard's coming."

Skip considered for a moment, whispering, "Can you distract him?"

Anika swallowed hard. "Uh, yeah. I can think of something."

"Good." Then he ducked behind the huge desk as feet thumped on the stairs.

Anika tried to keep from shaking, wondering why Skip didn't just ambush the man as he stepped into the office. Instead, she tried to compose herself as a man in his thirties, clad in dark blue, a submachine gun hanging from a sling, cautiously entered the room.

Anika cradled the bottle of champagne. *Distract him? How? Come on, what would completely occupy his attention?*

"So, you're my new jailor?" she asked warily.

The man cast a wary glance around the room, speaking into a throat mic in German. Then he turned his attention to Anika, a slight smile on his lips. "I'm going to like this duty," he said in accented English.

Anika read the interest in his eyes and she had it. "Look, I'm tired. Stephanie acted like an ass. I'm taking a shower, drinking a glass of champagne, and going to bed."

The guard shrugged. "You are not to be out of my sight."

"Not even in the shower?" Anika asked as if stunned.

"*Nein.* Not out of my sight."

"Hope you don't blush," Anika growled sourly as she started past him for the bedroom. "Because I'm sweaty and filthy."

From the corner of her eye, she saw the grin widen on his thin lips, a glitter of anticipation in his eyes.

He followed her into the bedroom, just as she'd hoped he would.

Anika unbuttoned her shirt and tossed it on the bed. As she stepped into the bathroom, she was unsnapping her pants, pausing long enough to hit the appropriate shower controls. As she began to slip her pants over her hips, the guard was in the doorway, eyes gleaming in anticipation.

"Don't think this is an invitation," Anika said in a chipper voice. "Not that you'd ever be distracted from your duty by a naked woman..."

A blur of movement behind the man was followed by an arm snaking around the man's neck. Then the fellow was yanked backward. Anika stepped forward, staring in disbelief as Skip Murphy lowered the guard's body quietly to the floor.

"Good work, Anika."

Anika snapped her pants, watching in amazement as Skip began peeling out of his jacket and shirt. "What are you doing?" She ran past him and retrieved her shirt from the bed.

"Dressed as him, I get you out of here."

Anika was pulling her shirt on. "They've got guard dogs. They're tracking you from your parachute. We don't have much time."

Skip stuck an arm into the guard's shirt. "Not my parachute, Anika. Someone else is here. I saw them drop in. One person, dressed in black.

Slender and moving fast when he hit the ground." He frowned at her. "Get a coat, your purse, whatever you need as long as it's small."

She yanked open the closet, pulling out her black coat and lunged for her purse. "How'd you get here? Can we get out that way?"

He checked his watch. "You ever read Homer? The *Iliad*?"

"You think you're Achilles and Zoakalski's Hector? You're going to challenge him to single combat?"

"Who? No, it was the horse I was thinking about."

"Classical literature isn't your strong point, is it?"

"Nope." He buttoned up the guard's shirt, wincing as it stretched the buttons over his thick chest. Clipping the throat mic to the collar, he fit the earpiece. He was strapping an equipment belt to his hips, when he said, "I won't lie. It's going to get scary out there. Are you with me?"

She gulped and nodded as he slung the MP5 submachine gun over his shoulder. "I'm my father's daughter." *I hope.*

"Yeah, I thought you were." Skip gave her a grin. "Come on."

He led her out to the office and flicked off the lights. At the sliding door, he raised a small radio from a holster on his belt.

He carefully slid the door open and said, "Ready." Even as he re-holstered the radio, Anika heard a *fssst* accompanied by a snapping pop. She swallowed hard, having heard that sound before: the sound of a high-velocity bullet hitting flesh. In her youth, it had always been a deer or antelope.

But there were no deer here.

"Come on," Skip said, stepping out onto the deck. "The rope's knotted. Can you climb?"

Anika jerked a nod, grabbing the rope. Driven by a fear she'd never known, she began to climb, Skip steadying the rope from below.

CHAPTER SIXTY-NINE

***

SKIP HELD HIS BREATH AS ANIKA CLAMBERED UP THE ROPE. THE TRICKY PART WAS WHERE it hung over the wood-shingled roof. But Anika managed. Then he muscled himself up, climbing for all he was worth. Anika was crouched at the top, and Skip paused only long enough to pull up the rope.

"What if they see us?" Anika asked. "They have cameras all over this place."

"I'm hoping they're shorthanded."

"They are. Food poisoning. Half the compound is down."

"Yeah. Maureen Cole will be delighted to learn her toxin worked." He was scuttling down the roof, the rope coiled over his shoulder.

By the time they reached the far end of the roof, they could hear shouts in the distance.

"What's all the commotion?" Anika whispered.

"My insurance policy." Then he listened as voices began bellowing orders in his earpiece. He turned and placed a hand on Anika's shoulder. "Just hold onto the rope. I'll lower you to the ground."

He unslung the rope and quickly wound it around her butt and thigh to create a belay. Then he placed her hands on the knots. "Hold tight. I won't drop you."

"I know." She maneuvered over the edge and saw Skip brace himself as he began lowering her.

When Anika's feet hit the ground, she scuttled back into the shadows and watched Skip descend.

"Come on," Skip said when he touched down. "Now, we're just walking normally. Two people out for an evening stroll."

"Where to?" Anika asked as Skip started down the walk to the trees.

He fished in one of the pockets of his tactical pants and found the key. "Hopefully, a rather uncomfortable ride out of here."

As they approached a line of conifers, Skip started as a man came trotting out of the darkness. "Be cool. Let me do the talking."

The man peered at them in the dim light, then straightened, saying in a German accent, "Mr. Murphy." The voice was in English now, the pistol pointed at Anika. "You will lower the machinegun. If I hear the selector click, Dr. French is dead."

Skip removed his hand from the grip, lifting it into plain view. "Very well, *Herr Gunter.*"

Anika had begun to shake like a deer in the headlights. Another of the distant shouts could be heard.

"The sniper is your work?" Gunter asked, head cocked. "Teams have already been dispatched to hunt your friend down. And we know the mountain better than he does." Gunter's smile hinted at nothing nice.

"Hope you told your teams to pack a lunch. They're going to need it."

"Turn around. Then, drop to your knees. Both of you."

"You might want to rethink that," Skip replied easily. "Helping us out of here might just earn you a very nice retirement. I'm thinking that house in the Bahamas would be a delightful place to spend the rest of your life."

Gunter gave a slight shake of his head. "Turn around. On your knees."

Anika caught the flicker of black as it emerged from the trees. In a low crouch—little more than a blur in the night—the form seemed to float toward them across the grass.

"Gunter," Skip called, "You really can make a fortune for yourself."

"Fortunes come and go. But the memory of a midnight execution, well, it stays with a man forever," he said reasonably. Skip watched him raise the pistol as the dark intruder slowed, straightened, and slipped an arm around his neck. Gunter was pulled back, arching.

Skip danced forward, using the HK to club the pistol from the man's hand. Then he stepped back, bringing the gun to bear.

Gunter thrashed, arms flailing, as his body was levered to the ground. Skip recognized the flicking motions as an artfully wielded knife did its work and was wiped clean on Gunter's clothing. Tall and lithe, the assailant straightened; the knife slid neatly into a belt sheath.

From under a balaclava, a female voice said, "Thank you for the distraction. I owe you one." She glanced down at the corpse. "With Gunter, it was personal."

"For Fetzer? The guy they found on the railroad tracks in Laramie?" Skip guessed.

A slight nod. "And then the attack in Italy."

"So what's next, Li?" He stepped in front of Anika, who'd been standing like a frozen deer. "Dr. French is mine."

She seemed to ignore the MP5 pointed at her middle. "We don't want her. Schott gave us everything we need."

"Then we're done here?"

She gave a nod and turned, long legs poised to strike in case he moved. "See you on the outside, Murphy."

He watched Mi Chan Li sprint into the darkness under the trees.

Skip grabbed Anika's arm. "You're not going to fold on me, are you?"

"No." She shivered.

Skip left at a trot, thankfully ducking into the trees. Crouching under the branches, he paused before stepping out on the other side. Yep, there it was, just like he'd hoped—silver and shining in the lights.

CHAPTER SEVENTY

***

IT HAD BEEN A REALLY SHITTY NIGHT: THE SECURITY OF THE COMPOUND BREACHED, Gunter and three others dead, Anika French vanished, and her dangerously concussed guard clueless about who brained him. And no one had been able to hunt down the sniper on the hillside. When Stephanie hadn't been dealing with one crisis or another, she'd been racing for the toilet.

She was in anything but a good mood when her cell rang. She fished it out of her pocket, blinked away her fatigue, and checked the number. Unknown.

"*Ja?*"

"*Stephanie? It's Mark Schott. Can you talk?*"

She glanced at Zoakalski sitting behind his desk, talking on his phone, so carried away in his own rage that he barely glanced up when her phone rang.

"Just a moment."

Zoakalski waved for her to leave the room.

Stephanie passed the security doors, nodded at the guards, and walked down the hall where no one could overhear. "Where are you, Mark?"

"*I don't have time for crap. Michelle Lee, as she called herself, doesn't work for the CIA like she told me. I got away in Venice. I've been on the run ever since. The whole fucking world thinks I'm a drug dealer!*"

"Easy, Mark. Take your time. Tell me what's happened."

"*They've had me working on the model. They had Anika's notes. And they told me my family's been kidnapped. Do you know anything about that? Tell me the truth for once.*"

"The news came the day after you were taken. We suspected that Li was using them as leverage. A means to keep you working."

"Your people don't have them?"

"Absolutely not."

She heard an exasperated sigh. *"Stephanie, what will it take to find them?"*

"I don't know."

"You have resources."

"We do." She paused. "What do you have in mind?"

"A trade. If you rescue them, I'll come back."

She considered the ramifications. Zoakalski was going to lash out as soon as his wits returned. And, with Simon dead, the person most likely to feel his wrath... She felt a cold chill run down her spine.

Bringing Schott in would be a small victory that might be sufficient to save her ass. At least until she could devise an exit strategy.

"Mark? Why did you call me?"

"I... I thought we had something together. Something special."

In a low voice, she said, "I thought so too." She hesitated, smiled to herself. "I've been worried sick about you. I didn't think it would affect me like this. I did everything I could. Traced you to a place in Italy where I thought you'd been taken."

"I know. I was there. Some goon tied me up and got me out in a truck." He paused. *"The gunshots? That was you?"*

She paused a beat. "Of course. I was trying to rescue you. Li and her people are still after you, by the way. She has the police alerted."

"I know. I'm being careful. I'm not cut out for this spy shit. Do you know Schongau?"

"I do."

"There's a church here. Maria Himmelfahrt."

"I know it."

"When I see your car, I'll call back. I'll be there in an hour."

"Mark? Mark?" Her cell told her the call had been terminated.

"An hour? Shit."

She opened her purse, checked to make sure her pistol was handy, and shook a couple of amphetamines into the palm of her hand. Did she try and take a team with her? Damned right she did. Pressing a number on her phone, she said, "I need two men in Schongau for armed cover. And I need them there fast. I'll have further instructions as the circumstances dictate."

Hearing an affirmation, she killed the call and dropped her phone into a pocket.

All she wanted to do was go back to her room and sleep off the aftereffects of both the illness and too many hours without sleep. Instead, she tilted her head back, gulped the pills, and shivered.

CHAPTER SEVENTY-ONE

MARK SCHOTT KILLED THE CONNECTION ON THE SATELLITE PHONE Q HAD GIVEN HIM AND wiped his face. Then he looked around the safe-house living room. Shaken, he lowered himself into one of the chairs beside the table.

"How'd I do?"

Q gave him a sober look, his thin face impassive. "It sounded good to me. I liked that slight quaver in your voice when you said you had something special."

"Yeah," Mark muttered. Then he glanced up. "She said they didn't have Denise and the boys."

"You're still in play," Q told him. "Whoever has them is going to hold them until they have you back or you're dead and no longer of use to anyone."

Schott gave him a dull look. "Thanks. That makes me feel so much better."

Q was watching his monitor, pointing. "There she is. Headed right for her Jaguar."

Mark bent to stare over his shoulder. "God, my hands are sweating. Do you guys ever get over this?"

"Hell no." Q grinned. "You never really know you're alive unless there's a chance you're going to be discovered and killed."

A pause. "Hey, do you have a real name?"

"Yes, I do." Q straightened. "There. See. She's through the trees, walking toward the car. She's got a bag with her."

Mark held his breath and watched the long-range lens focus on Stephanie as she hurried through the morning shadows.

She hesitated, then opened the driver's door, pitched the bag into the passenger seat, then slid into the Jaguar.

Q whispered, "It's working just like he said."

Mark felt his heart beginning to thunder. The silver Jaguar rolled out, and the long-distance lens lost it behind the palace. Then, it rounded the side road, heading straight for the entrance where the guards waited behind the great iron gate.

CHAPTER SEVENTY-TWO

***

MARK STARED AT THE CLOCK. HE'D MADE COFFEE BUT THE CUP RESTED ON THE KITCHEN counter, stone cold.

On the speaker, Helmut's voice announced, "Stephanie has arrived. She just drove past. As far as I can tell, she's alone. No chase cars are behind her. I'd call it a go."

Q glanced at Mark. "Time for the next call, Romeo. You've got the directions?"

Mark's stomach churned. "Yes." He lifted the paper with the scrawled directions, seated himself, and pressed the send button on the satellite phone.

CHAPTER SEVENTY-THREE

***

SLOWING IN FRONT OF THE CHURCH, STEPHANIE LET HER GAZE ROAM THE STREETS. CARS were parked along the Munzenstrasse; the faint morning light filtered through puffy white clouds that rolled off toward the east. The ancient church shone in the morning. She bent and peered back at the medieval town walls. The wooden walkways and towers were empty—the hour too early even for tourists. One by one, she cataloged the parked cars, looking for heads, seeing none. Only a few pedestrians were out for a morning walk—and they all looked like locals.

Her phone rang.

"Where are you, Mark?"

"A five-minute drive. Follow my directions."

"You'd better not be jerking me around."

"No. No. I swear. It's just that I've had one hell of an education lately. If Li's out there, I can't be too careful."

Stephanie put the Jaguar in gear. "Where am I going?"

She followed his directions out through the medieval gate with its guard towers, past the businesses and houses to Route 17. A kilometer and a half later, Mark told her to take a turn. Stephanie saw the road, wheeled the Jaguar onto a gravel track and ended up at a car park. A walking trail led off into the trees that lined the River Lech. She killed the ignition, reached for her bag, and asked, "What now?"

"I'm a couple of hundred meters down the path. Hidden in the trees."

"Why are we doing this, Mark?"

"To see if anyone followed you. Li hates you, you know."

Trap?

She killed the call, pulled her pistol from her purse and hit the call button on her phone. "Have you been listening to this?"

"Yes. We're at the turn off. Give us five minutes and we'll be in place," her cover team announced.

Stephanie stepped out of the car to carefully study her surroundings. To the left of the trail, the river ran full and clear, willows and other brush masking the shore. Tall oaks and poplars shaded the path.

She shouldered her bag, using it to hide the pistol, and walked slowly forward. One step at a time, she made her way down the path, eyes in constant motion. The adrenaline rush, the age-old companion of the hunt, washed the fatigue from her foggy brain.

"Mark?" she called softly, head cocked for any sound. Having gone no more than fifty meters, she looked back. The car was hidden by the trees.

Glancing at her watch, it was four minutes. Her team would be filtering in from the east, easing through the trees.

"Tell me this isn't a trap, Mark." She continued for another hundred meters, calling, "Mark?"

The only answer was birdsong in the trees. A sudden wariness made her step off the path and slip behind one of the pines. Lifting her phone, she punched the number.

"Yes?" a voice asked.

"Where are you?"

"Anders has a visual on where you just stepped off the trail. We see no one else."

Feeling better, she stepped out from behind the tree, shouting: "Mark? This is enough. I'm leaving!"

She listened to the morning, hearing water lapping at the river banks. In the distance, the sound of a motorcycle broke the morning peace. Stephanie tensed as cold realization flooded her veins.

Turning, she ran for all she was worth, charged into the car park, and saw her silver Jaguar. In the distance, the sound of the motorcycle was already fading.

Pressing her key fob to open the door, she noticed that the right rear tire was flat. The valve stem had been neatly severed at the rim and her trunk was ajar. She frowned and walked toward the rear to open it to peer inside. Nothing there, but she had the feeling that something was amiss... Things were in different places.

CHAPTER SEVENTY-FOUR

***

YOU OKAY BACK THERE?" SKIP CALLED OVER HIS SHOULDER TO ANIKA.

"Yeah."

Skip lifted his elbow and guided the Ducati up through a series of curves along a treed slope and risked a quick glance backwards. As they dropped down into the Amel River valley, the road remained clear except for a VW far behind.

He liked riding in Germany with its superbly paved and winding roads, green fields, forested patches, and neat, red-roofed towns. Before them, the Alps rose like great snow-capped teeth.

"What's next?" Anika asked.

"Getting you out of Germany and back to the United States. For the moment, however, we have to wait for DOD to figure out your extraction route. Innsbruck is one option. Milan another. Zurich is in Zoakalski's back pocket. Munich, we think, is too compromised by Zoakalski's people even if we give you diplomatic papers and try to take you out through the consulate."

"They wouldn't mess with the consulate, would they?"

"Of course they would. Who was it that messed with both Defense and the FBI when they took you? We're only beginning to understand how deeply Zoakalski's tentacles reach."

"Everybody's got the bloody model. Why does anyone care about me now?"

Skip chuckled. "Anika, the model was just the beginning. Now we're into something much more dangerous."

"More dangerous?"

"Yeah. There are things going on that you don't know about."

She leaned against him and yelled in his ear. "What things?"

He braked and downshifted, bending into the corners that would take him over the divide to Oberau. Picking his line, he leaned the Ducati, enjoying the stiff suspension; trail braking late, he gave it throttle.

As they crested the divide and began the tight descent down to Oberau, he answered, "There's a genetically engineered virus that running rampant through Israel. It only attacks men but it apparently causes sterility."

He felt Anika stiffen and heard her whisper, "First Israel. Then New York."

"What?" he called against the wind as he leaned into a corner.

Frantically, Anika yelled, "What's Israel doing to contain the spread?"

"Don't know. I haven't been briefed. We'll ask when we get back to the US. Why?"

"If you can find a way to let me contact Randall, I may be able to help."

Careful. Careful... You don't want your actions to be the fracture event.

CHAPTER SEVENTY-FIVE

***

"THEY'RE OUT!" MARK FELT A SENSE OF ELATION THAT TRUMPED ANY VICTORY HE'D EVER savored. He watched Q's previously professional expression crack enough for a weary smile as he huddled over the electrical gear that pretty much filled the wall. The man wore a rumpled white shirt, brown Dockers, and loafers.

Q rubbed his long nose. "Good work."

"You should have lived it from the inside." Mark walked over and tossed out his cold cup of coffee, putting new grounds in the machine. "Can you *believe* that? Murphy sneaked her out... in the trunk of Stephanie's Jaguar! If I hadn't just seen it, I never would have believed it. Not in my wildest dreams. Fucking Hollywood couldn't dream this up."

"Yeah, well, enjoy your moment in the sun. Now we have to get you out of Europe."

As Mark pressed the button on the coffee machine, Q was staring thoughtfully at his monitors. "So, who was the shooter last night? Someone was up on that hillside creating havoc."

"That was Helmut. He did time in Afghanistan with a German special warfare unit. And the other intruder? That's your Michelle Lee. That's a woman you don't underestimate. She wouldn't have just parachuted in without some sort of backup."

"Think she's really working for China?"

"Yeah, probably." Q rocked back in his chair. "It sure made our job easier. That whole compound was turned upside down. I wonder how Zoakalski's feeling this morning?"

Mark reflected on that. "I'd say he's pissed as hell. I met the man, Q. Stared right into his soul. He's not the kind to let you stick a finger in his eye and get away with it. Even Stephanie's scared of him."

"That's tomorrow's problem. One you don't have to deal with. Let's access the drone and see how Stephanie's doing." He entered keystrokes; the image refined to show a wooded area beside the Lech River. Stephanie's Jaguar could be plainly discerned where it sat in the car park beside the trailhead. The trunk was open, the liner folded back, and Stephanie and two men were in the process of jacking the car up to change the tire.

"So," Q mused, "She had backup. How'd they get there that fast? She must have been forwarding your directions. Now there's a lesson for us."

Mark nodded, seeing morning sunlight reflecting from Stephanie's blond locks. "Zoakalski's not the only one who's going to be out for blood. Drop your little drone airplane down, see if you can get a close-up of her expression. I'm betting she's mad enough to bend tenpenny nails in her bare hands."

"Instead of dropping down, how about we stay high and invisible." Q shot him a grin. "But I wouldn't suggest calling her up for a date anytime soon, if I were you."

Mark nodded soberly; the realization hit him like a brick: Playing Stephanie for a fool had gotten a lot of people killed in Italy. "Q, what's going to happen to me? I mean when I get home. I've got to find Denise and the boys. How do I do that when Stephanie's out there? She'll kill me without a second thought."

"Our people will figure something out."

"Like they did with Anika? Remember? The night Zoakalski took her right out from under the collective noses of the FBI?"

"You're probably going to have to change your name, disappear." Q chewed his thumbnail. "Sorry, buddy, but your days as a professor are over."

Mark stopped short as he reached for the freshly brewed coffee. Zoakalski—through agents like Stephanie—specialized in obtaining hard-to-get information. Make no mistake, the cunning bitch would be after him like a bloodhound on the trail.

Witness protection? With someone like Stephanie sniffing him out? She'd seduce, steal, or manipulate the information somehow. And when she finally found him, or Denise, or Will or Jake?

And what are you going to do about it, Mark?

He glanced furtively at Q. The man was using a joystick to guide his drone back to the field where Helmut would retrieve it.

Mark edged over to one of the lockers, quietly unhooked the hasps, lifted the lid.

Reaching down he removed one of the nine-millimeter pistols. His skin crawled at the feel of the smooth steel, his fingers curling around the cold plastic grip.

I'm never going to be safe…

CHAPTER SEVENTY-SIX

***

SKIP DOWNSHIFTED AS HE CLIMBED THE DRIVE TO THE MOTORCYCLE SHOP. FROM HABIT, he checked the huge sign dominating the roof. It was hard to believe they had a high-tech monitoring system behind those big letters.

"When I stop, keep your helmet on," he called over his shoulder to Anika. "Once you're inside, don't say anything. Zoakalski monitors the building."

"Yes, sir. All I want to do is find a shower and a soft bed."

He gassed the throttle as he took the last corner. "I have to check in first but if everything's good to go, I'll have you at the safe house by noon. Meanwhile, when the mechanics show up, you're my date. I picked you up at a bar in Munich. You're from California, here on vacation. Got it? Volleyball, surfboards, and hot bikes."

"Okay."

Skip noticed the KTM 450, canted onto its side stand, the handlebars cocked, its knobby wheels dusty. The bike looked forlorn all by itself.

He rolled to a stop before the garage door, put the bike in neutral, and killed the engine. Anika crawled off the back before he put the side stand down and walked to the door. With a key, he unlocked and hit the button that opened the door. Then, Anika following, he rolled the Ducati inside, stepped back, and looked up the mountain behind the shop.

Nothing on the hillside seemed out of place. The thick band of fir trees stood in the morning sun, branches tipped with new needles. Grass and flowers, occasional brush, and rock outcrops seemed crisp in the morning light.

Looks absolutely pristine, he thought. *Who'd guess?*

Turning into the shop, he hit the button that closed the door, gestured to Anika she could take off the full-face helmet, and punched the shop recording. Music and the sound of tools clanging on concrete could be heard.

"You can talk in a very low voice," Skip told her, seeing exhaustion in her puffy face. Damn the woman had to be running on sheer adrenaline.

Anika dropped to one of the mechanic's stools, shoulders sagging. "Skip," she whispered, "I need a phone. I have to warn Randall about New York and share the calculations about Israel that I've been running in my head."

"What about New York?"

"Just... I need a phone, please. It's complicated. I designed a model for effectively spreading a new virus in Rockland County, New York."

He walked over to a table and shrugged out of his jacket. "No phone, Anika. Too risky. That's my office over there. Remember it's bugged, so say nothing. At all. Period. If anything goes south, crawl up on the desk, open the trap door, and climb up into the dead space between the ceiling and roof. There's a bedroll there. But for now, there's a big chair. You're exhausted. I want you to go get some sleep while I figure this out."

Skip watched her walk wearily to the office, glance around suspiciously, and flop in the chair. He figured she was asleep before he pushed the send button.

Skip frowned, went over to open his toolbox, and pulled out his sat phone, then he walked out of Anika's hearing range and punched in the number. "Randall. What's the word on the post office? I've got a letter ready to be put in an envelope. Do you know what the postage is going to be?"

"*Glad to hear you can finally write. We were worried that you might have been detained by other obligations.*"

"Tell your team to take a close look at securing the *big apple* tree. I got a guy here who wants to do some picking. Probably an old grudge, having lost first prize at the fair. Your team can figure out where the fruit is the most vulnerable to worms and other pests."

He heard a long pause before she said, "*Which big apple tree. You got any idea when your guy wants to do his picking?*"

"The one to the north."

"Understood. We really appreciate you going the extra mile."

"Just don't forget the reason for the call. I need to know the postage."

"We'll have that for you as soon as possible." A pause. "Check the mail when you get home. Anything else?"

"Negative."

Skip heard the call terminated from the other end.

A delivery truck pulled up outside the shop, and Helmut stepped out and slammed the door. He had a plastic grocery sack swinging from his hand. He was smiling, whistling, his fake black mustache curled like a villain's. At the sight of Skip, he gave a thumbs up, then looked around. "Where?"

Skip pointed. "Crashed in the office chair."

"You've pulled one off for the books, my friend. Snatching your principal out from the jaws of… What's wrong?"

"Pretty sure communications have been compromised."

Helmut lifted a skeptical eyebrow. "How? It's a scrambled, line-of-sight, focused beam, magic quantum satellite phone. Q bragged, remember?"

"Yeah," Skip said and stared at the satellite phone. "Pray Randall works out a quick extraction for Anika and Schott, then—"

Skip's cell rang. *"Guten tag."*

"Alpen Motorrad?" Q's voice came through. *"Uh, I don't know how to explain this but I just lost a motorcycle."*

"How?" Skip asked coldly.

"It was here one minute and gone the next."

Skip sighed.

"More trouble?" Helmut asked.

"Schott's gone."

"What? What possessed him to do something so stupid?"

Q's voice came through the phone. *"Hang on. There's a knock at the door. Maybe it's him."*

Skip listened, hearing Q as he opened the door, saying, "*Yes? What can I…*"

Then came the sound of the phone clattering loudly as if dropped onto the hard floor. A sodden thump sounded. Then a crunching… followed by an ominous silence.

CHAPTER SEVENTY-SEVEN

***

AS HE WALKED DOWN THE STREET, MARK SCHOTT CAST FURTIVE GLANCES BEHIND HIM, trying to remember every spy movie Denise had forced him to watch. He'd hated those nights, sitting in the living room, eyes fixed on the TV, watching Matt Damon as Jason Bourne. Throughout the entire movie, he'd dissected every twist in the plot, every miraculous escape, and told himself how far-fetched it all was.

Now I'm god-damned living it.

Wracking his brain, he tried to remember every detail. Movies—fantasies though they were—still used consultants to create the illusion of reality. So, how many of the things he'd seen on television were actually based on fact?

"Why didn't I pay more attention?"

Because he'd been an arrogant professor and an intellectually superior prick.

He surveyed the street as surreptitiously as he could. And another fact came crashing down on him. He was an American, in a German city, who didn't speak a word of the language. He had a couple of hundred Euros, no identification, an illegal pistol, and a cell phone.

Mark stopped short, blinking, wondering at the limits of his stupidity, or even if there was such a thing.

"Come on, Mark. Figure this out."

Get your ass back to the safe house before you're arrested by the Munich police.

Instead, he walked into a coffee shop on the corner, ordered a cappuccino, and sat by the window, watching the street. As he sipped, a sense of desolation grew within him. Where the hell was Denise? He closed his eyes, trying to imagine it from her perspective. And Will?

Christ, he was only fourteen, bright and sensitive. And little Jake? What was it like to be nine, abducted, and scared witless?

"God, Denise." He rubbed his jaw, feeling his short beard. So, when a man had destroyed everyone he's ever been in contact with, how the hell did he atone?

He worked the problem.

Pulling Michelle's cell phone from his pocket, he blinked at it.

Work the problem...

CHAPTER SEVENTY-EIGHT

***

ARMS CROSSED, MAUREEN COLE BRACED HERSELF AGAINST THE DESK AND LISTENED TO the speakerphone on Amy Randall's desk. As Skip recounted the latest setback, Maureen watched Randall's expression turn anxious.

She felt as if a great weight had been lifted from her heart. Anika was free.

Randall's office was nice, accessed through a secretary out front. The place had wood-paneled walls, bookcases, a plush carpet, high ceilings, a huge desk, and a separate workstation. Photos of the president, the Secretary of State, and George Washington hung on the walls, while the photo of an older couple—who Maureen figured were Randall's parents—stood on the desk.

Skip's voice came through the speaker. *"Helmut reports that the safe house is trashed. Electronics are smashed and equipment scattered about."*

"And Nelson?"

"Who?"

"The CIA tech."

A two-second pause. *"Dead."*

"How is Anika?" Maureen called from across the room.

"Safe, but exhausted," Skip answered. *"Says she has information that will help Israel and New York. Best to get her out as quickly as possible."*

"We're working on that," Randall told him.

"I could get her to Ramstein, walk in through the A Gate, and place her on a military jet for home. No one would be the wiser."

Randall gave Maureen a guarded look, then added, "There are some additional considerations we've been forced to take into account."

After a short silence, Skip growled, *"What?"*

"You're just going to have to trust me on this. You're in a 'need to know' circumstance."

"Come on, Amy. I've been in the trenches before. If it was just my ass, I'd say sure, I'll take the risk but Anika didn't sign on for covert work. You need to get her home."

"Soon, but not now." Randall steepled her fingers.

"Madam Assistant to the Secretary," Skip's irritation was plain. *"I advise you to have a military transport waiting at Ramstein, because that's where I'm taking Dr. French."*

"I've already…"

Maureen vigorously shook her head, face cold as stone.

"Just a moment," Randall said, stabbing the mute button. "What?"

"Come clean with him," Maureen suggested. "Skip and Anika are both desperate."

Randall thumbed the button again. "Okay, Murphy, here's the problem: Anika's father is missing. We're fairly certain ECSITE kidnapped him. We're worried that ECSITE will use him—"

"Christ! Why didn't you tell me that when you first learned of it?"

Randall leaned forward. "Need to know, Murphy."

"All right. I'll explain it all to Anika."

Maureen heard the connection break and stopped pacing, trying to calculate the next domino to fall. It was probably in Israel but maybe somewhere to the north of Manhattan…

CHAPTER SEVENTY-NINE

* * *

SKIP STUDIED THE DISTANT COMPOUND THROUGH HIS HIGH-POWERED LENS. SINCE HE'D extracted Anika, the place almost appeared to be on holiday. Only occasionally did people cross the grassy area behind the palace. The usual line of morning commuters no longer queued at the gate for admission. Only the patrols were as active as usual, their dogs and machine guns reminiscent of a military compound in a war zone. Zoakalski seemed to have forted up.

Was this the same guy who'd shot up the Italian villa? The one who'd snatched Anika from the very arms of the FBI? What the hell was Zoakalski up to?

Stephanie's Jaguar hadn't made an appearance. So, where was she? Keeping a low profile until Zoakalski cooled off? Or had she ditched the Jag in favor of something less conspicuous? And, in that case, was she running or hunting?

"I don't know what to think." Skip pulled back from the scope and glanced at Anika where she lay on a sleeping bag, her hair pulled back in a ponytail. Even in the dim light, he could see she was scared silly.

"Skip, I'm not kidding. I have to get back to DC."

"I know."

"Why can't you get me home?"

Skip bowed his head for a moment. "I think Randall is afraid you'll stop cooperating with the government if ECSITE hurts your father."

"For God's sake, I already knew they had him. Zoakalski told me! I'm trying to get home so I can show them how to protect the country from my own model!"

"I understand that, I'm trying—"

"No, you don't," she hissed in a frantic voice. "I've seen their bioweapons lab. The number of diseases they have stored is huge. Zoakalski's team is working on my model as we speak and they're good. Really good."

Skip rubbed the stubble on his chin. "Actually, Anika, for the time being, I think you should focus on yourself because I have the feeling the DOD plans to use you for bait."

She seemed to be holding her breath. "Randall told you that?"

"Not yet. But I'm pretty sure that's where this is going."

She curled up on her side on the sleeping bag. "What do you think I should do?"

He studied her thoughtfully. "I can't advise you either way. I agree that Zoakalski is not the kind of guy you want to underestimate but getting you home may be beyond my ability."

"Why can't you just have someone drop me at Ramstein, like you said? I'll find a way to get home by myself."

Skip exhaled hard and studied the compound through the lens again. "Let me try to…"

His phone rang. Skip hit the button and placed it to his ear. "Yeah?"

"Skip?" Mark Schott said uncertainly. "I have a message for you. Mi Chan Li wants to know if you're familiar with Spago. It's a restaurant in Garmisch. She sends her regards and asks you to meet her there at five. A table outside has been reserved for the two of you. She says to ride the Ducati. Alone. Her people will be watching but you are guaranteed safe passage. She just wants to talk."

"About what?"

He heard Mark swallow hard before saying. "She would like to discuss a trade."

"Ask her how I can be sure of her good intentions."

After a pause, Mark said, "She said to tell you she owes you one. That you'll understand."

He severed the call.

Skip hit the end button and looked back at Anika. "Schott says Mi Chan Li wants to discuss a trade at a restaurant in Garmisch. Now, there's a twist I never saw coming."

CHAPTER EIGHTY

* * *

MARK HANDED THE PHONE BACK TO MICHELLE. HE STILL HAD A HARD TIME THINKING OF her as Mi Chan Li. Her 'associate', Yang, sat back in a chair, his arms braced on the back. His thick gray hair, square face, and hard eyes betrayed no emotion as he asked, "He will come?"

Mark shrugged, frightened half out of his wits. "I don't know. He sounded suspicious."

"He'll come," Li announced. "He's that type of man."

Mark glanced around the small room. No more than five paces by three, the furniture consisted of a bed, small table, and a chair. The walls were painted in scarlet. Red fluorescent lights added to the garish quality. The air carried the scent of perfume and, to his dismay, short ropes ending in loops hung from each corner of the cheap bed frame.

"Herr professor is uncomfortable in a whore's bed?" Yang said and gestured around. "What better place to remain out of sight than a brothel, eh? The locals are used to furtive men entering and leaving at all hours of the day."

Mark took a breath. He could hear faint music, occasional laughter and voices. Sometimes, people had passed beyond the door, their German unintelligible.

"Come," Yang said, rising from the chair, his stiff leg making the action awkward. "There are people waiting to see you."

Li leaned forward, her dark eyes close to Mark's as she flicked a knife open and severed the zip ties that bound his wrists and ankles. "Sorry," she whispered.

"Why?" Mark tried to read her expression. Now, he was even more scared than he had been.

He stood, tottered as circulation came back, and followed Yang out into an ornate hallway. Indirect, red lighting reflected from foiled wallpaper that depicted giant red roses. The faint scent of marijuana carried on the perfumed air.

Yang in front, Li behind, they made their way down the hall past closed doors. Passing an open one, Mark glanced in to see two young women in provocative lingerie sitting side-by-side on a bed. Both had cigarettes hanging loosely between their index and middle fingers. When they glanced his way, neither could have been older than twenty, their eyes flat and dismissive.

At the end of the hall, Yang produced a key and unlocked a padlock from a hasp. Then he input a code into a keypad set into the wall and the door clicked.

Mark was ushered onto a landing and found a stairway headed down.

Yang limped his way down the steps, unlocked a second padlock, and input his code into another keypad. "Double security," he said. "Wouldn't want anyone in the basement pounding on the upstairs door. Could lead to questions."

Mark bit his lip, dreading what he'd find behind that last door.

When it swung open, Yang stepped back and motioned for him to go first. "You'll want private time."

Mark gave the man a sidelong glance, wondering what would happen if he kicked him in the bad leg.

Michelle would slice my guts open with her knife. She'd stayed close behind him all the way down, her entire attention fixed on him.

Mark stepped into the dark room. Yang flicked on a light—and slammed the door shut.

Mark wheeled, grabbing the doorknob, trying desperately to open it. Then, in frustration, he slapped a hand against the heavy steel. The faint sound of steps faded into silence.

He turned, staring around. The walls were concrete; dark floor joists cluttered with cobwebs composed the ceiling. Boxes were stacked here and there and several old beds stood along the far wall.

The air carried a dank smell and the floor was featureless concrete with a single drain in the center. Pipes ran past the two fluorescent lights hanging from the joists.

Something moved on one of the beds, and he stared, seeing a

familiar face peering at him.

Mark cried out as he rushed across the floor, gazing incredulously at the bound figures on the beds.

"Jake? Will? Denise?" he dropped to his knees beside the bed, pulling the tape off Denise's mouth.

"Oh, God," Denise whispered. "Get us out of here."

Mark pulled strips of gray tape from Will's mouth, then Jake's. Jake was crying, his chest rising and falling. Will looked terrified, watching with bright, unbelieving eyes.

"Are you okay?" He pulled futilely at Jake's zip-tied wrists.

"Oh, God. Oh, God," Denise kept repeating. "Just get us out of here."

Mark staggered to his feet, looking around the room. "We'll be okay. Hang in there. I'll find something."

A search of the boxes turned up nothing useful. Most of it was old bedding, moldy and worn. Finally, on a lip of the concrete wall, he found a bottle. Its bottom was thick with some dried substance. Grasping it by the neck, he broke it on the floor and crossed to the beds.

"Hold still." He carefully severed the zip ties, helping Denise sit up. Then he went to the boys, cutting the bindings.

"Daddy?" Jake cried, flinging his arms around Mark's chest and burying his face.

"Shhh. It's all right. Everything is going to be all right."

Will flung himself at Mark. "Dad, where have you been?"

"I'm here now." Hot tears welled in Mark's eyes and for what seemed an eternity he clutched the boys to his breast.

Finally, he pulled free and looked at Denise. Her hair and clothing were filthy. She gazed at him like she didn't really see him.

Is she in shock?

He crossed to her with the boys following close behind him. Taking her hand, he asked, "Are you all right?"

With vacant eyes, she shook her head. "What did we do to deserve this?"

"It's going to be all right." He had no idea what to say.

"Where are we?" Denise demanded to know.

"Europe. Probably Germany. Maybe Switzerland. From the time they grabbed me, it wasn't long enough to travel to Italy or France."

"Dad?" Will asked, tears streaking down his face. "Why are they doing this? What do they want?"

Mark took a breath, trying to summon some kind of strength. "A computer model. One that charts the fall of civilizations."

"A fucking model?" Denise whimpered. "I don't know *anything* about any fucking model! Neither do the boys."

"Easy. Easy. Please, honey. Just relax."

"*Relax?*" Her face distorted, eyes tearing, her mouth twisted. "What are you going to do? You're a fucking coward. You always have been!"

Blinking, he looked around at the featureless basement. "I'll think of something."

CHAPTER EIGHTY-ONE

***

THE TOWN OF GARMISCH BASKED IN THE BRIGHT AFTERNOON SUNLIGHT AS SKIP WOVE around through the heavy traffic. Europeans had a much more reasoned approach toward motorcycles; lane splitting, passing, and maneuvering were accepted as a normal part of life.

Spotting Spago, Skip slowed and carefully backed into a space beside a lime-green BMW 1000RR. Kicking out the side stand, he killed the Ducati's engine and climbed off. Hanging his helmet on the handlebar, he glanced around at the buildings, taking in the windows. The sidewalk was filled with pedestrians, some standing around talking. No one seemed to be paying him the least attention. But then, they wouldn't have been professionals if they had.

Mi Chan Li was seated at a sidewalk table, sunlight sparkling in her long black hair. A colorful green motorcycle jacket hung from the back of her chair. She was dressed in a bright yellow t-shirt and form-fitting black riding pants.

She tilted her face up. "How's my Ducati?"

"Running much better now." Skip hung his jacket on the back of his chair. "When was the last time you had the valves set and changed plugs?"

"I didn't know you really had time to work on the machines given all the other things occupying your time."

"It's a compulsion." He studied her. How much did she know about Alpen Motorrad?

"I like Jurgen," she said, reading his mind. "We went riding one night and he showed me around the shop."

Why's she telling me this? Q hadn't swept the shop for days. Who the hell knew what she'd left during her tour? No wonder Washington thought security had been compromised.

Her dark eyes were fixed intently on his. What the hell was she trying to tell him? Something more than she was willing to say.

Okay, she's wired.

"Jurgen's pretty good with wrenches. He could probably coax a few more horsepower out of your Beemer."

She leaned forward. "We should go ride. I'd like to run the Ducati against the BMW, see which one has the edge in the twisties."

"Why don't we get down to why you wanted to see me?"

A faint smile formed at the corner of her full lips. "A simple trade. We know that Anika French and her team tested the model. We know a program was run."

"Too many bugs. Anika's on her way back to give it another shot."

Mi Chan Li gave him a disappointed look. "Which is why she was rushed off to the White House after the first run? Sorry. It doesn't wash. Whatever she found shook the President and cabinet right down to the roots. When Zoakalski grabbed French, it shook them even more."

"The FBI hates it when someone gives them a bloody nose and makes them look like fools."

Li placed her fingers on the tabletop and stared thoughtfully at him. "You'll be pleased to know that Washington Metro Field Office has had a shake-up. Lots of people were suddenly transferred to North Dakota."

"What's the trade?" He was mildly interested to note that passing men kept giving Li second looks. She had a curious magnetism which probably came from the fact that she liked to kill people.

"I'll trade you Schott and his family for French's model of Y-R1a virus distribution in Rockland County. No strings. We'll supply a computer to run the data, and when we know we've got the real thing, Schott, his wife, and kids will be turned over."

"Why should we care? He's a crummy anthropologist."

"Do you care about his innocent family? The wife is attractive. A pretty American woman would bring a nice price in an Arab country. And don't forget the boys. They'd be sold locally, of course." A beat. "It's a sordid world we live in."

Her eyes had narrowed slightly, intent on his again, trying to will him to see it all in his mind.

"You're a real saint."

The tightening in her expression, the thinning of her lips, told him volumes. She said, "I realize you will need to take our terms to Randall. You have until tomorrow."

"Why does China want the model?"

"Once they have French's model, their own model-makers will be able to reproduce it for other large cities. Providing it works."

Skip tapped the Ducati key on the table. "Tell you what. You ride up to the shop tomorrow morning, alone. I'll have an answer for you."

She nodded. "Acceptable."

Skip subtly looked around, noting the people standing on the street and in the café. "What have you heard about Zoakalski?"

"He remains a wild card. Stephie has managed to elude us as well." She gave him a meaningful sidelong stare. "If you happen across her, I'd really like to know."

"Right. I'll give you a call."

Her smile was teasing. "I didn't know you had my number."

"See you tomorrow at the shop."

She stood when he did, grabbed up her jacket, and walked with him to the motorcycles. She was giving him an evaluative look from the corner of her eye. "Do me a favor, Murphy. Make this trade happen. I'm a heartless professional but not even I can stomach selling children into slavery."

She slipped the helmet over her head, clipped the chin strap, and pulled on gloves and threw a long leg over the BMW. Inserting the key, she stabbed the starter and the four-cylinder exhaust spun a song of power.

Skip watched as she jerked a nod, toed the bike into gear, and smoothly pulled out into traffic.

Skip tugged his helmet on, used a heel to pull up the side stand, and thumbed the starter. As he engaged the clutch and gassed the bike, he once again surveyed the people around him, just taking note of anyone who left suddenly or was paying particular attention to him. He wanted to remember their faces, just in case he saw them again in more casual circumstances.

CHAPTER EIGHTY-TWO

***

SANTA FE, NEW MEXICO

In the dream, Dusty Stewart ran for his life through a desert full of giant sagebrush. Behind him, the wolf *katsina,* called *Kwewur,* leaped, howled, and snapped monstrous jaws with a sickening *clack.* The thing had a giant wolf's head, glowing red eyes, and a painted human body. With a rattle in one hand, a knife in the other, the Pueblo demon pursued with a vengeance.

The harder Dusty ran, the slower his legs became as if leaden and stuck in molasses. The jungle of sage had become thicker, the buff, sandy soil under his feet shifting. Dusty could feel hot breath on his neck, could smell a rotten odor—like that of a swollen carcass left too long in the sun. As the terrible monster katsina closed... a phone rang.

Dusty jerked, trying to figure out how a phone could be ringing. Some part of his dreaming brain analytically struggled to place its location in the aqua-blue sagebrush.

The second ring brought him bolt upright in bed, his heart pounding. Throwing the blanket back, Dusty careened off the wall of his antique trailer, banged off the door jam, and pounded down the narrow hallway, through his kitchen, and into the trailer's, small front room.

In his desperation, he flung dirty clothes off the threadbare couch, fumbled for the end table, and grabbed the receiver of his rotary telephone from its cradle. Lifting it to his ear, he stared around the dark trailer.

"Hello?"

"Dusty Stewart?"

"Yeah," he panted, blinking like an owl to clear both sleep and nightmare from his brain. "Who's this?"

"*It's Skip Murphy. I need to get a message to Maureen.*"

"What's wrong?" Dusty stood up straighter. "Last time you were around, people got shot."

"*That's what I'm trying to avoid. Can you get that message to Maureen?*"

Dusty rubbed his forehead. "Sure. I mean, I think so. But why can't you do it?"

"*Complications. I can't call Maureen directly without the computers tagging it. You're her boyfriend. When you call the base security office, tell them it's an urgent personal call. When you get her on the line, here's what I need you to say...*"

CHAPTER EIGHTY-THREE

***

"MA'AM?"

The voice brought Maureen awake. In the subdued gleam of her tiny barracks room, the uniformed officer looked like a shadow.

"What?"

"Phone call for you in the main office, ma'am. Says his name is Dusty Stewart... and it's urgent that he speak with you."

Maureen nodded and sat up. Urgent personal business, when it came to Dusty, could be anything. Once, after dancing with a stripper, he'd fallen on a barroom table covered with beer bottles and ended up with tens of stitches in his rear end. He'd considered that urgent personal business.

"Give me a minute, Sergeant. I just need to get dressed."

Five minutes later, she followed the sergeant to a spartan office with pale green walls. The man pointed to the phone. Maureen seated herself at the desk and asked, "Dusty?"

"Hey Maureen. Is this a secure line?"

"I doubt it." She closed her eyes. "What's wrong?"

"I just had a call from Skip Murphy." A pause.

"What did he say?" Maureen asked wearily.

Maureen listened, glancing occasionally at the sergeant. Her heart began to do the jackhammer against her ribs.

CHAPTER EIGHTY-FOUR

***

THE BMW'S HOWL GREW AS THE LIME-GREEN MACHINE RACED UP THE DRIVE FROM OBERAU. The rider was carving the corners like a GP racer, hitting each apex perfectly, heeling the bike from side to side.

Skip stepped out into the morning light, wiping his hands with a rag. Glancing around the corner, he noted that the plastic grocery sack he'd placed there was missing. There was a rock in its place.

He squinted as Mi Chan Li made the final corner, rolling the throttle, launching the 1000RR into the short straight. The front wheel lofted as she rode the wheelie into the parking lot, dropped the front end, and slid the bike to a stop no more than three feet shy of Skip's toes.

She killed the ignition, removed her black helmet, and stepped off. Unzipping her jacket, she shook out the wealth of her long black hair and said, "What's the answer, Murphy?"

Using the corner of the rag, Skip absently cleaned grease from under his thumbnail, then reached into his pocket and palmed a slip of paper as he walked over to shake her hand. She took it, showing no reaction. He bent down, pointing at her chain. "It's a little loose. Want me to tighten it."

She surreptitiously read the little note, crumbled it, and said, "No wires today. I can talk. I'm just here to find out if it's yes or no."

Skip stood, figuring that someone had a glass on them even if Li wasn't wired. He gestured absently at the machine as any bike nut would while discussing the intricacies of motorcycle elegance. "Tell me your angle in all this."

"Money," she replied easily, eyes on the sleek BMW. "I'm a private contractor. Chinese intelligence pays better than the corporate sector. Besides, Schott pretty much convinced me that the world is past saving.

What does French say?"

"The same. No going back. ECSITE has everything it needs. It's just a matter of time before Zoakalski's team uses her model to plan the demise of corporations, states, and nations around the world."

Li stepped forward, pointing to the handlebar where it was festooned with buttons for the traction control modes. "My dilemma is that my services are in high demand. Many parties in the world are itching to watch their enemies die."

He read the hard set of her jaw, the steel in her eyes and pressed the BMW's rear tire with his foot as if checking the inflation. "The answer is yes. The US will make the trade. The Defense Department dispatched an envoy with the French model last night."

Li took a deep breath. "All right, but we make the trade here. Same time tomorrow morning. That's non-negotiable." She waved up at the mountainside. "It's wide-open. No chance of a double-cross."

"Sure," Skip answered. "You said you'd provide a computer. Make it a damn good one. I'd suggest bringing a *very* competent statistician with you. This is higher-level thinking as I understand it."

"Of course. Yang wants to see how the model works to be sure I'm not jacking him around. Once he takes the New York model, gets in the van, you get the Schotts, and he drives away."

He gave her a sober look. "I hope so, Li. For your sake."

CHAPTER EIGHTY-FIVE

***

IN THE OBSERVATION POST IN THE ROOF BEHIND THE ALPEN MOTORRAD SIGN, ANIKA watched Mi Chan Li ride away, the motorcycle wailing as the woman bent the bike through corners.

Anika thoughtfully lowered the binoculars, her mind racing.

She heard Skip's feet on the desk before the hatch was pushed up and he climbed in. On hands and knees, he crawled over, staring thoughtfully across the valley at Zoakalski's compound. "You heard?"

Anika tapped her earpiece. "Yes. Tomorrow morning."

Skip propped himself on his elbows. "What do you think? A double cross?"

"Low probability." Anika ran fingers through her oily hair. Hiding in a rooftop wasn't conducive to her normal code of hygiene. "I read the file Randall sent on Yang. He's a long-term planner, talented at figuring out systems... making things work to his advantage with minimal personal risk. My impression is that once he has the program, he's running fast-and-straight for China."

Skip was chewing his thumb as he listened.

"Doesn't it taste like oil?"

He smiled. "Yeah, a little."

Anika took a deep breath. "All right. I've been going over the plan. By this time tomorrow morning, Mark, Denise, and the boys should be free."

"If your model works."

Anika's stomach muscles tightened. "Unfortunately, it does."

Skip pointed at her. "No matter what happens, you're going to be hiding beneath that tarp out in the fir trees, right?"

"Of course."

"If everything works out, I'll give you the all clear. If things go sideways, Helmut will retrieve you as soon as he can help you escape. As soon as you get up there, you'll discover I left a pistol under the tarp. That's a last resort. You only use it if you're discovered and desperate. Understand?"

Anika stared into his eyes. "What if they're about to shoot you down here?"

"Pull the tarp over your head and stay put."

CHAPTER EIGHTY-SIX

***

MAUREEN—PASSPORT AND COVID STATUS IN HAND—STEPPED THROUGH PASSPORT control and into the baggage claim. Having no luggage, she handed her card to the customs agent and exited to the main terminal at Franz-Joseph-Strauss Airport.

She took a deep breath. The lives of millions were at stake, not to mention the lives of French, Mark Schott, his wife, and two innocent boys.

"Hello, Maureen."

She glanced at the tall black-haired man, then did a double-take, looking over his shoulder at the four husky men approaching behind him. They neatly adopted a classic diamond formation, boxing her in. "Gave up being a dashing blond, have you?" she asked.

Helmut nodded and gestured to the men. "I'm taking extra precautions for your safety. The car's at the curb. The sooner we're gone, the better."

"Good to see you again, too. Seems like we never have time to just sit, have a beer, and reminisce about old times."

"I think Skip does this on purpose. But who knows, maybe after this is all over?"

"*Swineshoxen* at Der Franziskaner?"

"My treat."

Maureen followed him. The men marched in a protective huddle around her, their gazes roving, seeming to miss nothing.

"Any trouble?" Helmut asked.

"No. It worked just the way Dusty said it would. I ordered a car to take me to the Pentagon. Nothing unusual in that. They dropped me at the gate and, within minutes, a cab pulled up. Half an hour later, I was at Dulles. I picked up the ticket, went through security, and was airborne. By now, Randall must be frantic."

At the curb, three cars waited, bumper-to-bumper. Maureen was shuttled into the back seat of an Audi while the security detail clustered around her, vigilantly watching in all directions. As the door closed, someone slapped the roof.

Maureen craned her neck to see the detail pile into the chase car. As the small motorcade began to move, the chase car literally buried its nose in her car's back bumper. A move to keep anyone from pulling between them. Ahead, the blocking Mercedes was mere feet from the Audi's front bumper. Helmut, it seemed, took no chances.

"What's this all about, Helmut? Dusty just said it was, in his words, 'fucking important'."

Helmut swiveled in the passenger seat. "As I understand it, you're here purely for credibility. People are watching. Please play the part. Skip and Anika are taking a gamble on very long odds."

CHAPTER EIGHTY-SEVEN

***

MARK SCHOTT STARED UP AT THE BALEFUL LIGHTS ABOVE HIM. THE DAMN THINGS WERE never turned off. Now, he wondered if that wasn't just as well.

Facing his situation, staring at his hands where they hung from his limp wrists, knowing the bedding was filthy, and not caring, was easier in the hot white glare than it would have been in utter darkness.

Twice a day, a burly man brought a tray of food and an empty bucket. On the way out, he took the old tray and removed the bucket they used for a toilet.

"I hate you," Denise whispered after seeing the boys were asleep. Sleeping was easier for all of them. Once the brain had drifted off, the nightmares were only electrochemical phantasms spun by firing neurons or so he told himself.

"I hate myself," replied woodenly. It twisted his guts to know that her perfectly toned body might be the only thing standing between her and a bullet.

He couldn't bear to think about the boys...

Denise hung her head and filthy hair fell around her pretty face. "Was what we had in Laramie so bad? Was *I* so bad?"

"It wasn't you." He closed his eyes for a moment. "It was me."

She lowered her chin, staring vacantly at her feet where she'd pulled them up on the stained blankets. "Is anyone looking for us? Does anyone even give a shit?"

He took a deep breath. "I don't know."

"So what's going to happen? You're going to make this model for them?"

"I said I'd teach them how the model works."

She gave him that dead stare. "Then what? They'll just let us go?

Knowing what we could tell the world?"

He hung his head in defeat. "I'm so sorry, Denise. I wish—"

"Fuck you, Mark."

The faint sound of steps could be heard. Mark nerved himself, standing. He swallowed hard as the hasp rattled and the door clicked open. The burly man was accompanied by three hard-looking companions.

The boys started awake, sitting up with fear-bright eyes.

"Time to go," one said in a thick Asian accent. "One at a time, we're going to tie your hands. Walk straight to the van. If you shout or make trouble, you will be hurt."

Mark stepped forward, offering his hands as zip ties were produced. "Just don't hurt my family."

The man shrugged. "They be good, they don't hurt."

"Where are we going?" Mark asked as his hands were bound behind him.

"Maybe someplace different?" The man, day-old beard on his cheeks grinned. "Now I do your wife."

Mark caught the leer, saw the look in his dark eyes as he turned to Denise. His urge to kick the man squarely in the nuts was immediately dampened when one of the others stepped forward with a wooden club in his hand. Mark's bowels turned runny.

They did more than just bind Denise's hands behind her. She endured their groping fingers, eyes deadpan, as if her soul were absent. Will looked faint and Jake had tears running down his face.

The man with the club pointed at the door. "Go."

Mark turned, forcing himself to march forward.

CHAPTER EIGHTY-EIGHT

***

FROM HERE, YOU MUST GO ON ALONE," HELMUT SAID, OPENING THE AUDI'S DOOR FOR HER. "It's the building at the top with the big sign on the roof."

Maureen climbed into the vehicle and drove up the winding road. The alps were stunning this morning. The high peaks—coated with snow—stood against the blue sky. Lush green pastures, and the darker green of conifers, added to the contrast. Spring flowers in yellow, white, and blue accented the whole.

Skip, dressed in black tactical gear, stepped out the motorcycle shop's door just as she pulled up and turned off the engine. He paused long enough to pull a folded white plastic bag from under a rock. Then, grinning, he walked forward. "Good morning."

"Is it?" she said.

As he came forward to hug her, he whispered, "You're a DOD mathematician delivering French's program. Got it?"

"I didn't bring a program—"

"I've placed the flash drive with the program on the computer in the shop. There's a cubby hole right at your feet. If bullets start flying, you get your ass in that hole. The way the toolboxes are arranged, you should be safe."

"Where's Anika?"

"Safe and out of the action." Skip checked his watch. "Sorry I had to involve you in this but it had to appear that DC sent someone with the program."

"Credibility. I'm an emissary of Defense. I get it."

Maureen followed his gaze out over the town of Oberau, where red roofs gleamed with morning dew.

"Pretty spot."

"Yeah," Skip agreed. "Let's hope it stays that way." He pointed. "Here they come."

A gleaming Mercedes van began its climb up the winding drive.

"So, what do I do?"

"They're bringing a statistics expert. Just insert the flash drive into his computer and make him understand that this is the real thing."

"What if he's not as good a statistician as Anika? Skip, you've got to understand, Anika's program is very advanced."

He raised his hands in surrender. "I know."

Maureen turned to watch the white Mercedes van pull into the lot and Skip pointed to where he wanted it parked. An attractive woman was driving. When she stopped, two burly men dressed in dark t-shirts and clad in nylon tactical pants got out. They looked around, buzz-cut heads swiveling as they inspected the surroundings. Then a young man in a brown blazer opened the rear door. Blond, maybe thirty, he glanced around like a frightened owl, before he walked over to Maureen. "I'm Dr. Bier Fryung. You are the American mathematician, yes?"

"Yes. Dr. Maureen Cole."

The two guards told him to wait, then they both stalked like hunting lions into the shop. Through the door, Maureen could see them searching, opening doors, inspecting the office. When they finally emerged, they nodded, removed a laptop from the leather seat of the car and handed it to Fryung.

"Come on," Maureen said. "I have the program inside."

He followed Maureen into the shop and to the bench Skip had cleared. Setting the computer on the bench, Fryung clicked the power button and glanced nervously at Maureen. "I do not like this."

"Me, either. How did you get involved?" she asked as she reached for the flash drive where Skip had left it and handed it to him, watching as he inserted it in the slot and downloaded the program.

Fryung cautiously glanced around and whispered, "They kidnapped me from my office at gunpoint."

"Just do as they ask," she confided as the machine booted up. "I hope your machine has the capacity."

"It does."

She gave him a skeptical look. "You're a statistician?"

"Economist."

Maureen sighed. "Well, I'm about to take you on beyond zebra."

"I do not understand."

"That's what I'm afraid of. This model has been refined by the finest statisticians in the world. I hope you're of their caliber."

While Fryung pulled a calculator from his pocket, a gray-haired man, late fifties, eased out the passenger door.

Yang. She'd seen his photo in DC Maureen tensed as he approached and his predatory eyes met hers.

A faint smile curled his thin lips. "You are from DOD, yes?"

"Yes. Dr. Maureen Cole."

"I would not be happy if this is not the model." In German, he asked, "Fryung? Does the program look authentic?"

"I need more time. Economists use many of these same mathematics but in a different manner."

Yang gave Maureen a cold look and inspected her body as if it were a piece of meat. "Get busy explaining how this works, Dr. Cole."

Maureen—skin crawling from the look in his eyes—crossed her arms. To buy time, she said, "Let me get this straight. I bring you one of the most advanced statistical models on earth and you bring a novice statistician to evaluate it?"

Fryung looked insulted. "I am not a novice, Dr. Cole. I simply need clarification on a few points." He tapped the screen. "Here and here."

Yang withdrew a small Beretta automatic and aimed at Maureen's head.

Maureen experienced that uncomfortable tingle in her guts— the one that anticipates the impact of a bullet. She turned, bending down beside the now-pale Fryung. "All right, let's start at the beginning." She tapped the screen to return to the initial formula. "These are the high-value and high-priority nation-state targets that will engage with the pharmaceutical manufacturers using the frozen vaccine contaminated with the new virus."

Fryung licked his lips, watching her with sweat beginning to bead across his forehead. "This is a model for distributing a new virus?"

Maureen fought a shiver as Yang leaned close, following the pointer on the screen. "It's just theoretical, Dr. Fryung," she lied.

He looked up like he didn't believe her, then glanced at Yang's gun. "I understand."

Something creaked in the office. Maureen ignored it as she continued her explanation of one of the primary distribution statistics.

CHAPTER EIGHTY-NINE

***

SKIP TOOK ONE LAST LOOK AROUND, SATISFIED THAT NO ONE WAS SNEAKING ACROSS THE
fields, that no aircraft were approaching, and walked over to the driver's
side of the van.

"How you doing, Li?" From here, he could see Maureen, the stat
guy, and Yang bent over the computer monitor.

"Okay. So far."

For the morning's activities, she'd chosen an athletic black spandex
that conformed to every curve of her tall body. Skip did his best to
keep from staring.

"We're keeping our end of the bargain." She got out of the van,
grabbed the handle, and swung the side door open.

Skip stepped up and saw Mark Schott's bound body seated on the
bare floor next to a woman and two boys. They had hoods over their
heads, their clothing filthy, a definite odor wafting out the door.

"Not my idea," Li told him firmly. "But I'm not calling the shots."

"You really have to get better jobs."

"Soon, Murphy. Very soon."

Skip jerked a tight nod toward the shop. "Be out of Yang's employ
before I catch up with him."

"Is that a warning?"

"It is."

Thoughts churned behind her half-lidded eyes. Then, she walked
to one of the security guys, asking, "All's well?"

"Yes. Nothing moving. It's just like they said."

Li nodded and walked back to Skip, her eyes on the distant
compound. "Nothing cooking over there?"

"Zoakalski has had the place locked up like a vault." Skip rubbed the back of his neck. "It's not his style. Usually, cars and trucks come and go constantly."

"You think he's watching us?"

"Count on it. Hopefully this looks like a shop doing business. Just for appearance sake, your two guys might want to look more like customers instead of sentries."

Li motioned to the men. "Feel free to look at the motorcycles. I know you love bikes."

They took the hint, nodded, and began ambling around.

Skip turned back to the van. "Mark? It's Skip Murphy. Can you hear me?"

The hooded head bobbed, Schott making muffled sounds through a gag. "Just hang in there. Another fifteen minutes and this will be over."

The children started crying and Skip jerked his chin at Maureen where she bent over the bench with Fryung. "Hope your guy in there can understand that program."

"Me, too. Otherwise, this is going to get very messy."

CHAPTER NINETY

***

THIS IS CRAZY!" FRYUNG CRIED, THROWING HIS HANDS UP, "I DO NOT UNDERSTAND HOW these variables work."

Maureen, heart pounding, gave him a disgusted look. "It's just systems theory, right? All you have to—"

"Dr. Cole?" Yang asked ominously. "Your time is running out."

She barely heard a shoe grate on the floor behind Yang, and figured Skip was finally coming to her rescue, when a soft female voice asked, "Can I help?"

Yang turned and stiffened. Maureen saw a smiling blonde woman, tall, wearing a dark, form-fitting top, and smudged black slacks. A long suppressor gave her pistol an unbalanced look. The thing made a *pffft* sound, followed by the snapping of the slide and the melodic tinkle of empty brass on the floor.

Yang's knees buckled. The woman leaped forward and competently twisted the pistol from his hand and leaped back.

"It was a pleasure to see you again, Yang," the woman said curtly, then she turned both her attention and the suppressed pistol Maureen's way. "Not a sound, Dr. Cole."

"Where did you come from?"

"Trap door in the floor. It was a miserable cramped and cold night, and I'm in a really foul mood. Now, not another word."

Two men in black emerged from the office and slipped along the benches, ducking behind motorcycles, black submachine guns held at the ready.

Maureen started to yell, but the blonde pointed the pistol at Maureen's chest, and hissed, "We already have the model. I really *don't* need you alive."

In the parking lot, Skip stood talking to the black-clad Asian woman while they looked at something in the van.

CHAPTER NINETY-ONE

***

THE SOUND SKIP HEARD WAS LIKE A COMBINED COUGHING-AND-POPPING ACCOMPANIED by *shik-shick*ing. He threw himself to the ground and madly crawled for cover.

A voice called, "*Freeze!* Now!"

Skip shot a look over his shoulder to see Stephanie Huntz—flanked by two men—emerging from the shop door. The subguns—they held were at the combat-ready, stocks centered in the shooter's chests. Skip froze.

Li was in a crouch, hands extended, a look of disbelief on her face. Both of her men were on the ground, one gasping, blowing foamy blood from his mouth. The other stared sightlessly up at the sky as blood pooled around him.

Stephanie took a step to one side, glanced down at the dying guard, and coolly shot him in the head.

Skip swallowed hard. What the hell were his options? He glanced up at the band of firs up slope, then shook his head vigorously.

"On your knees, both of you," Stephanie ordered.

Skip carefully rose to his knees, aware that Li had dropped to hers. She gave him a measuring glance.

Stephanie stepped right up to Skip, placed the pistol to his head and ordered, "Where's Anika French? Call her out or Maureen Cole and the Schotts die."

Skip took a deep breath, then shouted, "Anika? Come on down! No choice here."

A disappointed expression came to Li's face when the young red-head rose from the ground beneath the firs and started down the hill with her hands locked behind her head.

"My insurance," Skip growled. "In case things went wrong."

"As a bargaining chip? Did you a lot of good," Stephanie said. As she stepped back, she kept her pistol steady as she shot a quick glance to the gold sedan that had just pulled out of the ECSITE compound gates.

"Who's that?" Skip asked.

"Who do you think?"

The two shooters started forward, subguns trained on French as she walked slowly down the hill. Anika was wearing oversized mechanics overalls, the dirty sleeves bagging where she had her hands clasped behind her head.

"So, Stephanie," Skip said conversationally, "How'd you figure this out?"

"When I was fixing my tire that day in Schongau, I heard the motorcycle leaving." She turned, looking down the drive. Skip could see the sleek gold sedan climbing the curves. "I just couldn't get it out of my head. Why a motorcycle?" She shrugged. "But then you've got a motorcycle shop full of them with a giant sign we can read from clear across the valley. Right where you could watch every move we made."

Anika, her face expressionless, jaw locked, stopped just short of the van. Her face was pale, contrasting with dirty red hair. She kept her hands clasped tightly at the back of her neck. The green stare she fixed on Stephanie was filled with loathing.

Stephanie laughed out loud at the dirt and oil covering Anika's clumsy overalls. "Look at you. You're a sight to see."

The gold sedan pulled to a stop, and when the door opened, a pale Mikael Zoakalski stepped out. The driver followed behind him, a Beretta Model 92 in his hand.

Zoakalski braced a hand on the car door and weakly pushed to his feet with sunlight gleaming in his shock of white hair. "Nice work," he said to Stephanie. "This day, you are back in my good graces. As we said in the Great Patriotic war, atoned for in blood." He arched an eyebrow. "Yang?"

"A simple shot to the heart," Stephanie said with a shrug. "Wish I could have made it last a little longer."

Zoakalski nodded and his gaze went straight at Anika. He slowly walked forward. "Dr. French, may I have a word with you in private?"

"What do you want?"

"Follow me over to the trees, please." He led the way toward the grove of pine trees. She followed, her hands still clasped behind her neck.

CHAPTER NINETY-TWO

***

ANIKA GOT A GOOD LOOK AT ZOAKALSKI'S FLUSHED FACE AS HE STOPPED AND TURNED. HIS skin was sweat-slick. *Fevered?* She studied his glassy eyes, the trembling in his limbs, his shallow breathing.

Zoakalski's knees shook as he stopped beneath the swaying boughs and spread his feet to brace his legs. The scent of pines perfumed the air. Across the valley, his compound gleamed in the sunlight, falling through clouds that leisurely drifted eastward.

After inhaling a shallow breath, he asked, "I suppose you think I'm careless."

Anika tried to gauge the man's temperature. One hundred and four? "No, but given your heritage, there was a high probability you'd be targeted—"

"We discovered that it was introduced on the same food contaminated with the enterotoxin." He fixed her with glazed eyes. "We were surprised that our vaccine did not work against it. Your idea?"

By now, she was dead anyway. What did it matter if he knew that she'd worked this out in DC when she'd decided to bring him down? "Vaccine makers can't account for all the mutations, especially rare ones. Your grandfather's heritage gave you a very unique genetic marker—the M204 mutation. It evolved in the Middle East and Caucasus. If I hadn't done it, someone else would have. You have many enemies, sir."

"Brilliant." He gave her an appreciative nod.

She paused to frown at him. Her arms were aching where she had them clasped behind her neck. "Were you aware that your grandfather's lineage was extremely rare?"

He staggered before he locked his knees to steady himself. He said,

"My family was hunted down by the old Imperial Russian eugenicists but they couldn't have known. They didn't have the technology." He blinked feverishly at the trees before he asked, "Is your virus deadly?"

"At your age, probably."

"I see," he said with a smile and finished, "Let me show you how I deal with treachery. Come. Back to the van."

Staggering and wobbling, he led the way to the van and gestured to the hooded people inside. "Drag *Herr Professor* out."

"No!" Anika pleaded. "Take it out on me, not—"

One of the shooters lowered his MP5, reached into the van, and dragged out Schott, and ripped the hood from his head. Mark blinked against the morning sun, then panic contorted his face when he saw Zoakalski.

"Ah, Dr. Schott." Zoakalski stepped forward, weaved on his feet. "We were grieved when Yang jerked you so rudely away from us. Please understand that we tried to get you back."

Zoakalski slipped a worn blue Makarov from his pocket and took aim at Schott's head. When Mark began to sob against his gag, Zoakalski said, "Be glad your death will be quick. As for your family…"

A bullet makes a distinct sound when it impacts a human skull. The loud *snap-pop* is simultaneous—a combination of breaking bone mixed with vacuum as the deforming bullet smashes a hollow through flesh. That hollow, called the temporary canal, slaps shut just as fast.

Anika heard when she unclasped her hands and pulled the heavy HK pistol from the holster. She'd clipped it to the neck of her overalls. At this range, she couldn't miss.

Zoakalski's head exploded with that sound, bits of brain, blood, and bone spattering in all directions.

Even as Zoakalski's body slammed onto the pavement, his pistol clattering away, Skip was shouting, "Anika, no!"

She ignored him, pivoting at the waist; she shot the closest of Stephanie's men with a single shot to the chest. Saw the bullet's impact through the ripple in the man's shirt.

The second was turning, bringing his submachine gun up. She triggered the HK as the front sight aligned with the top of his breastbone. Then fired again as he staggered backwards and toppled onto the howling Mark Schott.

In the process, Skip had stepped close. He wrenched the gun from Anika's hand and shoved her rudely to the ground, shouting, "Stay there!"

Then he whirled, taking two fast shots at the van's driver. The man slumped onto the wheel, then slipped sideways as he collapsed in the seat.

From the corner of Anika's eye, she realized too late that Stephanie had crouched, her pistol in an isosceles grip. She was staring at Anika over the sights, rage in her eyes.

Skip started to bring the HK around.

Too late!

Oddly, the barrel dropped an instant before Stephanie triggered the gun. Anika heard the impact, felt the spatter of lead and copper when the bullet's disintegrated on the pavement between her right knee and left foot. She saw the brass flung sideways. Stephanie's blue eyes widened as her mouth gaped in disbelief. Then, Li artfully kicked her in the side of the head, toppling Stephanie onto her side.

As Stephanie struggled for air, Li grasped the knife protruding from Stephanie's back. The way she flicked the blade back and forth, the keen edge slicing through lung, heart, and arteries, was quick, fast, and efficient.

Li withdrew the blade, carefully wiped it off on Stephanie's clothes, and—still in a crouch—whirled on the balls of her feet, searching for other targets.

In a combat crouch, Skip covered Li with his HK. Anika grabbed up Zoakalski's fallen Makarov, scrambled to her feet with her knees shaking. Bits of bullet stung where they'd ripped through her coveralls.

Skip ordered, "Anika, check on Maureen. But stay frosty."

"On it." As she started off, the Makarov ready, she heard Skip say to Li, "Nice work with Stephanie. Are we good?"

"We're good, Skip. You can lower your weapon, I'm here to make a trade, nothing more," Li replied, "That said, I'd better check on Fryung." Li headed for the shop, striding behind Anika.

CHAPTER NINETY-THREE

***

AS ANIKA LED MAUREEN OUT INTO THE PARKING LOT, SKIP NOTED THAT SHE WAS white-faced and looked shocked as her glance went from one bleeding corpse to the next.

Skip pulled his knife, cut Schott's bindings, then yanked the tape from his mouth. "You all right?"

Schott, who'd been weeping, finally gulped air, and said, "My... My family?"

"Safe."

Skip spun around at the sound of a single-cylinder engine. Down the slope, on the winding drive, he could make out the KTM 450 as it was ridden away. Long black hair streamed out behind the figure at the bars.

"Figures."

In his mind, he could imagine Mi Chan Li. She'd entered the shop, walked right past Fryung, then hurried out and found the KTM. The slope in front of the shop was open grass. She would have straddled the bike and coasted it down the hill. Only when she hit the road, did she turn on the key, shift to third or fourth, and let the clutch out to bump-start the bike.

"Skip?" Maureen called. "The flash drive! Damn it!"

Skip cursed. Down the long hill, Mi Chan Li caught another gear, and the KTM vanished among the houses.

Anika walked unsteadily, almost stumbling, the sunlight shining in her bright red hair. She had tears in her eyes. "It's downloaded on the computer, so we still have it," she said, then she bent double and vomited.

Skip called, "You okay?"

Anika shook her head. "No. And I don't think I ever will be. I feel sick."

"Hey, you did what you had to. If you hadn't killed those men when you did, we'd all be dead." Skip told her sympathetically.

Anika closed her eyes and took a breath, then shuddered as she exhaled and clamped her eyes shut against the tears. "You don't get it. I proved that my model could be used to genetically target individuals." Opening her eyes, she gave him a sober look. "The President of the United States with his Navajo ancestry? Any population with a unique genetic identity? Jews? Koi San bushmen? They're now vulnerable. Don't you see? *I* was the fracture event. *Me.*"

EPILOGUE

* * *

HIGH IN THE COLORADO ROCKIES, SKIP SAT AT THE BUFFALO BAR'S ANTIQUE BAR AND LOOKED up at the ancient mirror. Through the open door, he could see Idaho Springs' Main Street, where his BMW RT1250 canted on its side stand, the sun shining off the tank, fairing, saddlebags, and tour trunk. Three Harleys with short pipes made him wince as the big bikes prowled up the street. The too-loud exhausts were no-doubt shaking windows out of the historic buildings.

He tapped his bike key on the scarred wooden bar. Over the years, it had served generations of miners, tourists, locals, and countless motorcyclists like himself. The place was noted for great pizza and buffalo burgers.

He took another sip of his beer and rubbed the back of his neck. The sweet tremolo of tuned pipes caught his attention. He glanced out, seeing a lime-green BMW 1000RR pull up. The slim woman artfully backed the machine to the curb beside his BMW, deployed the side stand, and removed her helmet.

Skip gave her a grim smile as Mi Chan Li came walking in, flipping the wealth of black hair out of her racing jacket before she unzipped the cuffs and perched on the next stool.

"Nice place, Murphy."

"I thought it would work. You got the flash drive?"

She reached into her pocket and placed it on the bar. "You got the transfer ready?"

Skip pulled his phone from his pocket, pressed "send" and when he heard Maureen's voice, said, "Send it."

Li was staring at her own phone, a slight frown lining her forehead.

"Takes a while," Skip told her and laid his phone on the polished wood.

"Not that long," Li told him. She inspected the number in her Grand Cayman account, smiled, and tucked the phone into a jacket pocket, saying, "I enjoy doing business with you."

"I wouldn't wait too long to spend it. America's flat broke."

She ordered a Guinness, then asked, "Must have been an interesting time when you got back to DC."

"Let's just say we had a spirited debriefing. The Germans are taking Zoakalski's compound apart. Once he was dead and harmless, you'd be surprised how fast his employees turned on him. They gave up Anika's father in a heartbeat. Working through Interpol, Europe is dissecting Yang's network. Turning over that information on his sex traffickers bought you a lot of goodwill."

She gave a slim-shouldered shrug. "They paid well."

"Is that all that motivates you?"

She gave him that familiar penetrating look and smiled. "Not all."

"So…" he said, making conversation. "What's next for you?"

"I don't know yet."

He studied Li from the corner of his eye as her Guinness was placed on the bar.

She sipped and said, "I grew up in a different world than you did. Half way between Hong Kong and China. When I was recruited, I got to see all sides of China and, for a while, I was a true patriot."

"What happened?"

"I endured while my superiors squandered one opportunity after another. As difficult as it is to believe, Xi Jinping's bureaucracy is more corrupt and inefficient than yours. Initiative is rarely rewarded."

"True."

"How is Dr. French doing?"

"At home, in Wyoming, working on a model to halt the R1a virus that spreading around the world. The FBI has a wall of agents around her. No one wants her snatched again."

"I assume the government is going to hire her to find ways to counteract her own model?"

"I'm sure they'll try," Skip replied with a grim smile.

"And Mark Schott?"

"Denise divorced him and took the boys." Skip shook his head.

"And I don't know if he has the stomach to fix himself."

Li pursed her lips. "Well… Men are weak creatures."

He took another sip of his beer.

She ran her slim fingers down the sides of her glass. "So, what happened to Dr. Cole?"

"She's back in New Mexico with that archaeologist, Stewart. He's got her out in the desert somewhere, digging up pots and pueblos. I think that sort of thing heals her."

For a time, they sat, sipping at their beers.

Then Skip said, "What no one can figure out is why Zoakalski would target the Y R1a variant when he had it himself. He must have known that his family around the world would eventually be infected. How could a man do something—"

Li laughed softly. "You Americans are so myopic."

"How so?"

"Zoakalski was a Zionist at heart. He would never have threatened Ashkenazi men."

Skip sipped his beer and gave her a sideways glance. The lights behind the bar glittered in the bottles on the top shelf. "What are you saying?"

"I'm saying that you Americans are appallingly easy to mislead." She cocked her head to give him a plastic smile. "Just because the virus started in Israel doesn't mean it was the target."

A cold feeling invaded the pit of his stomach. "It wasn't?"

"All I'm saying is that the R1a haplogroup spans Eurasia, extending from Scandinavia and Central Europe to Southern Siberia. Lots of men fall into the R1a haplogroup." She cocked her head and gave him a penetrating look. "But less than two percent of them are Han Chinese."

A LOOK AT: DISSOLUTION BY W. MICHAEL GEAR

***

FROM WESTERN WORD-SLINGER AND ANTHROPOLOGIST
W. MICHAEL GEAR, COMES AN ENTIRELY NEW TYPE OF
WESTERN – A CONTEMPORARY APOCALYPTIC WESTERN.

For anthropology graduate student Sam Delgado, headed to the wilds
of Wyoming, this is his last chance to save his graduate career. He and
his urban classmates see this as the adventure of a lifetime: They are
going to horse-pack in the wilderness to map and test a high-altitude
archaeological site.

Until a cyber attack collapses the American banking system, and
an already fractured nation descends into anarchy and chaos. All
credit frozen, Sam and his archaeological field school is trapped in
their high-altitude camp. With return to the East impossible, Sam, the
woman he has come to love, and the rest of the students must rely on
hard-bitten Wyoming ranchers for their very survival.

Guided only by an illusive Shoshone spirit helper, Sam will discover
the meaning of self-sacrifice. Even at the cost of his life.

Haunting, provoking, frightening and prescient – in the end, all
that stands between civilization and barbarism is one young man's
courage and belief in himself.

AVAILABLE NOW

ABOUT THE AUTHORS

***

W. Michael Gear and Kathleen O'Neal Gear are *New York Times* bestselling authors and nationally award-winning archaeologists. They have published 75 novels and over 200 non-fiction articles in the fields of archaeology, history, and bison conservation. In 2021, they received the Owen Wister Award for lifetime contributions to western literature and were inducted into the Western Writers Hall of Fame. They live in beautiful Cody, Wyoming.